WINGS

OF

DARKNESS

BOOK TWO

M.S. Quinn

AUTHOR'S NOTE

Wings of Darkness is a fantasy romance novel that explores potentially triggering and dark themes. It is intended for an adult audience. A list of content warnings can be found in the back of the book.

For the tortured souls who give their heart, soul, sweat, and tears, and still don't believe they're enough.

You are.

VEIL FOREST
SHARD FIELD
ETERNAL
FOREST
HOAR
HOLLOW
HELL
REDEMPTION CIRCLE
PORTAL
LAKE
VERDANT
FOREST

Hierarchy of Angels

Seraphim

Leaders of the angels.

- Possess blue Glory and a unique, signature power.
- Cannot grace Elora or Earth without sever consequences.

Archangel

Military leaders ranked just beneath the Seraphim.

- Possess white Glory and a signature power, though less powerful than the Seraphim.
- Most angels report to them, as they are more accessible.
- Require Seraphim permission to enter Elora or Earth.

Below them are the levels of angels that are allowed in any dimension at any time, as long as they are following the laws of their kind.

Dominion

Military leaders in Elora.

- Telekinetic powers.

Powers

Military warriors.

- Elemental powers.

Thrones

Angelic Scholars.

- Photographic memory.
- Can discern truth and deception in any form of writing.

Virtues

Healers.

Nephilim

 Half-angels.

- Powers come from their angelic father.

Fallen

Angels that disobeyed Heaven's laws. (punishments may vary.)

- Wings are ripped or cut off.
- Banished from Heaven and the Ethereal Kingdom.
- Glory is removed.

Hierarchy of Hell's Military

Elite Squadrons

- **Dreads** – Commanded by General Ronen
- **Nightmares**
- **Infernos**
- **Tormentors**

Beginner Squadrons

- **Devils**
- **Trenchers**
- **Bowels**

THE SEVEN CIRCLES OF HELL

Souls are judged by the King of Hell and cast into a circle matching their sins. Redemption is possible—but only by enduring their torment and climbing the brutal, winding ladder back. The deeper the descent, the more circles they must conquer. Those who fail remain trapped, reliving their punishment until madness consumes them—or the Horde does. Few ever escape the Hallucination Circle or lower.

Redemption

The first circle of Hell and the domain of the King of Hell. This circle holds souls who have committed only trivial sins, those who have survived the deeper circles and are still paying off their debts, and the souls who are preparing to ascend.

Temptation

The second circle of Hell, reserved for souls guilty of minor sins. Here, they are tormented by temptations.

Glaciation

The third circle of Hell—a frozen wasteland for souls who have committed moderate sins. Their punishments come in the form of unrelenting cold, isolation, and ice.

Hallucination

The fourth circle of Hell, reserved for souls who have committed significant sins. Here, they are tormented by endless hallucinations—twisting their memories, fears, and regrets into waking nightmares. Most who descend into this circle lose all grip on reality.

Suffocation

The fifth circle of Hell, reserved for souls who have committed substantial sins. Here, the very air is stolen from their lungs. Every breath is a battle, and the weight on their chest grows until it feels like it might cave in.

Scission

The sixth circle of Hell, reserved for souls who have committed major sins. Here, their skin is filleted in hundreds of ways. Every slice brings a scream—and every scream brings more slices.

Immolation

The seventh circle of Hell, reserved for souls who have committed atrocious sins. Here, oil and tar are poured over them and ignited with Hellfire. The burning never ends—flesh melts, reforms, and burns again in an endless cycle. The air reeks of scorched skin and screams.

Note: *The Horde dwell here—grotesque beasts that feed on hopelessness. They devour souls whole, dissolving them in stomach acid. Once consumed, a soul is lost forever, stripped of all hope for redemption.*

Each soul that succumbs to despair breeds a **Hellhound**—a mindless beast of rage and ruin. But if a soul endures and escapes, they birth a **Soulhound**—a rare and powerful guardian forged from resilience.

CHAPTER 1

Lucille

Strong arms held me close to their chest, their heart racing beneath my ear. The rough leather of their clothing ground against my blistered skin. That was all I could register between the boiling heat ripping through my insides and the searing cold offering a breath of hope—until it sluiced through my veins, just as cruel.

"Put her on my desk. Now."

I wanted to scream *no*, but every step, jostle, and rise of their chest stole my breath, the agony forcing me in and out of consciousness.

A crashing noise split the tense silence. They moved me onto something hard, and I surrendered to the wispy darkness.

Pain never touched me here. The dark tendrils silenced the frigid cold and scalding heat. They wrapped me in warmth and made me whole. They cocooned me in their gentle, unyielding embrace and whispered words of protection.

I never wanted to leave.

A ferocious fire pierced my wrist and speared into my body. I woke up screaming and thrashing on a wooden desk, pinned by a tingling touch.

Aspen?

He claimed my last thought before I passed out again. But this time, I wasn't with the wispy shadows. Instead, the darkness flickered with a familiar purple and white light.

The lie hit me the second I opened my eyes. Not a lie—a dream-walk into a dream that wasn't a memory. Or so I assumed.

Wildflowers tickled my legs as I sat in a moonlit field. Their soft, delicate petals reflected the blue light and turned a shade of indigo every time I moved my head, captured in my dream-walking haze. At the edge of the field, giant pillars circled like silent sentinels. The weathered stone supported arches overtaken by vines, creating an artful wall of green. Firewings danced between the tall grass and landed on ancient pillars. Small zaps sounded every time their wings touched, sending sparks of orange into the air.

I'd dream-walked to Elora. But I'd never been here before.

If I wasn't in one of my memories, but I inhabited my own body, then what was this?

I felt like I'd entered an ancient elven realm that existed only in the pages of the books I'd devoured as a teenager. I moved to explore the fantastical land when a tingly finger brushed the curve of my lip, snapping my attention away from the magic.

My heart jumped. "Aspen?"

Moonlight streamed through the oak branches behind us, catching the wetness on his cheeks.

My smile dropped.

I cupped his face, brushing away his pain with my thumb. "What's wrong?"

"I couldn't save you," he whispered.

"Save me?"

He latched onto my hand, and a shot of heartache speared through our bond as he lifted it in front of my face.

What the... A long pink scar slashed across my palm.

"Michael," he explained.

Slowly, it all came back to me. Magda, Marcus, Michael's torture, my mom poisoned to sleep, and the male who swore before I descended into a sweet, relieving blackness.

I looked around at the magical perfection of this place and really considered what it could mean.

"Are we dead?"

"I feel like it. I can't sense our bond anymore." His low, haunted tone stunned me. This wasn't the Aspen I knew. He never sounded like this.

"But the tingles." I touched his cheek, emphasizing my words. He rested his head against my hand like I anchored him from drowning in the sea of his unending sorrows.

"I can feel you here. But it's just a dream, sweetheart. This is all just one big dream." His voice cracked at the end, wrenching at my heart. He slumped against the oak trunk, as if surrendering to the finality of his words.

"But you're alive?"

Aspen stared out into the field, silent, mourning.

I jerked his face to mine, forcing him to look at me. "Are you alive, Aspen? Out there?"

He nodded.

A slight breeze floated through my hair, rustling the oak's branches. Its leaves fluttered in the ring of my purple haze. This had to be another version of dream-walking. I would know if I'd died.

I brought my forehead to his, breathing in his crisp apple and fire scent. "So am I."

Sorrow bled into our bond, and he shook. His tears slid down my fingers, resting against his cheeks.

He didn't believe me.

"Aspen, open your eyes."

He did, showing me his vibrant blues surrounded by his angel rings.

"I'm alive, out there. Not just in your dream but in life. I'm alive." Although I couldn't promise I was safe or okay.

The weight of his grief still rested like a mountain on my chest.

"Have you ever heard of a dream-walker?"

Aspen's watery expression narrowed. "I read the word once in an old angelic text."

"That's what I am. I can revisit a person's memories—and my own—through dreams. And..." I glanced around the enchanting clearing. "It seems like a person's imaginative dreams too."

The sharpness of his gaze faltered.

"It's part of my..." I paused, realizing I hardly had time to process who I was or where my purple flames came from.

Aspen stared at me, waiting.

I wanted him to know, no matter what he thought of me.

"Do you know who the King of Hell is?"

"Yes." He nodded slowly. "Lucifer is Lilith's unwilling husband."

Well, Heavenly Shit. I never put that together.

I took a deep breath, then said, "I'm his daughter."

Aspen looked like he expected me to take it back. He took my chin and twisted it back and forth, analyzing my eyes. Then a foreign pain seeped into my cautious emotions.

He dropped his hand and stood, gazing down at me with a curling lip. "I only saw Lucifer once, when I was younger. But I never forgot the two white rings distorting his eyes. When I met you, I knew the double rings meant you were powerful. I knew you were something other than an angel. I just never imagined it'd be Hell's offspring."

Offspring?

"Aspen?"

Then I saw them—two Hell Runes cut deep in his skin, as if carved by an invisible hand. Or, more likely, as if someone carved them on him as he slept. They peeked from the sleeve of his tunic, causing the invading pain.

I lurched forward, covering his runes. The raised skin branded my hands with their vile heat, demanding I let go. Instead, I gripped tighter.

The soft breeze picked up speed, whipping my hair around. His eyes shifted between a cold mask and a storm of unspoken emotion.

"Stay with me."

He jerked on his wrists. "I'm sorry, sweetheart."

But I wouldn't let go. He was *mine*. Lilith couldn't have him.

His skin puckered horribly beneath my fingers. All emotion bled from his blue eyes. Lilith's chokehold swallowed his pain and resolve, leaving our bond numb and empty.

"Fight her! You're stronger than her, Aspen!"

The moonlight blinked out, leaving Firewings as our only light—until the savage wind roared and hurled the tiny insects to the ground. Darkness swallowed us whole, stealing Aspen from my sight—but not from my hold.

"Aspen, remember who you are," I begged. "Give me the moon."

"I don't know what the fuck that means. But if you're alive, we'll find you." He wrenched his hands out of my grip.

The vicious wind halted, and a glowing ball of purple-white light illuminated the still, empty darkness.

He was gone.

I sat there, staring into the abyss of my mind.

He couldn't stay like that. He couldn't continue to be her lethal pawn, following her every whim and forgetting who he was and where he came from.

His mom wanted more for him. She wanted me to save him.

The more I thought about Lilith, the more my sorrow morphed into a vicious vengeance. Itches scattered across my skin. Purple flames burst forth, and the glowing ball beside me pulsed.

What did Magda say?

Something about Hell's general being able to remove his runes. I'd have to find him and force him to help me.

I slumped, letting go of my power. I didn't know where I'd be when I woke up, or what state I'd be in, or where my mom was. How was I supposed to find Hell's general and ask him to help me save my guardian? The male, I lov—

I stopped that thought. *Was that what these feelings were?* I didn't know. But he was mine, and I needed to save him.

CHAPTER 2

Ronen

Quiet eased through the castle, the staff and few souls privileged to live here settling in for the night. I padded down the crimson carpet toward my room. The color resembled fresh blood under the silver moonlight streaming through the floor-length windows lining the hall.

The color followed me everywhere—in every corridor of Hell's castle, in the uniform that covered my military, in the wounds they carried or earned. In every crevice of my hands and the tendrils of my shadows.

Blood followed me.

My room remained my only reprieve from the potent, ever-present stain—and the library.

The chair beside my favorite shelves called to me now, urging me to turn back, to ease the tension coiling tighter with every step toward my room.

I had to pass *hers* to reach mine. And for once, I didn't want my shadows pounding at my body to escape.

A soft click sounded ahead. I stopped, knowing exactly what was about to happen.

The scrawny Nephilim stepped out of his room and tiptoed toward Lucille's.

I clenched my jaw and let the oblivious male sneak a couple more steps. Then released a shadow and tripped him. He fell ungracefully to the floor.

"I told you to stay in your room."

He peeked through his unmanageable hair, grinning sheepishly. "Did you? I don't recall."

His grin and green eyes made my stomach lurch. He reminded me of someone from my past.

He stood, inching toward her door.

"She needs to heal," I warned.

The Nephilim crossed his arms. "Does she? Huh. The slices down her limbs and her unconscious state must've slipped my mind."

My shadows whipped around me in threat. If he didn't share those oddly familiar features with the male who saved my life, I would've released them. Let them rough him up a bit. Instead, I passed by him, leashing my shadows before they slipped beneath her door.

"Get back in your room."

"Yes, Sir."

A door opened and shut behind me, sounding closer than it should've.

I guaranteed he went into her room, and I didn't have enough energy to go drag him out. Or, more likely, I didn't want to set foot in there.

I entered my sitting area and sighed in relief. It was empty. I walked over to the wall of weapons by my fireplace, removed my Soul Swords and daggers from my person, and placed them back on the runed wall. Raising my last dagger, I paused.

Sinking into the chair next to my fire, I twisted the handle of Tsal-mawet in my palms. This dagger could change my life—if only we had my feather. Lucifer would want to know I'd found the blade that sawed off his wings and created the world we now live in.

Hell.

The place the council claimed they wanted me. But they were lies. Etan would've kept me as his slave for all eternity. Fortunately, I escaped, and now I had a home in Hell's first circle: Redemption.

It used to be the least gruesome circle of the seven—until twenty years ago, when the gates closed and Hell began to devolve. The Seven Circles stopped recycling souls, making them overcrowded and allowing dangerous souls to pop into circles they weren't allowed in. And now... now everything was fucked, making my job as a general harder than it'd ever been.

I fingered the deadly blade, unable to resist the magnetic pull of the cold, lethal edge. Its power hummed against my fingers as if calling out to be used. But Tsal-mawet wasn't meant to be wielded by the hands of men or angels. It was the Weaver's to use—to create and destroy. And it certainly wasn't meant for torture.

My muscles tensed, urging me to find the Archangel that tore apart her flesh. My vision darkened as a wisp seeped from my hand, wrapping around the hilt of the humming metal. I wanted to destroy him. I wanted to make every blood vessel in his body burst and savor his screams as I filleted—

I hissed, cutting myself on one of the dagger's sharp quillons.

For fuck's sake.

Every time I so much as thought about her lying there, bloody and dying, unending cold rage seized my thoughts. All I could think about was revenge on everyone involved in her torture.

Lucille's torture.

My second problem.

Arms wrapped around me from behind, startling me from my thoughts.

"Are you going to play with your dagger all night or come to your bed and play with me instead?" Moira asked, pressing her soft lips to my ear.

Seven Hells, my shadows didn't sense her? Was I that distracted?

She slowly slid her naked arms down my chest. My muscles pushed at the thick material of my uniform like my shadows pushed at my body to escape—and go to... her. Not the female attempting to unbuckle my cuirass. The female down the hall.

The writhing wisps living inside me were both a part of me and an entity all their own. They craved the female like they craved the blood of our victims. They craved her, and I desired to have *nothing* to do with her.

I didn't want a romantic relationship. I didn't want a cordistella. I didn't want another fucking bond. The fact that I had one—and my shadows acted against me—posed a serious problem.

"Ronen," Moira begged, kissing down the stubble on my jaw. "Come to bed."

"I need to see the king." I shrugged her off and stood.

"Are you sure?" She drew out her words, each sound dripping with sex.

If I turned around, she'd be completely naked.

I rebuckled my cuirass. "Yes."

"Do you want me to join you?"

I could hear her disappointment. She didn't want to join me. She wanted me to stay and sink my cock into her. My shadows revolted at the mere thought.

"No. I'll be back later. Sleep."

Then I left, sheathing Tsal-mawet at my side and refusing to lay eyes on her beseeching baby blues or supple naked body.

I yanked my door open and strode into the hall. At the end of the corridor, my shadows jerked beneath my skin and eclipsed my eyes, begging to pool out of me and turn right.

I was sick and tired of this. The king should've kept her on his level of the castle. He could protect her just as well. I needed more space from her, not less—but I couldn't very well tell him that. In fact, I couldn't tell him anything about our bond. If he knew, it could jeopardize our arrangement. Not that I intended to claim her as my cordistella.

After going down three levels to the ground floor, I approached his hall. At his door, I raised my fist but hesitated, grazing my thumb over the dagger. Did he need to know? Nothing could change without my feather.

The frozen door handle melted. "Enter, General Ronen," he called out.

I slid my arm in front of the dagger and mentally berated myself for hesitating when he could sense me. Then I walked in.

"Lucifer." I nodded. That was as much as I'd bow to him. He may have given me a title and a place to stay, but he also knew what I was to him—or what I was supposed to be.

He nodded back. The same old song and dance we played with each other.

Since he asked me to come in, I knew he needed something from me.

"Yes?" I prompted.

He stood from his desk and turned to face the fire at his back. "Lucille needs training. She's weak and inexperienced."

I shoved my infuriating wisps deep inside my core, unwilling to deal with their temperamental bullshit. He was right. Yet for some reason, they saw his words as a slight, even when they were facts.

Well, not frail. Small and malnourished. But she still had muscle on her bones.

"And you want *me* to train her?"

No one ever wanted me to train them. My Dreads didn't even want to go through the drills I put them through, and they were my elite squadron.

"She will be placed in the Infernos."

"Lucifer," I protested.

He turned around and raised a brow. "I want her trained, Ronen."

I refrained from cracking my thumbs in my fist, squeezing them instead. "The Infernos are third from our elite squadron. She wouldn't last a day." He knew that. His eyes twitched and illuminated. He was about to veto me. "They won't tolerate her. You know how hard they've worked to reach the third squadron. You can't place her there like it's nothing."

He considered me, then nodded. "Fine. The Tormentors Squadron."

"Your daughter doesn't have the necessary skills to be in any squadron but the Bowels."

Lucifer's eyes narrowed, and the room dropped in temperature. "She doesn't have the luxury to start at the bottom. The Redemption Circle is becoming more dangerous each week. I want her in the Tormentors. If she has to train every second of every day to progress faster, then so be it."

"They will prey on her weakness—especially if they know who she is."

"They will not know who she is."

"Why?"

He gave me a measured look. "You haven't figured it out yet, have you?"

What was that supposed to mean?

"Have you sensed her power?"

I've tasted it in her blood, but he'd be less than pleased to hear that, so I nodded.

"She's my daughter. The first offspring of Hell. There's no telling all the power she contains. I learned of some when you bridged our minds together. Based on what she said and what I've seen, I believe Saraqael is her mother."

I stilled. What he said wasn't possible. Angels were created—never born.

"I don't understand."

He scoffed. "Neither do I. But if my daughter is telling the truth, then she is no Nephilim, and I somehow got Saraqael pregnant the last time she was here."

I remembered that day and still didn't know what to think about it.

"Do you think she planned it all?" I asked, thinking back to the odd way Saraqael acted, and the ice storm that shattered the windows when she stormed out of Hell and never returned.

Lucifer's eyes were glazed, most likely reliving the worst night of his life—when Saraqael chose Michael over him. "I don't know. That's why I need her to wake up."

Even with my power to manipulate the bodies and minds of others, I couldn't wake Saraqael. That was almost as surprising as the fact that Lucifer allowed me to taste her blood in the first place.

"What about the fem—Lucille? Can she tell you anything?" Her name curled around my tongue in a sweet caress. I grimaced, hating that I liked it.

"She's been in and out of consciousness this last week. But, knowing Saraqael, I doubt she knows much. I need Saraqael."

By the look on his face, he more than needed her. He yearned for her, obsessed over her, and would do absolutely anything for her—even after she stormed off and chose another.

That wouldn't be me. It was bad enough having to watch Lucifer pine for Saraqael.

No, I'd never allow someone to have that hold over me again. Moira satisfied me enough. She had low expectations for our situation and never pushed for more. We were both happy with the way things were. So the whirling darkness coiling inside me better enjoy disappointment.

"Give Lucille a couple more days to heal, then introduce her to her new life with your Tormentors."

"You're sure you want her with the fourth squadron?" Anyone else who dared to question the King of Hell would've suffocated on ice.

"Train her hard, make her suffer, but keep her alive. I don't care how you do it, but she needs to be ready. There'll be a reckoning in Hell for what's been done."

His ominous words stirred the shadows beneath my skin.

"What kind of reckoning?"

"The kind that will restore Hell to what it once was."

I slid my hand behind my back as I felt the whisper of my shadows tickle my palms. Lucifer was hiding something, and they didn't like that it had any relation to the female.

"I'll debrief you on her cover story in a few days. No one in Hell can know who she is. If someone tells the Council of Righteousness, those heavenly bastards will demand retribution."

Lucifer glared at the wedding band around his finger, connecting him to the Mother of Demons.

After Saraqael left him and Hell changed, he finally believed the council of Seraphim he'd once been part of had become venal. He should've come to that conclusion years ago, when I mentioned their immoral practices. But he chose not to believe or trust me. After all, I was a Dark Seraphim. My powers tortured and controlled. And yet, this Council of *Righteousness* created me. When the only being in existence who should be able to create angels was the Weaver and his dagger, which hid behind my arm.

But Lucifer provided me refuge, so I didn't question him.

Why he chose not to believe Saraqael, I had no idea.

"Add the Nephilim too."

I raised a brow. "The Nephilim?"

"She might as well have one friend watching her back. Put him with the Tormentors too."

Moira was going to roast my balls for this new development. I'd be going over her head to place two weak, tiny, unseasoned—not even warriors—in her squadron.

Seven Hells.

I sucked up my griping words and accepted my orders.

An unnerving smile graced his face as he dismissed me. One I recognized—and hated.

"Good luck."

I walked to his door.

"Oh, Ronen."

My hand paused on the door handle while my arm pressed firmly into the sheath hiding the Weaver's dagger.

"Yes?"

"Was there something you needed?"

Now was my chance. I could tell him we had one of the two items we needed for the Unmaking Ceremony.

"Just wanted to report we found no sightings of the Damned today."

The words just popped out. They were the truth, but they weren't the ones I should've said.

He nodded and waved me away.

The dagger burned a hole in my arm as I made my way back to my rooms.

Why didn't I tell him?

CHAPTER 3

Lucille

Grogginess weighed down my eyes as I blinked into a canopy of red and black fabric. I twisted to the right, tracing a line of deep red pillows that ended at a trio of floor-length, gothic windows. Pale light spilled through their decorative panes, casting shadows across the floor. A popping sound pulled my attention to a small fire flickering in a stone hearth.

I sat up.

Where was I?

Scooting over to the edge of the bed, I pushed off my blankets. A loose camisole fell over my chest, ending at a pair of tiny black shorts. I froze at the sight of the giant pink scars. They ran from the hem of my bottoms down my thighs, their stitched edges overlapping.

Who healed me?

I stood. Vertigo hit. I shot my arm out to steady myself and knocked over a water glass on the end table.

"Lucy? Are you awake?"

"Oliver?"

He stepped into the large bedroom. But he wasn't alone.

"What is that Soulhound doing here?"

Oliver approached. "She lives here."

As I met the beastie's deep, golden gaze, a blanket of safety enveloped me.

Going off instinct, I held out my hand. The beastie came bounding over, head-butting my palm with her wet nose and pushing me back into the bed.

"Huh, I expected a panic attack over her, not whatever"—he gestured to us—"this weirdness is. Do you know this Soulhound?"

"We've met."

"Oh." Oliver sank onto the bed. "She's sweet." He ran his hands through her shadow fur. "Aren't you, Rune?"

Rune scooted away from him and plopped down beside me, leaning into my side.

Heavenly Hell, she weighed a lot.

I smirked. "We met when I tried to escape Aspen and Brock." But the more I thought about it—the size of her, the ebony fur, the way she pushed into my touch—I wondered if that really was the first time I saw her.

"Right, well, if you weren't all broken and weak, I'd guarantee she'd be snuggled next to me and not you."

I rolled my eyes, then took in Oliver. Usually, his hair lay like a messy mop atop his head. But now it stuck up in every direction. He'd been stress-scrubbing—a lot.

"Oliver." My attention drifted to the intricately carved door near the crackling fireplace. "Last time I saw you, I knocked you out while you were under the influence of Magda, and now you're here, wherever *here* is. What have I missed?"

"You've been mostly unconscious and healing for a week. And..."

"And?"

Oliver ran a hand through his chaotic hair. "We're stuck in Hell for the foreseeable future."

"What?"

He sighed. "After Hell's general rescued us and your mom, I met the king. He told me it'd be at least another year before the gates opened again. Another year before he could help rescue my sister in exchange for returning you and your mom. So we're stuck here."

"No." There had to be a punchline.

Oliver ran his hands up his face. "We are. One more damned year to add to the ninety-five."

"No!" I wanted to stand and pace, to shriek, to—to do something! Aspen needed me.

"Trust me, I get it. I've done my screaming and might've destroyed a few things in the rooms I'm staying in."

"There has to be a way out!"

I couldn't let Lilith control Aspen for one more day—let alone another year—and Oliver deserved a chance to find his sister. She was all he had. He never talked about the angel who fathered him—only her. Thinking about his family reminded me of my own.

"You said my mom's here?" Dark wood trim framed the painted gothic roses blooming in reds and blacks on the walls. "Where is here, exactly?"

Oliver flopped onto his back, pulling me down with him. "She is, but I'm not sure where. You'll have to ask the king. We're in his castle."

I stilled. "We're in my father's castle?"

We were in Hell, like my mom's prophecy predicted, in the home of a male I'd only met through conversations in my head. A male with an authority complex, a cunning disposition, and little tolerance for my snark.

"The King of Hell is your father?"

I slowly nodded, but couldn't think about the male who sired me. Not yet. Not after Oliver's bombshell.

"You're the Princess of Hell."

Heavenly Shit. "Yep."

"How could you have kept that from me?" he accused.

I shot him a dry look.

"Right. Stupid question."

"A year, Oliver?" Disbelief rang in my tone.

He sighed again. "I know. But I guess Hell's been having issues. The gates used to open for a few minutes every day, releasing and gaining souls. Now it's a lot less—if ever."

"Is it all that bad? What soul wants to end up in Hell?" I muttered.

"Probably no one. But when I kill Marcus, I hope he ends up here."

"Yeah, I can think of a few people I want to send to Hell too."

We lay in silence, both lost in our thoughts, when Rune jumped onto the bed. She lay across the pillows and attacked my cheek with her tongue.

"Okay, okay!" I pushed her large head away.

Oliver snorted. "She sure does like you." Then he sat up. "Oh, fuck-a-duck."

"What?" I groaned. We didn't need any other earth-shattering reveals at the moment. I needed to find clothes, my mom, and a loophole to this new cage.

"Rune's eyes are glowing."

"So?"

His face scrunched in puzzlement. "So, it has something to do with him—her angel counterpart. I read something about Soulhound bonds years ago. They're connected somehow, like he can see through her eyes. And maybe more. I don't remember."

"And her counterpart is?"

Someone knocked—not on the door wide open to the bedroom, but on another, hidden beyond the wall.

"The oh-so-scrumdiliumcious male who rescued you and lives down the hall from us, and is the—"

A male walked into the room.

A sinfully hot male—in a slam-you-up-against-a-wall-and-satisfy-all-your-needs kind of way. His black button-up hugged every bulging muscle, sleeves rolled to reveal tattooed arms inked in black that curled into the open V of his shirt and wrapped around his neck.

A clean fade sharpened his dark hair, longer on top, neat at the sides. And when he moved, the gold accents on his sleeves caught the light—mirroring the burn in his golden eyes.

"Him," Oliver whispered in my ear. "The General of Hell."

Shit.

The general's eyes flashed with shadows. Not flame—shadows. What the hell *was* he?

He snapped his fingers, and Rune jumped down, placing herself at his side.

"Leave her bed, Nephilim." The same shadows that flickered in his eyes swirled around his inked neck, flowing past his button-up to wrap around his tensing arms and sheath his hands.

"Oliver can be wherever he wants to be," I said in his defense.

The general blinked and raised his chin. A shadow whipped out from his hand and snaked around Oliver's bicep, yanking him off my bed. He stumbled as the general forced him away from me.

"Who the hell do you think you are, barging in here and manhandling him?" I stood and reached for Oliver. Immediately, the room swayed, and my legs wobbled. Before I could fall, another shadow flew toward me—along with Oliver and a large, whimpering Soulhound.

Rune crashed into Oliver, sending him careening into my side. I grunted and tensed for the impact of the hardwood floor. But it never came.

The shadows that flew toward us cushioned our fall and slowly lowered us to the ground.

"You okay, Lucy?" Oliver mumbled.

Rune pressed her wet nose into my cheek, and I gave her a small glare. She didn't mean to slam Oliver into me and knock us down. She just seemed to have no idea how big she actually was.

"Yeah. You?"

"Well, I got a faceful of your bony shoulder, and I'm pretty sure Rune bruised my side, but I'm fine," he said, lifting his head to give me a goofy wink before flopping it back into my neck with a groan.

"*Leave*, Nephilim." Shadows overtook the unique gold of the general's eyes, turning them into dark, fathomless pits. "She needs to change and eat. Her father wants to meet with her in a couple of hours."

Oh, goodie. Another controlling, powerful asshat.

"And I was just getting comfortable too." Oliver sighed, untangling his legs from mine.

The general's expression narrowed. Two shadows shot out and snaked around Oliver's arms, forcing him to his feet.

His emerald eyes flashed with fire before settling to irritation. I sat up, meeting the general's gaze with a defiant stare—for Oliver's sake—but as much as I wanted to snap at him, I forced myself to hold back. Mainly because this was the male I needed to convince to help me, and we were already off to a disastrously bad start.

"Go, Oliver. I'll be okay."

"You sure?" A rebellious smile twitched at the corner of his lips. Oliver would try his damndest to stay if I asked.

We had come a long way in our friendship.

"Yes, I'll explain later."

His smile flattened, understanding I had something serious to talk about—something he probably wouldn't agree with. But the part about rescuing his sister would pique his interest.

"Alright. I'll be back later, then." Oliver turned, eyeing the general up and down as he left. The general took no notice of him, his drilling, dark stare directed only at me.

Wonderful.

I pushed to my feet, and his shadows helped to hold me up. Part of me wanted to tell him to get off me, but I couldn't stand without him. Lying unconscious in a bed for a week left me shaky and unstable. It also explained the ache in my stomach.

But I could do without the angry staring contest as I climbed back into bed. Well, angry for him. I'd shoved all my glares into a locked box, and keeping it shut took strength. Especially when his expression said I wasn't worth his time or energy.

"So, I guess thanks for saving me twice now. And saving my mom."

It was a pathetic attempt at gratitude, but I couldn't muster anything more, especially with the awkward tension thick in the air.

His eyes returned to their luminous gold. "Twice?"

"Yeah..." I tilted my head. "You and that female woke me up?"

I'd been so close to giving in to the Void when Marcus held me prisoner and poisoned me for Michael. But the general's voice—and the powerful emotion that bellowed out of him—woke me up. He'd acted like he knew me. But now, it looked like he not only didn't know me, but despised being in my presence.

Maybe I got it wrong. Maybe it wasn't his voice.

"I've been here in Hell for the past ten years. Last week, when I rescued you, was my first time out."

That didn't add up. Was he lying to me? If he didn't rescue me from my poisoned mind, then who did?

"Okay. Well, thanks...." I prompted for his name.

He crossed his large arms. "You can call me General or General Ronen. Your choice."

"What's your first name?"

"Ronen. But you're not allowed to call me that without my title."

Oh, Heavenly Hell. He wasn't going to make any of this easy on me.

"That's not your last name?" I gritted out.

"Angels and demons don't have last names. That's purely a human quality. You'd know that if you grew up around us."

And with that oh-so-pleasant but pointed comment nudging me to tap into my Infernus and chuck an icicle at his head, I said, "Get out of my room."

I didn't have to tolerate his disrespect or the disdain pressed into his lips. Sure, I needed to play nice—and I would—but I had no energy for that right now.

His shadows swallowed his eyes, and his nostrils flared. Aspen wasn't the only one who showed his anger through the power in his eyes. But from the pressure behind my own, I had a feeling they weren't alone.

"I may be weak right now, *General.* But that won't stop me from freezing your ass if you don't listen."

It was all bluster. The mere thought of pulling at my power made me want to pass out. But he didn't know that.

"Your father wants to meet with you in a few hours."

No shit. It's not like he didn't just mention that.

"Out."

I needed a second to gather myself and take in Oliver's information. I needed to process the fact that I was in my father's lands. I was the Princess of Hell. I was a born angel. And the person whose help I needed already hated me.

"Please," I pushed out through clenched teeth.

"Be ready." He gave me one last punishing stare, then left.

Rune sat in the doorway, panning between me and the general with her glowing golden eyes.

"Beastie, I'm not sure what the glowing entails, but if the general is watching through you, I'd prefer if you cut it out."

Rune's eyes returned to their normal hue, and I slumped back, feeling weak.

I patted my bed, and Rune jumped up, curling into my warmth without hesitation. My body sank into the sheets, but my mind... that was a different story.

Overwhelming thoughts circled with a vengeance, pressing down on my chest with each pass. I didn't expect to wake in *my father's* castle. The very thought of that term made my stomach twist. I knew he wasn't Michael, but that didn't change the fact that Michael tainted that word—and practically every other endearment regarding a father figure—with every line he carved into my body since I was five.

And the king wouldn't be any better.

My mother kept me hidden from him for a reason.

She always thought he'd kill me.

CHAPTER 4

Ronen

Punch after punch, I rammed my fists into the bag, changing up my combos but never slowing my speed or intensity.

"Okay, who got your wings wet this time?" Alexei gritted out, holding the punching bag for me.

Wet wings meant harder flight, losing altitude or tearing your muscles apart to keep from crashing to your death. It meant hours to fucking dry and dragging against the ground without the ability to dematerialize them until they dried or the torn muscles healed. Wet wings pissed any sane angel off, which was why if any of my Dreads chose to play another prank on me with water, they'd be demoted and running patrols in the Veil Forest, where Hellhounds and Spinewalkers crept through the thick fog. Lucky for them, I only manifested them seconds before flight, like most angels.

"No one." My right hook slammed into the bag, knocking Alexei back.

"It was Danny, wasn't it?" Alexei shook his head. "That prick's always doing something to piss you off."

He wasn't wrong, but no, it wasn't the squadron leader of the Devils. Not this time.

"No."

"Female trouble?" Alexei stepped back up to the bag, holding it steady. "Maybe if you didn't look the way you did, your life would be easier."

I scoffed, shaking my head at the golden boy who had females fawning over him weekly.

"And who will you have in your bed tonight?" I pointed out in between grunts.

He grinned. "I may have asked a few of my favorites to join me."

"A few?"

"It's so hard to choose. They're all so beautiful."

"And they agree to that?" I sure as hell wouldn't. I don't share.

Alexei shrugged. "I'll learn tonight. But I have a feeling it'll work out in my favor."

I laughed at my second and finished punching out my frustration until sweat soaked my clothes and sand clung to my arms. That was the one thing I hated about this enclosed arena—always feeling the gritty substance sticking to me like a second skin and digging into my boots. It didn't matter if I trained in my uniform or pants and a T-shirt; the sand always found a way in.

I also hated the floor-length windows lining almost every wall, like we were some spectacle to watch. This wasn't a gladiator arena, even if we were as brutal and vicious as those warriors. But the windows weren't for spectators, nor were they some punishment. Lucifer had created his castle with hundreds of them so he could gaze toward the heavens, where he'd believed Saraqael to be while she'd been away.

That was before he learned Saraqael avoided Heaven's domain like the plague and found a home on Earth.

"Here." Alexei slapped a towel into my chest, his eyes blatantly fixed on something to my right.

I shook my head. "Haven't you learned your lesson from staring at MJ's ass the last hundred times?"

MJ, my third, trained in the weapons range, pulling back her bow with precision before releasing two arrows. Both hit the dummy's heart from sixty meters away—about the same distance we stood from her in the sparring grounds.

He shrugged. "Doesn't hurt to admire."

I snorted. He knew damn well it did hurt him—frequently. Yet he always came back for more.

"It will once she notices."

Which she did. He deflected the arrow she shot at his face with a blast of wind, and it hit the punching bag, spilling grain everywhere. He smirked at MJ.

"Pick it all up, Alexei, and patch up the bag. We'll debrief tomorrow and check out the recruits for the Infernal Sixty," I said, walking past a few of my Dreads lifting weights.

"Can't wait for the new bait. I love the Infernal Sixty!"

I usually agreed with Alexei, but this time, *she'd* be a part of it. I'd had enough exposure to watching the Nephilim crawl all over her.

How many males did she have? First the damned traitorous pet, and now the Nephilim? She nearly rivaled Alexei—but no one could be as bad as him. Nor did I care who occupied his bed. Or hers. But my shadows sure as hell did.

We used to work as one, and still did—unless it came to her. If she entered the room or my mind even for a split second, they pushed and begged to be released. The last time I struggled this hard to keep them contained was when the council first created me—back when I was just learning about my semi-sentient power. Sometimes they had a mind of their own, did things without my command. But that was years ago. I thought we were past that petulant stage—until last week.

A soul groaned off to my left as I passed. A blood-banded warrior beat in his face, splitting his cheek. My lips pressed together, still unnerved by the fact the dead didn't bleed.

I gave the almost-empty arena a once-over before I left. Tomorrow, it'd be filled with new souls and blood-banded. Tomorrow, they'd realize exactly what horror they brought upon themselves.

Back in my room, I shucked off my sweaty clothes and hopped into the shower.

"For fuck's sake," I hissed, cringing as the icy water hit my back.

Someone must've pissed off Lucifer today. Hell was fortunate to have running water—unlike Elora—but unfortunately, Lucifer's moods controlled the temperature.

Stepping out, I paused on my only colored tattoo, like I did every day. The band of red circled my left bicep, a glaring reminder of my precarious situation.

As a living soul in Hell, to stay without consequences, I needed Lucifer's blood tattooed into my arm. He decided who among the living could reside in Hell before their time. But it came at a steep price.

I questioned the deal I made with Lucifer every day.

Having two alpha males with equal power in one domain amounted to a volatile atmosphere. But once we figured out our odd dynamic and he gave me a semblance of my control back, we came to a fragile truce. Then, when Saraqael left him, he no longer cared about changing leadership—and my guilt slid away.

The blood-band seemed like a saving grace for the last twenty years, even with Hell imploding. But after all these new developments with Saraqael and her daughter, the guilt snuck back in, sinking heavy in my gut.

I believed in truth—and yet, I never told him that if I ever found the items for the Unmaking Ceremony and replaced him as king, there was a chance he'd die.

I didn't think that made me a bad male—only a desperate one.

Because if I'd told him the truth, I wouldn't be a general. I wouldn't have free rein in the Redemption Circle. No—I'd be his slave. And I swore to myself, I'd never, *never* let that happen again.

I slipped on my uniform and strapped my dual blades to my back. After combing through my short hair, I glanced at Tsal-mawet secured to my weapons wall, then headed to the Hall of Judgment on the other side of the castle.

On my way, I tuned into Rune and felt a calm happiness from my Soulhound. The ease with which I connected to her mind gave me a sense of peace I hadn't had for the last ten years. I realized I had needed her back, and our connection restored.

I nudged awareness at her, forcing her awake so I could see the female. I groaned. No wonder Rune fell asleep. The female did too.

Wake her up, Rune. She needs to get ready.

Rune sent me a feeling of confirmation and licked the female's cheek. She smiled in her sleep, doing horrible things to my nerves. Rune, seeing the lack of opening eyes, slobbered all over her face.

I smirked, and the female laughed. I separated the visual connection the moment she opened her captivating, starry eyes and sent Rune a feeling of gratitude.

Hopefully, the female would be ready when I came to fetch her.

I really had to stop thinking about her as *the female*, or I'd start calling her that. But I needed something else besides Lucille.

My shadows sank their claws into the seductive syllables and darkened my vision. I shivered. This loss of control drove me insane. I didn't have the luxury to be anything but composed and unshakeable.

But the instant my shadows connected with her mind, the manipulative, revolting bond woke up. Immediately, I blocked her side of the connection—and my own. I wanted nothing from her, and I'd give her nothing in return. I'd have her trained and keep her alive, but it ended there. She was a job—only orders. I was lucky I didn't have to personally train her.

Now, if only my shadows would listen and quit challenging my restraint.

The tall doors of the Hall of Judgment came into view. Each one depicted a story. One door, blood red, illustrated souls begging for mercy in each of the Seven Circles of Hell on their journey to redemption. The other, pure white, illustrated joyful souls on their way to Heaven after paying the price for their sins.

Hell gained an influx of souls when the gates opened last week—so many souls that had been waiting in limbo to descend to Hell for their judgment. Now, Lucifer and I had to work overtime to send them to their respective circle.

Fortunately for them, Hell wasn't necessarily their last stop. They received the chance to redeem themselves—unless they were too corrupted and weak to ascend. Then they were stuck in Hell forever, suffering in the lower circles.

A Damned Soul.

A type of soul that shouldn't even be able to breach the Redemption Circle. Yet here I was, entering the hall to help Lucifer interrogate one.

I pushed open the door and made my way toward the dais. Lucifer occupied his two-themed throne with quiet authority. His hands casually rested on carvings symbolizing joy and agony.

"Bloodhound." Lucifer nodded.

His nickname for me eased the tension in my jaw. My cold shower wasn't a result of something I did. Someone—or something—else must've pissed him off.

"My liege." I nodded back, positioning myself at his side.

A couple of my Dreads brought in the Damned Soul. He limped in calmly, sandwiched between the uniformed warriors as if it were just any other day. Some of his skin wept with dark, bloody fluids, flowing from one burn to the next. He no longer had hair, and a grotesque, demented smile stretched unnaturally across the two pieces of dried-out flesh that made up his lips—wounds reminiscent of Hellfire from the Immolation Circle.

My attention lingered on his gums and the veins creeping through the exposed muscles in his arms and neck. They were *black*. Souls may not bleed, but their flesh remained red beneath their skin. Something was wrong with this soul.

I gave my warriors a sharp nod. They shoved the male to his knees at the foot of the dais. Immediately, the temperature dropped, and Lucifer rose from his chair.

"State your name," he commanded, his voice carrying an edge.

The Damned Soul laughed. "You don't remember me, Lucifer?"

The pressure in the room shifted. My ears popped as frost quickly coated the entire hall, and ice shards shot from the ground, encircling the soul. My uniform warmed against the deadly temperatures, holding my body heat in check.

"I am your *king*. I control your miserable existence. Name, now."

The soul's eyes glinted with madness. "You don't remember me confessing to the women I raped and killed? Or asking if there'd be more to play with in your circles, *Lucifer*?" He laughed again, the cackling echoing through the hall.

Lucifer's temper snapped. He sent a spear of ice through the soul's stomach, stopping his laughter mid-sound.

"How did you get into the Redemption Circle, Silas?" Lucifer demanded.

Silas smiled. What looked like black tar dripped from his mouth. "Wouldn't you like to know? But I'm not going to tell you," he sang, rocking back and forth on his knees.

"Bloodhound," Lucifer barked.

I extended my shadows, absorbing the Damned Soul's blood and bringing it to my mouth. Tar and ash stuck to my tongue. I forced back a gag and dove into his mind, finding it just as repulsive. Most of his memories were fragmented and disjointed—all but the ones about rape and his deserved suffering in the Immolation Circle. I dove deeper, prodding his neurons, only to find the echoes of madness.

"The King of Hell is on his throne, on his throne, on his throne. The King of Hell is on his throne, but not for long," the Damned Soul sang with unsettling clarity.

But the thoughts of the song didn't appear in his mind—as if they weren't there at all.

"His crown will fall, his kingdom will burn, kingdom will burn, kingdom will burn. His crown will fall, his kingdom will burn, and the sinners will sing. We'll tear the gates, break the chains, and rise again."

The words felt strange coming from a mind as broken as his.

It was as though someone else spoke through him.

"Xavier," I snapped. "Search him for runes."

Xavier stepped forward, moving through the ice shard circle, and ripped at the soul's tattered clothes. The soul didn't pause for a moment, continuing to sing the same eerie melody.

"What do you suspect, General?" Lucifer asked.

"An Imperium Voxus Rune. His mind is shattered, yet he speaks with clarity. Someone else is controlling his voice, overriding his broken thoughts."

Xavier paused, his fingers stopping near the soul's back. "General." He waved me over.

Lucifer and I stepped down from the dais and entered the circle. The soul didn't even flinch, unmoved by the danger he faced. Xavier pointed at a darkened spot carved into the soul's muscle.

Two runes.

One was the Imperium Voxus, and the other—

"Do you recognize the second rune?" I asked Lucifer.

Lucifer's gaze shifted, a flicker of something in his eyes. "No."

He was lying, but I didn't press him. Here, in front of others, I acted as his subordinate.

"You can't get anything else from him?"

I plunged back into the soul's mind, finding the same broken pieces. "Nothing," I answered, withdrawing.

Lucifer whipped up his hand and encased the soul in ice, silencing the incessant singing. With another swift motion, he formed an icicle in his hand and slammed it down into the soul's body, shattering him to bits.

Usually, the pieces vanished, sent wherever Lucifer deemed best—but this time they melted to black dots, coalesced into a slimy puddle, then seeped into the cracks of the black marble tiles.

"Has the Damned Soul left our domain?" I asked.

His silence made me nervous. I shot him a glance.

"Yes and no," he replied, glaring at the tile.

"What do you mean?"

"The darkness that has settled over the Redemption Circle has lessened—and grown."

"What?"

Lucifer rubbed his temples. "We need to find where they're coming in from, banish the invaders, and close the fissure before there's more."

"We've been scouring this circle with no results. Can you sense anything else?"

He should feel something from the land he ruled.

"I can't sense a specific location, only the stain of their ilk. Whatever they're doing, they're masking it well. Tell your Dreads to search harder."

I nodded. "Send in the next soul, Xavier. Then relay the message to our warriors."

"Yes, General."

He bowed to Lucifer, then left with the other Dread.

For the next two hours, I stood by Lucifer's side as he redeemed or recycled souls, only involving myself if the souls decided to cause problems.

I recognized a few from past judgments and wasn't surprised by their recycling. They lived near souls still fighting their own darkness—souls who hadn't yet freed themselves from their sins. That lingering corruption could easily rub off on those trying to stay pure. It was no wonder they slipped back into their old ways, even after enduring the trials of the circles.

But at least they were easier to judge, and we had less resistance from them.

Although, between the increase of corrupted souls and the Damned Souls invading the Redemption Circle, Hell needed to be fixed. But I had no clue where to start, seeing as we never figured out what caused the deterioration.

"Thank you, Bloodhound. You're dismissed. Please bring my daughter to me."

I left the dais, clenching my jaw as I went to retrieve the hellion.

Hellion.

It fit. The name had a certain bite to it—while also attesting to the problem she was.

CHAPTER 5

Lucille

With the help of Rune's giant body, I explored my room and discovered a walk-in closet filled with all types of clothing. I fingered beautiful gowns, pant sets, workout clothes, and more. They were so... modern. I hadn't expected that, even after the general had shown up in that too-tight button-up.

"What should I wear, Rune?" I asked, running my hands through her fascinating fur. She appeared to be half shadow and half soft fluff. The smooth wisps tickled my fingers, and I found solace in her warmth and steady weight.

She turned to me and tilted her head, looking as clueless as I felt.

Eventually, I picked out a soft pair of lavender leggings and a matching long-sleeve shirt. I grinned and undressed in front of my mirror. Then my grin dimmed.

My hand shook as I grazed a finger across every scar marking my body. The butcher's room jolted back to life—cold metal pressed into my back, warmth seeping from my limbs. My echoing screams covered the dripping of my blood, but not the shrieking metal as he outlined my body with his dagger.

Michael's *gifts* were forever imprinted on my skin.

Feeling drained despite our nap—and incredibly hungry—I nearly sank to the floor. Using the wall for support, I put on the purple set, enjoying the soft insides even when they brushed over my tender scars. I eyed myself in the mirror and considered hiding and never coming out. My outfit might cover up the wounds, but it did little to conceal my malnourished body. Closing my eyes and breathing back tears, I pulled on an oversized hoodie, hoping it would hide my trauma and pain.

"Foolproof plan," I whispered to my reflection.

Rune pressed into my side, offering support, and I gave her a small smile. Placing my hand on her spine, I steadied myself as we walked into another room.

A sitting area, I guessed, from the couches and chairs circling a table filled with mouthwatering snacks. I tripped over my feet, scurrying to them, while Rune tried to keep me from falling and eating carpet. She managed well enough, but I still ended up on the floor.

After shoving a few pieces of meat and cheese into my mouth, I snagged a chocolate truffle.

"Mmm, Rune," I moaned. "You have to try this."

That was purely the chocolate and exhaustion talking—she probably couldn't have chocolate, nor did she look inclined to try. She did glance at the jerky a time or two, and who was I to deny such a good beastie the pleasure?

I flung a piece at her. She caught it at the same time her eyes illuminated.

The door to the sitting area jerked open.

"Don't feed my Soulhound," General Ronen snapped as he barged in without knocking.

"Don't barge into places you're unwanted," I mumbled, ignoring him in favor of more chocolate. He didn't get the pleasure of ruining my heavenly sugary escape yet.

Plopping two more in my mouth, I closed my eyes, pretending I was back in the forest with Aspen the day we threw pieces of this sugary goodness at each other in hopes of catching them. I smiled at the memory, happy to have it back.

"Is that all you're going to eat?"

He wasn't there. He wasn't there.

"And is that what you're wearing to meet your father?"

The dark chocolate with a caramel center was my new favorite.

"You can't wear that."

"It was in my closet. Not sure why I can't."

Actually, the one that tasted like roasted marshmallows with a sprinkle of salt was my favorite.

"Hellion! Open your damn eyes and stop ignoring me!"

I slowly opened my eyes, then swallowed all the chocolate in my mouth, nearly choking.

His ebony hair glistened with a wet sheen, like he'd just showered, and he wore a white button-up instead of black. He might as well have been shirtless—the fabric clung to his body, practically see-through. Did he know how to use a towel?

I couldn't take my eyes off the dark artwork peeking through his shirt. Did they go lower, into his—

Flushing, I turned away. That was not a thought I wanted to complete. I wiped at the chocolate sticking to the corner of my lips.

"What did you call me?"

"Hellion. Because that's what you are. A problem, an annoyance, an irritating menace. Someone who doesn't know how to dress herself appropriately before meeting the King of Hell." His muscles coiled beneath his shirt, flickers of shadows wrapping around his crossed arms.

"Should I be in a gown with full skirts and some gloves? Do I need to go find my corset and bonnet, General?"

His expression narrowed. "Of course not. The king provided you with modern-day clothes. You're not a soul from the 1700s, so why would you suggest something so foolish?"

I licked my lips and stood. Rune immediately came to my side, letting me rest against her, which I both hated and appreciated. Hated, because the general noticed and glared—as if I were unworthy of touching his Soulhound. But newsflash: he left her with me.

"Didn't know the King of Hell employed such an asshole as a general," I stated. The shadows that eclipsed his eyes gave me great pleasure, right before succumbing to dread.

What was I doing?

Aspen needed him.

But why did he have to act like this? What did I ever do to him?

"Fine. Wear *that*."

The way he said it made it sound like I wore rags. But I only wore these clothes to cover my torture—not that the high and mighty general would ever understand. I didn't need his damned unsolicited opinion.

Before tears of frustration could destroy the carefully crafted glare I had going, he raised a hand and positioned his fingers like he was about to snap at me. Like I was a disobedient Soulhound needing to listen to her master.

"I'm *not* a dog. So much as move those fingers together, and I will risk passing out on this carpet in favor of smothering you in ice, *General*."

He dropped his hand, and the shadows left his eyes. "Fine. But your father is waiting."

"And my mother?"

General Ronen stilled. "Your father can tell you about your mother."

I moved closer to him with Rune's help. "What does that mean?"

He took in my leaning posture and scowled at the space where my body touched his Soulhound.

"I'm not going to damage Rune. Now what the hell do you mean?"

Needles prickled my hands, signaling my wayward Glory. Now was not the time for this, or the sudden squeezing pressure in my lungs that I had yet to deal with.

General Ronen stared at me, silent.

"Tell me!"

Why wasn't he answering? Did Oliver leave something out? Was she dead?

Oh shit, I couldn't breathe—I couldn't—

I let go of Rune, afraid I'd burst into flames and burn her, and sank to the floor, clutching at my chest. General Ronen followed me, watching with a look that was part confusion, part reluctant concern.

I heaved on the floor, hunched over my knees. He reached out to touch me, his hands swallowed in shadows once again. I flinched. He dropped his hands, looking down at them like he'd just realized the shadows were there.

"What's wrong?"

"She's having a panic attack," Oliver said from behind him.

I didn't even hear the door open.

Oliver crouched. "Lucy, calm your mind. It's okay. I bet your mom's just fine. Right, General?"

When the general didn't answer, the needles pushed at my Glory, flaring onto my hands. His shadows whipped out. Before I could pull back, they brushed my skin and—and—soothed away my flames. They quieted my fear and settled my breath.

My brows drew together. "What did you do?" I asked, staring at my lightless hands.

The general stood, silent and brooding. Fine. I didn't need to know what he did, but I did need to know about my mom.

"Is she okay?" I demanded.

He left the room, calling back, "Follow me and find out."

My Infernus called to me, enjoying the quick switch of emotions. I wanted to shove ice so far down his throat it pushed the stick out of his arrogant, controlling ass. But that'd get me nowhere, and I had no energy to use.

"I may murder him, Oliver."

He helped me off the floor. "My money's on you. So wait until I gather a big enough crowd to place my bet. I'll be rich."

"Think he's still waiting for us?"

Oliver nodded to Rune, whose eyes were glowing. "I'm sure he hasn't gone far."

"Right." It'd probably benefit us to figure out what the glowing eyes entail. But that was a later problem.

Despite Rune's whining, I gripped Oliver's arm to steady myself as we walked down a hall with red carpet and floor-length windows. I almost stopped when we hit the hallway. A foot of ice coated the outer black walls of the castle, bringing to mind part of Miriam's prophecy:

There once was a palace of crystallized ice awaiting the daughter to sacrifice. Unbalanced and sorrowful. Hopeless with no tomorrow.

Maybe it wasn't wise to meet the king—but I had to find my mom. And if he was going to sacrifice me, wouldn't he have done it while I was unconscious?

"How we're not freezing our asses off beats me," Oliver exclaimed.

"Magic?" I mumbled, shaking off my creeping apprehension.

"Probably."

We continued past the windows and followed Rune and the general to a staircase.

Shit.

"Need me to carry your scrawny butt down?" Oliver asked.

The general stopped at the bottom of the first set of stairs. Rune stayed beside me, whimpering and nudging me to use her before I descended. Maybe in a different circumstance, I would've taken

Oliver up on his offer. But with the general looking at me like I was worthless and couldn't do it, I didn't want to lean on Oliver or Rune.

Challenging the general to say a word, I stepped down. Again. My heart picked up speed. On the third step, I was about ready to smile in his condescending face when black dots stole my vision and weakened my legs.

I fell.

Teeth nipped into my back, catching my hoodie at the same time a chest barreled into me, gripping my shoulders.

I gazed up into piercing golden eyes, falling into the alluring molten depths. They held me captive with their intensity, as though they could see straight through me, tugging at something deep in my chest. I couldn't name the sensation—only that it felt unsettling and magnetic, drawing me in despite the sharp edge of his demeanor. Warmth smoldered there too, a quiet heat that contrasted with the coldness in his gaze, and I found myself wanting to explore it.

"Are you done trying to show off in your weakened state?" the general growled. His harsh words snapped me out of my captivation. I wasn't sure why I'd been so absorbed in him. He never smiled, his personality remained as dour as a storm cloud, and he seemed to have some vendetta against me I couldn't figure out.

"Only if you're done being an a—" I stopped myself.

His lips tightened. He knew what I was about to say—it wasn't hard to figure out. His golden eyes taunted me with their unnerving color, and I gritted my teeth, forcing myself to look away.

Instead, I focused on the disdain flattening his lips. Not that it was any better. The sight made me almost as angry as the strange pull

I'd felt before. There was only one male I wanted to affect me, and it wasn't the one staring at me like I was a pebble in his boot.

But I reminded myself I needed him.

No matter how much his expression, captivating eyes, or blunt words pissed me off, I needed him to save Aspen.

General Ronen lightened his hold as if he were about to let me fall down the stairs, but instead, he scooped me up and plopped me on Rune. She wagged her tail happily.

He stood there for a moment, like he expected a thanks or an apology. I didn't want to, but I had to make him like me.

"Thank you," I said, putting effort into sounding genuine.

He scoffed and turned.

I glared daggers at his back, flexing my fingers in Rune's fur. We continued down the stairs after him and through a couple more halls. Rune stopped when we arrived at a wooden door with a frosted handle.

The general knocked thrice in quick succession. The frosted handle thawed, and we entered a sitting room larger than mine. While mine featured shades of red and white, this one matched my bedroom—all dark reds and black. A crackling fire blazed in the back, next to two iced-over windows and a circle of comfortable seating. But no one was here.

"And she's riding your Soulhound, why, General?"

I jerked to my left, finding the king coming from a different room. Behind him, my mom rested on a bed.

"Mom?" I leaped off Rune. "Mom!" My feet hit the ground hard, and I stumbled, falling to my knees. *Dammit!*

Before I could crawl through the door, the king picked me up and deposited me on a loveseat beside the fire.

"Why is she still sleeping? What did you do to her?"

"You know I hate that tone of yours, daughter." He said *daughter* like it was both a term of endearment and an insult.

"Sounds like a personal problem. Are you going to answer me, *Father*?" Did he honestly think I cared what he did or didn't like while my mother lay in the other room, pale and still?

I stood, and ice covered my shoes, holding me in place.

"Let me go," I seethed, staring at the male who somehow made my birth possible. His white-blond, wavy hair sat a little wild on his head, like he'd just woke up. But by the suit gracing his form, that wasn't the case. He might be like Oliver, a stress scrubber. The bags under his double-ringed eyes sure spoke of some kind of stress.

"Your mother is unwell. She needs rest."

Did he think that'd placate me?

I jerked my legs, hoping to rip free, then almost smacked myself for thinking I was some helpless little girl again. I dove into my core to find where my Glory resided, but every time I reached for it and asked it to break the ice, my Infernus answered and created more. At least my purple flames protected my skin from the cold, but it wasn't what I wanted.

I wrenched against his hold, frustrated.

Oliver came up beside me, flipping a dagger and staring at the king with flaming emeralds. "Let her go."

The king raised a blond brow. "Are you threatening me, Nephilim?"

He shrugged. "Just a friendly suggestion."

"I'd put that knife away and sit before you find yourself encased in ice." The king smiled. "Just a friendly suggestion."

Oliver sheathed his knife and sat beside me, but the fire didn't leave his eyes.

"What did you do to my mother?"

The king turned his attention back to me. "I did nothing to her. She arrived unconscious. What did you and that Archangel do to her?"

"Michael gave her one bag of Nerium poisoning, but that shouldn't keep her unconscious," I said, narrowing my eyes.

"This isn't from Nerium poisoning. General Ronen could've helped with that. This is something else."

Was that how the general had calmed me earlier?

"Then what?"

"You tell me. What did Michael say to you? What happened before you were rescued?"

"Besides shackling me to a table, threatening to eradicate me from the world, and slicing me up every time I so much as whimpered—nothing too unusual. For him."

Can't believe Aspen let him walk away.

The tension in the room thickened. No one seemed to want to speak after that. But they'd rescued me. They saw the wounds and scars. Nothing I said should've come as a surprise.

Rune trotted over to me, wrapped her jaw around the thick ice covering my shoe, and shattered it. She did the same to the other, then sat before me and faced the king. Her tail stood still, her head lowered in challenge.

He gazed at Rune, raising an inquiring brow. "Troubles controlling your Soulhound, General?"

"Ten years with a disrupted connection has taken a toll."

Disrupted connection?

"Or living without obedience and roaming Elora and Earth at her own will. I expect you to remedy that."

Earth, huh?

Could that big wolf I saw in the woods have been her?

I looked back at the general and found a flat expression as he stared at the menacing king. After a tense second, he nodded. "As you wish."

"Tell me what else happened. Every detail from your life."

Peeking back at the door where my mother rested, I wondered if I could scramble there fast enough.

"If you tell me everything I want to know, I'll let you see her."

I curled my hands into fists at how he said *let*, as if I needed his permission. But I turned back to him, and instead of spewing insults and curses, I told him about our life—telling the general and Oliver in the process. I left out the parts with Aspen but described how Michael used to hit us and take a blade to my back one day every year.

Oliver grabbed my hand, squeezing it as ice crackled and the king's eyes glowed. Rune's fur whipped more aggressively. They only grew more tense as I gave more details of my capture.

"To protect her, I made a three-way deal with Michael." I yanked on the collar of my sweatshirt and showed the king my rune. "I told him I'd tell him my maker if he'd swear not to touch her again."

The king pursed his lips. "What exactly am I supposed to be seeing right now?"

I pointed at it. "It's right here. The rune. Don't you see it?"

"What does this rune look like?" he asked suspiciously, his eyes glowing and the ground slowly frosting over.

Apprehension crept in, and Rune tensed beside me.

"It's two elongated triangles with lines crossing through them and some dots."

The king stood, more ice crawling along the floor and ceiling. "Are the dots at the triangle's base or the point?"

I swallowed but held my spine beneath his intimidating stare. "The base."

"It's a Wrath Rune!"

My rune heated at his words, and his gaze shot to it like he finally saw it. A fierce wind shattered the ice across the floor. Before the shards could touch me, Oliver tackled me off the couch, and a torrent of shadows erupted, forming an impenetrable cocoon.

Glass shattered. Metal pinged. The fire hissed. Ice pelted everything outside our shield.

"Oliver," I wheezed. "Are you okay?"

"Yes," he mumbled into my neck. "Are you?"

"I'm having a hard time breathing. Can you get off?"

"Rune's on top of us."

I groaned. "Rune, we can't breathe."

A weight lifted, and I took in a lungful of air, rolling out from under Oliver.

The chaos softened, and we waited in the darkness.

"You can release them from your shadows now, Bloodhound. I'm under control," the king called.

The shadows stayed, brushing against my exposed skin like they were checking for damage.

"General Ronen!" the king snapped.

Light filtered through as the shadows wisped away. Oliver winked and sat up. Rune bombarded my face with licks, only stopping when the general snapped. She immediately pulled back and stood sentinel by my side while I took stock of the slushy sitting area.

The couches and chairs were shredded and dripping with water. Debris, ice chips, and puddles decorated every surface—except the king's chair and the circle of carpet we lay on.

I peeked back at the general over the destroyed loveseat. His golden eyes flickered, his face expressionless. Minor cuts marked his body. Red splotches seeped into his once-gorgeous white shirt, now shredded to bits.

Why didn't he protect himself during whatever the hell just happened?

"You let that Archangel put a Wrath Rune on the three of you?" the king spat.

I bit my tongue, dropping my gaze from the general and turning back to the king. "Let?" I sat up on the carpet. "I was chained to a table, bleeding out, and thought if there was a chance a deal could save my mother, then I'd sacrifice myself so he wouldn't touch her ever again!" I shouted. "I thought it was a rune for a binding agreement!"

The king stared at me, something close to reluctant respect entering his icy eyes. He nodded at my shoulder. "No, a rune for a binding agreement has the dots at the points. When the dots are at the bottom, it destabilizes the rune and turns it into that." His tone softened slightly. "A Wrath Rune." The rune heated again. "A specialized rune that's invisible unless you speak its name—which is why we never suspected it was the cause of your mother's coma."

Dread cooled the irritation warming my cheeks. "This is the cause of her coma?"

"Wrath Runes were designed to force energy from one person to another, but that's during a two-way bind. You said it was a three-way bind, with Michael as the lead, which changes the dynamic entirely. Michael either intended to steal your energy or transfer it to Saraqael, but it didn't work out the way he intended because you're awake. That means, as Saraqael sleeps, she's stealing your essence to stay alive. She won't wake unless she takes it all—"

"I need to die for my mother to live?" I whispered, horrified, staring at the door that blocked my view of her. I'd sworn I knew what rune Michael was placing on us. "Is that what needs to happen?"

Did he want me to die for her? Was *this* the sacrifice part of the prophecy?

I wasn't insulted. I had such low expectations for father figures— what was one more who'd rather see me dead than alive? At least this one carried possessive love in his unique, double-ringed eyes—for her, even after all these years.

I was nothing but a daughter he'd just learned about, one he forced to jump into a poisonous river without knowing if I'd survive. If I hadn't been his blood, I would've died. He gambled with my life. What was to stop him from doing it again?

As if reading my mind, he raised a brow and said, "I wouldn't have had my general rescue you if I wanted you to die. There's another way."

"Then what? How do we save her?"

"Michael needs to die," General Ronen said, stepping around the side of the loveseat and positioning himself next to Rune—and far too close to me.

"You can say that again," Oliver muttered.

I couldn't agree more. But we were stuck here for another year—one whole year—until the gates opened, and I had to save not only Aspen but also my mom. Again.

Michael ruined our lives. He needed to die. The thought of killing someone should've made me question my sanity. But part of me had no aversion to killing—a remorseless, dark part. The itches scattering across my skin and the music tickling my inner ear at the mere thought of what Michael had done made me crave his blood. Did this part of me stem from Hell? From the king's blood running through my veins?

"Michael's the head of the binding. Kill him, and the runes will release you both," the king confirmed.

"Then we need to get out of here and find him."

"No," the king said. "You need to train."

"What?"

He stepped closer, a cunning look glinting in his eyes. "You and the Nephilim will be placed in Hell's military, where we'll beat that human weakness out of your body and mind. And when you're not suffering with your squadron, you'll be in the library studying—or with me, training your powers."

I met his unflinching gaze with one of my own. "And if I refuse?"

"Then you won't survive."

CHAPTER 6

Lucille

After suffering through a few more minutes with the king, he finally let me see my mom. She lay beneath the covers, her small frame occupying little space on the giant bed. The black silk comforter contrasted horribly with her pale skin, like it was sucking the life out of her. In fact, the entire room felt dark and lifeless.

I reached out a shaky hand, smoothing back her black hair from her shoulder. Someone had placed her in a strappy nightgown, nothing she would've ever picked for herself. She needed her T-shirt and pants with the little chicks on them. She needed her obnoxious rooster eye mask. She needed—

A sob caught in my throat. I crawled across the mattress and curled up next to her. Tears slid down my cheeks as I wrapped my arm around her stomach and rested my head against her chest.

She needed to wake up.

I listened to her heart, guilt hitting me with every slow beat.

Why did this have to happen? Why couldn't it have been me, like I planned?

"I'm so sorry, Mom." My voice cracked. "I didn't know. I'm so sorry."

After kissing her forehead and wiping my face, I let Oliver help me back to my room. Rune and the general followed behind. There were no words of comfort. Even Oliver had no happy remarks, only a warm arm wrapped around my shoulder.

Right before my room, I paused at a large window—a cluster of buildings spread out in the distance. Unlike the small, thatch-roofed houses in Elora, these buildings were taller, wider, and had white caps on their slanted roofs.

"It's pretty frigid down there, and the people are something else to look at, but at least I haven't come across any demons like I expected I would," Oliver mumbled as I stared with a flat expression.

"What do you mean?"

Wasn't Hell supposed to have *all* the demons?

Oliver shrugged. "I mean, I haven't seen any scaly, bulbous, disgusting bastards anywhere. Some half-breed demons, but that's it. Not that the people look all that normal, but..." He shot me a look, then waved it off. "You'll understand once you see for yourself."

"Demons don't have souls. They aren't Hell's creations. You won't see them here. You'll only see their half-breeds," the general informed us.

"Okay." I didn't have the energy to say anything else.

I pulled Oliver to continue toward my door. I needed time to digest everything—and eventually discuss an escape plan.

Rune and the general hovered behind us, but neither would be allowed in. Not that the general ever was. Rune's tail curled happily at my attention, making me regret keeping her out. The general, on the other hand, seemed deep in thought.

"Sorry, Rune, but you and your angel aren't coming in this time."

Clarity sharpened the general's gaze. "Yes, we—"

"General, your clothing is in tatters, and you have blood all over your face and chest."

He glanced at his shredded shirt, then back at me, lips pressing into a hard line.

"Rune's staying."

"No, she isn't." I could only imagine he'd want to leave his Soulhound with us to gather information. "She can come back later, but for now, I'd like time alone with my friend, please."

The general held my gaze, something tightening in his face before he turned away. "Okay," he said softly.

I stood there, stunned. He actually agreed. But why? Did my bloodshot eyes and puffy cheeks move him? I highly doubted that. He hated me—so then what?

I didn't get a chance to ask. Oliver tugged me through the door, locked it, and then helped me to the settee.

"You're unusually quiet," I said.

He flopped next to me, picking up slices of dried meat leftover from earlier, and handed me a couple. "Your father is scary. Your mom is eating away at your energy. The general hates you. And now we've been signed up to train with both scary and pissy for the foreseeable future. It's a lot to take in."

I slumped deeper into the couch, munching on a piece of meat that tasted like salty mush. "That's not all."

Oliver snorted. "Why am I not surprised? What else is on Oli and Lucy's shitstorm of a plate?"

"Lilith carved more Hell Runes on Aspen's wrists," I whispered, hating even voicing it aloud. The urge to help him and my mom pressed down on my chest, almost crushing me. Frustration pricked my eyes at the fact that we couldn't. We were stuck, the general was an ass, and I was weak.

Oliver shoved another piece of meat into my hands and laid an arm over my shoulder. "We live fucked-up lives."

I smiled a somewhat watery, defeated smile. "We do."

"You want to save him, don't you?"

My silence was answer enough. He already knew I did.

"I still don't think he's good for you, Lucy."

"I don't care."

"It'll be dangerous."

"I know, Oli. So will finding your sister and killing Michael."

He stilled. "Did you just give me a nickname?"

"You've been by my side all this time and nearly got shredded by ice to protect me. You never let me give up on my mom, nor did you leave me to save your sister when you could've. Oli, you're the best brother I've never had."

He smiled and pulled me into his skinny frame for a big hug. "And you're the sister I've always wanted."

I let myself smile into his chest, taking one moment in my brutal life to appreciate our friendship. Then Oliver, being Oliver, found my head and gave me a good-natured noogie to finish off our sweet moment, and I laugh-cried as he did.

He wiped my cheeks. "I want to say it'll all be okay, but I don't know if it will be. But I'll be here with you one way or the other, okay?"

I nodded, having no words.

"So what do we do first?"

We were in way over our heads. Munching on the meat and cheese plate, we mulled over our predicaments. Oliver was right. Everything we needed to do would be dangerous. Which meant the King of Hell was also right. I couldn't go anywhere in this state. My mother continued to drain my energy to survive. My legs were twigs, and I needed to learn more about my powers. I didn't want to stay here another second, but I also didn't want to go out there and die the instant we faced anything.

"We need to train," I said.

"Uh—"

I stopped his protest with a smack on his leg. "Your running stamina sucks, Oli. And who knows about your fighting skills?"

"Like hell. The only reason my stamina sucks is because I'm carting your ass around. And I'm a badass fighter."

"You're a twig."

"So are you!"

"My point exactly." I sighed. "Plus, we don't know how to escape. Until we find a way, we can train. But we're not staying here a year."

Oliver groaned again.

"If I have to suffer through General Ronen's pissy personality, then so do you."

"At least he's nice to look at." Oliver grinned and wiggled his eyebrows.

I rolled my eyes.

After discussing plans and options, a maid with a bandage on her neck brought more food up. We devoured the juicy chicken, let Rune back into the room, then cuddled in my huge bed and slept.

A warm tongue lapped against my face, and a sharp poke woke me from my sound sleep.

"What?" I moaned, swatting at Oliver's hand.

"Rune's eyes are lit up, and someone knocked on the door."

I lifted my head. "It's not even light out yet," I complained, shoving my face back into my pillow.

"Don't think he cares."

No, he didn't. Especially since he stormed into my room, lacking the decency to wait for an answer. I swore I locked both doors too.

Standing at the foot of my bed, he scowled, his jaw tight as he gazed between us. Was he upset that Rune slept here? That didn't make sense. He knew where she was and could call her back at any time. Unless he was upset Oliver slept here? But that made even less sense.

"I didn't say you could come in."

Not like that mattered. He came and went as he pleased, with or without my approval—even if it was my damned bedroom.

What if I slept naked? What would he do then?

I almost wanted to test it. Just to witness his embarrassment.

"Get up and get dressed. Your father's waiting for you two." He turned his scowl on Oliver. "Go to your room and change."

I latched onto Oliver's hand before he could move, yanking him down to whisper in his ear. "Don't leave me."

Oliver quirked a brow. "I don't think he was asking."

He pried my fingers off his arm and climbed out of bed, grabbing his pants as he left.

Oliver liked to sleep in boxers, just like I preferred shorts and a camisole. I didn't care what he wore to sleep; he'd never make a move on me. The whole "lacking a dick" kind of put a stop to that. Even if he wasn't gay, he was my best friend—and not my type.

Still, I couldn't shake the feeling that a flicker of black flashed in the general's eyes, as if Oliver's attire had somehow pissed him off.

I shifted back in bed, wishing Oliver would hurry up and return. I didn't want to deal with the awkward tension building between me and the general.

He watched me, his expression guarded and cold, lips curling in a way that only frustrated me more.

I didn't deserve his condescending judgment. He didn't know me—we'd barely spoken. Sure, I may have insulted him several times, but the moment he barged into my room, he already had that glower on his face. Then he proceeded to force *my* friend out of *my* bed.

I sat up straighter and lifted my chin.

If he wanted a stare-off, then he'd get one.

Neither of us blinked. I fixed on those unique golden eyes like I could burrow into his brain and make him see me—really see me— for who I was, not what he assumed. But I didn't have the ability to manipulate minds, and his expression remained unchanged. If anything, his eyes narrowed, as if he were even more displeased. Worse, that same pulling sensation stirred, urging me to lose myself in him—again.

Digging my nails into my palms, I broke our little game and shook my head. If I lost this battle of wills, so be it. I didn't want to admire his irises—or worse, drown in them. My gaze landed on the red roses decorating my walls, and flustered, I blurted out the first thing that came to mind.

"Roses are red, violets are blue, General Ronen needs to get the—" I shut my mouth when I saw the blue hues of dawn reflecting off the snow weighing down the evergreen trees.

Blue was a color I only associated with one person.

Blue was a flame so hot it could melt cuffs to rescue you.

Blue was a flame so fierce it could destroy the chains holding you prisoner.

Blue was Aspen—the one who saved me. Or at least, tried to.

Subdued, I turned to the general. "What do you need?"

If possible, his expression grew colder. *Heavenly Hell.* What was his damned problem?

"Stand up, go to your closet, and change before I make you run until you puke tomorrow."

I bit my tongue. *Disrespecting ass.*

Rune whined at me, shoving her nose into my shoulder like she wanted me to move too.

"Traitor," I muttered, flinging the covers off and standing. A wispy shadow grazed my leg, pulling my attention to my tight boy shorts and camisole.

"What are you doing?" I didn't want his shadows anywhere near me.

"That's what you wear to bed with the Nephilim?"

I couldn't tell if he was surprised, angry, or curious. His eyes were pitch-black as he cracked his thumbs, the tension in the air practically suffocating.

"I didn't know what I wore—or who I wore it around—was any of your business," I replied, trying to sound casual. It took a lot of effort to keep the bite out of my voice, but I had to be careful. Polite. Nice. It was the only way if I wanted him to help me.

"Be ready in ten," he barked, then turned on his heel and left.

"How do you put up with him?" I asked Rune.

Her cute little tail curled in response. I rolled my eyes and entered my closet.

Never in my life had I owned this many clothes. And while I loved all the different textures and endless color options, I didn't care about any of it—not when I resented the state of my body.

I refused to look in the mirror, keeping my gaze away from my scars as I pulled on an oversized sweatshirt and pair of sweatpants. With a little more energy than yesterday, I put my hair into a high ponytail.

As I gathered my wild waves, my fingers brushed my ears, and my stomach sank. Memories of Brock resurfaced as I grazed a finger along the healed cartilage. My thick hair usually covered it, so I managed to forget, but the scar permanently marked me—a reminder of that despicable fallen angel and another male's abuse.

I sighed, pushing the memory aside, and instead made a conscious effort to place my hair in a low ponytail, carefully covering the wound I wasn't ready to face. I pulled a happier memory to the surface.

A time when I wore my hair like this—a memory that returned to me.

My first kiss.

It didn't happen in the Drune Forest when my powers consumed us. No, my first kiss occurred long before that.

Did I go too far? He could break an ankle with the trap I set for him. But Aspen had gotten too arrogant with his ability to make me fall on my ass every time he blipped into existence, so I wanted to repay the sentiment.

Knowing he always zoomed in as close as possible to shock me, I used that to my advantage. With my hair pulled up, I waited for his blur of movement to flash in front of my face.

But it never came.

"Boo," he whispered in my ear, almost startling me into my own hole—but he caught me around the waist.

Dammit. He was supposed to come in front, not behind.

Dedicated to my plan and all the effort I'd put into it, I did something bold and crazy. I twisted around and bounced onto my tiptoes to press my lips against his.

For the first time.

Tingles erupted between our pressed skin, dancing down my spine, making me crave more. For a moment, he stiffened—then melted into the kiss, grabbing the back of my neck and pulling me flush against the hard length of him.

Shit.

My nipples pebbled beneath my shirt as I dragged my tongue across his mouth, intensifying the tingles. He moaned, almost distracting me.

But I had a score to settle.

With a soft whimper, I pulled away, a devious smile curling across my face. I took a large step back, teetering dangerously at the edge of my hole—but righted myself.

His vibrant eyes flashed with light, and he followed, his gaze locked on mine, distracted, mesmerized by the way I slid my tongue across my lips—so distracted, in fact, that he stepped right into my trap and tripped.

"Look who's on the ground now." I laughed, not hiding a single ounce of my smug smile.

His mouth twitched in response, and a cunning expression replaced the outrage.

Oh no.

"And to think I finally caught you before you fell," he said, latching onto my arm and yanking me down. My chest collided with his while the rest of me lay outside the small hole. He angled my face and dove back onto my lips.

"You're benefiting from it, though."

"You're right. Maybe I'll let you make me fall more often."

He deepened our kiss.

"Hellion! You have one minute before I drag you out."

I gritted my teeth. I truly hoped I didn't kill the general before he could save the male I ached for.

CHAPTER 7

Lucille

General Ronen led us to the second-floor library. We paused at the entrance. The gold-framed doors towered from carpet to ceiling, inlaid with a red, black, and white mosaic. I frowned at the intricate glass pieces.

The mosaic depicted an unsettling image of a demon and his victim.

At first glance, it looked like a sensual embrace—the demon about to kiss the female—until I noticed the rows of razor-sharp teeth pressed into her flesh. Black glass formed a network of veins spreading from the puncture site, echoing the veins crawling up the back of the demon's neck.

I couldn't distinguish their faces—only her long back hair and uniform, and his short white locks, suit, and curling horns.

"If Hell doesn't contain demons, why is there a whole doorway portraying one?"

Oliver glanced at me, his brow furrowing in confusion. "Where do you see a demon?"

I gestured toward the doors. "Right there."

General Ronen turned, his eyebrows raised in silent question.

"You don't see it?" I asked them. "The demon, biting her?"

Oliver looked concerned and reached out, placing his hand against my forehead. "Do you need more rest?"

I swatted his hand away. "I'm fine."

Neither of them saw it, and I couldn't make sense of that. Oliver's concern was tangible, but General Ronen looked confused, as if debating whether to comment or simply move on.

Before either could speak, the heavy doors creaked open with a groan, revealing a bald male in white and gold robes. His sharp gaze locked onto mine with unnerving intensity.

I didn't like that.

The bald male dipped his chin to General Ronen. "Leave us."

"With pleasure."

The general snapped his fingers and pointed toward the door. Rune sat, her eyes fixed on her master.

He gave her a brief nod before turning, not sparing us a second glance. Poor guy. Dropping off the *hellion* must've been traumatizing. Now he could enjoy his miserable life in peace. Considering how much of a struggle it had been to escort us one floor down, he deserved the day off—maybe a massage.

We followed the bald male through the door. As it closed, I heard Rune whine, her head peeking through the narrowing gap.

"Rune, you know the rules. Stay," General Ronen barked down the hall.

Rune's head dropped, and she obediently sat back out of view.

My chest tightened. The doors shut, and I turned my attention back to the bald male. "Why can't she come in?" I asked.

"I don't allow any creatures, food, or thieving hands in my library," he replied, his tone matter-of-fact as he continued his purposeful walk.

Of course the grumpy male didn't.

We walked along white marbled floors, past towering dark shelves packed with books in every imaginable color. Gilded labels glinted from the glass orbs dangling overhead, each flickering with fire.

The romantic atmosphere of the library tugged at the corner of my lips. I tilted my head back, following the rows of books up to the skylight.

"Lucille and the Nephilim."

My head jerked back down, finding the king standing near a table, clasping the bald male's arm.

"He does have a name, you know," I chided.

"This is Cato, our Throne. In writing, he can distinguish between fact and lies and retains everything he reads. He'll be teaching you the ins and outs of our world. When you're not with him, you'll be with me, learning about control," the king said, completely disregarding my comment.

Control? Should he be the one teaching me about control when he almost pulverized us with his ice yesterday?

He must've seen the attitude on my face because he stepped closer, his white-ringed eyes burning into mine. "Make no mistake, Lucille—I am not Michael. But I am the King of Hell, and any grief you give me will be repaid in your training."

"Understood," I bit out.

He smiled knowingly, then nodded. "Before I leave you with Cato, you and the Nephilim need blood-bands, and you need an Evanescent Rune."

"A what and a what?" Oliver asked.

My thoughts exactly. Not sure I wanted either.

Cato lifted the sleeve of his robe, revealing a thin red band of ink.

"He's as tall and scrawny as I am. Maybe I should shave my head and become a Throne," Oliver whispered in my ear.

I elbowed him in the stomach, smirking at his gasp of outrage. The king ignored our antics and pointed at the tattoo.

"That, Nephilim, is the only way you don't cease to exist or cycle to the lowest level of Hell. Assuming you don't want to be burned alive for an infinite number of years, I'd think you'd want the blood-band."

"Now that you mention it, I think red really goes well with my green eyes. I'll take it," Oliver said, nodding like he was possessed.

"And me?"

"My blood and will allow certain beings to reside in my lands. Seeing as you are my blood, there's potential you don't need it, but I'd rather not take the risk."

Sounded like a good enough reason. "Okay."

"I'll be taking that blood-band now." Oliver held out his arm.

The king's lips lifted in a cunning smile. Pulling a knife from a sheath at his side, he slit his palm. Cato drew a stick from his pocket with a needle on the end, dipped it in the king's blood, and stabbed Oliver with it.

"Fuck-a-duck, that hurts," Oliver exclaimed as Cato continued. *Blood*-band. Right.

Cato finished Oliver's tattoo and wrapped it in a strip of thin material. "Every six months, you'll need it redone," he told Oliver, moving to me and pulling up my sleeve.

I winced at the first bloody poke. "And the Evanescent Rune?"

"A disguise," the king explained. "You are one of a kind. The knowledge of who you are and how you came to be could be danger-ous—not just for you, but for your mother and this realm. I don't want any redeemed soul sharing information with the Seraphim when they ascend, or for the Damned Souls to use you to get to me. The Evanescent Rune will hide the white ring in your eyes from everyone who doesn't know who you are."

"Damned Souls?" I asked, watching and wincing with each stab of Cato's needle.

"Souls dark enough to be sent to the lowest circle. There, they burn endlessly, choking on the stench of their flesh until the Hordes of Hell consume them," he said, clasping his hands behind his back. "Lately, we've seen more of them in our circle."

"And that's not normal," I surmised, noting the strain in his expression.

"No. I reside in the Redemption Circle—the final circle, where souls are purified on their way to Heaven. Most won't risk anything to prevent their ascension. But in the last few years, Damned Souls have been sneaking through, causing havoc."

Sneaking through. So, he didn't know how they were getting in.

"What kind of havoc?"

The corners of his eyes tightened, and his white rings flashed with light. He didn't answer, but he didn't need to. Damned Souls were condemned to burn forever in unending torture by his hand. Add that to the fact they were corrupted enough to be sent there in the first place, and I could only imagine the horrors they'd wrought in this circle. Horrors they were *still* causing, considering he hadn't figured out how they were getting in.

No, I didn't want them to know I was the Princess of Hell either.

Knowing he wouldn't answer, I brought up another issue just as Cato finished my tattoo.

"What about Michael? He knows. He'll tell the Seraphim."

The king's nostrils flared. "The Seraphim would demand proof of his tale. Proof we won't give them. Only the people in this room, Saraqael, and General Ronen will know you are a born angel and the Princess of Hell. To everyone else, you'll be a warrior in training, attempting to prove yourself and work off your debt to stay in my castle."

"And Oliver? What's his cover story?"

"Your companion is sharing the same debt."

The funny thing about our cover story was that we really were going to train—and since the general hated me, we would probably train *hard.*

Cato wrapped my blood-band, and the king took out an angelic feather.

"What do you know about angelic feathers?" he asked, his gaze skeptical.

"Only Archangels and Seraphim have them, and they're used to carve runes."

He paused briefly. I'd surprised him.

"Yes. They are the only feathers pulled from our wings, forever dipped in Heaven's inkwell. They can only be used by an Archangel or Seraphim. Any other angel who attempts to use one risks killing themselves—even the Dark Seraphim, since he is of a different breed entirely."

"The Dark Seraphim?" I asked.

The humorless smile on the king's face did nothing to calm the nerves that name stirred.

"General Ronen."

I swallowed.

The king walked around me and pulled down the collar of my sweatshirt. He dug his feather into my shoulder and carved.

"What is a Dark Seraphim?" Oliver asked while I tried not to cringe or squeak in pain.

"A Seraphim with wings as black and deadly as his powers—representing the corruption of souls."

"His shadows don't seem that deadly," Oliver mused.

The king chuckled. That wasn't a good sign.

He finished the curling rune, wiped at the tender spot, and released my sweatshirt just as Cato dropped three thick books on the table.

"Books on runes, Hell, and Elora, like you asked, Sir." Cato bowed.

The king nodded. "I have souls to judge. So today, you and the Nephilim will read. Tomorrow, you'll train with the Tormentors. And the next day, I'll see what information you retained."

"You expect us to get through all three of these in a day?" I asked, eyeing the books. Each one was the width of my head.

"You should've already learned this by now," the king replied, his voice clipped.

I opened my mouth, ready to explain my lack of education, but before I could speak, he cut me off.

"How old are you?"

The metal table and Michael's birthday gifts flashed in my mind, and I swallowed, fighting the pounding in my chest. "Twenty."

His eyes narrowed, considering my words. Then he spoke, each sentence calculated.

"Angels begin their instruction on the language of runes during their seventh year of creation. They have it mastered by their eighth year. Have you mastered the language of runes?"

Heat rose to my cheeks. I didn't like where this was going. "No."

"Angels study the dynamics of each dimensional world and retain all the information by their fourteenth year. Do you know anything about Hell, besides what I've told you?"

I dug my nails into my palms until they ached. "No."

"Angels diligently practice and hone their powers every day, and most have them mastered by their eighteenth year. Do *you*?"

My frustration boiled with each jab. It wasn't my fault! My mother kept me from all of this. She'd done everything in her power to hide it from me.

"Angels—"

"I'm not an angel!" I yelled, the words leaping from my mouth before I could stop them. I was born on Earth and raised as a human. I didn't have wings. I wasn't created.

The king stepped into my space, his eyes glinting with icy flame.

"No, you are *my* daughter. As your father and king, I will raise you as I see fit—seeing as I lost twenty years of that. Heaven only knows why." His voice grew cold, cutting through the air. "Begin your studies."

With that, he stalked out of the library. I stood there, feeling the weight of his words press down on me like a heavy stone.

"Read," Cato drawled, his robes swooshing across the pristine white floors before he faded into the sea of books.

I'd forgotten he was even there, along with Oliver, who threw an arm over my shoulder.

"I get it now why your father employs assholes. He is one," he declared, bumping me with his hip.

I gave Oliver a small smile. Maybe. But the king wasn't wrong.

Sighing, I sat at the table and pulled over the second-largest book: *The History of Hell and Its Creation.*

Oliver grabbed a different one: *Elora, Hell, and Heaven: The Three Celestial Dimensions.*

"Seeing as there's no way we'll finish reading these thousand-page books in one day, I say we read some and then go find breakfast."

"Okay, but we'll probably have to sneak out and make it quick," I said, resigned.

The silence stretched, and I lifted my head to find Oliver watching me.

"He's right, Oliver."

Understanding flickered across his face. He squeezed my hand before we dove into our books.

CHAPTER 8

Ronen

Bonny, our floor maid, walked toward me carrying a basket of my dirty sheets. She hid behind her messy orange hair, her eyes lowered. She never lifted her gaze above my chest. Never had since she came here a few months ago. I unnerved her. Angels unnerved most of the blood-banded humans that had to pay off their debt in Hell. Not the human souls that were sent here, though. But that had something to do with the fact that they were dead.

"Bonny."

She halted in her tracks, keeping her gaze on the basket. "Yes, General Ronen?"

"Can you send a message to Moira that I'm looking for her?" It was time to tell her the news.

"Yes, General. Right away." She bowed and scurried off.

I shook my head and walked into my rooms. She had a bad habit of bowing to me and any other angel she talked to, as if she owed us her deference.

I stripped out of my clothes and stepped into the shower. After rinsing off and drying, someone knocked on my door. I wiped myself down and put on loose pants, walking out of my bedroom just as Moira let herself in.

"Ronen." She smiled, eyeing my chest. The heat in her eyes did little to arouse me, but she wasn't here to satiate my needs.

"Moira." I grabbed her arms before she wrapped them around me. "I have news you're not going to like."

She stepped back. "Oh? Does this have something to do with how you've barely touched me this last week, or how you're always working now?"

Her whining grated against my patience. But she was right. I'd become distant. Not that I thought she'd ever voice her concerns.

"I've been under a lot of pressure from the king. But that's not why I had you come here. You need to demote two of the weakest warriors in your squadron. The king intends to replace them with two recruits."

She tensed, and the crystal on my coffee table vibrated.

"You can't do this."

"King's orders, Moira."

"Who? Who could possibly be better than Dusty and Matt?"

Those were her two weakest? Fuck.

"It'll only be temporary." *I hoped.* "We'll put Dusty and Matt in the Devils as first and second."

She snorted. "So, you're going to demote Danny and Lou?"

Demoting Danny would piss him off for sure, and Lou followed him like a shadow. Did I care about their ranks or hurting their feelings? No. Suffering was part of their daily punishment. This was Hell, after all. But he held a grudge against me for replacing the last general who treated him like a spoiled prince. Well, not replace—I killed him and took his spot during challenge week. So, I understood Danny's grudge.

But I had no other options unless I wanted to go back and beg the king to reconsider. The higher-level squadrons were set at a number limit for management and training purposes.

"Yes. Maybe it'll teach them a lesson."

She rattled the swords on my walls, her temper seizing control of her Dominion powers. "Don't do this, Ronen."

"Go tell them now. Your two recruits start tomorrow."

She stormed out of my room, slamming the door shut.

I released a sharp breath, changed into my uniform, and went out to find Danny and Lou.

After searching the enclosed arena and asking a few patrols, the sounds of yelling finally led me to their squadron.

They were at the edge of Verdant Forest, circling a small frozen pond. Two warriors from their squadron faced off on the ice, pummeling each other. Squadmates booed and cheered in equal measure as one sent the other to the ground and smashed in his face, while others shifted uncomfortably on their feet.

Danny and Lou stood with their backs to me, collecting Hellmarks from their booing members.

We didn't have many rules in our military. But currently, they were breaking two.

I slid out from behind a tree and stalked toward the pond. They didn't hear me coming, and I made sure to blend in with the shadows of the evergreens so they didn't see me either.

A couple yards away, I unleashed my shadows, absorbing the blood from the warrior's knuckles and immobilizing him before he murdered their unconscious squadmate. Danny and Lou whipped their heads around, searching for me, and everyone else stilled.

"Kneel," I commanded, stepping into view.

Every single warrior sank to their knees—except Danny.

Oh, how I loved disrespect. Always enticed the bloodthirsty beast within.

I smiled, wrapping my shadows around his neck and forcing him down. He fought me the entire way until his knees slammed into the compact snow. Stepping forward, I forced his head to tilt back. His dark skin flushed, and his nostrils flared.

I tsked. "Gambling against your warriors? How long has that been going on?"

Danny pushed his tongue into his cheek and shrugged.

I crouched before him, then turned to his follower, Lou. "How long?"

Lou swallowed, his face leaching of color making his freckles stand out like tiny bull's-eyes. "I—uh—" he stuttered.

"Yes?"

"About two—" His voice cut off on a gurgle, drowning in a mouthful of pressurized water.

"Oh, Danny." I latched onto his neck, digging my fingers into his pulse point. I could've easily used my shadows to strangle him, but I wanted to feel his struggle for air vibrate through my palm. "I know

I'm nothing like your last general. I bet he let you say and do whatever you liked." I stood, bringing his face within inches of mine. "I just figured you could've scraped two brain cells together to figure that out for yourself."

He gasped and clawed at my grip, making me bleed. For a moment, I eased up, giving him a second to suck in air and speak. Instead, he used his second to spit in my face—before surrounding it with his water.

Grinning through the blurry sphere trying to suffocate me, I lifted him higher, then threw him down on the pond, bashing his skull against the ice. Blood pooled across the frosty surface, and his water splashed to the ground, releasing me and Lou.

"Did you kill him?" Lou gasped after hacking up water.

"No." Unsheathing a dagger at my hip, I ran it across Danny's neck. Blood spurted in rhythmic bursts, coating my hands before slowing to a drizzle. "Now I did."

Lou gaped at me as I stood.

Danny's warriors stared at me with mixed expressions–wary respect, shock, and some even looked relieved.

"I'm going to give most of you a pass and assume this was all Danny's doing. After all, he was your leader—he knew better than to gamble with your lives and pit you against your own. And he paid for it with his life."

"Most?" Lou whispered.

"Dusty and Matt are taking your places, and you've been demoted to third."

Although I should demote him to the Bowels Squadron, Lou knew better too. But I had a feeling Danny threatened him, so I let it go.

This wasn't the original way I planned to change their leadership, but it worked nonetheless.

"And you," I said, pointing to the male immobilized at the pond's center, "didn't Danny tell you that murdering one of your squadmates is against our rules? Did you want to die?"

I released him, and he slumped next to the unconscious male sprawled on the ice. "No, General."

"Didn't think so." I turned on my heel and yelled over my shoulder, "Someone burn your dead leader so he can cycle to the king to be judged." I left them, not feeling an ounce of remorse, and hoping Danny's soul descended to a lower circle.

I headed back toward the arena in search of Alexei. Once inside, I spotted him in the back, near the weights and several attractive souls.

"Alexei," I called out.

He stood, widening his eyes, taking in my soaked hair. "Did they get your wings?"

"No, never materialized them."

"Shame. I've been wanting to test my aim." Alexei held out a pair of boxing gloves.

"If the Devils didn't burn Danny's body, he still may be back in the Verdant Forest for you to fry." I shucked my bloody gloves for the ones Alexei handed me.

Alexei's brows raised. "You sure he didn't get your wings wet?"

"Only my face with his spit, then his power, after I found him gambling against his squad's lives."

Alexei groaned. "And you're telling me I missed his beatdown and murder? Why do you always keep me away from the fun?"

Fun wasn't the word I'd use. Danny's death was a necessity—a reminder of what happened when they broke the rules or disrespected me. Moira may be furious I murdered her friend. But this was the way of Hell.

"Next time. Now let's box, or tomorrow I'm making everyone sprint through Veil Forest."

He smirked, putting in his mouth guard and gloving his hands. Once ready, I came at him hard, throwing combinations and putting my weight behind my jabs. He grunted with each hit but came back at me with just as much force. We both relished the intensity of our fights. Alexei liked to call them our therapy sessions, and I agreed. My thoughts, worries, and anger all fell away—even the connection to Rune muted. Just me, Alexei, and our fists.

Pure bliss.

CHAPTER 9

Lucille

After meandering the halls on unsteady legs, Oliver, Rune, and I stumbled upon the glorious kitchens. A sweet female named Dorus gave Oliver and me a slice of quiche, and Rune a big hunk of raw meat. On our way out, she handed us a handful of truffles, lightening the weight on my chest caused by the king's words. We snuck our forbidden treats into the library but left Rune outside the doors before settling in to read—she was harder to hide.

By lunchtime, I'd finished ten chapters—a tenth of the book. Oliver, however, was nearly halfway through. But his method of reading consisted of a quick glance before flipping the page. I wasn't even sure that was classified as reading.

I was drawn to the sections about the King of Hell—how he analyzed the depths of souls before deciding whether to send them to a circle or redeem them. After all, he was my father. I wanted to understand the male who not only made my birth possible but whose land we were stuck in.

"Did you find anything useful?"

Oliver froze. "Uh..." He dragged his finger across line after line. "Maybe. It says that Hell has a lake that acts as a portal to different dimensions, but it doesn't state the dimensions." He checked the previous few pages and the ones ahead. "It doesn't elaborate on the dimensions anywhere."

"We should ask Cato," I suggested.

Oliver hummed. "Can we trust him not to report to your father that we're looking into Portal Lake without asking why?"

I grimaced. "Fine. Then who else could we ask?"

"Someone who isn't close to the king or the general."

"And that'd be?"

Oliver ran a hand through his wild two-toned bangs, having no answer.

Right. "We'll just have to ask him for more books on Hell."

"Yeah, okay. What have you been reading?"

"Not much besides how the king judges souls and everything you'd never want to know about the Seven Circles of Hell."

Saying the words aloud brought to mind another piece of Miriam's prophecy:

There once was a daughter of seven circles, hidden, protected, avoiding the hurdles.

That part came true. But that didn't mean the rest of her prophecy would. Clearly, the king didn't want me dead, or else I would be.

"Like?" Oliver prompted, bringing me out of my thoughts.

I found the perfect paragraph to read for him. "Like… The Scission Circle—the sixth circle of Hell—favors slicing and maiming. The lord and his servants preside over the circle and take particular pleasure in using their sharp instruments on sinful souls—especially rapists. For males, the Scission Lord bludgeons the balls until they are pulp, then skins the pen—"

"Yep, nope." Oliver stole my book, slammed it shut, and handed me the third book we'd yet to touch. "Time for something lighter."

There was nothing light about the third book—*Celestial Powers, Weaponry, and Warfare.*

We read late into the night, then trucked up to bed with Rune as our escort. Once snuggled under my sheets, I stared into my fireplace, ruminating on thoughts of escape and Aspen until my eyes closed.

I beheld the tall, ivy-woven arches with a sinking stomach. I didn't want to be here. My heart still ached from Aspen's cruel words. But I had little control over my dream-walks.

"Lucille?"

I stiffened, my pulse ratcheting. Cringing from the course field grass, I slowly turned toward his voice.

He stood beneath the oak tree. His dark uniform and cloak billowed in the breeze among the tree's falling leaves.

"Aspen," I said, wary. A strange urge screamed at me to go to him, but I held myself back.

He gave me a small smile. It seemed genuine, but I'd been fooled by him before. As he stepped closer, I instinctively backed away. A sharp rock stabbed the arch of my foot, and I lost my balance.

Aspen luscelered forward, catching me before I could hit the ground. He steadied me as I drank in his blue eyes—eyes that held no anger, no disgust. They were filled with concern and disbelief. As if he couldn't believe I was real.

"See? I catch you when you fall," he whispered. His calloused hands tingled against my bare skin. I glanced at his wrist, finding only white scars from previous inactive runes. The Hell Runes were gone.

"But—how? I don't understand." My head spun, trying to reconcile the Aspen before me with the one from before.

He righted me, and I winced, wishing I'd dreamt up shoes—or anything other than what I'd fallen asleep in. Barefoot in tight boyshorts and a strappy camisole, I had little protection from the goosebumps raised by the cool breeze or rough field grass beneath my toes.

A second later, as if someone had heard my mental plea, a pair of boots covered my feet.

I gaped. "What's going on?"

Aspen grabbed my hand. "We have some things to talk about."

I let him pull me toward the oak tree as I scrutinized his tilted lips. He seemed himself, but I didn't trust it.

Aspen sank to the ground, leaning against the tree. He tugged my arm when I didn't immediately join him. But I couldn't sit.

He sighed, accepting my resistance, and let go.

"You dream-walked into my nightmare. Every night since they took you from me, similar scenes have played out in my mind. I'd hold you in my arms, and we'd talk until—" He paused, averting his gaze.

"You'd die. Either by someone else's hands or"—his voice softened—"my own, when I was Hell Runed."

Unable to stand the ache in his tone, I lowered myself next to him. But I couldn't bring myself to touch him—not yet.

"I didn't think anything of it when the scenery in my nightmare stilled or our conversation diverted from what my subconscious usually imagined. You kept telling me you were alive, and all I could think was... not for long."

A tear slipped down his cheek, and despite my need to reach out and comfort him, I couldn't. I wanted to believe and trust him, but the vividness of the last dream-walk sank its claws into my mind. It had felt so real.

"Then you brought up the term dream-walker and told me you were the daughter of Hell, and I knew something was off about my nightmare. But that didn't change the direction of my subconscious." He glanced down at his wrists. "The Hell Runes were carved into my skin, and I turned like I always did. But before I could kill you in my nightmare, I woke up. I'd never been able to wake myself up—I always had to watch you die.

"The moment I opened my eyes, I knew something was different. I followed my gut, searched our library for the term, and found nothing. It was odd, seeing as I swore I'd seen it in one of our books before."

"So the Hell Runes weren't real?"

"No."

"But I felt your pain."

He turned to me. "I thought I was about to kill you." The shame and horror twisting his expression only made me question myself more.

"But I can't feel any of your emotions now." I wasn't sure why I continued to doubt him. His expressions seemed genuine, his words sincere. He didn't act like he was hiding anything from me or about to turn on me. Everything he said made sense. So why didn't I trust him?

He shrugged and pressed his hand to my cheek. "I can't feel our tether anymore, sweetheart. That's why I thought you were dead." His hand trailed to my lips, sending tingles across the sensitive skin. "Sometimes I still wonder if you are, or if my nightmares have taken a turn for... well, I'm not sure if this would be better or worse."

If he couldn't feel our tether, maybe my ability to feel his emotions was cut off too. But what did I feel before? Was it a fluke of the dream-walk? I didn't understand this type of dream-walking. Or was being in Hell disrupting our connection?

"It was only a nightmare, Lucille. I'm fine."

I was so close to giving in to his words, yet a small part of me still wanted to question him. He must've seen my wavering doubt.

"Watch," he said. The top of his uniform vanished to reveal a pale, muscular chest. It was exactly what he'd done to my feet with the boots. A second later, thousands of Hell Runes appeared across his skin.

I recoiled, but they were gone just as swiftly.

"Whatever powers you use to come here, allow me to change things. I had suspicions when I woke up and confirmed them earlier with your boots."

I bit my lip, holding back my creeping hope. "A nightmare?"

He smiled and slowly reached for my face, giving me time to pull away. I stayed put, and his smile widened as he removed my lower lip from abusing teeth. The playful lightness in his blue eyes chased away the last of my doubt.

"A nightmare," he confirmed.

Delicious tingles spread across my skin as his thumb brushed along my mouth. His eyes followed the motion, enthralled. Desire overtook his expression, turning his smile into something more heated.

"I want to kiss you," he murmured, his voice low and husky.

I opened my mouth wider, letting his thumb graze my tongue. His eyes shot to mine.

"Then why don't you?"

He laughed and shook his head before winding his hand through my hair and pulling my mouth to his. The tantalizing buzz of our skin warmed my body and calmed my mind. The tingling intensified as his tongue danced with mine, and I moaned.

I forgot how good it felt to kiss him.

"Have I ever told you what you do to me when you moan?" Aspen breathed, nipping my lip.

"No," I gasped as he lay back on the ground, bringing me with him. His hard length pressed against my stomach, sending a shot of heat to my core.

If only it were lower.

"It makes me insane." He trailed his mouth down my neck, passing my clavicle, and pausing just above my camisole. "It makes me want to do many, *many*, dirty things to you."

"What things?" I whispered as he palmed the underside of my breast, his mouth hovering just above my covered nipple. All the while, his hard length throbbed against me.

We'd never gone beyond this. We'd only kissed in the woods near my house. The time when my powers took control was the closest we'd come to being truly intimate. And now, more than ever, I desired to take things past that—at least a little.

"Things with my fingers." He flipped me over, then bit my nipple through my camisole before lowering his mouth to the top of my shorts. "Things with my tongue."

Wet vibrations grazed the line of my waistband. I arched into his mouth, hoping to bring him lower, hoping he would place his tongue on my needy center. He smiled against my skin, peering up at me through hooded eyes. They flickered with fire and held a taunting edge. He knew exactly where my thoughts had taken me—but instead of easing the ache, he made it worse.

He kissed a path back up to my breasts, pulling up my shirt as he went. Then he paused, gazing down at me. One second. Two seconds. I writhed on the third. What was he waiting for? A smugness glinted in his heated, dark eyes. Slowly, he descended and wrapped his mouth around one nipple, biting. I jolted from the pain, but he quickly soothed the ache with his tongue. The combined sensations with the vibrations from our bond made me moan.

He groaned and crawled back up my body. "Things with my cock."

I rubbed myself against him, craving friction. "So what's stopping you?"

Immediately, my shorts and panties vanished. I gasped. I was completely naked beneath him. The only piece of clothing separating our bodies was his pants.

His eyes danced with sinful intent. "Nothing."

My core throbbed, my mind overridden with need. I spread my legs wider, showing him exactly what he had done to me, showing him where I needed him.

He stared at my drenched center, taunting me as he lowered his mouth, brushing his lips against my core before moving back up to my ear.

"Aspen," I begged.

He smiled against my cheek, then his tingling fingers grazed my clit, and stopped.

"Don't stop," I groaned.

I couldn't handle all this teasing.

"Moan for me, sweetheart."

"I can't just moan on—"

He plunged his fingers inside me, and I came alive. My head dropped back, my eyes fluttered, and I homed in on his scintillating touch. His fingers thrust in and out, hitting a spot that made me beg—made me grind against his hand, calling out his name as pressure, unlike anything I'd ever felt before, built inside me.

"That's it, sweetheart. Take what you need." He continued his relentless pace, the sounds of his fingers inside my body obscene. He sank deeper, hitting a spot that took me higher, then sucked my nipple into his mouth and bit down. I cried out and split apart as the aching pressure shattered. I pulsed around his fingers, and he continued his ministrations until my body relaxed and my moans quieted.

"I don't think I'll ever get used to that sound," he said, removing his hand and slipping his fingers into his mouth. He groaned as he sucked me off his fingers, and my core throbbed again. "Or this taste."

I didn't know it would feel like that. Nor did I expect to want it again so soon.

He read the desire on my face and started unlacing his pants. Heavenly Hell, he was such a tease. Seconds from imagining them away, a noise sounded in the distance, and we stilled.

The flowers and dark sky blurred around us.

"Lucille? What's happening?" Aspen's form wavered, his voice dropping, as if he were fading away.

"I think it's some kind of noise... from where I'm sleeping. I'm waking up."

He gripped my arms. "Waking up where?"

"Hell."

CHAPTER 10

Lucille

I groaned, rolled over, and hit a warm body. Something tickled my face as an ungodly noise sounded.

Was that a trumpet?

I cracked one eye, finding a face full of Rune's shadow fur. Curling my fingers in her soft, tickling depths, my soul settled. I didn't know why, only that I'd come to crave the peace she gave me.

The trumpet blared again, and Oliver whined from Rune's other side.

"What the hell is that noise, and why is it waking us up at the ass crack of dawn?" Oliver pulled a pillow over his head. "Tell them to go away, Lucy."

"Like anyone here would ever listen to me," I grumbled, wishing I could return to Aspen. What he did to me... I shuddered.

Someone knocked on the door to my sitting room. "Wake up! You have ten minutes to get dressed for the Infernal Sixty! Wear something you can exercise in." Whoever yelled through the door had a deep voice and too-chipper attitude.

Oliver and I both groaned. Neither of us moved until Rune, whose eyes flashed golden, started bombarding my face with slobber.

"Okay, okay," I said, pushing her away and elbowing Oliver. "I'm pretty sure I don't have your size in my closet, so get a move on before we're dragged out by our ankles."

He groaned again, slid off my bed, and stomped out the door like a toddler. I laughed as I pushed off the comforter. Rune lay with her head between her paws, her tail wagging like she was excited for the *almost* day. I couldn't say I felt the same. I would've rather stayed in my dream with Aspen.

Walking into my closet, I stripped off my bed clothes and dressed in a baggy sweatshirt and leggings. Taming my wild waves, I wove them into a low braid, covering my ears.

"Luce, you ready? I just saw the trumpeter on his way here."

I met Oliver outside my closet. "I'm surprised you're not wearing green."

He shrugged down at his T-shirt and black sweats. "Would if I could, but whoever supplied my wardrobe has a thing for boring neutral colors. At least it's not a tunic."

Someone banged at my door and blew a horn. My hands jerked over my ears. "Is he using an airhorn?"

"As much as I want to say yes, Hell isn't *that* modern."

"Right."

I laced up black sneakers and walked with Oliver and Rune to my sitting room door. Oliver opened it, and we found a muscular blond guy about to place his mouth on a long animal horn.

"Yes, please blow out our eardrums. Maybe then I can sleep through your noise," Oliver said.

The blond smiled, lowering his horn. "Get used to it, Nephilim. This will be your new routine for the foreseeable future."

"Oliver."

The blond held out his hand. "Alexei, General Ronen's second. I'll be seeing a lot of you two. But hey, no complaints here. I'd take castle living over the barracks any day."

Oliver shook his hand and stared at Alexei without saying a word or letting go. I jumped in before it became awkward.

"Lucille," I said. "But you can call me Lucy." I already loved his easy smiles; I didn't mind throwing in my nickname for him.

He removed himself from Oliver's resisting grip, then kissed both of my cheeks. "Or I could call you beautiful."

I blushed and fumbled for a response. Did I compliment him back? Did I smile and say thanks?

"Are we off to training?" Oliver interrupted.

Alexei gave us a long look, lingering on our shoes. "Yeah... Do you two have anything warmer? Maybe a pair of boots?"

I surveyed his thick, red-and-black leathers. "Exactly what kind of exercising did you say we were doing?"

His eyes glimmered. "I didn't."

"I guess we'd better find some thicker clothes and boots, then."

Alexei tilted his head, his flirty grin lighting up his face. "Beautiful *and* smart."

I rolled my eyes, and Oliver scoffed before we both returned to our closets to change. Dressed in the thickest clothing I could find and boots, I met a similarly dressed Oliver at my door minutes later.

Alexei nodded. "Better."

We followed the general's second to the first floor, down a few hallways, through more doors, and into an enclosed arena.

The tile gave way to sand, and the temperature dropped. Like the castle, the arena had rows of tall windows, and natural light illuminated a sea of people.

Most wore red-and-black uniforms similar to Alexei's, but a different group stood in the far-right corner, beside a towering wall of weapons. They wore no uniforms—just an eclectic mix of clothing from various cultures and periods. Together, their differences formed a strange, unified whole.

Oliver and I should've been with them. Instead, we stood out from the uniformed warriors like chihuahuas in a pack of Soulhounds.

"What's with everyone's outfits?" Oliver mumbled.

"Hell doesn't discriminate on culture or dress. Some souls choose to stay in the clothes they died in. Others don't. Blood-banded can bring whatever clothes they desire to Hell. Don't worry, you'll both receive uniforms if you pass the Infernal Sixty," Alexei explained.

"And what is the Infern…" I trailed off.

What was that?

A red mark glistened across a female's face in the far corner.

Was she wounded?

No. She wasn't bleeding, nor was she alone. Others also had odd markings. Were they scars or paint? From this distance, I couldn't tell.

I squinted, then turned to the uniformed members before us, but they were all facing forward.

"Attention, warriors and recruits. Welcome to the worst sixty days of your lives," General Ronen announced from the front of the arena. He stood on an elevated surface in all his intimidating black-and-gold glory, staring me down as if his words were meant for me alone. "We will assess your strengths and weaknesses through a series of drills and courses to see where to place you. Most of you won't make it further than the Bowels Squadron, and some of you won't make it at all."

The way he deliberately looked away when he said *strengths,* only to pin me again at *weaknesses,* said it all. I held his condescending stare, frustration simmering in my veins. The molten gold of his eyes beckoned like an abyss, daring me to surrender. I resisted—or thought I did. A warmth stirred in my chest the longer I held on. My breath hitched, and I hissed, jerking my gaze away.

"Recruits." He pointed to the corner. Everyone looked, their faces twisting into predatory sneers. At that moment, I was glad Alexei hadn't led us to the mob of outcasts. "We will test to see if you will join our lowest squadron, the Bowels. The rest of you—Bowels, Trenchers, Devils, Tormentors, and Infernos—this is the time to try advancing to the next level. Remember, Tormentors, Infernos, and Nightmares have a specific number for their squads, and a spot needs to open before you advance. Nightmares, you must prove yourselves to hold your current spot—and maybe one of you will shine enough to elevate yourself to my hand-picked squad of Dreads."

Someone in the back coughed and raised a shaky hand. The general slowly lifted a brow, as if surprised that someone had enough courage to interrupt him.

"How do you advance to the next level?" the male squeaked.

The general's grin sent needles stabbing across my skin.

"There are three ways. The previous warrior either advances or dies, and you have to be at a level to take their spot. Or, in the final week, you can challenge them to a one-on-one, no-rules match for it. This is Hell. You prove yourself, or you die.

"For the blood-banded, that is. For the souls in attendance—you can't die, but if you're not redeemed, you can recycle. And there's a much higher chance the Horde will devour you."

Murmurs swept through the arena. Oliver shot me a wide-eyed look that I mirrored. We were both blood-banded—which meant we could die and be sent to whatever hellish circle our souls ended up in.

"Hell doesn't have many rules, but our military has two. First, no killing is allowed within your squad. Save it for challenge week. Second, no gambling or betting against fights. Break either rule, and you forfeit your soul to a lower circle of Hell."

"So I'm thinking you use your clout to convince the king to exempt us from this. We can get stronger another way," Oliver whispered.

Alexei shot us a considering glance. "Ronen told me you guys had a debt to the king, and you're living in his castle. Whatever clout you had has likely been used up since he placed you in the Tormentors. That's our fourth-best squadron."

Oliver's eyes widened further, and my skin prickled with irritation.

No wonder the general had looked so unimpressed with me. The king didn't mention we'd be placed in an upper-level squadron. We were better off trying to make it in the Bowels with the rest of the haunted faces, shaking legs, and non-uniform-wearing beginners. Not... I surveyed the sea of black and red. There was a clear distinction where the lower-level military began and ended.

The lower levels watched the elites with hungry, eager expressions—like they'd be more than happy to kill an elite member to join a higher tier. But the elite squadrons tauntingly smiled back with blazing eyes as if to say, *Try and you'll die.*

"Well, what circle do you think we'll end up in after this?" Oliver asked.

I jabbed him hard in the ribs. "Not funny."

After the rest of the general's speech, he called for the squadron leaders to find their groups and congregate. Bodies moved left and right while Oliver and I stayed put, shifting on our feet.

"You both will be with Moira—the Tormentors' leader." Alexei gestured to the front, where an attractive blonde stood. Her uniform had an added breastplate that accentuated her curves and cinched her waist. Add that to her heart-shaped face, two perfect ears, and eyes the same crystal blue as Alexei's, and Moira was gorgeous.

"Damn, she's hot," Oliver said.

"Really? Because there's a noticeable *lack of bulge* in the area you like," I teased.

Oliver snorted. "You're right, she's not my type. Doesn't mean she's not hot."

Alexei stared at Moira as if she'd put a bad taste in his mouth. "That's good. She'd eat you alive, spit you out, and then stomp on your remains. Besides, she only has eyes for one plaything." He nod-ded to the general, making his way to Moira. For some reason, their pairing made a lot of sense.

"They look like they could fuck and murder in the same breath," Oliver commented.

I snorted my agreement as I watched Moira give the general a brilliant smile. He never returned it. The dour male probably didn't know how to smile since he had a large fist up his ass. Maybe she could soothe it for him like she did his shoulder.

The placement of her massaging touch and perfectly manicured fingers provoked my Infernus. It whispered, flowing from my ears and scattering across my skin. I shook it off and shoved their songs away. "So what do we have to look forward to?"

Alexei brushed a wayward black wave from my cheek. "Nothing good, beautiful. The higher you rise, the more ruthless we are."

That meant Alexei was at the top of the ruthless hierarchy. But as he shamelessly flirted with me, it was hard to see. His warm smile and the glittering playfulness in his expression said *charming flirt*, not *touch me and die* like the general's expression always seemed to say.

My cheeks flushed at his attention, but before I could politely step out of his reach, Rune butted between us, forcing Alexei away, and sat pressed against my leg.

Alexei frowned down at Rune, glanced at the general, then waved us forward. "Come on. Better not keep General Ronen wait-ing."

"Yay, off to our death," Oliver groaned.

CHAPTER 11

Lucille

I knew the moment Moira laid eyes on us that we were screwed. Screwed in the sense that she was about to make our lives absolutely miserable, or we wouldn't survive the Infernal Sixty.

"So these are the two *warriors* replacing Matt and Dusty." Pure disdain bled through her words and leached into her face. Warriors clearly wasn't the word she wanted to use. Did standing next to General Ronen make her think twice? Not sure why. He didn't care what she called us, not when he had similar feelings.

"You could place us in the Bowels," I suggested, hopeful.

"No, we can't," General Ronen snapped, silencing whatever Moira was about to say. Her expression darkened at his words. But the anger she was directing at us should've been directed at the general or the king. It wasn't like we chose to be here.

"And that's my cue to leave," Alexei said, smiling. "See you later, Nephilim." He nodded at Oliver, then winked at me. "Lucy."

My cheeks flushed again. Gah, I couldn't control the annoying things. I gave him a flustered smile, then returned to our angry circle. That wasn't an exaggeration either. Moira looked ready to stab me in the eyes. The general looked disgusted. Even Oliver looked annoyed.

But it finally made sense as he continued to gaze longingly after Alexei.

Oliver liked him—or at least found him attractive enough to want him.

I bumped his hip and leaned in to whisper, "I'd never stand in your way. He's just... flirty."

Oliver gave me a small smile, then pulled back when the general whistled at us. *Freaking whistled.* I shut my eyes and breathed deeply, calming the sudden itches breaking across my skin. I opened them when the pressure behind my eyes receded.

"Squad Leader Moira, these are your two recruits, Oliver and Lucille." The general grimaced. "Play nicely. Recruits, you'll listen to everything your leader says and do everything she demands. Don't whine or come to me for help. The Tormentors Squadron is one of our four elite squadrons, and the king seems to think you're both tough enough to be here." He flicked his gaze over us. "I suppose we'll see if that's true." He left with Rune, leaving us with Moira.

"Line up behind formation, recruits. We'll start the Infernal Sixty with a ten-mile run." She smirked, then headed to the front of the squadron.

"Did she just say ten miles?" Oliver surveyed the arena. "So Hell's entire military will witness our wheezing disgrace as we run around this sand bowl?"

Shit, I hoped not.

"I'm definitely luscelering," Oliver muttered as we lined up behind two females with long black hair.

We could cover ten miles in about ten minutes if we luscelered. It'd be easy. Yet, the mere thought of cutting corners filled me with anxiety. We wouldn't become stronger by cheating.

"Oliver, we can't—"

One of the females in front of us turned around, and my stomach dropped at the sight of her face. Angry red burns marred her forehead down to her jawline. A milky white cloud covered one of her eyes, while the other gleamed a honey brown.

"Should you lusceler, Moira will punish you accordingly. You'll only prove to everyone you don't belong here," she said with a slight accent.

But we didn't.

"I've never felt the urge to prove myself to anyone, to be honest. What exactly is her punishment?" Oliver asked.

The second female turned around. She was the mirror image of her sister—the same honey-colored eyes, face shape, and hairstyle—but without any wounds. Or so I thought, until my gaze fell to her neck. I cringed, seeing the deep gash splitting her flesh, revealing glistening muscles beneath.

Why didn't it bleed?

That must've been what Oliver had meant earlier—how people here didn't exactly look... normal.

"It would be unwise to provoke Moira. Her punishments are severe," she warned. "This is Ni"—she pointed at her twin with the giant neck gash—"and I'm Ichi."

"Oliver"—he gestured to me—"and this is Lucy."

Then, because he couldn't help himself, he said, "So I keep seeing weird shit like that on people." He pointed at Ni's neck. "Do you just run on zero circulation, or does living in Hell give you some kind of immunity to having your neck sliced open?"

I internally cringed at his blunt humor, hoping they didn't take offense. The last thing we needed was to make enemies within our squad when we already didn't belong.

Ichi's lips twitched. "They're our soul wounds." At our confused expressions, she clarified. "They're our death injuries. Our souls take our wounds with us as we pass to Hell, and the closer to redemption we are, the more they fade. Or you can petition the king to have a Soul Mender heal them. We don't have the Hellmarks for that, but we like watching our wounds fade—it gives us hope." She nodded to her sister. "I used to be completely blind, but now I'm only partially. And soon, Ni will regain her tongue so she can speak again."

"I'm so glad I didn't have breakfast," Oliver mumbled, and Ichi responded with another polite smile. Ni, on the other hand, shook her head, unamused.

"You've angered quite a few people by ending up in this squad," Ichi said. "I strongly recommend you keep your heads down and attempt to survive." She glanced at our shoes. "At least you're starting well. We'll be running through slush for the next hour."

Oliver laughed and reached out to Ichi, patting her shoulder like she'd told a good joke. She stepped away, his hand flopping to his side.

"You're not joking." Oliver's laughter dried up. "We're running ten miles in the cold, and you think we can do it in an hour?"

"Yes, every morning from here on out. It's our warm-up," she stated, glancing toward the Bowels Squadron across the arena, her lips twisting with pity. "Our leaders usually don't tell recruits the specifics of the Infernal Sixty."

We followed her gaze to the far corner. Half the Bowels Squadron wore thicker clothing and boots—the ones who'd been here longer. The other half wore various exercise gear in different degrees of coverage. Some looked prepared for the outdoor run. Others were about to regret it. One guy even sported shorts.

Oliver grimaced at the group. "Separating the wheat from the chaff."

Survive or die. Wasn't that what the general had said? Even Ichi mentioned survival. So why should I be surprised by the lack of information, or by Alexei's misleading words of *wear exercise clothing*? This was Hell. No one came here for the sparkling snow and evergreens. Most were forced here because of their sins.

If I was surprised by anything, it should be Alexei's advice on our clothing. If he hadn't said anything, we'd be part of the chaff, slogging through slush, barely surviving the cold.

I glanced over at the blond warrior. He stood by General Ronen, conversing with a few others. Why he took pity on us, I wasn't sure. But from now on, we'd need to always expect the unexpected—and probably worse—when it came to this place.

Moira yelled over all the noise, getting her squad's attention. "Tormentors! To start, we'll run to the Upper City of Hoar Hollow and back. Then we'll have weight training. Easy first day."

"Easy my ass," Oliver remarked.

Moira started to turn, then stopped. "Oh, and since we have two recruits who think they're so *elite*, we'll make things interesting."

Heavenly Hell, I hated her smug tone.

"Last ones to the arena will be scrubbing the kitchens with Dorus for the next week." She leveled me with a knowing look. "Happy running."

I tilted my head, returning her saccharine smile while grinding my nails into my palms and shoving my Infernus's whispers away.

"This just keeps getting better and better," Oliver grumbled.

We all knew who'd be cleaning the kitchens with Dorus this week.

"Under no circumstances should you stop. Even if you have to walk," Ichi advised.

I sighed and followed the Tormentors through the doors. Cold air blasted my face, instantly freezing the moisture in my nose. I tucked my hands into my coat sleeves, wishing I had gloves, and stood atop a large, snow-covered hill overlooking Hoar Hollow.

Below us, angular snow-capped roofs dotted the landscape, stretching wide and blending into the gloom of the gray, frigid day. From here, the city looked farther than a five-mile run. I just met Moira, but I wouldn't put it past her to lie about the distance. I'd rather run around the arena.

Turning away from the slushy, endless path to Hoar Hollow, I stared longingly at the behemoth behind us.

The king's castle didn't compare to the stifling farmhouses and cabins I grew up in. Its gothic architecture jutted into the sky, stirring a sense of the unexpected. The black, iced-over walls shimmered with eerie reflections, and the floor-to-ceiling windows—like dark, glowing eyes—beckoned to the part of me that longed for something more. For adventure, danger, *life*.

And yet, beneath its grandeur, it was another cage—one that thrived on *death*.

"Lucy! Get your ass moving!" Oliver called out.

I slogged through the slush, feeling it splatter my thick pants and boots as I caught up with Oliver. He was surprisingly good at keeping his feet as we ran down the slick hill.

"Okay, we can do this." Ichi and Ni were only a few yards ahead. So far, so good.

"Doesn't take much skill to run down a gravel road, Lucy."

A second later, Oliver hit a patch of compacted snow and slid, cursing. I grabbed his elbow before he could fall and raised an eyebrow at him.

He rolled his eyes. "Whatever."

The hill gradually leveled out, and at the bottom, someone called, "Faster."

Everyone picked up speed at a set of gates.

"Fuck-a-duck."

We increased our pace.

My lungs burned after mile one. Thick phlegm and the taste of copper invaded my mouth, and no matter how often I spat, it always came back. Ichi, Ni, and the rest of the Tormentors were way ahead of us, and we barely heard someone call out mile two a few minutes later.

Two miles. Two freaking miles.

I wanted to give up.

Every breath felt like a battle. The air dried out my throat, making each inhale a struggle. My feet—encased in weatherproof boots—burned with the cold. My heart pounded in my chest, my lungs screamed for relief, and I was pretty sure death was near.

I wanted to quit. I wanted to cheat.

But I couldn't.

My mom and Aspen were counting on me—even Oliver's sister.

To lusceler or stop would be worse than any punishment. The raging storm inside my chest would consume me if I failed. If I gave up now, I'd be everything this kingdom thought I was—an unskilled liability placed in a squadron because the king said so, unable to rescue my loved ones.

I couldn't stop. *We* couldn't stop. Despite my legs begging to collapse, the light-headed dizziness threatening to overwhelm me, and our ragged breaths filling the air, we kept running.

Our pace slowed as we continued, and we lost sight of the Tormentors. Oliver fell back, looking like he was about to take a break.

I snatched his hand. "No stopping." I regretted the breath I'd used for those two words. But they were as much for him as they were for me. The more we slowed, the more my body begged me to quit. If one of us stopped moving, I knew it'd be over.

He gave a weak nod.

The rhythmic crunch of our footsteps blended with the distant whisper of wind through the evergreens. The landscape stretched endlessly before us. With each bend in the road, I clung to hope that just around the corner would be a glimpse of the city—just one building, any sign of progress. We'd be halfway done. But with each turn, my legs grew heavier, my vision hazier. My hope dwindled.

Ahead, a burly male with orange hair and his wiry, brown-haired companion rounded the corner. A flicker of relief sparked in my chest. We had to be close to the halfway point.

They ran toward us, their footsteps steady and sure. I opened my mouth to ask how far we had left, but before I could speak, the burly one shot a sly grin at his friend. They barreled into us without warning, knocking the wind from my lungs.

We slammed down onto the slushy gravel. Rocks and ice sliced open my palms, the gritty slop soaking my clothes as I slid.

"Suits you right, Hell-whores. Moira should kick your asses out," the ginger said, grinning as he blasted us with water.

I gasped as the frigid liquid drenched my back, my muscles seizing against the cold.

His friend snickered, and they ran off, heading back toward the arena. I curled my nails into my palms. My Infernus raged in my veins, itching along my skin. Cracking ice and a low, seductive hum pressed at the edges of my mind, urging me to retaliate.

But what could I do?

If I used my Infernus against them, I'd only cause more issues. I couldn't risk revealing myself. Besides, they were part of an elite squadron, nearly finished with a run we could barely manage. They'd already proven they could put us in our place.

"I fucking hate Powers and their elemental bullshit," Oliver snapped and stood, gazing down at his drenched clothes with flaming green eyes. He flung the water and grime from his hands and glared at the two sprinting males like he wanted them to experience their worst fears.

I hissed as I pushed myself off the ground and joined Oliver, matching his glare as my body trembled. The music of my Infernus still whispered in my ear. Soaked through, shivering, sore, and unable to feel my toes, hands, or face, I let my purple flames coat my skin for a split second once they were out of sight. Feeling slowly returned—and my split second turned into minutes. I didn't want to let the warmth go.

"Come on," Oliver said. "Before I break the rules and lusceler after those assholes."

I glanced up at Oliver's scowl and flaming eyes. "Thought you didn't like to use those powers."

"I don't. But carrot-top just poked some old wounds I thought were buried."

I raised a brow, and he rolled his eyes. "I'll tell you on our long-ass walk. We're going to be last regardless." Oliver sighed.

I knew he was right, yet my gut churned at the thought of walking. Our pace would earn us nothing but slow suffering in the cold—probably why I hadn't let my Infernus go, despite the risks.

But we needed a break. After his explanation, we could run again.

He heaved a breath. "After my mother's murder and my sister's kidnapping, I developed a habit of drawing them in a journal. Any memory I could drag up, I'd draw. That's how I coped with their loss as I bounced between foster homes." He shoved his fists beneath his coat, burrowing them into his armpits. "I never expected much from foster care, but after losing everyone I cared about, I thought I'd get some kind of reprieve. It's too bad the powers that be didn't feel the same."

I squeezed his arm in support, but quickly snatched it back when ice began to crust his sweatshirt. "Sorry," I mumbled. "My Infernus is keeping me warm."

Oliver snorted, his teeth chattering. "My second foster home had a son named Forest. A big ole carrot-top, like that Power. One day, Forest—who already hated that I was eating their food, taking up his parents' attention, and whatever else—found my journal. I begged him to give it back. I told him I'd do anything. And he said he would, in exchange for two things."

I didn't like where this was going.

"The first, to pack up, leave, and never return. That one was easy." He bowed his head, then continued, almost as if the next part hurt more than he wanted to admit. "The second, to lick the bottom of his boots. Said I was a 'gay piece of shit' and should know my place."

I stopped in my tracks, understanding what his bowed head meant. "Tell me you didn't."

"That journal was everything to me, Lucy. *Everything*. I was so lost. And I was willing to do anything, even that... So I did. I licked his boots—which were smeared with dog shit—just to get it back." He shook his head, his face a mask of disgust. "And while I puked on his bedroom floor, while he laughed at me, Forest pulled out a lighter and burned my journal to ash."

I clenched my hands into fists, enraged. "Tell me something horrible happened to him."

Oliver's voice softened. "Something horrible did happen to him." He paused, his eyes distant. "I was so angry, I tapped into my powers and touched him. We both relived his greatest fear."

His face twisted—drawn and haunted.

"You know what his greatest fear was, Lucy?"

"What?"

"Getting raped by his father."

"What?" I whispered. "Why would he do that to you then? If his father..." Ugh, I couldn't even say the word. It was difficult enough to think about when I was almost raped not long ago.

"Evil breeds evil."

I wrapped my sopping arm around his waist, keeping my flaming hand away from him. "I'm so sorry, Oli."

He sighed and leaned his shivering body into mine. "It was a long time ago. But I've got a thing against bullies now. Especially bullies with carrot-tops."

The sound of crunching gravel and pounding feet had us pulling away from each other. The rest of the Tormentors rounded the turn ahead. I immediately dropped my Infernus, and the cold rushed back in. The chilling wind brushed against my half-frozen clothes. Numbness worked its way back through my toes, and goosebumps spread down my spine from my dripping hair. I shook just as much as Oliver did.

They cursed, spat, and kicked slush at us as they passed. No one blasted us with water this time, but their message was clear. We weren't welcome here.

The only two who passed us amicably were Ichi and Ni.

Then came Moira.

She eyed us up and down, a slow smile spreading across her face. "Maybe I'll enjoy training you more than I thought." She pointed behind her. "You have two more miles until you turn around. I usually wait for my squad at the halfway point, but since you two are so *special*, I thought you could figure it out alone." She smirked. "Oh, and you've got thirty minutes to get back. If you're late, you'll be our honorary targets. Hope you don't freeze to death before then."

With a flick of her wrist, she pulled up her fur-lined hood, effectively dismissing us. But I still caught the cunning, vile twinkle in her eye as she jogged away.

"I'll owe you big time if you make her live her worst fear," I stuttered, coating my body in my Infernus flames once it was safe again. My eyes felt heavy with the warmth, but I couldn't stand the cold for one more second without my powers.

"If we could get away with it, I would," he replied, hunching into himself. His lips were blue, and his cheeks had taken on a bruised shade of red.

"How are your toes and fingers, Oli?"

He gave me a weak wince. "What toes and fingers?"

I stared down the winding road, my frustration mounting. We hadn't even made it halfway yet. But if we didn't turn back soon, he'd become hypothermic. My mind screamed to keep going, to prove I could do this, but my body ached with every movement.

"Oli, we need to lusceler back. Running will take too long, and we need to get out of the cold."

"What about what Moira said? Or Ichi and Ni, for that matter?"

"We are both frozen through, and only one of us has the power to stave off hypothermia. That is, until I pass out from exhaustion. Then we'll both be left here to die."

Even now, I could feel the weight of my powers pulling at my energy, my focus. I shouldn't keep using them.

"That's a little dramatic."

I gestured to his shivering body and stiff clothing. "Your lips are blue. We're luscelering back."

"They're going to think we're weak."

"News flash, Oliver, we are! They want us to die out here! Let's not give them that satisfaction."

He grumbled something under his breath, and then we luscelered. Our feet barely touched the muddy slush, although the wind pummeled our faces. My powers shielded me from the chill, not the wind. Tears stung my eyes from the force, and my vision blurred. But when I blinked, it didn't clear.

A hazy hill loomed ahead, and Moira flickered in and out of my sight. That should concern me, but I couldn't remember why. Sand weighed down my feet, slowly spreading through my body. When we reached the middle of the hill, my legs gave out, and I collapsed into the snow.

"Lucy!" Oliver shouted.

I tried to blink the dots from my vision, desperate to see him or the black bounding form behind him, but the dots only grew larger.

"Lucy!" Oliver stumbled back to me, his voice frantic as he grabbed my shoulder. "Hey, open your eyes."

I felt him struggle to drag me against his quaking body, but it was useless. He was in no shape to help, and the world around me faded.

What was the King of Hell thinking, placing us in an elite squadron? What skills did he see in us that made him think we could ever be close to this caliber? Did he want the entirety of his military to know we didn't belong?

Because we didn't. We weren't warriors.

CHAPTER 12

Lucille

A grin spread across my face as I stared at the familiar moonlit field of flowers, the soft breeze playing with the tips of my hair and rustling my coat.

"Sweetheart, how did you end up in Hell?" Aspen's voice broke the serenity, and my smile widened.

Before I answered, I tilted my head to the night sky and imagined the one thing I continued to miss from Earth. A second later, twinkling specks of silver sprang from nowhere and gave life to the darkness. I giggled, the sound filling the quiet.

Turning away from the sparkling sky, I found Aspen standing beneath the oak tree. I walked through the field, my fingers trailing over blooms, and startled when my winter clothing melted away—replaced by a form-fitting green dress. The bodice dug into my ribs and pushed up my small breasts, making them look larger than they were. Aspen even changed my hairstyle, unweaving it from its braid to let it spill around my face.

Was this what he found attractive?

I much preferred pants over long skirts that snagged on every blade of grass and tangled around my legs.

"This is... different," I remarked, meeting him beneath the tree.

Shadows and moonlight slashed across his leathers, giving him a striking, almost otherworldly appearance. He stood still, watching me as if waiting for something. The weight of his gaze and lack of explanation made my smile falter. He lifted a hand, brushing my cheek softly, but his lips were pursed, his brows furrowed.

"Are you going to answer me, sweetheart?"

"That's where the general took me when I was dying. To my father."

Aspen's frown deepened, his eyes searching mine for more. "Lilith always said Hell was locked. No one can enter or escape."

"Well, for some reason, it opened that night."

His fingers twitched against my skin as he mulled over my words. "Why? No one has been able to—for what? Nine, ten years?"

I shook my head, frustration bubbling beneath the surface. "I don't know."

But he had a point. What made that night different? And how did the king know Hell would open—unless he'd been gambling with my life again?

Aspen gripped my shoulders. "Regardless, you're not safe there, Lucille. You need to find a way out."

Safe? The word dug under my skin, sharp and irritating. My thoughts spiraled back to my homes on Earth, to the moments that still left a bitter taste in my mouth. I remembered crying when I had to leave my friends. I remembered fighting with my mom just to get a taste of life outside the house—begging to see humans, to breathe air that didn't feel so... oppressive. The constant arguments. The suffocating isolation. Always wanting more freedom, more connection, more anything—but the walls closing in around me.

I'd been safe for half my life—protected from anything that could hurt me. I didn't know how to live, to fight for what I wanted, to push to be more than I was. I'd been weak, and now I was stuck trying to fix it.

"What has being safe ever gotten me?" I shot back, my voice clipped.

"The air in your lungs." He shook my shoulders, his voice rising. "Your life!"

I scoffed. "I lived in a comfortable prison, Aspen. That wasn't a life."

He flung his hands into the air. "So what? You're going to flounder about in Hell for the foreseeable future, and I'll just have to wait and see if you're still alive every time I fall asleep?"

"Flounder about? Is that how you see me?" The words stung more than I expected. "Is that why you imagined me in this suffocating gown?"

Only an innocent damsel would wear this.

But could I blame him? He'd had to rescue me so many times, and I still barely knew this world—even with my memories back.

"I can't protect you in Hell if I can't get to you," he pleaded.

The flicker of vulnerability caught me off guard, making my chest tighten. I took his hands and peeked at his wrist, relieved to still see them bare of those vile runes. But for how long?

"What about you, Aspen?"

He hesitated. "What about me?"

"Who's protecting you while you're back with Lilith?"

He pursed his lips into a thin line and glanced toward the arches, confirming my assumptions. The tension in his shoulders spoke louder than words.

In our last dream-walk, he'd said he searched *our* library. Aspen had been raised in the Tenebrous Kingdom. So it was safe to assume the only library he'd claim as his own was the one he grew up with—which meant he'd returned to her.

"I've got it handled," he insisted. "Don't worry about me. Worry about getting out."

I let out a frustrated sigh and pressed my hand against his cheek, coaxing his gaze back to mine. "Of course I'll try to find a way out. But I need you to be honest with me. You're not alone in this."

His eyes flickered with something unreadable before he dropped his gaze. "I'll be okay. Just find a way out."

"I will. And then I'm going to rescue you and kill Michael."

His head shot up, eyes flashing with blue fire. "That archangel I found mutilating you?"

Images of Michael slicing me surged into my mind. I curled my hands into fists, digging them into my palms, grounding myself to push the rising panic away.

"Yes," I forced out. "He put my mom into a coma. The only way she wakes is if we kill him."

I didn't mention the other part, the darker truth—how my mother was eating my energy. Or how she could wake if I died. I didn't want to admit my mistake and give him more proof of my floundering.

Something shifted in the air—an unsettling ripple of shadow near the tree line. I frowned at the wispy blur, but Aspen's voice pulled me back.

"I'll figure out where Michael is," he said. "But promise me you'll keep dream-walking to me so I know you're okay. And if you find a way out, come to me. We can kill him together."

His strength and resolute tone steadied me. This was the Aspen I was falling for—not the one who said I was floundering, but the one who wanted me next to him when we killed Michael.

I stepped closer, pressing my body against his, and he responded instantly, bringing his mouth down to mine. Our breaths mingled, and the world narrowed to the two of us.

Aspen moved, pinning me gently against the tree and removing the space between us. A soft moan escaped my lips, and our slow, tingling kiss deepened, growing hotter. I felt him harden against my stomach, sending heat pooling low in my belly. He groaned when my hand grazed him over his leathers.

I smiled against his mouth.

He dropped to his knees, running his hands up my legs and bunching my skirts. "Do you know the best part about dresses, sweetheart?" he challenged. His fingers trailed higher, nearing my throbbing core. "The ease with which I can touch you."

I gasped, throwing my head back as his fingertips slid against my center. Before he reached my clit, a sudden rush of noise broke through the moment—and his face blurred.

"Dream-walk to me again soon!" Aspen's voice reverberated through my mind as everything went dark.

"Wake up!" someone shouted, shaking my shoulders with a bruising grip.

"Quiet down. There are other patients here, you know."

"Leave us. You healed her. Now she needs to answer my questions."

I opened my eyes to the general standing over me, the shadow of his body blocking the ambient light streaming through the high, vaulted windows. The warmth from my fresh clothes and the blankets covering me slowly leached away under the cold wrath in the general's face.

"What—" I moved my arms to push myself off the cot and found them restrained by wispy black shadows. "What the hell is going on?"

Oliver lay on a cot beside me with his eyes closed. I jerked on my restraints. "Oliver?"

He didn't stir.

"Oliver!" I shouted. When he didn't respond, I whipped my head back to the one holding me captive. "Is he okay?"

The general stared at me, something vicious writhing in his cold gaze.

"Is he?"

He crossed his arms. "Tell me if you're working for Lilith, and I'll let you know if your other precious boyfriend will live, *sweetheart*," he spat.

"Will live?" I demanded.

What happened after I passed out?

"Are you a traitor?"

"How can I be a traitor when I'm not part of anything?" I yanked against my restraints, and for a moment, the scenery changed, and I was begging for my life as Michael cut me open.

"You're working for Lilith," he accused, tightening the wisps around my wrists.

Why was he bringing up Lil— And then I figured it out. That had to be what the dark, wispy shadows were, like when he sent a ball of them into Aspen's back and knocked him unconscious in the butcher's basement. Somehow, the general who knew absolutely nothing had snooped in my dream-walk.

What else could those shadows do?

My skin flushed, and my vision kept flipping between past and present—between rage and embarrassment over what he'd witnessed. My hands trembled in their restraints, my heartbeat thundering in my chest. I needed him to release me. I needed him to release me *now*. Heavenly Hell, I was about to hyperventilate.

"Let me go."

"Tell me what I want to know."

I couldn't think. The knife sliding down my thigh, making a squelching noise as my flesh split, invaded my senses. Blood pounded in my ears, and my breath became uneven.

"You were there. You saw how Michael used me as his personal knife sharpener," I seethed between breaths, trying to stay strong and keep the panic at bay. Hopefully, he thought my uneven breathing was from rage and not the undeniable images and sounds of my torture flashing through my mind.

Black swallowed the gold in his eyes. "Yes."

"It wasn't a question. It was an accusation. For someone who saw what torture I endured while bound and immobile, it takes a real *small* male to restrain me—not even a couple of weeks later."

Instantly, his shadows released me, but his cold expression never changed.

I swallowed a shaky breath, hoping he didn't notice the relief in my drooped shoulders or the extra second I shut my eyes.

I wasn't sure if comparing him to Michael would do any good, but at least now I knew there was a shred of something more inside him.

Pity? Maybe. Or something else entirely.

"Are you working for—"

"Why would I ever be working for a queen who wants to torture and kill me to use my powers to get out of her cage? Why would I ever be part of something that harms other females? Why, oh-so-smart General, would I want to work for someone who forced Aspen to take me against my will? I thought you were more intelligent than this, being in the position you're in, *General* Ronen."

He had no comeback to that. Of course he didn't.

Why did he have such a problem with me? It really hurt my chances of helping Aspen escape Lilith, especially since he seemed to detest us both. I saw how the black had thickened in his eyes at

Aspen's name, and how his shadows had wreathed his neck, curling down his body—like when he first met Oliver.

The general gave me one last penetrating stare, then stalked away.

"Oh, and Ronen," I said, forgoing respect.

He jolted to a stop, as if hearing his name shocked him.

"Please, stay the hell out of my head."

He stood there a moment before striding through the doors. They shut with a resounding bang.

"Lucy one, General zero."

I whipped over to find Oliver smirking.

"Have you been faking sleep this entire time?"

His smirk widened.

I shook my head and sagged into the cot. "I can't believe you."

"I woke up halfway through your argument and let the conversation roll. Happy I did. You gave him a tongue-lashing. Never knew you had it in you."

"Me either," I said, rubbing my face. "So what happened? How did we end up here?"

"Well, you so kindly passed out. My legs were no longer functioning after freezing my ass off in soaking clothing for who knows how long, and Rune saved the day by carting us to the healers' wing."

"And?"

"And you and your friend are lucky," a male interrupted.

He had curly chestnut hair and a freckled complexion. I'd say he looked boyish and cute if it weren't for the sternness in his expression or his tall, authoritative stance.

He wore a loose-fitting charcoal shirt and pants. His clothes matched those around him—others who walked between the line of beds and curtains.

"He almost lost his toes. It took several sessions to heal his flesh and a couple more to stabilize his body temperature," he said, confirming my assumption. "And you." He jabbed a finger at me, drawing attention to a yellow crystal the size of a baby's fist dangling from a chain wrapped around his knuckles. Similar crystals graced the necks of the other personnel, but in different colors.

"Divine Wasting is serious. You almost drained yourself dry. If you don't know how to use your powers safely, don't use them—or find a teacher."

"I only used them for ten minutes. If that." I didn't think such a short time would cause me to pass out.

He gave me another scalding look. "Your powers come from your soul's energy. The same energy you exercise with. You exhausted yourself during your run, barely leaving anything to tap into your powers. Luscelering should've been the last thing you did."

"So what?" I shot back, feeling the edge of my frustration rise. "Should we have just continued running in our wet clothes and died of hypothermia instead?"

His nose wrinkled. "Of course not. Oliver had enough energy to lusceler himself back, and he could've found another member of your squad to come help you."

I opened my mouth to argue, but he cut me off.

"If you use up all your energy, you'll die. I'm sure you felt some signs of degradation. Those are warning signals—telling you to stop."

He sighed, shaking his head, as if he could tell I was only taking half of what he said to heart.

"I've healed you as much as possible, but something is not allowing me to heal you fully. Every time I try to replenish your energy reserves, it doesn't stay filled like it should. Have you run into this problem before?"

"A problem with my energy? No, I don't..." I trailed off as my shoulders dropped.

My mother. How could I have forgotten?

"Say someone was draining your energy... what happens to them if you use too much of your power?"

He scrutinized me, placing his crystal back around his neck. "That depends—"

"Would it hurt them?"

"In most cases, no. Usually, it's more harmful to the person being drained," he said slowly, his eyes narrowing. "Why, is someone draining your energy?"

I hesitated. "No, just a hypothetical question."

He studied me. He didn't believe me. "I don't normally do this, and it's not a solution, but it will help."

He reached into his pocket, pulling out something small and gripping it tightly. Yellow light gleamed through his knuckles before settling. A small yellow crystal rested in his palm when he opened his hand.

"Here." He handed it to me. "Squeeze it only if you absolutely need to. It probably only has about two uses, but it'll replenish your energy when it gets too low."

"Thanks." The crystal hummed faintly as I grasped it, a comforting sensation swirling through my palm. I tucked it away in my pocket with a grateful smile.

The tightness in his pursed lips told me he wanted to press further, but he didn't. After a long pause, he cleared us to leave on the condition that we rest and refrain from going back outside. I forced a tight smile. I could appreciate the order, but a part of me still boiled with frustration at our failed run.

Once he left, I gave Oliver a questioning look. "And that joyful male was?"

Oliver gazed after the healer with a peculiar expression. "His name's Sam. A Virtue, like the rest of the healers here. Or at least like the rest of the ones wearing an amulet."

I assumed they all wore a necklace, but I'd found some healers without them.

"Is it a rank of some sort?"

Oliver shrugged, turning back to me. "Maybe. Sam used his when he healed us. So it channels their powers, but I'm not sure why the different colors. I'm assuming the healers who don't have them either don't need them, aren't Virtues, or aren't qualified for them."

Shifting to the side of the bed, my sweatpants bunched at my waist and pooled past my feet. They were huge.

"What am I wearing?" I plucked at the thick, black long-sleeve swallowing my small form, smelling of crisp winter air, balsam, and a sharp note of cloves. My eyes fluttered, and a genuine smile lifted my lips as I brought the shirt to my nose.

Home.

The scent reminded me of the rare times my mom and I felt free—when our burdens fell away, and even Earth's suffocating homes didn't feel so stifling. Every winter, soft snow blanketed the evergreens and carpeted the grass in a sparkly white sheen. My mom would light a balsam candle, and we'd string up lights and fresh greenery while her terrible jazz music played in the background. And on the nights snow fell thick, she'd pull me from bed before sunrise, and we'd bundle up, make snow angels, and giggle under the twinkling stars. The hot chocolate afterward sealed it as one of my favorite traditions.

This scent was all that—but also spicy and sharp. Toe-curling.

Oliver smelled his own shirt, nodding. "I mean, yeah, the general smells great, but I didn't think it was moan-worthy."

Instantly, I let go of the shirt, giving Oliver raised, incredulous brows.

"Sam suggested warmer clothing instead of the thin, papery gowns they give patients, and the general complied by donating a couple of shirts. That semi-kind gesture happened before I fell asleep and woke up to him flipping his shit."

"The general doesn't know how to be kind, Oliver. The king went to great lengths to get us here, and if we died from hypothermia training in his Hell Squadron, it would be his ass. He gave us warm clothes because he needed to, not because he was being kind."

"*Ohkay*, you're probably right. Now, do you want to tell me why he flipped out about Lilith?"

Sighing, I stood, holding onto the general's sweatpants so they didn't fall to the ground and show my bare ass. Oliver had to do the same. At least his didn't pool by his ankles. "Not here. I'll tell you in our rooms."

Rune met us outside the healers' wing and followed us back. Once we shut our door and both sank into the settee, I told Oliver about my dream-walks with Aspen—leaving out the sexual details.

"Be careful, Lucy. He still could be under the queen's influence. You can't trust him completely."

I considered his words and the dream-walks. The first one made me suspicious, but Aspen explained himself, and it made sense. Everything he said and all his reactions added up. But Oliver was right. Even if he wasn't runed, he was still near Lilith.

"About that... you do know Ronen's the general Magda talked about, right? I assumed you did." But by his expression, he'd totally forgotten what the witch told us. "He's the one who can save Aspen. Lilith has the general's feather."

Oliver laughed—and laughed some more. I knew what he was about to say before he even said it.

"Hate to break it to you, Lucy, but when the general was rescuing you, he was two seconds away from ending Aspen. He only stopped because you were dying. The general hates him. By the sound of it, all of Hell hates Aspen and Lilith. We're better off trying to steal his feather back and using it ourselves."

Oliver was right. But if we went up against Lilith without the general, we'd die. We weren't warriors. We were... flounderers.

Rune rested on the plush rug at our feet. Her fur undulated like the general's shadows, and as the sinking dread set in, I wished I had as much sway over the general as his Soulhound.

"I don't know what to do," I admitted. "Oli, what do we do? I can't leave him like he is. He can't stay there doing heaven-knows-what for *her*. I can't—I think I might... I..."

"Stop." Oliver took my shaking hand. "I'm only saying this because I have years on you, but before you say what I think you'll say, I need you to wait."

"Why?" I tugged on his hold, not liking where this was headed.

"Why do you have feelings for him?"

"He cares about me. He protects me." *He makes me feel like no one ever has.*

Oliver pursed his lips, frustration thickening his voice. "I didn't know carting you to his evil queen was protection." I opened my mouth to protest, but he didn't give me a chance. "I care about you. I try to protect you. Do you love me?"

"Not like that."

"So, is it his good looks? Because if it is, you might want to reconsider—I'd say the general ranks above the prince in that department."

My irritation spiked. "You know the answer to that. Aspen..." My voice faltered as I tried to explain. "He makes me feel safe. Seen, like I matter. He's different."

"Seen how, Lucy? What do you even know about him? What does he even know about you?" Oliver pressed.

I gritted my teeth. Why did it matter to him?

"What is the point of this conversation? Are you jealous? Do you want me like that?" I blurted, knowing it was absurd the moment I said it.

He sighed, a long, weary exhale. "No, I love you like a sister, Luce. But someone needs to look after you the *right* way. Your family's coping mechanisms are messed up—abuse, overprotective to an extreme, and possessive indifference—it's not healthy. If you love the prince, fine, love him. We're rescuing his ass either way, I know that." His voice softened. "But seriously, Lucy, ask yourself why. I may not know all that's gone on between the two of you, but I do know the look in your eyes when you speak of rescuing him scares me."

"What look?"

"The look where you'd give absolutely everything for him—even your life."

My head dipped as shame burned in my gut—and something else I couldn't name.

"Would that be so bad?"

"Didn't we already talk about giving too much of yourself? *Your life* is on that damned list, Lucy. And I just..." He trailed off, a deep unease settling into his voice. "I have this feeling."

"A feeling?" I pulled away and stood. "That's what you're going off? A feeling?"

The expression on Oliver's face put pressure behind my eyes. I didn't want his pity. When he opened his mouth, I knew I didn't want to hear anything else he had to say.

"What if it's the bond?"

"How do you know about that?"

"He told me after you were taken. That's how he got me to trust him enough to follow him."

I backed away. "That doesn't mean the bond is forcing my feelings," I snapped, turning sharply and heading to my closet to find different clothes.

"Okay, fine. Then let's talk about someone you haven't mentioned since you saw her. Your *mom*. Are you going to give her all your energy so she lives and you die?"

"Of course not!" I'd never see her again if I did that.

"And while we're on the topic—how is Aspen, who's under Lilith's thumb, going to find Michael for you? And what if he doesn't? Who will you save first?"

I ripped off the general's shirt and pants, chucking them at the wall. Sam's crystal bounced out of the pants pocket and across the floor.

"Will you leave your mom in a coma while we attempt to convince the general to help us save Aspen and my sister? Or will we save them second and try to kill Michael first?"

I yanked on new clothing and pocketed the crystal, my hands shaking from the overwhelming weight of his questions.

"Did you ever consider we can only save one at a time?" Oliver's voice was quieter, almost gentle, as if he knew what he was doing to me.

"No," I whispered from my closet, my eyes wide with horror as the implications of his words settled like lead in my stomach.

"What if we have to choose, Lucy?" he asked, his words piercing my chest. "Who would you choose?"

Choose? Like I was picking out something to wear for the day. This wasn't some simple answer. I couldn't just pick one over the other. How could I possibly choose?

"Who has more time? How long can you and your mother last with a Wrath Rune? Or how long can Aspen survive under Lilith's control?"

"Stop," I gasped, his words choking me. I didn't want to hear any more.

"Have you thought about the consequences of going one direction or the other?"

I splayed and clenched my shaking hands, trying to steady myself, but my vision blurred. "No. Stop! Please, just stop talking."

Oliver's drilling, heart-wrenching questions pressed on my chest, and I couldn't take it anymore. I stormed out of my bedroom and wrenched open the door to the hall, not caring where I went—just needing to escape.

Rune lifted her head, and Oliver shot up off the couch. "Where are you going?"

"Don't follow me. Please."

I wasn't sure who I was begging—Oliver, who wasn't trying to be cruel, or the general who suddenly illuminated Rune's eyes, who definitely saw the tears streaming down my face after I'd tried so hard to be strong in the healers' wing.

I ran out of my room, slamming the door in Rune's face, and kept running until I collapsed in front of the library.

My hand clamped over my mouth, holding back my whimpers. I'd never considered I might have to choose who to save—but now that I was forced to think about it, the ache in my chest was unbearable.

Because deep down, I knew.

And the guilt threatened to destroy me.

CHAPTER 13

Lucille

Eventually, I calmed myself enough to think about my choice, but the guilt never faded. I didn't think it ever would.

I went through so much in Elora to save my mom, and now look at her. I didn't save her—I condemned her. All because Michael wanted my life and to possess my mom. A mom who now lay unconscious in the king's rooms. I haven't even tried to visit her after the first time. The shame and weight of how little I knew about the worlds she kept me from—no! That I kept *myself* from—put us in this situation. I should've tried harder to find and unlock her books. I should've never believed Michael would do what I wanted.

Why didn't I trust my instincts? Why didn't I know more?

I slammed my hands on the carpet.

And Aspen. The first male to capture my heart was being abused and used by an evil bitch. His mom asked me to save him. I told myself

I'd find the general and save him! Everything inside me pulsed with the urgency to rescue him. So much so—I'd put him before my mom.

But how?

A slobbery, warm tongue slid up the side of my cheek, taking away my tears but leaving a wet line of saliva. I looked up at Rune and her illuminated golden eyes.

"I said not to follow me."

Rune licked my other salty cheek in response.

"I wasn't running away to join Lilith's little gang, if that's why your spy hound is here."

Rune sat back on her haunches, and they watched me. It seemed unfair that he could see and potentially hear everything I said or did, but I only had Rune's head tilts to contend with—and I couldn't be irritated with her. Worse, I had no energy left to force them to leave.

"You probably think I'm weak right now. A weak, scrawny little girl, crying on a carpet." I bowed my head, no longer willing to look at those illuminated eyes, and stared into my hands. "I just want to save the people I love, Ronen. That's all."

I realized I hadn't used his title, but it wasn't like he was here to discipline or berate me for it.

"I want to be strong enough to do what it takes to save and protect everyone who means something to me. I'd never join Lilith. I'd rather die than be part of her plans. I didn't know about any of this or the rune."

My voice cracked, and I swallowed back the ache in my throat. "I didn't know it would put her in a coma. The king and Aspen are right. I am floundering," I whispered, lifting my head to Rune.

The mosaic doors rearranged behind her, revealing a scene that would be burned into my mind forever. I dug my nails into my trembling palms. It was one thing to live through it—another entirely to see it captured in such stark, cruel detail.

If I hadn't been me, I would've sworn the female chained to the metal table, lying in a pool of her blood, was already dead. Michael stood over her, the image so raw and brutal it felt like I could reach out and touch the horror.

What were these doors?

I stood, forcing myself to take in the scene despite the urge to look away. The more I stared, the more an overwhelming need pounded through my blood, demanding more from me—demanding I *be* something more. I clenched my teeth. The girl who lay upon that metal table, exposed, weak, helpless, and dying—that could never be me again.

"I'll see you tomorrow, General. Tell your girlfriend we'll be ready for her punishment. We did come in last, after all."

With that, I patted Rune on the head and entered the library.

"Cato," I called out. My voice bounced off the towering dark shelves and into the high ceiling. If he didn't hear me, he sure would in a second. "Cato!"

Someone tapped me on the shoulder. I whipped around. Cato stood there wearing his robes and a dry, irritated expression. Sure, I yelled in a library, but it wasn't like anyone was ever here.

"Yes?"

I gestured to the doors. "What are those? Why do they show what they do?"

Cato clasped his robed hands before his body and pursed his lips.

Seconds passed. Then a minute.

"Well?" Heavenly Hell, I didn't think an answer would take this long. If he were an all-knowing Throne, shouldn't he already have one?

He shifted his pursed lip a millimeter and walked away.

"Hey!" I yelled. "I asked you a question."

Cato faded behind a shelf, and I stood there in disbelief. When the soft thumps of his feet also vanished, I plunked down at the table where Oliver and I had left our reading material. Before I so much as touched the cover of a book, Cato appeared out of nowhere and dropped two books onto the table, startling me.

"I think you need to wear a bell," I muttered.

"Or you need to be more observant."

I frowned at the titles: *The Doors of Moirai* and *The King of Hell.*

"I wanted straight answers, not—" Cato was no longer there. "Books." I sighed. So much for the all-knowing encyclopedia being helpful.

I tilted my head to the glass ceiling. The dark sky, empty of twinkling lights, added to the sorrow and guilt lingering in my throat.

Was Earth the only place with stars?

I didn't know why I wanted to see them so badly—why the glittering of flaming gas soothed something inside my dreaming soul. Maybe their light gave me hope, or perhaps they reminded me of the nights with my mom, staring into the sky and making wishes.

Pursing my lips, I readied myself for another long night of reading and opened the book on the doors. The first page displayed a curving script and dedication:

To the reigning King of Hell.

I turned to the next page and was happy to find my answer.

The Doors of Moirai, otherwise known as the Doors of Fate, were created the day Heaven decided it needed a counterpart—Hell. Housed inside the doors are the powers of three: the Spinner, Allotter, and Unturning. The things that were, the things that are, the things that may be.

When Heaven chose Lucifer as the ruler to reign over the dimension of Hell and all the souls who'd end up there, the doors followed—connected to the king. For only the king could judge the souls of the dead, and judge them fully.

With the Doors of Moirai, the past, present, and future are presented to the reigning ruler upon Judgment Day. They do not need to look upon the doors to know and see. But the past shows the sin, the present shows the growth or lack thereof, and the ever-changing future shows the consequences. Judgment can't be placed solely on a future that could change. The majority of judgment must come from the things that were and the things that are.

So the doors showed the past, present, and potential future. But why could *I* see the images? Because I was the daughter of Hell, or for another reason?

Tonight, I saw a moment of my past.

But what about the other day with Oliver and the general?

It looked like a demon biting a female. And not just any female—someone from Hell's military. But that didn't make sense. The general had said there were no demons here unless it was a half-breed.

So, a half-breed demon had either bitten, was currently biting, or was going to bite someone in Hell's military. But why did it matter? Why show me this? Was it intentional, or some twisted happenstance?

My head fell against the book as I groaned.

"You're not going to find your answers that way."

I shifted my head to the side, glaring at the Throne who definitely needed a damned bell. "Is there anything you can tell me about the doors?"

"No," he replied, ignoring my glare. "But if you'd read the book, you'd know who to ask."

He meant the king. And he was right. It clearly stated that the King of Hell and the doors were connected. I was just hoping the *all-knowing* Throne would tell me what I wanted to know, and I wouldn't have to resort to the king.

I fiddled with the book's page, dreading how that conversation would go. My stomach twisted thinking about it. So far, every conversation with him had been miserable. It always came back to how naïve I was, like some unavoidable label.

But why should that surprise me?

He wasn't much different from when he'd spoken in my mind in Elora. Back then, he called me naïve, and I hadn't exactly been reading any books since my mutilation or recovery. I sank lower in my chair.

I couldn't avoid talking to him—he'd be training me to control my powers, after all.

"Rest assured, the king is nothing like Michael," Cato said, as if reading my mind—or, more likely, my nervous fidgeting and the scowl on my face.

I turned toward the Throne. "So he's not a self-serving bastard who gambles with his daughter's life?"

Cato's eyes flashed from brown to black, silver sparks gleaming in their depths. It was there and gone so fast, I almost thought I imagined it. Angels' eyes usually erupted with flame when emotional, not... whatever that was. But then again, how would I know? General Ronen's eyes shifted to swirling shadows, so maybe it was a Throne thing.

He stepped closer, and I leaned back as far as I could in my chair, intimidated by the quiet severity of the Throne boring down on me. "Your father didn't gamble with your life."

Right. And Michael didn't carve me open either.

Cato's gaze sharpened, clearly reading my disbelief. "Your father knew about you the moment you manifested your Infernus. Or rather, he suspected, when he sensed someone outside his domain using the icy powers of Hell—a power only he should have. Lo and behold, when he had General Ronen connect your minds, he found a young female living with his cordistella and fighting off the same male she left him for," he continued, his voice firm. "He knew you wouldn't die in that river because he knew you were his daughter."

I froze, barely breathing. Cato's words hung in the air, and I stared at him, searching for the lie. I wanted to argue. I wanted to rip apart every word he'd just said. To me, the king had always been callous and cold-hearted. Once he sent me into that river, I'd assumed my life meant little to him—just another game piece to play or discard. But Cato's words... they made me hesitate.

I'd almost forgotten that moment—the cold, commanding voice that had infiltrated my mind and helped me freeze Michael. The king had saved our lives. I didn't know it was him at the time, but I remembered feeling strange gratitude toward the mysterious male. And if that wasn't enough to make me question everything, I'd seen his love for my mom. She was his cordistella—his soulmate. It all made sense now. Every glance toward his bedroom door, like she'd disappear on him if he didn't check every few seconds. The raw, helpless fury he unleashed on his room when he learned what Michael had done to us.

He loved her because she was his other half.

The memories, combined with Cato's words, slithered into the cracks of the steel fortress I'd built around my opinion of the king, forcing me to reconsider who he was.

But if they were cordistellas, why did she leave him? Why did she end up with Michael?

So many questions swirled in my mind, but the ones that escaped my lips felt like the words of a small, shriveled child clinging to an unfair past she couldn't understand. "If the king knew about us—if my mother was his bonded—why didn't he ever come for us? Why didn't he ever save us from Michael's abuse?"

How different would our lives have been if I didn't have to hear my mother's cries, the sickening slap of skin against skin, or the clattering of furniture? If I didn't have to feel the cold blade split open my back, or—

I swallowed hard, forcing the ache down, and pushed aside the memories of Michael.

"The king isn't allowed to leave the Redemption Circle," Cato answered, his tone somber. "Even before Hell's gate issues."

What about his military? He couldn't have sent someone to find us?

Bitterness slapped the back of my throat. I was wallowing in self-pity, and it'd do me no good. "The past happened," I snapped softly to myself. "You can't change it."

He considered me for a moment more, then nodded to the book I had yet to open. "You'll be meeting with your father in the morning. It'd be wise of you to brush up on what you know about him and your Infernus."

"You know about my Infernus?"

"I'm a Throne," he deadpanned.

Right.

"What do you know?"

He turned his back on me, swishing his robes as he did, and padded away. "Read and find out about them."

"Them?" I called after him. He faded into an aisle of dark shelving and books, ignoring me. "For a Throne, he's really choosy with what information he gives me," I grumbled beneath my breath, flipping open the book on *The King of Hell.*

The opening paragraph explained the creation of Hell and the need for balance in the celestial world—an opposite to Heaven. The passage continued, saying Hell had once been without a ruler. But then the following paragraph discredited that information, stating Hell was created when the council chose Lucifer to be its ruler. It didn't add up.

But that was nothing compared to the blacked-out paragraph at the end of the page. Was the author trying to hide a mistake? Or had someone deliberately erased it?

I held the page to the light, squinting to make out anything beneath the thick ink. Whoever had blacked it out had been thorough.

I skimmed the rest of the history, finding more blacked-out pages, and noting the celestial world's obsession with balance, then moved on to the section about our Infernus. I spent hours reading, absorbing everything I could, until my eyes grew heavy.

Our powers came from the Seven Circles of Hell: Redemption, Temptation, Glaciation, Hallucination, Suffocation, Scission, and Immolation. Each circle contributed a piece of itself to the king—and, by extension, me. The book didn't clarify what powers we received from each circle. Still, it mentioned that the king had once possessed immense power until he willingly divided it, giving parts of his power to the lords of the circles to ensure their obedience—and to maintain balance and a connection to each dimensional circle.

I pursed my lips, a begrudging respect for the king creeping up inside me. To once hold such power and give it away took strength. Sacrifice. Michael would've never done that. He wanted to murder me for prestige and to regain my mom's wings—wings she never once mentioned to me. She seemed content without them.

Maybe Cato was right. Perhaps the male who fathered me wasn't as bad as I thought. He obviously cared for my mom—without hesitation or conditions. Maybe he just wanted me to be stronger, to teach me the ways of his world.

But something still nagged at me. Why put me in an elite squadron when I wasn't ready? Why demand I read thousand-page books in a day?

He was rushing me to be better. I felt my own urgency to grow stronger and understand more—but I had my reasons. What were his?

I chewed on my lip, my eyes drifting in and out of focus as my thoughts circled, following the sentences without retaining the information. Then my gaze landed on a distinct passage:

You'll hear their whispers when they come,
they'll stretch your skin when you're one,
but know this ruler, and know this well,
the circles have a counterquell.

The whispers I assumed were the odd melodies I would hear. The stretching of my skin must be the itches. But what in the world did *counterquell* mean?

I read for a few more hours, even some of the books the king required us to read, all the while resisting the sagging of my eyes. At one point, I knocked my head against the table, nodding off, and knew it was time to leave.

Walking through the Doors of Moirai, I found Rune curled up in front of them.

"Rune?"

She lifted her head, blinking sleepily, then yawned and stretched like a cat. She gave me a wet lick on my cheek with a soft nudge. I smiled and ruffled her shadow fur.

"Let's go to bed. I'm assuming I only have a few hours before I need to get up." I refrained from groaning—and refrained again when Rune's eyes lit up.

"You really can't help yourself, can you? I'm off to bed, General. Follow along if you like."

Rune and the peeping general trailed me as I returned to my room. I said nothing else to him, and if I didn't look at Rune, I could almost forget he was there. *Almost.*

At my door, Oliver's snores vibrated through the wood. My lips twitched.

"I'm going to bed now, and Rune's—" I almost told the general his Soulhound was sleeping with me. But Rune wasn't mine, and I had to keep reminding myself of that, even if she was near me almost 24/7. "I'd like it if Rune slept with me, and you didn't invade her mind." *Or mine again.* I left that part out, though.

"And by the way, Oliver prefers males. That's why I let him sleep in my room." My face heated at how much I was sharing. I must be drained. "It comforts me to have someone I know who's there for me and isn't trying to use me. So, not a boyfriend. And—" I paused, knowing I needed to do this, but not entirely feeling he deserved it. "I'm sorry for insulting you. Goodnight, General."

CHAPTER 14

Lucille

A strange gurgling noise jerked me awake. My heart raced as I scanned the dim room. Rune slept soundly beside me, her shadow fur curled around her like a soft, soothing blanket. But Oliver... he was gone. His side of the bed lay undisturbed, perfectly made, like he'd never been there at all.

"Oliver?"

Did he go to his room?

Throwing off my covers, I sat up—and found myself clothed in a Hell Squadron uniform. My brows furrowed.

Purple didn't ring my vision, so it wasn't a dream-walk. But then... where did this uniform come from? And who dressed me?

A choking sound sputtered through the cracks in the door—ragged and desperate, like someone gasping for air.

I shot out of bed, my gut twisting at the horrifying noise.

"Oliver?" I shouted. The word rang out as I slammed open the door and froze. "Oliver!"

He lay on the settee, his neck sliced.

Without thinking, I luscelered to him, my hands shaking as I pressed them to his wound. Blood seeped between my fingers, and Oliver's terrified eyes locked onto mine, his lips parting in a desperate attempt to speak.

"Stop! Don't!" I yelled, pressing harder, but the blood kept flowing—hot and thick—dripping down my wrist and soaking the velvet cushion. His chest heaved as he gurgled and choked on the blood spilling from his mouth.

This wasn't real. This couldn't be real.

"Help!" I shrieked. His pulse was fading. "Someone! Please!"

But no one came.

"There are three classes of power in our world—physical, mental, and runes. Which do you suspect this is, daughter?" The king's voice rebounded off the walls of the sitting room.

I whipped around, searching for him, but he was nowhere to be found. My hair prickled, every strand standing on end as his chilling presence pressed in on me.

"Help him, please," I begged, turning back to Oliver—and found an empty settee. The floral pattern was undisturbed. Pristine.

I shot to my feet. "What—"

The room dissolved, shifting into a different nightmare—one I'd already lived.

Cold metal chains pinched my skin, their unforgiving grip splaying me out for Michael's eyes. He circled me. A grin twisted his lips as he turned his black blade this way and that, eager to press it into my flesh.

The king's words vanished, replaced by suffocating panic.

"No," I whispered, shaking my head vehemently against the table. "You're not real."

My heart pounded, lungs straining as I fought to breathe. Michael's eyes twinkled with disgusting relief, like he'd finally get to unleash his pent-up sadistic nature.

"You're not real!" I shouted, my voice trembling. My body betrayed me, trembling harder.

I had to wake myself up. I couldn't live through this again, nightmare or not.

He laughed in my face, raising the dagger.

I recoiled, twisted in my chains. Uncontrollable tears slipped from my eyes. I wouldn't beg. I refused. But I knew what happened next.

"Answer the question, Lucille, and it'll stop," the king's voice sliced through the fog of my panic, making the scene waver.

I froze, latching onto the disruption. Something about it tugged at my mind, demanding I remember. The thoughts hovered just beneath the surface—so close I could almost reach them. And then Michael's dagger glinted.

It plunged toward my arm.

"This isn't real," I choked out, losing my moment of clarity. "I need to wake up."

"You're right—it's not real. But if it's not real, then what is it?" His words were like pebbles dropped into still water, fracturing the nightmare's surface.

The dagger hovered inches from my skin, the scene blurring again, and with it, everything—Michael, the chains, the dark basement walls—distorted, shifting in and out of focus. For one fleeting moment, I felt the tight grip of confusion.

It's not real. Shifting in and out of focus. Distorted.

I'd seen those words. I'd read them late last night.

There are three classes of power in our world—physical, mental, and runes. Which do you suspect this is, daughter?

Michael's dagger solidified, sinking into my skin. The fiery slice tore through my arm. "Mental! Hallucination!" I forced out as Michael dragged the dagger up my arm, sawing apart my flesh. I screamed and screamed, my voice raw. I couldn't take this. I thought he said it'd stop. I thought answering would make it all end.

But then, just as quickly, it came to an end.

Something—someone—released the hold on my mind, and the hallucination dissolved.

I jolted awake, my body thrumming with the aftermath of the pain.

The King of Hell sat in a chair near my bed, casually resting his head in his hand. His legs were stretched out, his posture too comfortable for someone who'd just subjected me to two horrific hallucinations. If not for the lingering white glow in his irises—or all the information I'd gathered about his powers—I might've convinced myself I'd dreamed it all.

I flung off my blankets, my pajamas sticking to the sweat sheening my body, and stood in front of him, heart pounding.

"What the hell was that?"

He straightened in the chair, his eyes narrowing. "Watch your tone with me."

"Tone? *Tone*?" I scoffed, not giving a damn if he was my father or the king. He'd forced me to reliving the worst moments of my life. What kind of father does that?

"I haven't even started with my tone. Why did you put me through that?" I demanded, curling my hands into fists to hide their spasming.

His gaze flicked to them, but he didn't acknowledge it. He rose from the chair, towering over me.

"I'm beginning your power training," he said, his voice flat.

I stared up at him, shaking my head in disbelief. I hadn't expected an apology, but his lack of empathy hit harder than I thought it would. Last night, Cato had given me the tiniest shred of hope that the king might be different. That maybe, just maybe, I could have some kind of relationship with my father.

But after what he'd just done? After he forced me to experience Michael's torture, Oliver's death? I was kidding myself.

"So these torture sessions will continue?" I accused.

"Yes. You've pushed me from your mind before. Until you learn to keep me out, we'll continue with the hallucinations."

The urge to argue clawed at my throat. I had no qualms about snapping at the king. But the longer I glared at him, the more I noticed his no-nonsense expression—the same one my mom wore. A pang hit my chest, and I ended our stare-down, refusing to waste my breath.

"There are three classes of powers in our world—"

"Mental, physical, and runes," I interrupted, barely containing my bitterness. From his icy silence, he didn't seem pleased by my interruption, but I didn't care.

"You can use all three: your hallucination and glaciation powers, and the power to give runes. The rest of your Infernus you gave away," I added, proving to him I'd done my reading.

He nodded, and I almost thought the quick gleam in his expression was approval—but I refused to hope. Casually, he adjusted his suit jacket and waved a hand over the door. A glossy layer of ice coating the wood evaporated, and the frosted door handle returned to a metallic black. I frowned.

He'd locked us in?

"The majority of beings who live in our world have physical powers. Only some have the ability to control the mind or use runes."

His words stirred a memory, pulling my focus from my unease. "Like your general?"

"Yes. But he's not the only one who can influence the mind. And as you well know, anyone with the ability to carve runes can control you."

I grimaced. How could I ever forget?

"Are you saying that learning to shield will help me resist runes?"

"Some," he answered, giving me a knowing glance. "But not all."

"Not a Wrath Rune."

The brief tightening of his jaw told me all I needed to know.

I shook my head, wishing it could've been that easy.

"Do you not wish to shield your mind against those who would influence it?" he asked, as if he were disappointed in me.

"I do," I shot back. "It's your methods I hate!"

"My methods?" he mused, his hand resting on the doorknob. "Did you read all the details of the powers of hallucination?"

"Yes," I said immediately, though the words felt hollow. I couldn't quite recall everything. I'd nodded off, and half the information I retained from the last hour was fuzzy.

"If you had, you'd know that hallucinations can be created one of two ways: by projecting a scene into someone's mind, or by projecting an emotion and allowing their subconscious to create the scene." He gave me a cool side-glance. "Now, how could I have projected a scene of Michael's torture if I was never there?"

"You could've stopped it!" I exclaimed.

Facing away from me, he opened the door with a flick of his wrist. "Yes. And you could've as well."

Oliver fell in with a loud thud, offering a sheepish grin. The king glanced down at him briefly, grunted, and stepped over his sprawled body.

"Retain more of what you read, daughter. I'll find you for our next session in a couple of days."

Hearing my second door close, I sank back onto my bed, dropping my head into shaky hands, hoping they'd be still by the time we went to the arena.

Oliver scrambled over to sit beside me. "That was the longest hour of my life," he muttered, running a hand through his hair. "I didn't know whether I should've called for help or... just wait."

Alexei's ungodly trumpeting started.

Oliver nudged my shoulder. "You good?"

"Yeah." I sighed. "I'll be fine. Just had a rough power lesson, is all."

"And... we're good, right?"

I lifted my head from my hands. His concern tugged at my heart. I grabbed his hand and squeezed.

"Yes, Oli. We're good."

He'd only asked questions I never wanted to think about. That didn't make him the bad guy—just a smart one.

He squeezed my hand back, warm and reassuring. "You sure you're okay?"

I gave Oliver a small smile. "The king's hallucinations were..." I swallowed. "They were difficult to experience."

I continued to hold his hand, unwilling to let go, needing to feel the warmth of his skin and steady rhythm of his pulse. The gentle pressure calmed my racing thoughts, grounding me back to reality. I glanced back at my mattress, noticing the wrinkled bedding and faint impressions where Rune and Oliver had slept. The reminders that they'd only been hallucinations eased some of my trembling.

"If you say so."

I was grateful he didn't press further.

"Where's Rune?"

"The king kicked us out of the room. Told me I could stay in the sitting area but sent Rune back to the general."

"Interesting," I muttered. The king didn't exactly seem to like Rune, but maybe it wasn't Rune herself. Perhaps it was the fact that the general could snoop through his Soulhound.

The trumpet blared again. I didn't want to leave yet, but I knew we needed to.

"We'd better get going, Oli. We're already on everyone's shit list as it is."

He groaned and stood, releasing my hand. I refrained from snatching it back.

"Fine. See you in five."

After changing and taking a few more deep breaths, Oliver and I met up with Alexei outside my door, then headed to the training arena.

"Welcome back, recruits," the general called out over the whispering sea of bodies below the dais. Alexei and a red-haired female stood on either side of him, both wearing flat expressions and Hell Squadron uniforms with fewer accents of red. Behind them, three more males stood at attention, their faces and uniforms matching—his Dreads. "Most of you made it to your second day of the Infernal Sixty."

Most?

That sobered everyone up, quieting the whispers coming from the non-uniformed recruits. Some even looked a little pale.

General Ronen lifted a brow, scanning the faces of his military. "Did you think I was kidding yesterday? Half of you are here for penance. It's demanded that you go through suffering. You make it or recycle. The other half of you are here because of the deals you've made. You make it or die." He paused, letting his words sink in. Nervous shifting and tapping feet filled the heavy silence. "That being said, we still want you to succeed. We need more hardened warriors in our military, so I have an incentive for you."

He stepped aside for Alexei, who pushed his shoulders back and shot out his hand. The hairs along my arms rose in the thick atmosphere, and in the next second, a flash of silver cracked through the air, striking something over our heads. We all jolted at the re-sounding crash and stumbled back when something fell—only to realize it was a large, rolled poster.

It unspooled to reveal the title of each squadron and four blank spaces beneath each. The two at the top were highlighted in red.

"Over the next two months, General Ronen, I, and a few other Dreads"—Alexei gestured to the four behind him—"will be watching you."

I didn't know if it was from his lightning trick or his playful personality, but I could almost hear the smile in his voice as he spoke.

"As we watch you train and pass drills and challenges, we'll rank you. But there are only four slots per squad, and ranks will change. If you manage to hold a spot before the last week of the sixty days, you'll earn a favor regarding challenge week—within reason. If you happen to place in the top two red slots, you gain our respect and a gift."

"Not sure I'd want a gift from Hell's military," Oliver muttered.

"Souls—if you're placed at the top, you can mend your wounds for free, and you'll gain favor from the king when it comes time for your next judgment. Blood-banded, the king will expunge the foolish deal you made with him, allowing you to cut your time with our military in half and, when you're able, leave Hell. And if that doesn't pique your interest, General Ronen will grant you a favor—again, within reason."

The energy inside me, already buzzing with the need to be stronger, surged. Oliver and I didn't have a *real* deal to expunge or soul wounds to heal, but we needed the general's respect and favor.

And so far, we hadn't made any progress in that area. But if ranking could earn us the help we needed to save Aspen and Oliver's sister, then we needed to rank.

I panned around the room, taking in the leather uniforms hugging the seasoned military members, then glanced down at Oliver and me, clad in layers and thick clothing for our inevitable run. We were bulky while they were sleek and pristine. We were staring around like the rest of the clueless recruits in the Bowels Squadron, while others stood with chins raised and confident gleams in their eyes. They were honed warriors, ready to do whatever it took to gain the Dreads' respect, the king's favor, and their reward. Oliver and I had the motivation—but not the muscle or skill. We'd ended up in the healers' wing after our *first* run. Ranking in two months felt daunting. Nearly impossible.

It would require nonstop training, late nights in the library, and—honestly—a new damned game plan. Because there was no way in this dimension, or the next, that the scraps of strength and skill we could scrape together in two months would be enough. Our squad already itched to tear us apart and stomp on our weak, little pieces. They could crush us, and they knew it. Hell, we knew it too. The only advantage Oliver and I had was our powers. But I needed more control. And technically, I couldn't use mine unless I wanted to expose myself. Oliver... I gave him a quick once-over, biting my lip. Oliver would have to overcome his aversion to using his ability.

He side-eyed me, feeling my gaze. "I don't like that expression on your face."

"What expression?" I asked, my eyes wide and innocent.

Oliver scoffed. "Your bug-eyes can't hide the smell of your stinky guilt. You've come up with some kind of scheme that somehow involves me, and you know I'm not going to like it."

My fake smile turned sheepish.

"If you get us killed, I'm forcing the king to place us in the same circle so I can annoy you while they torture us—for the rest of time," he said, running his hand through his moppy hair, his nerves blending the black and blond strands of his bangs.

I squeezed his free hand. "Wouldn't have it any other way."

"That's it for today. Find your leaders and follow their instructions," General Ronen concluded, snapping my attention back to him and straight to his piercing golden gaze.

I held it for a second—one second—and that same magnetic feeling pulled at my chest, begging me to move closer. He wore no smile. Gave no pretense that he liked me. If anything, he only tolerated me, even after I opened up to him. So what was this damned attraction I didn't want? And how did I stop it?

I needed his respect, which meant I'd have to hold his gaze for more than a few seconds eventually. More than that, I'd have to break through whatever resentment he held against me.

So his pretty little face didn't matter.

"Lucy." Oliver tugged on my arm, pointing toward our squad. "The pack of hyenas is congregating."

"If they're hyenas, what are we?" I asked.

"Roadkill."

Accurate.

We dragged our feet toward the Tormentors—not alone in our reluctance. Many other recruits seemed unenthusiastic about starting their second day. Half the Bowels Squadron looked petrified. They must've witnessed a squadmate's death or recycle. The smug expression twisting Moira's perfect face made me want to turn and leave, but I held my ground.

"Oh, look. My favorite two recruits," she purred, her voice sweet and mocking as we joined the others.

Everyone circled us. Some smiled. Okay—most smiled. Except Ichi and Ni, who stood silent, lips tight in disapproval.

"So, what's our punishment?" Oliver asked, cutting straight to the point.

"Target practice," Moira replied, her tone dripping with superiority. "Come along, recruits. Theon and Cyrus will be helping me out today. The rest of you—spectators."

The ginger and his wiry friend's smiles deepened, and my stomach dropped.

"Wonderful," Oliver muttered.

This wasn't a coincidence. She must've known about our last interaction—or even instigated it. The urge to rake my nails across her golden skin overwhelmed me.

We followed behind our squad, walking next to the twins. The concerned creases in their lips never changed.

"What's target practice, Ichi?" I asked.

She gave me a side glance, shaking her head with a heavy sigh. The weight of her exhale pressed on her drooping shoulders. Her sister wouldn't even look at us, like she was ashamed.

"Target practice is quite literal," Ichi said softly. "You're the target, and we are instructed to practice on you. Sometimes with weapons, other times with powers. Moira decides the conditions."

Her expression turned distant. "She started it a few years ago, after a couple recruits disobeyed her. Ever since then, anyone who displeases her becomes an example, and we're her tools."

My jaw tightened. Sounded like we'd be her example every day from here on out. "And the general allows this?"

Ni finally shifted, her face saying everything.

Ichi sighed. "She's dating the general. And this is Hell—"

"Suffer or die," I finished, the bitter truth sliding off my tongue. She nodded.

"Are we moving targets or..." I trailed off at the twins' matching expressions. "So, no. We're just supposed to stand—"

"In a damned public bathroom and let carrot-top and his weasel friend show us how glued their lips are to Moira's bleached ass," Oliver finished for me, stopping at the threshold of the showers.

"Move, recruits. We have other things to do today."

To hell with what she had to do.

"Move! Or I'll let all of them punish you."

Oliver, having other ideas, pulled me into the open area and stopped at the wall Moira pointed at.

Theon and Cyrus swaggered into place, their eyes glinting with smug satisfaction.

Moira gestured to us. "Have at it, Theon. And if they even flinch, you can restrain them, Cyrus."

The beefy carrot-top—Theon, I assumed—whipped up his hands. Two powerful streams of water shot out, slamming into our chests and sending us back into the wall.

My head cracked against the tile. I bit my lip, holding back a cry of pain.

"Hit their faces," Cyrus suggested.

It took everything I had in me—plus squeezing Oliver's hand in a death grip—not to move an inch. After this morning, I knew I wouldn't be able to handle another restraining without either having a panic attack or revealing my Infernus.

I weathered the blast of frigid water, clenching my teeth against the bruising pressure. The third and fourth blasts barreled into my stomach harder than the last two.

Our squad jeered and belittled us, enjoying our torment. Each laugh, each curse, seared through my veins. But that paled in comparison to the unholy rage pounding in my chest from Oliver's broken, hollow expression. I wanted to latch onto my Glory and burn the arena to the ground—to watch their sneering smiles blister and turn to specks of useless ash.

Even now, my Infernus begged to escape, enticing me with its music. It wanted to trail across the tile, slide up the ginger's legs, and crawl down his throat. It wanted to watch Theon suffocate on his burning flesh. It wanted—

I squeezed my eyes shut, ignoring the haunting melody. But the more I did, the louder it became. The taunting whispers turned to an addictive noise, forcing me to listen. Theon blasted us with a harder stream, and itches scattered across my skin.

No. Shut up. *Shut up!*

"That's enough, Theon," Moira called out, halting the water.

My Infernus quieted the moment Theon released us from his power, and the itches dissipated. I sagged against the wall.

"It's time for our run." Moira ushered the squad out of the bathroom. "Faster, recruits," she said, pointing at us, grinning.

"We're soaked," I snapped.

Moira laughed with disbelief. "You think I care? We might not be allowed to kill you, but if the elements do it for us, it's not our problem."

I grabbed the side of my soaking pants to refrain from punching Moira—or tackling her to the bathroom tile. Oliver placed his hands on my shoulders, understanding that I might actually attack her and lose.

"Move," she ordered, turning as the last of the squad left the showers. The smile in her voice needled at the melody I'd just put to rest.

We followed them out, then luscelered to our room to change.

CHAPTER 15

Ronen

My Dreads and I split up and rounded on the six Hell Squadrons, observing their skill levels and assessing our leadership. Rune padded silently at my side, ever watchful as we evaluated the recruits.

Each of us carried a piece of parchment marked with a Scriptum Ostendere—a rune that linked our papers, allowing us to share our thoughts and observations in real time. By day's end, I planned to use the second piece in my pocket, linked to the poster overhead, to rank our warriors and give them a clearer sense of their competition.

I paused near the Devils Squadron, where groups of recruits sparred in hand-to-hand combat. I glanced down at my paper, fighting the urge to roll my eyes at Alexei's latest addition to our notes. And it had to be Alexei. He was the only Dread who'd think to draw a crude stick figure of a female with exaggerated curves and, predictably, a list of her hair and eye colors. We didn't know all the names in the lower-level squadrons, so we relied on physical descriptions and—in Alexei's case—personal embellishments.

I scanned the Devils, bypassing Lou's drilling stare, and found the female Alexei had so expertly drawn, shaking my head when I did. She had a half-bare face, the skin stripped from her neck to her temple, revealing slick muscle. Bone jutted from half her nose, and her teeth gleamed as she took blow after brutal blow from her opponent. Alexei should've noted her soul wound, not her curvy body—but knowing him, I wasn't surprised. Still, he wasn't wrong to note her.

She took hits to the face and kidneys and didn't flinch. Not a grunt, not even a hiss of pain. Her remaining eye, fierce and determined, locked onto her attacker as she absorbed the hits to her ribs. Then, with an almost casual efficiency, she knocked the male off balance, drove him to the ground, and hammered him with her fists. I nodded, impressed, and placed a tally next to her name.

Rune bounded off to the far end of the arena, grabbing my attention, only to lead me to *her*.

She stood bundled up, shivering, and heaving against the Nephilim. Surprisingly, my shadows didn't react. I refused to think about why. Like I refused to think about what her words had done to me the other night. Not her worthless apology—she could apologize from dawn to dusk, and I wouldn't give her a moment's attention. At least, not more than I had to. Even if I found myself checking in on her more than I should. No, it was before that—her defeated honesty that struck a chord. And damn it, I hated how it made me feel.

Gritting my teeth, I glared at the wet sheen in her heavy, dark waves and her undeniable shivering. My shadows shoved at my control, wanting to shoot out and tamper with her neurons to warm her up.

Why the fuck was her hair wet again?

"Tormentors Leader," I called out, walking over to the iron yard.

Moira set down her weights. "Yes, Ronen?"

"What did you call me?" My shadows seeped from my feet, secretly sliding up her leg and lifting a dagger from her sheath.

My lips pressed into a line while hers lifted in a taunting smirk. We both agreed at the beginning of this arrangement that she wouldn't drop my title during training. I didn't want anyone thinking she had special treatment. But it seemed she no longer cared—still snubbed by the unfairness of her situation, the murder of her friend, and probably the fact we hadn't fucked since we rescued the hellion. It hadn't been without trying, but every time she came to my room, I would either leave, sleep, or try to please her and lose interest, leaving her to pleasure herself. She had reasons to be upset, but she was testing my restraint. Her devious little mind once intrigued me, but now I found it off-putting.

Her lip twitched, as if we were playing a game. "Ro—"

I nicked her neck, and my shadows drew her blood to my mouth. Quickly, I shut down the neural pathways to her temporal lobe, silencing her.

"Here, I am your general." I stepped into her space, towering over her as the shadows swirled in my irises, deepening my vision. "Not your punching bag. Not your *boyfriend*," I spat. "Your general. If you want to continue down this path, you can join Danny in the lower circles. Understood?"

She slowly nodded, her nostrils flaring with anger. I shouldn't let this disrespect slide. I usually didn't. But there was something else that needed my attention—something gnawing at me enough to tighten my chest and stir the anxious shadows under my skin.

"Your new recruits have returned." I nodded to the door, releasing Moira from my control.

"Worthless. Both of them," she seethed.

I forced my shadows back.

They had nearly torn me apart, trying to break free and comfort the female when she'd ended up unconscious in the healers' wing, her lips blue, her clothes damp and frozen. When Sam suggested I retrieve her warmer clothing, I luscelered away, grateful for a task that would not only put distance between us but also ease the restless hunger of my shadows. It aggravated me how much they were affected by her.

When I returned, I couldn't hold them back any longer. They dove into her mind, and her powers wrapped around mine, caressing and seducing them, pulling me into a scene that would forever be seared into my brain—the *pet* and her.

My blood simmered with lingering rage.

I had to listen to them. To *see* them.

I shoved the memory away. "Explain the state of their hair."

Moira eyed them from head to toe, seeming satisfied by their misery. "They probably tripped into another puddle. They're not the brightest."

That was what she had said yesterday.

"They tripped and fell only on their heads?"

Moira shrugged. "Maybe they took a shower before the run. I don't know, General. I'm busy training a squad, not trying to look after two worthless bodies of flesh."

A shower?

On a good day, Hell peaked at thirty-two degrees Fahrenheit, but lately, it hovered closer to the negatives, reflecting Lucifer's mood. Even the seasoned warriors, with their Hell Squadron uniforms designed to regulate temperature, knew better than to shower before training outdoors. Those with at least half a brain understood the risk, while the ones who didn't—like a couple of dead Bowel recruits— paid the price.

The hellion and Nephilim made their way over to us. A black wisp circled my palm, begging to leave me and infiltrate her brain. I clenched my jaw and locked it back inside my body.

"Ni," I commanded. She marched over with her twin.

The Dojigiri twins never left each other's sides. And after hearing their stories, I didn't blame them. Somehow, after killing a famed demon leader, the council didn't reward the two upon death with Heaven—but with Hell.

"Dry those two off."

Ni nodded and met the hellion and Nephilim a few yards away. Ichi explained Ni's powers, then her fire magic thawed and dried them. The shadows in my core settled when the hellion's lips pinked along with her cheeks.

"Train your recruits better, Squad Leader. If you can't keep them out of puddles or showers before a freezing run, then how do I expect you to lead them at all?"

Outrage infused her expression before smoothing over to cool indifference. "Is this not Hell, General? Suffer or die, right?" she said, throwing my words back in my face.

My shadows rattled inside me. But I wasn't my shadows, and this was Hell. "Right."

The cunning gleam settling on her face stoked my possessive power. It slammed against my barriers, demanding out, demanding to protect the hellion.

I glanced at her again, flashing back to her broken voice as she kneeled in front of the library. Her vulnerable words had tugged at a part of me I continuously denied. I scoffed. She didn't deserve my sympathy.

Shame slapped a bitter taste at the back of my mouth. Nor did she deserve to be called a traitor or pinned to that cot. She had been right. I was the general for a reason. I'd been inside countless minds and could spot people's motivations. The hellion was never going against Hell; she may not be for it, but she wasn't a traitor.

She just *kissed* fucking traitors.

But seeing her there at those doors, so overcome by the weight of her sorrows, it took every ounce of my will to fight my shadows and not go to her.

My Soulhound didn't have those reservations. I gazed at Rune and the excited black wisps curling around her tail. She sat by the hellion's side, completely content.

Rune was the only piece of my soul I'd allow the hellion to have. Not that I could ever stop Rune. From the glimpses of Earth I saw through her eyes and hearing about the hellion and Saraqael's story, I realized Rune had found our cordistella way before I did. She loved the hellion, and nothing would keep them apart. I just hoped the hellion never figured it out.

Although if she knew, she wouldn't care. After all, she and the pet looked pretty fucking cozy in that dream-walk.

In all my years, I had never heard of the term or experienced something like that. It didn't make sense. But for all I knew, that form of communication stemmed from some Hell-born power.

My nostrils flared at the information the pet could be gaining, while my shadows rioted at the images of him *touching* her.

For fuck's sake.

I gritted my teeth and strode away. I didn't want to be near her any longer than I had to.

After observing the training sessions and ranking five recruits in each squad, Alexei and I left with the Dreads to patrol and search the Lower City of Hoar Hollow for Damned Souls. Eventually, I commanded everyone to split up.

Alexei, MJ, and I circled the outskirts of Veil Forest, searching through the gnarled dark limbs. Spinewalkers crept through the mysterious, never-ending fog, their elongated black bodies as spindly as the trees. If not for their jagged spinal columns protruding from their ten-foot backs or the large ovals that represented their faceless heads, they could easily be mistaken for the trees themselves. Fortunately, the disturbing creatures were harmless—as long as you didn't touch them.

The wind carried the Spinewalkers' wails through the branches and snuck beneath our uniforms.

"MJ." Alexei raised his gloved hands and batted his eyelashes. "Warm me up. I'm freezing my balls off, and you're the only one who can fix it, sweetness."

Sighing, I whipped up a wall of shadows immediately after MJ threw a fireball toward Alexei's head. I was in no mood to see who would fry the other faster.

Alexei smirked. Bastard knew I'd step in.

"You know I'm not always going to be the buffer between you two. So you'd better come to terms with being shriveled and bald or refrain from taunting her."

Alexei flashed a wry smile and flicked his fingers, sending tiny sparks of lightning crackling toward MJ.

He managed to duck before the next fireball singed his head.

A sharp scream pierced the wailing wind, ceasing their childish behavior.

Alexei drew his daggers, I unsheathed my swords, and MJ readied her bow.

"Why do the screams always come from Veil Forest?" Alexei muttered. "Isn't the unnatural wind, fog, and Spinewalkers enough?"

"Don't forget the Hellhounds," MJ added.

"How could I ever forget those bastards? A pack of them is probably waiting for us to step into their domain and drain our blood."

MJ shrugged and strode into the barren woods with balls the size of a Soulhound.

"MJ," I commanded, stopping her in her tracks.

Sometimes, I wondered if she had a death wish. Her confidence bordered on recklessness these days. But after her cordistella was killed, half of her soul died—and she no longer feared death. She sought it.

"Alexei's right. We need to take to the sky first."

She nodded, and the three of us summoned our wings. We shot into the air and circled the forest. The vile wind howled around us, a living thing that slipped beneath armor crafted to withstand the extreme cold of the Redemption Circle. Our uniforms never protected us from Veil Forest's wind, whether above it or in it. For Alexei and me, at least. MJ, as a fire Power, never seemed to feel the cold.

"Look there," MJ called out, pointing at a body dangling from the branches of a tree.

We flew to it.

Not *it*—her.

"Scout a circumference for threats. I'm going to attempt a body count."

My second and third nodded before flying off.

I sent out a dark stream of my power and immediately battled against the wind. It blasted through my wispy tendrils, scattering them into inconsequential pieces. I pushed more strength into my shadows, and the wind roared, slamming me back. My wings strained to keep me airborne as the Veil Forest fought me tooth and nail. Releasing more shadows, I managed to weave a tendril across the forest floor, searching for blood, heat signatures, or movement.

It picked up a pool of blood beneath the female's body and a trail leading away from her. Before I could follow it, the wind blasted my shadows apart. I pulled back my power, and the wind eased around my wings.

MJ and Alexei flew back.

"All's clear. Did you find anything?" Alexei asked, sounding doubtful.

"No Hellhounds or creatures in the vicinity. Only a trail of blood leading from her body."

They nodded, and we dropped to the forest floor, unsummoning our wings.

Blood and grime obscured the female's face, but I recognized her. "Bonny?"

"You know her?" Alexei asked.

"She's the human maid who works on my floor," I said, surveying her shredded body and the uniform hanging off her in scraps.

Both raised their brows.

"Who the hell brought her all the way out here?" Alexei asked, throwing his blade and slicing through the rope holding her neck at an awkward angle.

Bonny dropped, and I caught her, knowing she was dead.

MJ summoned orbs of fire. Their heat seared through the thick fog coiling around our shins. We caught sight of the glistening pool of blood—and something darker—before the wind roared and snuffed out her flame.

An angel might survive that much blood loss, but a human would not.

"Do you think they infiltrated the castle or captured her outside it?" MJ asked.

"The king would know if someone infiltrated his castle," I said confidently, lowering Bonny.

"Just like he knows how the Damned Souls are infiltrating the Redemption Circle?" Alexei countered.

He had a point, but his comment didn't sit well with me. I'd have to post a few Nightmares near the castle entrances.

Fog crept over Bonny's body, swallowing her from sight. If not for my hand on her shoulder, I wouldn't have known she was there.

Flame whipped from MJ's hand, slicing through the fog and wind, bringing Bonny back into view. She pressed her fingers to Bonny's neck, checking for a pulse. But we all knew she wouldn't find it. She shook her head. "Dead."

"I've never seen cuts like these," Alexei said, pulling back the soaked fabric.

My stomach dropped when he revealed the expanse of her skin.

"That's because they're bite marks."

"From what?" MJ asked, revulsion lifting her lip.

"They're too small to be from a Hellhound. But they—" Something about her blood seemed off near her exposed chest. "MJ, hold your flame here."

She summoned it, battling the pissed-off wind. Her flames flashed in and out of view as the wind shoved against her, whipping her hair.

"What the fuck is that?" Alexei exclaimed.

Black veins surrounded the bite marks, and dark gunk oozed out, mixing with the blood between her breasts.

Dread settled in my gut. Silas had similar veins—but I didn't remember any bite marks on him when he was interrogated.

"That's enough, MJ."

She pulled back her power, and the wind stopped attacking.

A branch snapped. All of us stood, weapons drawn, eyes scanning the dark trees. But aside from a few Spinewalkers in the distance, nothing stirred.

Then the hum began—slow, soft, and unnervingly familiar. The sound swelled, growing louder until it cut off sharply as a Damned Soul emerged from behind a tree.

I shot MJ a quick nod, and she released two arrows. They whizzed over our heads and pinned the Damned Soul to the trunk. He gurgled a laugh.

"Damn, they just keep getting more repulsive," Alexei said, slowly approaching. "Remind me to ask the king not to send me to the Immolation Circle when I die."

The male's naked, hairless body glistened with a pinkish sheen, black gunk weeping from his wounds.

Alexei narrowed his eyes at the fluid. "Is it leftover from whatever the Immolation Lord uses to burn them with?"

"That doesn't explain the veins," I replied. "Or his horns."

"Are we sure he isn't a demon?" MJ asked, though her voice lacked conviction.

Demons might be the only creatures with horns or grotesque features, but they couldn't survive in Hell without a soul. They belonged to Lilith. We'd wiped them out centuries ago, and the few who remained resided in Elora and her kingdom.

A few feet away, I lifted one of my Soul Swords, hearing the metal hissing as it met the Damned's exposed skin.

He remained unfazed by the searing of his flesh. He didn't act like he was in pain at all. It was possible he wasn't. In rare cases, souls in the lower circles could lose all sensation from repeated torture—so their lords would heal them just enough to make them feel again.

His wild eyes darted around, and his grin stretched wider, exposing pitch-black gums and razor-sharp teeth—teeth that matched the bite marks on the female's skin.

"Did you kill her?" My voice darkened, pressure building behind my eyes like an impending storm.

"No. She's my next follower," he rasped, glancing down at her body as he ran his tongue along his teeth.

Follower?

"She's dead," Alexei said with disbelief.

The Damned Soul laughed, the sound ragged and wet. Black liquid flowed from his chest, staining his already ruined skin.

"Is she?"

"MJ," I snapped, my pulse hammering against my ribs. "Check her teeth and hair."

Every instinct screamed that I already knew what she'd find, but I fought to hold on to the sliver of hope that I was wrong.

"No change in her teeth," MJ said slowly, "but... she's growing horns."

Fuck. *Fuck!*

How was that possible?

The Damned could infect others.

Lucifer needed to know—immediately.

"Is biting the only way you infect each other?" I squeezed the hilts of my Soul Swords. The Damned smiled, as if savoring my panic. I pressed one of my blades into his neck. "Is it?"

"Scared your little mind invasion with Silas will have consequences, General?"

How did he know about that?

The Damned jerked up his hand, grabbing ahold of my chin. I refrained from ending him then and there—I needed answers.

Alexei snatched the Damned's arm and slammed his dagger into his hand, pinning it to the tree trunk. MJ did the same to his other hand with an arrow.

The Damned hissed through bared teeth, but there was no pain in his face, only anger.

"Come closer, General, and find out," he taunted, chomping at the air. A slimy pink substance leaked from the points of his teeth, sliding down his chin. Slowly, his skin blackened where the fluid touched.

Like a demonic venom.

Their maker must've weaponized their teeth.

"How did you get to the Redemption Circle?"

"By the time you figure it out, Hell will have fallen."

I pressed my blade harder against his neck. "You know what this is?"

"A soul-eater, Ronen."

A chill shot down my spine at the casual way he spoke my name.

"Then answer me."

"Even if you trap me in your blade, it won't stop us." His confidence clashed with his erratic heartbeat, which vibrated against the metal of my sword.

"Who is us?"

He didn't respond. The silence of the forest pressed in around us. Lifting his chin in defiance, exposing more of his throat, he began humming that same soft, twisted tune.

"Tell me who," I demanded, digging my sword in deeper. The black liquid oozing down his neck caught my eye.

It had been a couple of days since I'd ingested the Damned Soul's blood, and I hadn't seen any dark veins creeping beneath my skin. Bonny couldn't have been infected long—meaning the transition was fast. Still, the last time I drank their tainted blood, I'd puked it up hours later, my throat burning as it came out. I knew it would make me sick again, but we needed answers.

"You won't find what you're looking for in my mind," he said, noticing the direction of my gaze.

He might be right. But I sent out my shadows anyway, absorbing a single drop of the poisonous blood before the wind could stop me. It would be enough for a few questions—long enough to dig for something useful, before I'd have to risk more to hold his mind longer.

I dove into his memories, burrowing deep into his deteriorating mind. "Who do you work for?"

Fragments of figures—blurry, disjointed—flashed by. I caught glimpses of blond, black, then red hair. Tall and short shapes. But nothing substantial. Every image bled into the next before vanishing completely, too fast to make sense of.

I pushed deeper. "Where are you coming from?"

A solid black void swallowed the fragments, devouring every trace of color and shape.

"I told you." He grinned. "You won't find what you're looking for inside my mind. They were prepared for you, General." His smug expression bled into his thoughts, taunting me.

Enraged, I tore apart every neuron in his brain, savoring his sharp, ragged gasps. When I finished with him, I had two choices.

I could let MJ burn him, sending his soul back to Lucifer for a second judgment—*hoping* the disgusting soul would land in the Horde's stomach, dissolving for years or centuries until he ceased to exist.

Or I could take matters into my own hands—slide my Soul Sword across his neck and condemn him to eternal agony.

Both options were brutal. One would trap his soul in the Horde's relentless void, his existence erased when they deemed him ready to be unwritten. The other would bind him to an endless torment, his crimes remembered by those who survived him. Either way, he would suffer.

But I didn't know which was worse—my sword or the Horde. Eternity in hopelessness... or horrific agony, followed by a permanent end, forgotten by all.

This time, I couldn't take the chance. The Horde might spare him. Or, worse, bits of his soul might bleed into the ground, like Silas's had. Even if Lucifer sent his soul straight to them, the Horde devoured as they saw fit.

The Damned Soul's grin faltered, a flicker of understanding crossing his eyes. He knew.

He struggled against the arrows pinning him, jerking up and down, but never forward—like he thought he could somehow kill his own soul and recycle.

But in Hell, souls could only recycle once their bodies were destroyed by slow decay, fire, or—in the king's case—ice.

"Enjoy agony." I decapitated the Damned Soul.

His body turned to ash, then sifted into my swords, vanishing from sight.

"I need to report this to the king." The air pulsed with raw energy as I summoned my wings. "Take her out of here and bring her to the dungeons. He'll want to see this."

"Ronen, that's the fourth Damned this week," Alexei said, picking up Bonny.

"I know. Keep searching. Capture any soul or blood-banded who's infected. Only kill them if you must."

MJ and Alexei summoned their wings. "With pleasure," they said in unison.

CHAPTER 16

Lucille

My legs, arms, abs, and feet all ached in ways I didn't know were possible—and we still had seven weeks left. The general had perfected the art of avoiding me like I had some kind of disease. Then there was the lack of progress in finding an escape.

The days blurred together—a mix of punishing water abuse, freezing runs, weight training, and the king's illusions. My exhaustion went beyond muscle pain. And that wasn't even including the daily library visits, or my mom draining me to survive. I could've used Sam's crystal to help, but I was saving it for when I absolutely needed it. So I suffered, the weight of the world and my decisions threatening to crush me. But I couldn't stop.

On our one so-called day off, Oliver and I scrubbed the kitchen. Like our bruised ribs from that damned carrot-top weren't punishment enough.

Half asleep, I dragged my arm across the metal counter. Oliver wasn't much better off. His head rested in his hand as he half-heartedly scrubbed the sink. After several minutes of mindlessly wiping the same spot, I sank to the floor beside Rune.

She gave me a nice wet lick and nudged me back into her large body, as if encouraging me to rest. Maybe she knew how exhausted I was.

Unable to help myself, I cozied into her warm shadow fur and fell asleep.

"Watch," the familiar voice whispered.

I opened my eyes, expecting to see the female in the red and black cloak who'd helped me regain my memories in Elora—but stopped short.

Chains dug into my limbs, binding me to a bed designed for luxurious comfort. It was oxymoronic. Buttery silk sheets, crafted of the finest threads, draped over my legs, while my head rested against a plush velvet headboard. The softness of the fabrics mocked the rough chain links pinching my skin. The room around me—though difficult to take in with my neck held in place—seemed vast and decadent, from the faint glow of the crystal chandelier to the gossamer purple fabric swaying above my head near a tall, arched window. And yet, amidst all this luxury, panic shoved at my lungs, and a dark hole of nothingness threatened to consume my fear.

A door squeaked to my left. I twisted my head as much as I could and stiffened.

I'd only ever seen her once, but once was enough. I could never forget those scarlet-ringed eyes that twinkled with cunning and menace, or her unearthly darkness that drew me in. The Mother of Demons was both captivating and terrifying—a cataclysmic force of nature.

She glided toward me, dressed in a sensual gown as dark as her black mane. Her painted lips spread into a wide smile as she revealed an ebony feather in her hand and pressed it against my wrist.

I jerked as the tip stabbed me, but I couldn't go anywhere.

"Don't," I rasped—then something shifted.

The dream changed.

It was no longer me on the bed, but Aspen. I stood by the bedroom door, watching Lilith brush the tips of her nails down his cheek. She sank onto the edge of the mattress, rattling his chains.

"Do you have anything you'd like to share?"

He clenched his jaw, staring at her with defiance.

"Oh, my darling prince, I thought you had learned."

She pressed down on the feather. Every muscle in his body tensed, veins popping. Lilith's lips twisted into a satisfied smile as she dragged the feather down, splitting his flesh. He screamed, wrenching at his restraints as blood dripped from his wrists.

Shaking off my shock, I sprinted to the bed and tackled Lilith to the ground—then the dream changed again.

"Keep watching." The female's voice echoed, everywhere and nowhere at once.

I tried to find her, but someone else caught my attention.

She sat on the edge of a blue pond, surrounded by white Celestrus, her long black hair flowing down her favorite sweaterdress.

"Mom?"

She twitched, as if hearing my voice, but continued to swish her legs in the water and stare ahead.

"Behind you!"

Still, she didn't turn. It was almost as if she drifted farther away, yet neither of us moved. Panicked, I ran toward her. But no matter how fast I moved, she always slipped farther out of reach.

"Each ripple alters the course for what's to come. Remember that, Lucille," the female said.

"Who are you?" I shouted. But my words were lost as my dream shifted into a nightmare.

My back pressed into a cold metal table, filling me with dread as I stared at the rusted butcher chains dangling from the ceiling.

I knew where I was. I knew whose footsteps sounded behind me.

I swallowed hard and squeezed my eyes shut.

"It's just a nightmare," I whispered to myself.

But everything felt too real, and shutting my eyes only made me more aware of the heavy metal pinning me down.

A blade screeched across the table, and I tensed.

"Open your eyes," the female said.

"No." I squeezed my lids tighter.

"You need to open your eyes. Remember!"

"Like I could ever forget!"

The terrible squeal of the blade drowned my words. Then it stopped. I knew what came next, and I didn't want to watch as Michael drove the blade into my flesh.

In my nightmares, he didn't talk. He didn't demand answers. He only stabbed me—over and over and over again.

"It's just a nightmare," I begged myself to believe. "Wake up!"

"You are not helpless! Listen to me!" she demanded. "Look and remember my words!"

I couldn't look. I could only shriek, enduring his abuse forever.

"Lucy," someone said.

"Please!"

It needed to end.

"Lucy!"

Something zapped me, and the torture dissolved.

Alexei crouched in front of me, mini lightning bolts zinging between his fingers. "There's Sleeping Beauty. Having a nightmare?"

I jerked up and swallowed, my pounding heart throbbing in my ears. "Alexei?"

I looked around, spotting Rune's glowing eyes and Oliver sitting beside me, looking horrified. Rubbing my wrists, I gulped down air, trying to calm the terror prickling along my arms. "Why are you here? What's going on?"

He nodded at Rune. "She interrupted my boxing match with Ronen after she and Oliver couldn't wake you. You were screaming."

The lightning between his fingers vanished, and he helped me off the ground. "You okay?"

"Yeah," I lied.

"Bullshit," Oliver snapped.

My hands shook, and my skin felt clammy. I probably looked like a mess, but I wasn't about to talk about it in front of Alexei or the general. Even if I explained everything to them, what could they possibly do?

Maybe it was from the king's illusions, or from Moira constantly threatening to restrain me, but for the past week and a half, instead of dream-walking, I dreamt of the same three things: Aspen, my mom, and my torture. And the horror always started with that female's voice.

I wanted to believe they were just nightmares, but a part of me wasn't sure.

I never dreamed. I only dream-walked or slept through the night. So what were these?

Was she doing it—the female who guided me to Elora? Would Cato or the king know?

"I'll be fine," I said, biting my lip and glancing at Rune and the general watching us.

Alexei raised his brows, tilting his chin down as if to say he didn't believe me. "Why don't I show you two around town?"

"I—Why?"

First, Ronen had Alexei come wake me up—which, if he despised me so much, I figured he'd let me suffer. And now Alexei wanted to take us out?

He stepped closer, fingering a piece of my hair. "Can't I just be a nice male who wants to take a beautiful lady and her friend to a warm spot with good food and drinks?"

"You could. But my track record says that's not likely."

Alexei smiled. "Then you'll just have to figure out my ulterior motive while we're there."

I narrowed my gaze.

"Come on." He laughed. "I bet you both are hungry. Plus, you two need to see something other than the castle and arena."

I was hungry. And by how dark it appeared outside, Oliver and I slept through lunch. But more importantly, Alexei was always by the general's side. Even if he had an ulterior motive, maybe we could use it to learn something.

"Okay, sure," I said. "Oliver?"

"Anything to leave this castle."

After bundling up, Alexei led us to a large outdoor barn. Long, black wooden planks lined the building, and brown trim broke up some of the darkness. Unlike the castle, the barn had the right number of windows. The castle almost had too many, making me feel exposed as I walked down the red-carpeted halls.

He opened two dark wooden doors. "This will save your legs for your next run."

Black sleighs with red detailing lined the barn.

Genuine joy lifted my lips, pushing away the aftershocks of my nightmares.

"So is this how the souls and blood-banded move around when you're not trying to torture yourselves with running?" I mused, stepping into the building.

Alexei snorted. "Actually, when we're not in the mood for torture, we enjoy flying—or we blood-banded who have wings do. Angelic souls, unfortunately, lose their wings and powers if they're sent to Hell, so sleighs are their best friends."

I frowned. "But Ni used her power—"

Alexei cut off my question. "Hell is all about punishment and sacrifice, but also redeeming. So it depends on what Lucifer decides to take from you when you die. Most angels' wings are ripped off like

Lucifer's were when Hell was created. But as angels ascend and make it through the Seven Circles of Hell, they can earn them back."

"And if he takes their power, will they earn it back?" Oliver chimed in, looking more intrigued than he should.

"Depends. Usually, you can only earn both back when you ascend to Heaven—if you ascend."

"Are you able to choose which you earn back?" I asked.

"Not sure on that one. That's a question for the twins or another dead angelic soul," he said, then put two fingers in his mouth and whistled.

"What was that for?"

Alexei gave me a handsome smirk, his crystal blues sparkling with mirth. "Something has to pull the sleigh, beautiful."

Rune's shadow fur whipped around as if she were agitated. She sat staring into the snowy trees at the end of the building.

Three large felines with gorgeous white, speckled fur and eyes as crystal blue as Alexei's prowled into view. My mouth dropped open.

"Snow leopards?" Oliver asked in awe.

Alexei crouched down, and one of the felines broke away, sprinting toward him. My Glory prickled, then slowly eased when I noticed Alexei's wide-open arms. He chuckled when the large cat tackled him to the ground.

"This is my girl, Jaz. She's a Hellcat. They look like Earth's snow leopards but breathe ice and blink."

"Blink—"

The last two Hellcats sprinted toward us, but unlike the one currently purring on Alexei, the other two disappeared mid-sprint and reappeared right in front of our faces. Oliver and I both fell on our asses. Rune growled, pressing closer to my body.

"So their blinking is like teleporting," Oliver said, laughing when the Hellcat butted his chest with its head, pushing him into the ground.

Alexei chuckled along with Oliver, shoving off his Hellcat. "Rosie, get off him." Rosie stepped back, then circled Alexei, purring. "Yeah." He gave Oliver a hand. "That's a good way of putting what they do. These are the triplets I've raised. Rosie, Jaz, and"—he pointed at the one in front of me—"Scarlet. My favorite ladies."

I reached out a hesitant hand and slid my fingers against Scarlet's spotted face. Rune growled, and I glanced at her. "Don't be jealous. You're still my favorite."

That seemed to appease her enough to stop her growl, but her teeth were still bared. Scarlet didn't seem to care. Her purrs vibrated my hand, making me smile.

"They're going to blink us around the city. Less walking, less cold, and more sightseeing."

Oliver rubbed his gloves together. "I'm game. Where are we going first?"

Alexei matched Oliver's smile. "The Hoar House for some food."

"We are talking about real food and not some kinky euphemism for food, right?" Oliver asked, seeming intrigued but also wary.

"Trust me."

We helped Alexei harness the triplets, apparently headed to the Whore House. Rune, deciding she would neither be left behind nor harnessed up front with the Hellcats, crammed herself into the sleigh.

Oliver was pressed against Alexei, while I squished between the rail and Rune. Based on the barely contained giddy smile on Oliver's lips, I don't think he was all that upset by our positioning.

The triplets pulled us out of the building, pausing atop the hill. On the nearside of the castle, straight ahead, an expanse of snow led to a sharp drop-off. The Hellcats flexed their claws in the snow as if preparing to run.

"We're going off that cliff, aren't we?" I asked, my Glory prickling again.

Alexei's eyes twinkled with amusement. "To the Hoar House, ladies!" he shouted.

Jaz, Scarlett, and Rosie sprang into a sprint, forcing my back against the sleigh and running straight for the drop-off.

I pressed closer to Rune, and her shadows seeped across my shoulder and brushed my cheek, soothing my nerves. But they did little to muffle the shriek I let loose as the Hellcats leaped. We were airborne for a second—then we were in a snowy city, in front of a brick building covered in frost.

I laughed, both amazed and recovering from the jolt of adrenaline.

"New favorite mode of transportation," Oliver said, and I agreed.

Alexei gave us a smug smile. "If you had wings, you wouldn't be saying that. But it is the next best thing."

Gazing up at the unique, frosty building, I realized Oliver and I had reached the wrong conclusion.

"*Hoar* as in hoarfrost," Oliver said in an aha moment, taking in the building with a similar appreciative expression.

Ice frosted the vines crawling up the brick facade. The sparkling white-and-blue surface glittered beneath the flaming streetlamps, looking like a foggy coat of glass. Next to the other partially frosted brick faces, the Hoar House stood out—a beautiful oddity in a sea of normality.

Here, in what I assumed was the heart of Hoar Hollow, the cold piercing my cheeks faded away in the splendor of the magic surrounding Hell's city. Colorful sleighs lined the cobbled, snowy street, with Hellcats at the forefront of each carriage. Other sleighs blinked in and out, startling me with their sudden appearance and departure on this busy street. And the splendor of Hell didn't end there. Above our heads, angels with gorgeous feathered wings in varying neutral colors flew overhead. If what Alexei said was correct, most of them must be blood-banded, given permission from the king to live in his world.

Before this moment, if anyone had asked me if I wanted to come to Hell, I would've said no, expecting fire and gruesome torture. And while our squad leader was torturing Oliver and me, this almost made it better. It was as magical as the time we walked through Damatha Forest—totally unexpected, and mesmerizing.

Alexei laughed. "Ronen thought you two might like the inner city."

I whipped my gaze back to Alexei. "The general?"

He grimaced. "Guess there goes the mystery of my motive. He suggested getting you out of the castle. It wasn't actually my idea—I was just following orders..." He trailed off at my gaping mouth.

What was the general playing at?

CHAPTER 17

Lucille

A blast of rich, warm spice hit my face when I stepped through the door of the Hoar House. I had never been to a tavern on Earth or in Elora, but I assumed they didn't look like this.

Icicles protruded from the ceiling, their sharp tips glistening in the flickering flames of glass orbs hanging between each cluster. Vines dusted in frost crawled up the walls, intertwining with twinkling lights that seemed to move and hum. When one light fanned its wings, I realized the strand of lights was glowing butterflies. I shook my head in shocked wonder. This place looked nothing like what I expected a tavern in Hell to look like.

Sparkling icy floors and ethereal lighting? No. Dark, threatening, and bloody? Yes.

I expected the tables to be worn and stained with food and blood, not made of glass and frosted with a crystal votive as the centerpiece.

I expected the bar to be decorated in reds and blacks and lined with jars of body parts, not the soft frosted whites and blues of ice and glass shelves displaying an assortment of liquors in various shapes and sizes, none of which I recognized. They could've been Hell's special concoctions or Earth's finest for all I knew.

The Hoar House might have been something I expected to find in Damatha Forest, but its patrons made up for the lack of gruesomeness with their open soul wounds, weapons, and bloody uniforms.

"What are you doing here? And why in the seventh circle is *Rune* with you?"

Recognition stiffened my spine. I turned. Tucked in a secluded booth beneath an ice-carved arch sat Moira, surrounded by her simpering admirers.

Before I could respond, Alexei came over and wrapped an arm around my shoulders.

"Lucy, Oliver, Rune, and I have some business to attend to. Nothing to worry yourself about, Momo."

I bit my lip hard to keep my grin at bay as Moira's face pinched into a dark scowl. Even better, I knew Alexei outranked her, so she couldn't say shit, which she proved by nodding with thinly pressed lips.

Once he steered us to our frosted table, I let my grin loose.

"I think I'd like to marry you after that," Oliver joked.

Alexei clapped him on the back, laughing. "I've never liked Moira, which is unfortunate, seeing as she's sleeping with Ronen. But to each their own."

I grimaced. Rune pressed against my leg, licking my hand.

"So, how are you liking Hell so far?" Alexei asked, waving over a server.

"Before, I thought it was an ice prison with a bunch of psychotic warriors. Now I think it's an ice prison with a bunch of psychotic warriors and some potential," Oliver said, gazing at Alexei like he wouldn't mind if he were dinner tonight instead of whatever the tavern had.

"I can't say I disagree. And you, beautiful, what do you think?"

"I think—"

Our server came over, stopping my thoughts. Her copper corkscrews, amber eyes, and gorgeous bronze face sparked something in my memory, but I couldn't place it.

She gave Alexei a soft smile. "Same as usual?"

He smiled back. "You know me too well, Lini."

"And for you two?" she asked.

But for the life of me, I couldn't speak. I was forgetting something important, something about this female. She shifted on her feet.

Oliver elbowed me and handed me a menu. "Stop being weird. Look and order."

I glanced down at the menu, still unable to shake the feeling. "I—"

Luckily, Alexei saved me. "She'll have what I'm having."

Oliver ordered next, and Lini left to put in our order, my gaze trailing after her retreating form.

"You okay?" Alexei touched my hand and held it there.

"I know her, but I can't remember from where."

"Really? Lini's a soul who's been in Hell longer than you've been alive. And you're how old?"

That couldn't be. I'd seen her somewhere.

I sighed and pulled my hand from his lingering hold. "Twenty."

Alexei sat back in his chair, shaking his head. "Damn, you're young."

I snorted. "Let me guess, you're like three hundred?"

The corners of his mouth twitched with barely concealed amusement, a gleam of mischief threading through his crystal eyes. "Give or take."

"And the general? How old is he? Has he been in Hell long?" I asked casually.

Alexei's playful expression tightened, his lips forming a skeptical curve. "Why do you want to know?"

I needed to learn everything I could about him—what made him tick, what got under his skin. I had to figure out what he liked, what he hated, and what he respected. Honestly, I'd take anything that could give us an edge, anything that might convince him to help us. Every scrap of information could be a step closer to getting what we needed.

Alexei crossed his arms, staring expectantly at me.

Before I could come up with a sufficient answer, a different server delivered our food and drink.

Turned out Alexei's *usual* was a deep red martini called the Devil's Cocktail that misted with smoke, and for his meal, the Fiery Feast.

Spice curled from the steam of my bowl. I took a hesitant spoonful and smiled. The stew wasn't half bad. A second after I swallowed, I coughed, the spice burning the back of my throat. My face flushed, and I dabbed at my runny nose, giving Alexei an accusatory glance.

He snorted. "I like my food spicy—the same way I like my sex."

I choked on my next bite. Alexei laughed, and Oliver pounded my back.

"Good thing this wasn't actually a whore house or our dear Lucy might've keeled over," Oliver teased.

I swatted at him in good-natured outrage and took a large drink of the red cocktail to soothe my throat. The burn of the alcohol was instant on my tongue. I gagged and slapped a hand over my mouth to avoid spitting it out, forcing it down.

"Hell, Alexei," I gasped. "What is that?"

He smirked at my torment, then took a sip from his cocktail. "A lot of tequila with some other odds and ends to give it an extra punch. You're supposed to sip it, not gulp half of it down."

"Noted," I said, sitting back. My stomach warmed pleasantly, tempting me to reconsider my aversion to the drink.

Alexei set his spoon down, a smile lingering in his eyes—though it was more calculated than warm. "You didn't answer my question. Why do you want to know about Ronen?"

I shot a glance at Oliver. His attention was wholly absorbed in his meal, leaving me to fend for myself.

"I need to impress him. To rank."

Alexei lifted his brows, a flicker of understanding chasing away his suspicion. "And you think getting to know your general will somehow gain you favor and respect?"

"More or less."

He nodded, panning between us. "It won't work. For one, it took me ages to gain his trust and friendship, so you won't pull any information from me. If you want to get to know him, talk to him yourself. Secondly, he'll see right through you. Don't you think everyone is trying to fight for his attention so they can rank and win their spoils?"

"But we're at a disadvantage being in an elite squadron," I said, gritting my teeth.

Alexei hummed in thought. "Some would say you're at an advantage. You have less competition and more skills to gain from experienced warriors."

I slammed my spoon into my stew, splattering the broth onto the table. "Don't you see? That's the problem. We aren't experienced warriors! How are we expected to rank against them?"

Alexei glanced toward the tavern door. "Well, if you have complaints or want to try your hand at buttering up Ronen, here's your chance."

I twisted to see the general walking into the tavern. He scanned the room before settling on Moira's table. His posture was rigid, every step deliberate and controlled as he joined her.

Moira wasted no time making her possessive claim. Her manicured hand slid around his back, creeping up to trace the muscles of his neck as she pressed her body against his stiffened form. He shrugged her off, shifting to the edge of the booth. She scooted closer, angling her body to rub her leg against his.

Itches scattered across my hands, and ice crackled in my ears. My gaze narrowed on the points where they connected, watching her fingers trail across his body, each touch seeming to make his jaw tick.

Moira tugged on his head and puckered her desperate lips, demanding a kiss.

Was she not getting the hint?

The icy crackling surged with intensity. He muttered something to her, then wrenched himself free, making his way to the bar. I smiled at the pinched expression Moira tried to hide with a wave of her hand as she turned back to her friends, my Infernus settling.

My eyes trailed after the general, curious to see how he interacted with people out of uniform. He didn't smile or laugh. He kept his distance, never staying long enough to engage in real conversation. The most he gave was a stiff nod, every inch of him locked up, like the simple act of socializing caused him physical pain.

"Why is he here?"

"We come here often when we want to unwind."

Unwind? The general didn't look like unwinding was even in his vocabulary. His tense shoulders, his clenched jaw—it was more like he was bracing for something rather than letting go.

As his eyes flickered briefly toward me, unease flashed in his gaze. The same look he always wore, whether escorting us to my father or silently observing our squad during training. It never changed. It wasn't the social setting that made him uncomfortable.

It was me.

Alexei grabbed my hand, pulling my attention back to him. He turned it over, studying my palm and brushing gentle patterns along the sensitive skin. "I was kidding, by the way," he said, looking up with a teasing smile. "There's no way to butter him up, beautiful."

Maybe. Maybe not.

Rune sat up, her attention on Alexei. A low growl rumbled in her throat. I gave her a confused look, then noticed Oliver pounding back his drink and avoiding our interaction.

I pulled my hand back, realizing Oliver was jealous—and knew what I had to do. I copied him, tipping the rest of my martini back. The burn hit me as hard as the first time, and I coughed, trying to maintain some semblance of composure.

Alexei studied me for a moment. "How often do you drink?"

I hesitated, unsure of how much I wanted to admit about my sheltered life. "Eggnog. Once a year. My mom was... a little over-bearing."

Oliver snorted quietly into his empty glass, shaking his head.

Alexei's lips twitched. "Once a year, huh? Was she strict with all aspects of your life?"

My answer hung in the air, unspoken. He had no idea. Nor would he ever.

He grinned, the glint in his eyes turning mischievous. "I'm going to take that as a yes, beautiful. Need any help curing that... inno-cence?"

Rune growled and bared her teeth at Alexei, her shadow fur stilling.

"No, thank you." I could only imagine what the golden warrior had in mind.

Standing, the world tilted a little too much, forcing me to steady myself with the table. But the dizziness didn't fade like I'd hoped.

Oliver sighed. "You're so out of your element."

I shot him a wry smile. "Well, then I guess it's time I change that," I said, turning on my heel and heading toward the frosted bar. "The general isn't going to butter himself up."

I weaved through tables and lively patrons, my gaze glued to the general's back. With each step I took, I swore the tension in his shoulders increased as if he could feel me coming. He probably could. A foot from his back, I side-stepped him and plopped myself down on a glass barstool, bringing our arms within inches of each other.

"Is there something you need, Hellion?" he asked, his voice low and irritated. He stood, twirling a tumbler of amber liquid, staring resolutely at the glass shelving of liquor behind the bar.

"No," I lied. "I just wanted a drink." I locked my gaze on a bartender and waited until they came over. "The Abyssal, please," I said with confidence, acting like I knew what I liked, and ignoring the large description beneath the drink.

The general side-eyed me. I flicked my gaze to him and back to the bartender, who nodded and walked away.

We sat in tense silence—or I sat; the general stood—his shadows slithering around his palm and the unusual letters tattooed into his wrist.

The warm fog from the martini Alexei ordered me didn't give me the courage I'd hoped for. I had no idea what to ask or how to approach buttering up General Storm-Cloud. Still, this was the perfect opportunity. He wasn't walking away, nor was he grating on my nerves with his usual disdain.

I needed to ease into it. Ask something easy.

"What does this mean?" I traced my finger over his wrist, the motion so casual that I barely registered the shock of contact until we both flinched. He stepped back, and my face flushed, my mind scrambling.

Why the hell did I do that?

I didn't need a second martini after all, but it was too late to cancel my order. A moment later, the bartender appeared with my pitch-black drink. I said a quick thanks. The general handed her a few coins, and my flush deepened, burning all the way through me. I'd forgotten about the whole payment thing.

"Sorry, I—I didn't realize. Thanks," I muttered, keeping my gaze locked onto my unusually dark drink as I pushed my hair to cover my face. I waited for him to leave, knowing he only stuck around to pay for my drink. When I heard him move, I shook my head, a soft laugh escaping. "I knew it'd never be that easy," I whispered to myself.

"Aletheia."

I froze.

Turning slowly, tension knotted in my stomach. He stood there, fully facing me, his golden eyes unreadable as they burned into my face. My pulse quickened, but I forced myself to bear the weight of his attention.

"What?" I asked.

He unbuttoned his cuff, revealing dark, bold lettering circling his right wrist. "It's ancient Greek. It means truth." His eyes narrowed, holding mine with a depth that made the word feel heavy—like it was meant for me, like it carried a warning or a challenge.

"And your other tattoo?" I asked, trying to keep my voice steady as I pointed to his other wrist.

General Ronen stared, as though weighing whether I was worthy of more information. His fingers lingered on the button of his other cuff, and for a ridiculous moment, I had the sudden urge to help him. To uncover whatever secrets lay hidden in the black ink swallowing his tanned skin.

I shot a glance to meet his gaze. But it wasn't quick, not when I got lost in the gold. It didn't matter if they were unreadable. It didn't matter if a frown creased his brows. They pulled me in.

Everything I'd been carrying—the weight of my decisions, the urgency to help Aspen and my mom, the gnawing frustration over how far behind I was—lifted. My chest expanded, my breath coming deep and steady, and for the first time in ages, I felt something close to peace. And, hell, I wanted more.

Before I could stop myself, I was on my feet.

He stiffened and pulled back. *Shit.*

I quickly grabbed my martini and took a sip, pretending the movement was casual, as if standing had been my plan all along. But my sip turned into a big gulp. I was so sick and tired of finding him attractive, of getting lost in his stupid eyes. Peace? I thought I'd felt peace? No. The only peace I had ever found was in Aspen's arms, and I needed that back.

"Aphesis. It means liberation," he stated, unfazed by my sudden lack of interest.

I polished off my martini, focusing on the spiced blackberry taste and the burn that pushed the invasive feelings away.

"And what exactly would the big, bad Dark Seraphim want to be liberated from?" I asked, my voice tinged with irritation.

He stepped closer and brought his face inches from mine. "You."

His sharp retort made me laugh.

The alcohol had a serious role in my laughter, especially as he lorded over me. He was at least a foot taller, and the fierce intensity of his proximity should've made me nervous, but I couldn't have cared less. The glare furrowing his brows only made me laugh harder.

"That's right, General Storm-Cloud." I faced him. "What were your words exactly? I'm a problem, an annoyance, an *irritating menace*," I said, booping him on the nose and sniggering at his glare. "Which is so funny, because last I checked, you knew little about me. You've made assumptions on heaven only knows what to fit whatever terrible image you've crafted in that stormy mind of yours." I patted him on the chest, as if to say I forgave him for his misgivings, the warmth of the martini I downed severely taking over my actions.

He dropped his gaze to the hand I'd yet to remove from his soft button-up, the tips of my fingers pressed against his exposed skin by his collarbone. Enthralled, I traced my fingers over the inked design, then toyed with his top button, curious what lay beneath his shirt. The thought stopped me short, and I had enough clarity left in my muddled mind to take back my hand before the shadows swirling in his irises devoured it.

Walking around him, I copied his move and tiptoed up to his ear. "But do you know what I think, General?" I whispered, raising goose-bumps along his neck. "I think you're intrigued by me."

"Is that so?"

I shifted closer as I moved to his other ear and stumbled. My hands latched onto his hard sides to steady myself, and he tensed.

Damn, was he just pure muscle beneath his clothes?

It took me a couple seconds to regain my train of thought and release him. "Why else would you stay to talk to me?" I asked, my voice dripping with smugness. I blinked away the darkness encroaching on my vision. But it didn't help. "Would you please put your shadows away?"

He grunted, grabbing my arms and forcing me back onto my stool.

Why wasn't he doing it? Was he trying to make the whole bar go black?

But the longer I focused on the darkness, the more I realized it wasn't his shadows—it was my vision. Suddenly, the general, the bar, everything slipped away.

My stomach dropped, and I grabbed his arms. Surprisingly, the contact helped to calm my rising panic, but not enough to stop the piercing tingles along my arms. "Ronen, why can't I see?"

"The Abyssal martini. You didn't read the warning." His voice was matter-of-fact, like he knew I hadn't.

That was what that long, hard look was for. He knew. He knew, and he stayed not just to pay for my drink, but because of its effects.

I squeezed his forearms harder, my frustration boiling. "What was the warning?"

"The martini steals your senses."

"For how long?" I demanded.

"Until it passes from your system. A few hours."

Unbelievable. I dug my nails into the soft fabric of his shirt, my pulse thundering in my ears. "Why didn't you say anything?"

His warm breath brushed my cheek, sending a shiver down my spine. "Because I wanted to see how far you'd go with your little game. Now, how about you tell me the truth about why you came over here?

Then maybe I'll help you out," he whispered, his voice carrying a thread of danger.

"Help me out how?"

"I'll bring your senses back," he taunted.

He didn't find me intriguing—he saw an opportunity to get the answer he hadn't gotten earlier. I shouldn't be surprised. He was the general, after all. By definition, he was a strategist—calculated, methodical—the kind of male who never acted on impulse, who weighed every action like a chess move.

For a second, I almost didn't want to tell him. I could just suffer through the darkness—senses stripped away, unfeeling, unseeing, unhearing. My skin prickled with a sharp sense of dread.

Damn him!

"What sense is going to go next, Hellion? Time's ticking."

I dug my nails into his arms, refraining from doing something crazy like slapping the smugness from his tone. I shoved the panic crawling up my throat back down, forcing myself to think clearly.

I knew he wouldn't help me unless I were honest.

"I came over here because... I want you... to train me," I blurted out, realizing that pausing to think after saying *I want you,* after rubbing my hand all over his chest, gave the wrong impression.

I was never drinking again.

My words hung in the air. The silence and tension in his forearms made my palms sweaty.

He pried my hands off his arms and stepped out of reach. I was left clutching the edge of the bar, needing something solid, regretting the anxiousness that came from the sudden absence of his touch.

Something tickled my nose, and within seconds, my vision returned. The tension in my body eased, but the weight of his power swiftly replaced that relief. He restored my senses as easily as flipping a switch. And the thought of how much control he had over the mind made my stomach twist. If he could return my vision in an instant, I could only imagine the horrors his shadows could do in the same heartbeat.

My heart picked up speed, and I stared at the disbelief on his face. He stood there acting like I'd just asked him to wrestle a Hellhound.

"The time I'm required to spend with you is enough as it is," he said, his voice flat, dismissive.

"What's your problem with me?"

"Nothing."

I scoffed, unable to hide my frustration. "Liar." I took a step forward, meeting his gaze with defiance. "Why won't you train me?"

"I don't play favorites. Find someone else."

"I want you," I said, snatching his wrist before he took off. My fingers brushed a raised part of his skin. Something was familiar about the shape of it. But without seeing it, I couldn't be sure what it was.

He jerked his wrist away and waved his hand to the bartender. "Nalini, give her some water. She'll need it while I go fetch her escort," he said, before turning and walking away.

I wanted to call after him, to stop him, but his use of *that* name stunned me.

Nalini, not Lini.

I turned around and laid eyes on Aspen's first love, handing me a glass of water.

I wasn't sure how I'd forgotten about her. Maybe because the last time I saw her wasn't in person—it was in Aspen's memory while I dream-walked to him. And the reason her amber eyes looked different was because I remembered them dull and unseeing—dead.

Now they were filled with life and light, or I suppose as much light and life as a dead soul could have living in Hell.

My muddled brain had no idea how to react to that eye-opening information.

Before I could so much as lift my jaw off the floor, Alexei appeared, and Nalini went to help another patron.

"Causing problems, beautiful?"

I glanced at Alexei's smile, then at the general, who'd found his way back to Moira and her wandering hands, then to Nalini.

"Hey." Oliver came up on Alexei's other side. "You okay, Lucy?"

Was I okay?

My head throbbed inside my skull like it was threatening to break free.

"Alexei said he'd take us around Hoar Hollow to check out more sights if we wanted," Oliver said. He sounded eager, and I caught the hopeful glance he shot toward Alexei. I almost hated to spoil his fun.

"I think I'd rather go back to the castle."

Especially when the general wanted absolutely nothing to do with me unless the king required him. Aspen's first love was dead, in Hell, and working with a gentle smile in the bar. And we were no closer to our goals.

What the hell did I do with any of that?

CHAPTER 18

Lucille

That night, the same three nightmares tormented me, but unlike every other time when Oliver or Rune woke me, this time, a swath of shadows soothed and gentled my pain, easing me into a blissful, deep sleep. Sleep I hadn't had in a while.

Finally.

When I woke up to Alexei's trumpet, I groaned, crushing my pillow to my ears. Though I was thankful my sheets weren't soaked through with sweat and Oliver wasn't hovering over me with that helpless expression, I could do without the headache.

Speaking of Oliver, why didn't I hear his groaning? I peeked over at his spot in bed, finding the blankets made, and sat up. Neither Rune nor Oliver was next to me.

Was this another hallucination?

"Oliver?" I called out, half expecting to hear him choking on his blood.

He walked into the room, dressed in warm clothing, with a coffee in his hand. I blinked a few times, not sure if this was a different tactic the king was trying out.

Oliver laughed. "I've only been up for like five minutes. Don't have a coronary."

I rolled my eyes and flopped back in bed, my head throbbing. "Did the king show up this morning? We were supposed to have our lesson today."

"Not unless he showed up in the two minutes I left to change. But Rune almost broke down the door to be let out, then raced away, so maybe the king and the general have something more pressing to deal with."

Weird. But I couldn't say I was all too upset by the fact I wouldn't have him prying into my mind while it slammed against my skull.

Alexei blared his trumpet again, longer than usual, like he was determined to make my head split open.

"Make it stop," I whined, burrowing under the covers.

"Enjoying that hangover, Luce?" Oliver asked with a smile in his voice.

I sank into my Infernus, pulling on my power to form an icicle to chuck at him, but the moment I felt the itches, my stomach revolted. Shoving away my blankets, I sprang out of bed and sprinted to the bathroom, making it just in time to puke in the toilet.

Oliver leaned against the doorframe, grimacing. "That good, huh?"

"Think Alexei will let me stay back?" I moaned, resting my cheek on the toilet seat.

He snorted and handed me a towel. "If death isn't off the table during training, then I'm pretty sure puking because someone can't handle her alcohol isn't either."

"Death seems like a better option right now," I mumbled, staring at my hair, now a casualty of the puke's path.

Unfortunately, Alexei didn't care about my hangover and threatened to carry me out of my room if I didn't dress in the next five minutes.

The day only got worse from there.

Like the last two weeks of training, we started in the bathrooms. Carrot-top blasted us with his water during our drenching hour while some of our group watched. My head pounded, and I gagged back bile, having nothing left to puke up after this morning.

Although I almost wished I did, just to see the look on Theon's face.

After we jogged to our rooms to change and dry our hair as best we could, we ran-walked our ten miles and lifted weights. Fortunately, by the time we started lifting, my hangover had metabolized out of my system, and I was able to enjoy the little progress I made that day.

"Tormentors, finish up your last set. We're moving to the weapons range," Moira called out.

A group of ten warriors finished up drills in the weapons range. They were securing an arsenal of weapons—swords, axes, daggers, javelins, spiked balls—onto a towering wall, their steel gleaming in the light streaming through the high, arched windows.

Oliver and I walked behind Cade and Zera—two group members we hadn't interacted with much besides seeing their taunting smiles during *the drenching hour*. Usually, the twins were in front of us, but they were curiously absent.

We passed the Bowels Squadron practicing in the sparring grounds. The size of their group occupied a good fourth of the area, not including the stone seating that their leader had half of them running up and down. I wish that was our daily warm-up and not running miles in ice and snow.

We moved on, passing more squadrons and the dais where General Ronen should've stood, but he was also absent today, leaving Alexei and four other Dreads to watch our progress.

"How good are you with weapons?" I asked Oliver.

He ran a hand through his hair. "Daggers, decent. Swords, I can get by. Anything else... I'm trash."

So, we wouldn't be impressing anyone today.

"For *most* of you, this week of weapons training is all review, so feel free to test out new maneuvers," Moira said, singling us out. "To start, we will split into pairs and rotate archery, swordsmanship, close-combat weapons, throwing, and hand-to-hand with powers. Pick your partner, pick your station, and wait for my whistle."

The enthusiasm on everyone's faces, and even Oliver's face, did not match my increasing heart rate and frown. It worsened when Moira called us over.

"Since I know you two are, in fact, worthless, it would be careless of me to keep you paired up." She motioned to Theon. "Lucille, precious, I think you'd be best with Theon at the hand-to-hand station. Seeing as you have experience with his element, it may be easier for you."

Her baiting smile had pressure building behind my eyes, which only made Moira's smile widen further.

"Which leaves Cyrus with Oliver and close-combat weapons." Moira took a step back from our group and called out to the Tormentors. "We'll do forty-five minutes per station, take breaks as you need them, and try not to kill anyone who doesn't deserve it." Then she blew her whistle in my face.

I guaranteed she hoped Theon *accidentally* killed me.

Theon and Cyrus headed toward the stations, but I remained rooted in place, my gaze locked on Moira. Oliver stepped between us, nudging me back a few paces with a firm hand and shooting me a warning glance.

"Your eyes are glowing purple, Lucy, and unless you want shit to hit the fan with you-know-who, and everyone else, rein it in. You're lucky your disguise works, or it wouldn't just be purple Moira and everyone else would see. And if she found out what you are, I can guarantee she'd use it against you to benefit her. Stop playing with fire," he whispered.

It probably wouldn't be a good time to comment back that I wanted to play with ice, not fire. But Oliver had a point. I ground my nails into my skin, needing the pain to stuff the anger back in its cage. "She makes it hard."

He snorted. "Oh, I know. She's a bitch. But one we have to listen to." He grabbed my shoulder, ducking down to look me in the eye. "When you fight with Theon, you can't show anything but the flames in your eyes, you know that, right?"

"I have control, Oliver. And the majority of angels I've interacted with have difficulty keeping their power out of their eyes."

His face scrunched in an odd way I didn't like. "You aren't part of the majority, Luce. There is only one of you, which means you have to be more careful."

"Move, recruits!" Moira snapped.

I squeezed Oliver's hand. "Don't worry about me. I have control."

Oliver huffed and mumbled as he left, "Someone's got to."

Walking over to Theon, I tried my best to keep the dread off my face, which was hard when his eyes sparkled with the promise of pain. I was weak. He knew it. They all knew it. They all saw how much we lifted and how far we could run. They abused us for our slow time every day.

"Ready, weakling?" Theon asked, adopting a fighting stance.

"Very original. Bet that took a lot of brainpower to come up with," I said, mirroring his stance and enjoying the way his smile flattened. "I suppose not every elite member of Hell's military needs to be intelligent."

Theon swung at my face, surprising me with his speed, and I dodged it. His eyes widened—and he wasn't alone. I hadn't expected to react so quickly. He threw a combination at me, and I ducked and pivoted away from each punch. I beamed. I may have lost most of my muscle, but I hadn't lost the muscle memory of sparring with my mom. For once, I had the slightest bit of hope.

I flicked my attention to the figure standing behind Theon, and my hope grew. Alexei stood on the sidelines watching. He wasn't the general, but he was the next best thing. If I impressed him, the general would have to notice me. And if they ranked me, I would gain the general's favor.

Theon's nostrils flared. Whether from my comment or the fact that he hadn't knocked me out yet, I didn't know.

"Did I hit a nerve? What, the Powers thought you were too insignificant for their games, so you had to crawl to Hell to find someone who'd tolerate you?" He didn't have any apparent soul wounds, but he could've died and become a redeemed soul, earning back his power and healing his wounds, or he was blood-banded.

His pale face flushed, almost matching the brightness of his hair, and he flew at me. I twisted out of the path of his fists, only to have him come at me faster. My body knew what to do before my mind could catch up. I weaved to the side and snuck through his guard, sending a hook into his ribs. It connected, and a full-blown smile took over my face, teeth and all.

Theon stumbled back, more from shock than my weak punch, I assumed. Veins bulged in his arms and neck, his fists clenched white-knuckled, and his glare could've killed. He had no idea I could fight. He probably thought I'd be out cold by now. Hell, I wasn't sure my body even remembered how to hold up after all this time.

His weight shifted forward, and suddenly I was fifteen again, standing in our yard as my mother forced me to study every subtle shift and twitch in her body, to anticipate how she'd strike.

I let him close the distance. He lunged, and I pivoted to the side, kicking in his knee.

He slammed to the ground, rolled, and blasted me with his power. I whipped up my arms to protect my face. Theon stood, smashing his fists into my ribs. I gasped, hunching over, and had an unnerving sense of déjà vu. I could almost hear my mother's voice snapping at me to move and widen my stance. I was off balance and in a weak position. But I didn't—now or in the past.

Theon threw a powerful hook to my jaw, connecting and sending me to the ground. My head hit hard, specks of light dancing in my vision. For a second, there was no pain, until my vision cleared and blood pooled into my mouth. I groaned.

Theon stood over me and smiled. "You almost look good down there, Hell-whore. But you just need one more thing," he said, then spat on me. "There, much better."

The scene flickered, replacing the black and red uniform with white, and ginger hair with blond. Crackles of ice whispered in my ear, begging me to let my Infernus free. I dug my nails into my palms, blinking away the image of Michael.

I glanced at Alexei and swore I saw him nod in encouragement. I had to get up—I had to show them.

"Unfortunately, you don't look so good from down here," I said, grimacing at Theon's groin.

As expected, he lurched forward, taking my bait. I scissored my legs around him, pulling him to the ground with his momentum, and immediately straddled him. Before he raised his guard, I punched his nose twice, hearing the satisfying crunch of his cartilage.

"Bitch," he said, arching his hips to throw me off.

He knocked me forward instead of off, positioning me inches from his face. I spat blood and grinned. "My favorite endearment."

Enraged, he smashed his forehead into my nose, returning the favor, and sent me flying back with a blast of water. Stunned, I had a difficult time shaking away the black specks. But I needed to stand.

I tried to roll when his boot slammed into my stomach, snapping something. I cried out, shoving at his leg. He stepped off me and smirked as I scooted away. After taunting me with a few inches of space, Theon followed.

I looked to the side, expecting Alexei to step in. Weren't there rules to these fights?

But he only watched, flipping a dagger as if he had no cares in the world. The general and Rune were still gone, Oliver and our squadmates were too busy fighting or practicing, and Moira gave two shits as she smiled at me from afar.

Fuck.

Theon formed a sphere of water in his palm, bouncing it with each languid step. It grew until it was just bigger than my head.

"It's too bad we have an audience. Makes killing you a little hard," he said, pouting. "But that doesn't mean I can't give you a taste of what your future holds."

I stopped scooting and grabbed a fistful of sand, letting him close the distance. I didn't have much of a plan besides distracting him.

The moment he got within reach, I lashed out, throwing the sand in his face. Immediately after, I clenched my teeth and stood, but it was no use. Theon's water wrapped around my head and stole the breath from my lungs.

I dropped to my knees, clawing at the water. He loomed over me on the other side of the blurry surface, laughing.

"You want to play dirty? I can play dirty, Hell-whore," he said, his voice muffled and distorted.

The whispers in my ears raged at me to do something. It was no longer the crackling of ice but the haunting melody of my Hellfire seeking retribution. The more I suffocated, the more I let the melody take over.

Theon's eyes gleamed, pupils blown wide as if he relished every breath he stole. His mouth lifted in a savage grin. He looked drunk on my torture, and something in his expression told me he wasn't going to release me.

He was going to kill me.

Itches spread across my skin, but before my flame erupted, the air shifted behind me, and shadows circled my wrist, their touch gentle and soothing.

His presence seared into my back. "I know how to play dirty too."

Even with the water muffling my hearing, it didn't stop the goosebumps from spreading down my spine from the general's deadly tone.

A band of shadows coiled around Theon's throat, his face bulging as he gasped for air. His control over the water slipped, and I seized the moment to inhale deeply, blinking water from my eyes. I twisted to the general—and a fierce-looking Rune. Her shadow fur lashed around her as she growled at Theon, copying the general's whipping shadows, a dark echo of their power.

The general's face was cold, his posture rigid. He forced Theon to the ground, unsheathed both of his swords from his back, and prowled toward him.

"No," Theon choked out, throwing out his hand and squirming away with no luck. "Please."

General Ronen cut off his cries as he replaced his shadows with a sword against Theon's neck.

"Please. I was only trying to teach her a lesson," he begged.

The general pressed the edge into Theon's flesh. It didn't slice him, but his skin sizzled, and he whimpered.

What kind of blade would do that?

"General! What are you—"

The general pointed his second blade at Moira, stopping her question.

"Don't worry, Squad Leader. I'm only teaching him a *lesson*," he said, tone soft and mocking, putting pressure on his sword.

A puddle of liquid spread out on the dirt beneath Theon, and when I glanced back at Moira, I saw a similar fear holding her tongue.

"Stand, Hellion," the general commanded.

I did, but a bit too slowly for his liking, since his shadows helped me. Then Rune pressed in close, holding me upright.

General Ronen raked his gaze over me, holding his attention on the arm wrapped around my ribs. Shadows seeped from his body, encircling me, him, and Theon. Moira, the other squads, the arena— all vanished. His pitch-black eyes lifted to my face, held there, then he crouched next to Theon, avoiding his pee.

"I'm assuming by your piss puddle you understand what this sword will do to you?"

Theon gave the tiniest of nods.

"Good." The general pointed his free sword at me. "You ever play dirty with her again, I'll trap you in fucking agony for the rest of your miserable life. Understood, blood-banded?"

"Understood," he whispered.

"Find a shovel and clean up your mess." The general's shadows dropped, and he sheathed his swords. "Squad Leader."

"Yes, General Ronen?" Moira said, wary.

"From now on, Lucille will be paired with Ichi, and Ni with the Nephilim until they've improved. Understood?"

Moira's face flushed. She pressed her lips together as her chest heaved. Metal rattled on the weapons wall behind us. She looked ready to burst.

He lifted a brow in challenge.

"Yes, Sir," she finally gritted out and stormed away.

I held back my smile, a sincere thanks on my tongue for saving my life and pulling rank on his girlfriend. But the moment I met his pitch-black eyes and saw the ruthless, quiet rage still there, the words died on my lips.

He prowled toward me, and all our previous interactions flashed through my mind. He may have defended me from Theon, but he'd also called me a traitor and made it clear he wanted to be free of me.

I stepped back, Rune close at my side. The general's shadows whipped around him as if ready to strike. One shot toward my arm, and I flinched, but it only brushed tenderly against my skin, somehow soothing my shaking hand.

Weird.

It was like my body knew the shadows wouldn't hurt me, even as my brain screamed to get the hell away. I considered luscelering for a split second, but then I backed into the weapons wall, swords rattling behind me. He stepped forward, pushing Rune aside and caging me in. My chance to escape vanished.

"Is it your turn to threaten me now?"

He tilted his head. "Why would I threaten you when I just finished protecting you?"

"I'm still trying to figure out why you intervened at all. Alexei didn't."

The general stared at me, drilling right into my soul, unnerving and entrapping me all at once.

His shadows shot toward my face, and I jerked back. But they only tickled up my nose, making the pain disappear.

"I thought I told you to keep your shadows away from me," I said half-heartedly.

He raised a brow. "You didn't seem to mind them at the bar."

"Yes, well, it was the least you could do after letting me drink a cocktail that steals your senses."

"Maybe next time you'll give me the truth up front and I won't have to watch you make a fool of yourself."

I bit my tongue to hold in the curses I wanted to spew. I even kept the glare off my face as I held his gaze. It was the same silent game—a battle of wills through eye contact. And he had the upper hand. Because holding his eyes made me feel like I'd only been breathing with one lung for the past twenty years.

But he held no respect for me. And he wasn't Aspen.

Guilt pierced the magnetic pull, forcing me to look away—once again.

"Did you force me against this wall just to demean me?"

"Did you not want relief from your pain?" he countered.

"I've been in worse pain than this."

"I know." His voice softened, doing things I didn't like to my nerves. The shadows dancing around him sank back into his skin. "You have a broken rib and nose, but no internal bleeding. Go to the healers' wing and ask for Sam."

He turned to leave, and I snatched his wrist, my fingers brushing that curious bit of raised skin.

"You care enough to rescue me but don't want to train me? I don't want to end up suffocating on water again."

The general's eyes dropped to my hand on his wrist, then dragged back up to meet my gaze. "The king told me to keep you alive. I wouldn't call that caring. I'd call that a job. And Theon won't be a problem anymore. I made sure of that."

No wonder he wanted to be rid of me.

Whispers drew my attention. Most of the warriors were still practicing, but some were definitely staring, particularly at my hand on his wrist.

I released him. "What about my next opponent?"

"Don't worry, Hellion. I'll do my job."

It took every ounce of my willpower not to smack the self-confident ass. I didn't want his rescuing. I wanted his favor. But the only ways I knew to gain that were by ranking or building a relationship with him, and I highly doubted the latter would ever happen.

"I want to rank."

"Hellion, unless there's something I haven't seen, you'll never rank. Even with the accelerated muscle growth and recovery from your angelic blood, you're still years behind your squad's skill level."

"That's why I want you to train me."

"You'll never catch up in two months."

"You have no idea what I'm capable of," I snapped. He didn't know me. I'd do anything to protect the ones I loved.

"No," he said firmly, then left.

For a moment, I just stood there, watching him go. He met up with Alexei, who glanced at me, then whipped his hand toward Theon. From his sharp gestures and serious expression, I doubted he was saying anything good.

I shook my head and ran my hand through Rune's fur.

This wasn't over.

CHAPTER 19

Lucille

After Sam healed me, I went to the library. I asked Cato to enlighten me on two specific Ancient Greek words, along with anything he could tell me about the general—his powers, weapons, fighting techniques, and strategies.

I read late into the night. The words blurred together, and the weight of exhaustion pulled me under, darkness slowly claiming my thoughts.

Snow crunched beneath my boots with each step through the evergreen forest. At the edge of the tree line, I paused. The branches parted to reveal a familiar house. Smoke curled into the starry Earth sky, inviting me with its warmth and memories of a different time—a time when my life was simple and secluded. A time when my mother wasn't in a coma, I wasn't battling nightmares and Hell's military, and I wasn't locked away in a dimension, unable to help the people I loved.

I shot a hopeful glance up at the stars, wondering if by chance they'd answer the prayer I had never dared to speak aloud.

I had been avoiding her and her condition for weeks, too scared to revisit her. But now, standing in front of the house from my previous life, I hoped this was my mother's dream.

At our front door, I stared at the handle like it might save me or damn me. Although, I already felt damned. It should be easy to push through the door and suffer the possibility that she wasn't in there.

But what if she was? What would I say to her? Would she remember what Michael did? Would she know I made a bargain that sentenced her to life in a coma?

Steeling myself, I twisted the knob. The smooth rhythm of jazz music met my ears, tugging at a piece of my heart and pulling me into our house.

Greenery decorated the cozy fire crackling in the chicken-themed fireplace like background music to the soft piano and saxophone. Balsam and clove infused the air, twining with the scent of burning wood. I closed my eyes for a moment and breathed it in, feeling a settling in my soul.

After removing my coat and boots, I walked farther into the living room and spotted two steaming cups of hot cocoa. One was piled high with marshmallows—courtesy of my mom's marshmallow addiction—and the other had a melting chocolate ball in it. Smiling, I drifted toward the kitchen, where voices murmured behind the wall.

Hope fluttered in my chest. I crept forward, paused at the doorway, then stepped into view.

And found another version of myself talking to my mom, who was wearing her favorite sweater dress.

"What the hell?"

Was this a memory? But I wasn't nauseous and didn't feel the disorientation of being in two places at once. My dream-walks continued to both confuse and surprise me.

My mom straightened, and the other version of me vanished.

"Lucy?" She pressed a hand to her mouth, her eyes brimming with tears. "Is it really you?"

"I—"

I stood frozen.

She didn't hesitate. She skirted the counter and pulled me into her arms. "Oh, Heavenly, I thought you were dead," she cried. "I thought Michael killed you." She ran her hand down my hair and buried her face in my neck, tears soaking into my skin. "I thought he killed you."

Her shaking shoulders and broken sobs shattered my frozen state. "He didn't, Mom," I whispered, squeezing her tight. "I'm okay. I'm alive."

She was here. I could talk to her, hold her, smell the vanilla in her hair. Heavenly, how I missed that smell, missed her hugs.

Buried grief surged, choking my breath. My hands trembled as I clung to her, burying my face in her shoulder. We held each other fiercely, the ragged sounds of our breaths mingling with the music.

Eventually, Mom led me into the living room and handed me the hot chocolate.

I sat in my favorite chair, took a sip of the sugary goodness, and teared up again. "I can't believe I dream-walked to you."

She gave me a gentle, grateful smile. There was no confusion on her face, no question at the term, as if she'd known from the beginning. Just like that, a bucket of icy realization washed away her hug and reminded me my mother had kept secrets—lots of them.

"You've always known, haven't you?" I lowered my mug, my smile fading.

She bowed her head, unable to meet my accusing stare. "You did it when I was pregnant with you," she admitted, her voice barely above a whisper. "You did a lot of strange things to me while I carried you—even changed the color of the flames in my eyes. At first, I thought the baby in my dreams was just my imagination—until you started doing it at four years old, and I sensed your vast power."

I dream-walked at four?

"I tried to ignore it, but then I started researching and figured it out. You'd do it when you had nightmares. You'd project into my dreams, crying." She stared into her fidgeting hands, her voice lowering further. "Sometimes I let you cry it out. But other times... I'd force myself awake so I could wake you, in case—"

"Someone sensed my *vast* powers," I finished for her, bitterness coating my tongue. She'd kept so many things from me. I was sure there were more.

She nodded. The weight of her silence spoke louder than words, and a faint tremor in her hands betrayed the guilt she couldn't hide.

"I'm sorry, Lucy. I did what I thought was best. But I didn't know Michael was working with Marcus. It never occurred to me he would ever ally with a demon..." Her voice cracked as her attention drifted to a long scar on her hand.

The scar from Michael's knife.

The purple halo around my vision darkened, and I squeezed my cup. "He gave that to you."

"Sweetie, it's okay. See? Gone." The scar vanished.

Heat rose up my neck and pushed behind my eyes. I was so sick of her trying to protect me with lies. None of this was *okay*.

"I'm not thirteen anymore! You can't just cover it up and hope I'll ignore it—like when I burned our house down. I was there when he slammed that knife into your palm, and I'll never forget—"

She reached out and touched my hand, stopping my heated words. A gentle, cooling energy soothed my boiling blood. Maybe she was right. Everything was ok—

I jerked away, breaking the emotional hold she had over me and spilling hot chocolate.

"Haven't you learned your lesson?" I banged my mug down on the coffee table and stood. "We can't hide from everything anymore! You poisoning and calming me to keep me safe backfired! Everything you tried to protect me from went to hell! In fact, we're both there right now!"

"I'm sorry, Lucy," she whispered. Her eyes were puffy and bruised, her posture slumped.

And, dammit, how could I stay mad at her when she looked entirely broken?

I sank back into my chair. "You left me so unprepared, Mom. You're unconscious because of my deal with Michael, and I'm trying to survive while I train and live in a place I'm only beginning to understand—surrounded by beings who hate my guts because I'm worthless and weak! I can't use my powers without endangering myself, you, and potentially the king. We're stuck in Hell, unable to kill Michael to save you and I—I don't know what I'm doing."

I dropped my face into my hands.

My mom knelt before me. She lifted my chin and looked me dead in the eye. "You're anything but worthless and weak. Now tell me everything from the beginning."

The tenderness in her voice wrapped around me, and I nodded.

I told her nearly everything that had happened up until today, and she never interrupted. Her eyes would occasionally glaze over, or she'd reach out and squeeze my arm with a trembling hand. But she didn't try to control the whirlwind of emotions inside me. I think she just needed to reassure herself that I was still here.

I left out details about Aspen, focusing instead on Lilith's general kidnapping me and the significant events that followed. I couldn't explain our relationship or what I was planning. How could I? How could I admit that saving him might come before saving her, when my heart was already so heavy with guilt? I couldn't explain the pull I felt toward him—the raw need pushing me every day to find a way out of Hell. I didn't understand it myself. But I knew it wouldn't fade until he escaped Lilith.

When I finished, she gave me a watery smile and hugged me.

"I'm so sorry, Lucy. I never wanted any of this for you. I just wanted—"

I pulled back. "You wanted us to live as humans and stay safe and sound in our little mountain home." I surveyed the perfectly imagined house, taking in all the chicken-themed decorations. This was my mom's haven. But standing in the middle of it, surrounded by all those familiar sights and sounds, I knew it wasn't mine. "That dream of yours has died, Mom. Even if I wanted that life again—which I don't—there's no going back while we're trapped in Hell."

Her pink cheeks paled. "You were never supposed to end up there."

"Because of the prophecy?"

She pressed her lips together, the soft notes of her favorite jazz music filling the silence. I took it as a yes.

"I clearly haven't been sacrificed. And unless someone kills me in training, I'm not sure you interpreted Miriam's prophecy correctly." I couldn't outright say it was wrong— after all, nearly everything else had come true. I was the hidden, protected daughter of the Seven Circles of Hell. Elora had been concealed from me, and I assumed the whispering ice was either my own power or the king's, whenever he contacted me. "Lucifer and his general want me alive."

"Miriam is never wrong."

I sighed, frustration creeping in. "Mom, did you ever think 'awaiting the daughter to sacrifice' might mean Hell was waiting for me to sacrifice something—not my life?" Her fear still ruled her. It creased her forehead and the corners of her lips.

I gently took her fists, slowly uncurling her shaking hands, trying to ground her. "You're in a coma. We're stuck in Hell. The only way is forward. There is no more locking me away to keep me safe, okay?" I said softly.

Her gaze slid away, avoiding mine.

"What else are you keeping from me?"

Silence.

"When will the secrets end, Mom?" I shouted, standing and stepping back. "I don't need your protection anymore! Your secrets have gotten us nowhere. What I need is help—help training my body and powers, and figuring out how to get on the general's good side! Things I'm sure your secret angelic life before me could actually help with!"

She continued to stare at the wall like she hadn't heard me. I dug my nails into my palms, wanting to throttle her. When I entered this dream, I just wanted to see her. I hadn't realized how much anger I still carried.

But why, after everything that had happened and everything our choices had cost, did she still think it necessary to keep her secrets? What was she hiding?

I shook my head, unable to feel empathy while she remained so blinded by fear. Turning away, I headed for the door, desperate to wake up from this dream-walk before I said something I'd regret.

"Fine."

I stopped.

"I'll help you train when you dream-walk to me. But I'll only share things with you when I'm ready. Deal?"

I turned. Pure white armor materialized on her body, hugging every curve, and a long sword peeked out over her shoulder—her Archangel uniform. I'd never seen her wear anything like it. It was strange, seeing her look so... imposing. During our sparring lessons, she always wore loose-fitting exercise clothes.

"Do I even have a choice in the matter?"

She placed her hand on my shoulder and met my gaze. "There are few instances when you don't have a choice." Then my shirt and pants shifted into a Hell Squadron uniform—black with accents of purple, instead of the usual red. "Your choices now are simple: take the deal and I'll train you, or don't and get nothing from me."

For the first time, I saw the version of my mother that existed before I was born. Growing up, I'd caught glimpses of her—but never like this. Never in her armor. Never with that fierce expression.

"Now let's go dissect the fight you had today and see how you could've won."

I twisted, frowning as she strode out the door. I wasn't sure what I was getting myself into, but I followed her out into our snowy front yard.

"Show me your stance and explain the fight in detail," she said, squaring off in front of me.

I separated my feet, raised my fists, and tensed my core, then began explaining, leaving out Theon's insults and my taunts.

My mom nodded her approval, then jabbed at my face just like Theon had, only faster.

I bobbed to the side. She clipped my chin, pulling her punch at the last second. I'd forgotten how fast she was.

She must've seen the shock on my face. "Sweetie, I trained as an Archangel for hundreds of years. If you can dodge all my punches, you'll be more than a match for most of Lucifer's elite squadrons." She circled me, and I mirrored her.

"Okay, but it's not just sparring. I told you Theon used his water against me. How do I combat that when I can't use my powers on him—or anyone else, for that matter?"

My mom hummed in thought before mimicking Theon's punches. Except each one of hers connected, and they stung.

"If you can't use your powers, then you need to cause enough pain to distract him."

She flew at me, and despite expecting it, she still broke through my guard. I tried the same footwork I used with Theon, but had to remind myself—she'd taught me those moves. And I'd never once beaten her in a sparring match.

"Ready for the tackle?" she asked before slamming into me, sending me crashing to the snow faster than I could dodge.

I groaned, the impact jarring through my spine. I lay there, letting the snow kiss the nape of my neck. The sensation was soothing until it began to burn.

"I'll take that as a no."

I rolled my eyes and pushed up onto my forearms. "I thought the purpose of this was to show me how to improve the things I did wrong, not beat me at the things I did right."

She reached out a gloved hand, her armor glinting in the porch light. I took it, but she didn't pull me up.

"No. The purpose of your training is to make you faster and more equipped than Lucifer himself," she said firmly, the seriousness of her gaze making me pause.

"Lucifer isn't going to kill me."

She ignored me and pulled me to my feet.

It wasn't that I thought it was impossible. Lucifer had an agenda—why else place me in an elite squadron? But Cato's words had slithered into my mind, making me question the king's intentions.

"Isn't he your cordistella? Your soulmate? Why would he kill me if it meant losing you?" At least emotionally. I suppose if he killed me, my mother would wake from her coma.

My mom tilted her head to the stars and sighed. "We're no longer cordistellas. Our bond was severed when Lucifer was made King of Hell."

"Okay, but he still loves you."

Her eyes locked onto mine, but there was a quiet sadness in the downturn of her lips. "Sometimes love isn't enough."

"So you turned to Michael?" The words escaped before I could stop them, but I just couldn't understand how he fit into all this. Lucifer would do anything for my mom—he acted like he wanted the best for me, something Michael could never claim. "I don't get it."

My mom's eyes narrowed, and she swept her leg, sending me back into the snow. "If and when I am ready, Lucille Chiara."

I gritted my teeth, wanting to know what she was hiding. She had a whole life before me, hundreds of years' worth, and I knew an infinitesimal part of it.

Her hand fell in front of my face, and for a moment, I considered refusing it. But despite how frustrating her terms were, I knew I needed whatever help she could offer. I slapped my hand into hers, and a flood of overwhelming love and security washed over me, momentarily silencing the chaos in my mind.

I sprang to my feet and into her arms, hugging her tightly. "I love you so much."

She pulled away abruptly, shoving me back and raising her guard as she circled me. I smiled, arms wide, hoping for another hug. But instead, she punched me.

Her fist slammed into my side, then my stomach, and I gasped, stumbling back. For a split second, confusion cut through the overwhelming love, but it quickly faded.

"Lucy, remember what I told you earlier. How do you fight off someone's power?"

Her words resonated with something I needed to remember, but it was buried beneath the sticky love clouding my thoughts. "I don't want to fight you," I admitted, the words tasting wrong as they left my mouth.

She sent another combination into my body, carefully avoiding my face, as if she knew I wouldn't be able to block it. But I *could* block. So why didn't I?

Each painful punch jolted me, pushing harder against the haze in my mind. They came faster, and with each strike, my frustration bled through the love. I raised my arms, barely managing to block a few.

"Good. Fight it, but remember what I said."

I needed to make her feel pain, to pull her focus away from her power. But how? Even with my mind fully in control, I couldn't land a punch. Then, an idea sparked.

I forced myself to focus, drawing on the whispers of my Infernus, willing the purple flames to flare to life in my mind. It felt foreign, like a muscle I hadn't used in ages, strained and hesitant. Back when we used to argue, I'd sheath my skin to keep her out, though it was an accident, triggered by my anger. But this time, I didn't want her to see me resisting—if I could manage it.

My head throbbed as I struggled to envision the shield, each punch she sent my way disrupting what little progress I made. Sweat trickled down my neck, and I panted, hoping she'd think it was from our sparring.

At the last second, just before giving up, I managed a thin, wavering barrier. It barely held back her influence, and her powers still probed at the cracks. But it was better that some snuck through, knowing she could feel emotional shifts. I needed her to *assume* she still had control. Still, I gained enough mental ground to quiet the overwhelming love that had silenced my clarity. I kept the stupid smile plastered on my face, my hands awkwardly held up in front of my chest to maintain the act.

"Fight it, Lucy. Or you'll never win." She threw a punch at my face, and I let it connect. There was half a second where I could've stopped it, but I didn't.

I whimpered, and it wasn't entirely faked. She hit hard, and my head wouldn't stop throbbing, but I exaggerated the reaction. I dropped one hand, clutching my jaw with the other, pretending to be stunned. Her attack faltered, and I seized the opportunity. With a swift twist, I brought my dropped hand up in a controlled uppercut, landing it squarely on her chin.

She stumbled back, the emotional probing of her power falling away from my mental shield. I swept her legs out from under her, sending her into the snow with a satisfying thud.

Pride gleamed in her smile as she looked up at me, and for a brief moment, I felt the weight of it settle in my chest. It had been a long time since I'd felt that kind of acceptance from her. Even before I was kidnapped, our relationship had been rocky. I wasn't sure what it was anymore—but I missed that look.

"Good." She took my outstretched hand and stood. "But using my concern for you against me won't work on most of Hell's elite military. You'll have to find a different manipulation tactic."

"I've read about others in a strategy and warfare book," I admitted, pretty sure I was still sleeping on it as we spoke.

She nodded. "And if manipulation doesn't work…" She threw a punch at my face, catching me off guard.

I fell on my ass, avoiding the hit, and my metal barrier crumbled.

"You'll need to move faster and react faster. It's you or them."

"I'm well aware, Mom."

"You should also stay away from Lucifer and Ronen."

"Mom, Lucifer and the general have saved my life at least two, maybe three, times now," I added quickly, counting the river incident in my mind. "Stop being paranoid. The only ones trying to kill me are my squadmates and the squad leader. So teach me how to survive against *them*."

She seemed to agree, though reluctantly, and we practiced—well, I couldn't tell how long, since time worked differently in dreamwalks—but it felt like hours. Most of that time, I ended up flat on my back.

When I woke up in the library, I was surprised my body wasn't one big throbbing bruise. And even more surprised that it was still dark outside.

CHAPTER 20

Lucille

"I hate you," Oliver whined, zipping up the collar of his coat and throwing up his hood, which continued to fall in the wind.

"I know."

"I hate you."

"Oliver! Shut up! I got it the last forty times you said it!" I panted. "Suck it up. We've only run half of the way so far."

He groaned. "Ran-walked."

Ugh. "I know!"

Change didn't happen in the blink of an eye. I didn't expect to be able to run the entire ten miles after barely managing five. So of course we ran and we walked through the negative-degree weather to achieve our goal.

Or at least I did—and I hadn't even gone to bed, not counting the nap in the library. After deciding to wake Oliver from sleep to train, he half-assed his run behind me, kicking every stick and pebble along the way. I should've left his grumpy ass in bed, but he needed this as much as I did. Every minute counted, and if one of us could rank and gain the general's favor, we'd be halfway to rescuing Aspen and Oliver's sister.

And if we didn't rank... well, there was always befriending the general. The thought almost made me laugh out loud, but I had no air in my lungs for that.

"We could've at least waited until there was no freeze-your-face-off wind chill. And not in the middle of the fucking night!" Oliver's complaints were on a never-ending rotation, sandwiched between the I hate yous, the you're crazys, and the I'm not carrying your passed-out ass up that hill again.

"This is our new reality. Every day, every night. So get used to it, and take it like Rune is."

She ran next to us with an ease I both envied and adored, her tongue lolling out.

"Rune was created for Hell! I was not!"

Strangling him sounded tempting. I was about to rip into him when a mischievous smile graced his face. He hadn't smiled once since we got out here, and now he was?

"Oliver," I warned. "Don't you dare—"

He luscelered away.

"Cheater!" I yelled.

Exhaustion tugged at my eyelids, tempting me to lusceler after him, but I couldn't.

For one, I'd probably would pass out if I did, running on the little energy I had left. For another, I needed to accomplish this. The groaning trees and their shadowed depths might've unsettled me, but it didn't matter. This was Hell, yes, but I had Rune—and my powers, as a last resort, if things went wrong. I wasn't stopping. Ten miles. No shortcuts. Even if I had to crawl.

By the time I reached the bottom of the hill with two miles to go, my run had turned into a hobbled shuffle, and dawn crept upon us. Rune pressed close, like she thought I'd collapse, and though it sounded like it with my ragged breaths, I didn't stop. About halfway up the hill, I stumbled, almost going down. Rune whimpered, her illuminated eyes twisting to me.

The general was watching.

I put on a burst of speed, my vision clouding with dots and ice, but I refused to collapse in front of him with only one more mile to go. I pushed, giving everything I had to that last stretch, ignoring the agony. When I reached the arena door, I couldn't summon enough energy to smile. My vision blurred, and my knees buckled just as the door swung open.

Strong arms caught me and slowly lowered me to the threshold.

"Dammit, Lucy, I thought you'd follow me," Oliver said, his voice laced with concern, and sounding farther away than expected.

"I can't—lusceler—without passing out—cheater." My words came out in broken gasps as I rested my head against his sternum, blinking to clear my vision.

"So running until your fucking body collapses is the next best thing, Hellion?"

I stiffened. That wasn't Oliver's voice.

Slowly, I tilted my head back—and there he was. The general. Holding me in his arms.

I found myself kneeling between his legs, my hands resting on his solid thighs, his hands securing me in place.

His expression was impassive, but his gaze burned with something darker. I swallowed, my throat tight, and quickly averted my eyes. My heart raced, and I shot a pointed glare at Oliver, who stood frozen behind us.

"You took too long," Oliver said, grimacing. "So I had him check on you through Rune."

I fought the urge to shake my head. He could've luscelered back to meet us if he was so concerned. I didn't like the idea of the general seeing me struggle—or worse, giving him more proof of my ineptitude.

I lowered my head, pretending to catch my breath, when really, I was hiding. Giving myself one fleeting second to bask in this accomplishment before the general could ruin it.

Six whole miles of straight running. It wasn't the full ten. But it was progress.

I smiled. Hopefully, by the end of the week, I could reach eight.

"You didn't have to stay," I said as my breath finally evened out and I dropped the smile. I pressed against the general's hold to stand, but he resisted.

"I did," he said, his voice tight. Shadowy whisps swirled within his gold irises, giving away his displeasure.

My palms turned clammy against the rough leather of his thighs, heat from his skin seeping through the fabric. His gaze burned through me, consuming. The world around us fell away. All I could smell, hear, and feel was *him.*

Surrounded by his delicious, spicy, balsam scent, it became harder to tear myself away from the overwhelming need to know him. To unravel the thoughts that hid behind those molten depths. To see the male beneath the general's mask—to know all of him.

It wasn't about getting under his skin for Aspen's sake. It was something deeper.

His eyes called to me in a way nothing else ever had. They pushed Aspen—and the unrelenting need to get to him—to the furthest reaches of my mind.

I leaned forward, holding my breath, not sure what I was about to do. His arms and legs tensed, startling me back to reality.

Heavenly Hell!

I jerked back, rubbing my hands against my pants, desperate to shake off the feel of his warmth. "I'm fine," I insisted, shoving at his hold.

Finally, he released me. But when I struggled to stand, his shadows wrapped around my legs, lending their strength, while Rune pressed against my side, steadying me.

The general stood, his body rigid and mask firmly in place. "You sure fucking look fine," he said, voice mocking. "Do you honestly expect to be able to run another ten miles in an hour?"

My muscles and lungs screamed no, every fiber begging for rest. But the urgency that had momentarily faded in the general's arms— the same burning need that only grew stronger with each day I went without Aspen—flared back to life.

I lifted my chin. "I'll do whatever it takes."

Something flashed in his expression. Begrudging respect? Pride? Surprise? I couldn't tell. And before I could make sense of it, it was swiftly buried beneath a layer of anger.

"Go to your rooms and rest."

"What? But—"

"This isn't a negotiation, Hellion. Go. Lucifer has requested extra time with you. I'll let your squad leader know you won't be training today."

"No." I understood we missed my power training lesson, but I didn't want it to cut into my time with the Tormentors. "I have to—"

The general stepped closer and removed his shadows from my legs, cutting off my protest. I slumped into Rune, shaking too much to hold myself up. His shadows whipped around him chaotically before swarming back to me.

"Bed. Now."

I opened my mouth.

"Nephilim," he snapped. "Help her to bed and make sure Sam comes up to check on her."

Oliver hurried to my side and wrapped his arm around my waist. The general watched us in silence as Oliver and Rune led me out of the empty arena, the heavy echo of our footsteps filling the quiet hallway as we entered the castle.

I gritted my teeth, understanding I needed rest, but having no patience for it. Frustration simmered beneath my skin, and I wanted to go back and lay into the general.

"This isn't a joke, you know," I snapped. "You can't lusceler when it's too hard to run. Did you happen to forget that the only way into Lilith's kingdom is with Ember Manacles? Manacles that suppress our powers, Oliver. What will you do then?"

"The ten miles just stressed me out. I'm not good in the cold, Luce, and you woke me up in the middle of the night. To *run*."

I scoffed. "So if it's too cold or in the middle of the night, you'll leave your sister to what? Suffer at the hands of Lilith until it's a balmy seventy degrees and just after lunch?"

Oliver let go of me, forcing most of my weight onto Rune.

"And what about you?" he said, his emerald eyes flashing with fire. "Are you going to push yourself until there's nothing left of you?"

"I'm getting stronger!"

He shook his head. "You look really strong right now, Lucille." He jabbed a finger toward me, each word sharper than the last. "If you didn't have me or Rune, you would've been dead from hypothermia at the bottom of that hill. How many times have you pushed yourself to the point of passing out? Today was the first day without me, and you didn't even make it through the door. Anyone else would've left you out there to suffer or die. You can only push yourself so far."

I couldn't believe I was hearing this.

"We need the general's favor if we have any chance of helping Aspen or Melanie! The only way we do that is if we rank!"

"Yeah, fine. But you need a healthy stopping point."

No. There was no stopping. Not until Aspen was beside me.

"What I need is for you to take this seriously and stop complaining. It's no wonder you haven't rescued your sister in ninety-five years."

Oliver jolted as though I had struck him, the hurt snuffing out the flames in his eyes.

"Rune can help you to bed. You can find someone else to carry your unconscious body up the hill," he said, turning away.

I reached out, my voice catching. "Wait. Oli!"

He shrugged off my hold, walking away without a backward glance.

When Rune and I finally made it back to my rooms, Oliver wasn't there, and the rising sunlight peeking through the windows seemed duller because of it.

Sam came by later, looking as sullen as I felt. He gave me some ice packs, heating pads, and some kind of hydrating pills, then left after scolding me. He didn't even replenish my energy like I hoped he would. Either Oliver or the general told him not to, or there was some other reason he didn't.

Eventually, after beating myself up for what I said to Oliver, I fell asleep.

"There you are, sweetheart."

I closed my eyes, the urgency that wouldn't let me relax easing the slightest bit at the sound of his voice.

"Aspen." I sighed. Heavenly Hell, I was grateful to see him.

He stood in his usual spot beneath the oak tree, his uniform hugging every inch of his muscular build. A breeze rustled through the leaves, whipping at my thick coat and pants, sprinkling debris into his brown waves.

I smiled, and he walked over, wrapping me in his arms and squeezing me tight. Breathing in his apple scent, I relaxed into his embrace, needing this—needing to feel him, to know he was alive.

"Sweetheart," he breathed into my hair. "Two weeks is much too long for me to wait for you." He crushed me tighter to his body, and I savored every second.

"I'm sorry. I don't know how to direct the dream-walks," I admitted.

"You don't?" He pulled back—or tried to. But I wouldn't let him, continuing to meld my body to his. After the fight with Oliver, I wanted comfort.

"Lucille," he prompted gently.

Sighing, I eased up on my hold. "No. And with all my time focused on training, I never thought to ask anyone how."

"But you've tried?"

I stepped out of his arms. The tightness around his eyes made my stomach sink. He doubted me.

Every day since I ended up in Hell, I'd been trying—trying to complete ten miles, to impress the general, to rank, to suffer through my power training, to read as much as I could, to be as knowledgeable as everyone else, to find a way out of Hell—all to rescue him. I wanted to scream in his face: *I've been doing nothing but trying!*

Instead, I said, "Of course."

"What have you tried?"

He still didn't believe me.

"I think of the person before bed and see if I'll dream-walk to them. Sometimes it works, sometimes it doesn't." Saying it out loud made me cringe. My words lacked confidence and determination. It didn't sound like I was actively trying—it sounded like I was letting it happen, as if I wasn't pushing myself hard enough.

Aspen's expression confirmed my thoughts. I could almost hear him thinking: do better, be more, try harder.

"Maybe if it's not working, then you need to try something else."

"Like what?" I threw my hands in the air.

"Like," he drew out, his irises flashing, "maybe it's not the person your dream-walk seeks out. It's something else. An answer to a question. Knowledge."

He sounded so confident, like he knew for a fact that was how it was done. But if that was the case... how would he know that?

"Is it?" I asked, suspicious.

He shrugged, then stepped toward me with a hungry look in his eyes. I moved back.

"I don't know. Could be. Or maybe it's comfort."

He did it again, and I mirrored, stumbling when my camisole vanished.

"Or need," Aspen whispered, his voice low.

My shorts vanished next, along with his leathers, exposing an expanse of naked skin on both of us. We only had undergarments left.

"Desire."

Heat raged in his eyes. He closed the rest of the space between us, pulling me against his body and silencing my lingering suspicions with the crash of his lips.

His ferocity surprised me. But as he nipped and sucked, the tingles sending shockwaves to my core, my thoughts melted into need.

I opened for him, and his tongue immediately ravaged mine with expert strokes. Hell, I thought the vibrations of his moist lips were addicting, but his wet tongue sending tingling sensations inside my mouth was a drug I never wanted to end.

Moaning, I pressed closer. Everywhere our skin touched, tingling ignited. The only place it didn't was where his cock strained through his undergarments, throbbing against my stomach.

He was so hard, and I was so wet. I couldn't help but push to my tiptoes and grind against him. He moaned, grabbing my ass, his fingers settling close to my core. Mere inches prevented him from touching me. It was agonizing. I squirmed, wanting his teasing fingers lower—inside me.

Instead, he moved them farther away. I whimpered, my cheeks heating at my neediness.

Aspen pulled back and gave me a smug smile, his hair falling into his dark lashes.

The rest of my clothes vanished, leaving me completely bare before him. He dropped to his knees, unfazed by the crunching grass or rocky ground.

"Tonight, I want you to take my tongue instead of my fingers," he said, gazing up at me, the blue hue of Elora's moon illuminating the sinful intent in his eyes.

I bit my lip, intrigued but also nervous. Were we moving too fast?

My nerves and doubts were quickly forgotten when he licked up the center of my core.

The fantasy of his tongue had seduced my mind since the day I tackled him off that carriage and felt it slide through the seam of my lips.

And now, living that fantasy, I came alive.

His tongue stroked through my slickness and paused at my clit, sending vibration after vibration shooting through me. I threw my head back in a gasp, my knees buckling.

So much fucking better than a fantasy.

He chuckled, gently pushing me to the ground and onto a blanket he imagined. His eyes were hooded.

"Are you ready to feel me inside you?" he whispered, the warmth of his breath teasing my wet skin.

I bit my lip and nodded.

He flicked my swollen clit with his tongue, making me arch, then used the angle to plunge it inside.

"Aspen," I cried out, fisting his hair in my hands.

He did it again and again, pushing the vibrations deeper. I rode his tongue, writhing on his face, moaning his name.

Encouraged, he gripped my legs and spread me wider. His tongue thrust deeper and faster.

I could barely think around the mounting pleasure. All I wanted was more.

"Don't stop," I begged, my voice raspy. *Hell, please don't stop.*

He didn't. He devoured me with his mouth and tongue, wringing cries and moans from me, until he nipped at my clit and drove inside me. I shattered, pulsing around him.

"You make the sweetest sounds," he murmured, sitting back and licking his lips.

Boneless, I smiled at him kneeling between my legs. His cock still strained against the fabric of his undergarments, full of unfulfilled desire.

I sat up and pressed my hand against him. His eyes tightened before being overtaken by a smug grin.

"No, sweetheart. Tonight was just for you."

"But last time was also just for me. I think it's time I pleasure you."

He rose to his feet, bringing me with him. In the next breath, clothes reappeared on us both.

"Next time," he said, tucking my wild hair behind my ears.

My brows furrowed. There was something in his gaze that made me question him.

"You sure?"

Aspen raised a hand and smoothed out the lines in my forehead.

"I want you to savor your pleasure, without having to return it, sweetheart. You're new to this."

"Okay." But I didn't believe him.

Was it his tone? His words? He sounded considerate. Although the last part rubbed me the wrong way. I didn't think he meant it negatively. Still, it reminded me how little I had lived, and that there was probably a giant list of all the females he'd had—like... Nalini.

Heavenly Shit.

How the hell would he react to knowing she was a soul living in Hell? Aspen loved Nalini, and her death destroyed him. I felt it.

He lifted my chin. "Are you okay?"

I opened my mouth, panicking.

"Earlier, you seemed upset when you came into my dream."

Being the coward I was, I took the out he gave me.

"Oliver and I had a fight after our late-night run, and I don't think he's speaking to me," I said, feeling yet another weight on my shoulders.

Aspen pulled me into his arms. "The Nephilim will get over it."

"Yeah." But I wasn't so sure.

The dream's scenery flickered, and Aspen stepped back.

"Dream-walk to me again soon, sweetheart."

Everything dissolved into a background of darkness, and Aspen vanished, leaving me with an illuminated ball of my power and a weird feeling.

CHAPTER 21

Lucille

After my dream-walk, I wasn't able to sleep. Aspen and his actions plagued my thoughts. I couldn't shake the feeling he was... off? Hiding something? I wanted to trust him. I *should* trust him—especially if I thought I loved him. But was love really this rollercoaster of want, confusion, frustration, and lust?

The questions rolled around in my head as I limped my way to the library. Each step tugged at my sore muscles, reminding me I should be resting and icing my legs.

Rune followed along. I couldn't make her stay in my room or go to the general's.

I paused at the Doors of Moirai, studying them closely. They depicted Ni standing in her Hell Squadron uniform. Odd. Besides the vacant expression replacing her normally inquisitive gaze, she looked the same. Although... I stepped back, noticing something off about her neck. Black veins crawled around the gash as if it were infected.

The Doors of Moirai were supposed to reveal glimpses of the past, present, and future, but I couldn't tell which this was. I saw Ni a couple days ago, and there was no sign of this infection.

"Is there a purpose to what you show me? Or are these images for the king?"

The tiles didn't spell out the answers to my questions like I hoped. I stood there, talking to the doors, probably looking insane to both Rune and—judging by her glowing gold eyes—the general.

I usually hated that little power of theirs. But right now, I couldn't hold back my smug smile.

"I bet you're seething in your little boots, aren't you, General?" I teased. "But don't worry, I'll be resting as I read. If you get a chance, let my father know I'm here."

I sat down in my spot and read about Elora, Hell, and a little of the Tenebrous Kingdom, but none of it gave me any clues on how I could get out of the Hell dimension. I found a little more information about the lake Oliver mentioned. But all I learned was that it was linked to the Seven Circles of Hell and was a way for the king to oversee his lords and their duties. It also stated something about how it connected to Earth, but as I frantically flipped the page to find more information, the chapter ended.

I sat back in my chair, squeezing my fists. We needed answers, and reading was getting us nowhere. But the only person I knew who could give me those answers was the king—or...

"Cato!" I yelled, peeking between the rows of books. Cato had this habit of sneaking up and scaring me. But today, I was prepared to catch him. I positioned my chair so that my back rested against a shelf, and I had a full view of the library.

A tap-tap on my shoulder made me jump. I whipped around to his unamused expression and a slight twinkle in his eyes.

"One of these days, I'm coming back with a bell."

"A bell wouldn't help you, Princess."

"I'm probably wasting my breath telling you to stop calling me that."

A title like *princess* carried weight—it meant I had sway over Hell's lands and its people. It came with duty, obligation, and sacrifice. Or so I'd gathered from all the books I'd been reading. But none of that resonated with me.

He gave me his favorite dry expression.

"Right." I rolled my eyes. "What can you tell me about Portal Lake?"

The time for beating around the bush had long passed. I wanted answers, and I wanted them now.

Cato nodded to my mini library of books resting on the table.

"Everything you have there."

I tapped my fingers against a book, analyzing him. "I don't believe you."

He blinked. "Pity."

Heavenly Hell. "The king—"

"Your father," he interrupted.

I gritted my teeth. "*Lucifer* said you can retain everything you read. Assuming you are a few hundred years old, give or take, I can imagine you've read a lot."

"Naturally," he drawled.

"So if you've read as much as I think you have, then you can't tell me you have no more information on Portal Lake."

"And why are you so curious about Portal Lake?" Lucifer's voice echoed through the library.

Luckily, I'd already thought about an answer to that question. "How else will I escape to find and kill Michael?" I said, turning to Lucifer.

One thing Oliver and I never considered was the fact that everyone believed we were stuck here for another year. And if they didn't think we could escape, then what was the harm in asking a question they thought wouldn't matter?

Lucifer strode toward me, his white-and-black suit perfectly tailored to his build. The coloring matched the rings around his eyes.

"You barely escaped him alive last time, and you think two weeks of training has transformed you into a warrior who can take on an Archangel?"

I was so sick and tired of everyone doubting me—of calling me weak, floundering, or unskilled.

"And what are *you* doing to find and kill Michael?" I fired back, rising. "Sitting on your royal ass while my mother suffers?"

White light flashed in his gaze. He walked right into my space, leaning down until his face hovered inches from mine.

"Don't for a second think I haven't been to Portal Lake and our gates every morning and night, carving open my flesh so I can send the general out to bring that repugnant angel back here to pay for his sins."

Pressure built behind my eyes, and my Infernus sang in my ears, my anger rising with his.

Straightening, he continued. "I'm the only one with the blood to access Portal Lake, and even then, it has not answered me. So you'd do well to rid yourself of your fantastical imaginings and focus on something more practical. Like controlling your powers."

His eyes settled back to their normal state, and he gazed down at me with a superior air.

It frustrated me to no end, but at least I received an answer. Now I knew his blood was the key to opening the lake—and, it sounded like, the gates too. Although he had a point. What made me think *we* could escape when Lucifer couldn't?

My shoulders slumped. Lucifer frowned, looking almost regretful.

"Your mother will be okay for the year. Cato and I have a temporary solution," he said, like he was trying to be reassuring.

"Are you sure it'll just be a year?"

The general had said he was locked in Hell for the last ten.

"The gates used to open annually on the same day for a short time. Then it stopped—and started again when we rescued you. I'm sure the pattern will repeat itself."

If he knew the pattern repeated, wouldn't he *state* that? Why say *I'm sure*, like he was making an assumption?

"Did you know they'd open when the general rescued me?"

Lucifer's expression said it all.

"You didn't." I sat back down, feeling like a fist had slammed into my gut.

I'd hoped that if Oliver and I didn't find a way to escape sooner, we'd at least have that year. It would be torturous and horrible to wait that long, but it was a backup plan. But now? We might be stuck here indefinitely. My mom couldn't stay in a coma. And Aspen... I wouldn't allow him to remain with Lilith. I needed him out of there.

"Are you sure you've tried everything to open the gates?"

He considered me, the minutes awkwardly ticking by as my father pierced me with his lofty gaze.

"We have tried to understand why the gates closed. We scoured the library for information, used dangerous runes, ripped apart the ground, bashed in the iron rods, and used every means we had to try and pry open Hell's gates or use Portal Lake. I even blamed it on your mother at one point after she left me, but she doesn't have the power capable of closing Hell," he spat, icicles growing from the glass ceiling. "We have tried *everything*. Now, we can only pray to the Weaver that the gates will open once more next year."

I straightened. "Is *that* what you did for me as Michael carved me open?" I raised my voice. "You *prayed* to your Weaver they'd open and gambled on our lives?"

He narrowed his eyes at my tone. "You were supposed to go north, where I had connections who could help you until we could retrieve you. You disobeyed me."

"I was trying to rescue my mother! Like I am now!"

"And *I* was trying to rescue *you* with the only means and information I had at the time."

Me? He was trying to rescue *me*?

I stared at him, hearing the remnants of the undeniable sincerity in his voice and seeing it in his softened expression. It was strange. Lucifer wasn't cuddly or warm. He wasn't the fatherly type—and I wasn't exactly sure what it even meant to *have* one. But hearing that he was trying to protect me, and seeing the truth in his face, shifted the bitterness I held onto.

Cato was right. Lucifer wasn't like Michael. And my mother, despite her beliefs, was wrong. Lucifer—my father—wanted me to survive. He cared about me, not just her.

"Why did she leave you for him?" I whispered, needing to understand why she'd traded someone who would bleed for her for someone who made her bleed.

Hurt tightened his eyes before he could mask it. "She told me she wanted him. I think... she thought it was the only way to protect you."

"With *Michael*?"

Lucifer shook his head. "I wish she'd wake up so I could ask," he said so softly, I knew he wasn't talking to me.

This was the most sincere emotion I'd ever seen from him, and the ache in his voice made me uncomfortable. "I spoke with her. She seems good." As far as I could tell.

"How?" Cato asked, assessing me with a sharp gaze.

I had forgotten he was still here.

Lucifer scrutinized me just as hard, the same question on his face.

"Do you know what a dream-walker is?" If anyone knew, it'd be them.

Cato stepped forward, his eyes narrowing. "Where did you hear that term?" he asked slowly.

"From Michael."

Lucifer's irises flashed. "I wouldn't trust a thing he said."

"I'd agree, but he's right, isn't he? That's what it's called when I enter people's dreams or memories?" I looked at Cato, who seemed to understand what I meant.

"Yes. And you're better off never using those powers again," he snapped, then turned and left, his robes swooshing as he stormed away.

I sat back, startled. That was the most emotion I'd ever seen from him. Even Lucifer looked taken aback, staring after his Throne.

But Cato knew about dream-walking. I had half the mind to run after him. I considered it, then dropped the thought. I knew if he didn't want to talk, he wouldn't.

"This is how you contacted your mother?" Lucifer asked, pulling my attention from Cato's retreat.

I nodded.

"Can you do it at any time?"

"No. And I'm having a hard time directing it. Sometimes I dream-walk to the person I want, and other nights I don't."

"Interesting," Lucifer mused. "I'll speak with Cato later and see what I can find out."

"Thanks," I said, grateful for his help, even if he was only curious because I could talk to his lost love.

He gestured for me to stand. "Come. Let's practice."

Lucifer led me to another part of the castle, strolling by my side as I limped. I would've used Rune to help, but he didn't want her to come along, commanding her to find the general. We ended up in a sort of greenhouse.

I walked through the frosted glass doors, feeling a chill instead of the balmy heat I expected. Flowers of every color and shape were encased in transparent ice. Sunlight shone through the greenhouse, glinting off the ice and casting prisms of color across the stone path.

"This used to be your mother's favorite place to come when she was here, but without the ice," Lucifer said softly, grazing a finger over the icy petal of a yellow rose. "When she left, I froze everything. I thought if I always had this piece of her, there'd be hope she'd come back to me." He sighed, leading me to a bench.

The moment I sat down, warmth seeped into my bottom. My eyes widened, and I glanced at Lucifer, who was smiling. It was small and weighted, but a smile nonetheless. And more of my hardened heart melted. I liked my father's smile. He seemed more... open and approachable.

"The bench is runed. I come here often. And despite my cold lands, I do enjoy warmth."

I nodded, gazing at a place touched by both my parents.

"You can come here whenever you like. But from now on, I'd like our training to be here."

I gave him a slight nod, and he patted my hand. But the movement was jerky and hesitant, like he wasn't sure what he was doing.

I laughed. "You don't have to try so hard. I don't have many expectations for a father. So just do what feels normal. Be you," I said, sounding cliché and weird. We both weren't good at this, I guess.

"Alright." He straightened and handed me a pink rose. "Freeze it," he said, his demanding voice back in place.

I sighed. I told him to be himself.

Opening myself to my Infernus, I gave it my want, and it answered. The whispering of ice came first, then the itches, and within seconds, the rose was completely encased. Though mine was more frosty than clear.

"Fast study," he said, approval ringing in his tone. "We'll practice more with your glaciation powers in the Shard Field. For now, let's return to blocking. I'll send your subconscious an emotion, and it'll create a hallucination using my Infernus. I want you to try to block it as soon as you see the scene."

I didn't even close my eyes before I was slammed with the image of me, Michael, and my mom in that butcher's basement. But this time, Michael was slamming his dagger into my mom's stomach. Even knowing it wasn't real, I screamed. She was unconscious, and each strike had her body jolting, blood spurting.

"Stop!" I shrieked. Heavenly Shit, I couldn't see this.

"Block, Lucille. Shield me out."

I couldn't. I couldn't stop watching, couldn't stop screaming as Michael mutilated her. She was dying.

"Lucille!" an icy voice boomed. "Shield! You've done it before."

I closed my eyes, the squelching noise of the knife in her flesh filling my ears. *Shield!* I screamed at myself. But I couldn't concentrate. The knife kept suctioning in and out of her skin. "Stop. Stop!" I begged.

The hallucination dissolved, and I doubled over, heaving.

"You have a minute to gather yourself. Then we go again. You've pushed me out before. Why can't you now?" His words were clipped and impatient.

Oddly, his tone helped to steady me, and the memory of those times flashed back. "You made me angry before, not scared." At least not *that* scared.

"Your enemies won't care how they break you. Fear, anger, sorrow... they'll use anything to take you down. Again."

"That wasn't a min—"

This time, the scene shifted. I wasn't strapped to the table anymore. Instead, I was the one holding the dagger, plunging it into my mother's stomach.

I squeezed my eyes shut, screaming so loud it drowned out the wet suction.

Shield. Shield!

I'd done it before—not just against Lucifer, but recently with my mom. I *could* do it again. I pulled at my Infernus, and it resisted.

Come on!

I pulled again, forcing it to the surface of my mind with everything I had. Something flashed behind my eyes, and I opened them to see purple flames engulfing the butcher's basement. Slowly, the scene faded away, and the greenhouse came into view.

"Better. But I told you not to force your Infernus."

"It wouldn't come otherwise."

He pursed his lips, displeasure written all over them. "You doubt yourself, so it doubts your wants. You need to understand—your Infernus is almost a sentient being inside your body."

"What?"

"The more powerful you are, the more your powers take on a life of their own. It will answer to your confidence and need—but even the slightest bit of doubt, and it won't. Again."

We practiced on and off for the rest of the day, breaking only for lunch and dinner, which were brought to the greenhouse. He didn't let me leave until I blocked him three times in a row. That took until nightfall.

By the time I stumbled into my room, my mind throbbed as much as my muscles. There was no way I'd dream-walk tonight. Every part of me was utterly spent.

CHAPTER 22

Lucille

Finding Oliver in formation, I slid up next to him and gave him an apologetic frown. "I'm sorry."

He didn't acknowledge me, and I couldn't take it anymore. For the last two days, he'd been avoiding me, not stepping foot in our bedroom and ignoring me at every turn.

"Oliver." I reached out and touched his arm.

Moira opened the door, and he jerked out of my hold, running ahead. I caught up to him, and he continued to suffocate me with his silence. Of course I expected him to be hurt, but I figured an apology would be enough to remedy his cold shoulder. He had to know I didn't mean what I said. I was just frustrated—with the general, our progress, and his cheating. I couldn't voice that part now, though, not as my breaths turned ragged and my lungs struggled for air.

Oliver slowed to a walk.

"No stopping," I heaved, waving him on.

He didn't respond, keeping his gaze on the winding road ahead as if I weren't there.

But I couldn't stop for him. He knew that. And he was using it against me to get away.

I swallowed the lump in my throat and continued without him, blinking rapidly to clear the sting from my eyes.

The Tormentors soon lapped me, their mocking shouts echoing down the slushy road. I kept them in sight as best I could, pushing myself through the pain. At five miles, my body screamed for a break. Numbness crept into my feet, and my vision fuzzed. A part of me knew I should stop, but an invasive urgency shoved the instinct aside, pressuring me to continue.

In one blink, my legs gave out, and I slammed my head into the gravel.

When I came to, something pressed against my neck. I blinked away the frost from my lashes and found Oliver's face.

"Oliver?" I said, forcing myself up, ignoring the pain in my skull. "Heavenly Hell, I passed out again, didn't I?"

He crossed his arms.

I stood, brushing my forehead and wincing when my fingers came away bloody. "Thanks for staying with me. Does this mean you forgive me?"

He raised a brow, snorted, then jogged away.

I sighed and jogged after him.

The next few miles were brutal, each step heavier than the last. My limbs dragged, and I stumbled and zigzagged more than I ran straight. Oliver stayed in sight, but he never once looked back. Even when I approached the hill, he continued, leaving me to struggle up it like he'd said he would.

I bit my lip to stop it from trembling, squared my shoulders, and forced myself to jog the final two miles. Oliver entered the arena, and nausea slammed into my stomach. I tried to hold it back; I only had a few yards left. But it bubbled up and out, splashing onto the snow just as another squad bulldozed through the arena doors.

"Oh, lookie here, it's the Hell-whore," a male sneered before kicking the backs of my knees and shoving me to the ground.

I hit the snow hard, catching myself on my hands and narrowly avoiding my puke. My fingers closed around a jagged lump of ice. I'd made it so easy for him to knock me down. Practically wore a sign that said *Weak. Doesn't belong. Punish her.*

And they would.

I'd already seen one Bowel member try to murder a Trencher just to take their spot. But even with my nausea, spinning head, and ragged breaths, that wasn't going to be me.

I'd fight.

Their laughter echoed as their boots pounded away.

"Should've slit her throat, Dusty," one of them called over the wind. "Could've gotten your spot back."

Surprised they left, I pushed to my feet and released the ice. My wary glare tracked Dusty and his friend as they jogged down the hill.

"And have the general's Soul Sword at my neck? No thanks." Dusty scoffed.

So the general's spectacle didn't just stop Theon; it made everyone else hesitate too. No wonder Oliver and I hadn't had more attempts on our lives.

"She must give him good head."

Good head?

"Either that or she's fucking the king," Dusty added, his voice fading as they ran.

They thought I—

"Gah." I gagged and shoved open the doors before I could puke again at the thought.

Inside, the air warmed, filled with shouting, slapping skin, and clanking metal—a cacophony of violence and skill. I walked over to the Tormentors, keeping my eyes trained on Oliver. He glanced up from his weights but quickly looked away, offering me nothing—not a nod, not a word.

Fine.

After strength training, before Ni led Oliver to their station, my gaze flicked to her neck. Her red gash still gaped and shone with mucus, but there was no sign of black infection. Maybe the doors had shown what Ni's neck used to look like before it started healing. But what purpose did it serve to show me the past? Unless the image had been meant for Lucifer and his judgment.

A javelin flew through the air toward me, startling me out of my thoughts. I caught it two-handed and found Ichi gripping her own with her dainty hands. I opened my mouth about to question her, and in one fluid movement, she lifted her javelin, took a few running steps, then threw it.

The javelin sliced through the air and slammed into a bull's-eye seventy meters away.

I gaped at her.

I think I had a girl crush.

I shouldn't be surprised by her ferocity. But Ichi stood at least three inches shorter than me, with a small physique and solemn gaze. She didn't have a hardened personality, nor a weak one—just a quiet, balanced presence.

What really made me second-guess her strength, despite countless training days, was her composed and respectful demeanor. Nothing about this military was soft-spoken or polite. Most of them were brutal, self-serving asses stronger than me.

But that didn't make Ichi lessor. If anything, the way she carried herself was a testament to her resilience and power. I was sure she'd been mocked and mistreated by the other squads as she rose through the ranks.

"Your turn." She nodded to me, a small smile softening her half-burned face.

I smiled back, unable to hide my awe. No one smiled around here—unless I counted the sneers or ignored the mockery behind them. Ichi was different. And I respected her more for it.

Focusing through the glare of sunlight, I mimicked her movements, hoping to impress her, only to stumble as I threw. The spear dropped halfway to the target, skidding across the ground.

When did it get so bright in here?

Ichi gestured at another javelin. "Again. Keep your grip firm, your core tight, and shift your weight to your front foot as you release—then maintain your balance during the recovery."

I threw again with her guidance and missed. She politely critiqued my form, then said, "Again."

That was Ichi's favorite word. She used it at least a hundred more times, only stopping when I finally nicked the target.

She'd get along well with my father.

"Good. Let's move on to daggers."

Throwing daggers would be easier. Or so I assumed.

It wasn't. Even though the target was closer and the weight lighter, I struggled. And my stomach still churned with nausea.

Ichi showed me over and over what to do, and I still couldn't get it right. Frustrated, I dug my nails into my palms when the dagger fell short.

"This isn't working!"

Hands pressed against my stomach and back, straightening my spine. I knew who it was the moment I smelled the spicy scent of clove and balsam and felt the brush of shadow on my forehead.

The general brought his lips to my ear. "Maybe because you have a concussion, Hellion. Mind telling me what happened?" he whispered, his body rigid behind me.

"I fell."

"During your run."

It wasn't a question, so I didn't answer.

He reached around and grabbed my chin, tilting it back to meet his pitch-black irises. "You want to see me seething in my *little boots*? Keep ignoring your limits, and you'll get to experience it firsthand."

"Oh? Is this another part of your job? Because last I checked, a concussion won't kill me," I snapped, attempting to jerk from his hold.

He squeezed tighter, his gaze boring into mine. "Don't test me, Hellion."

One of his shadows whipped out, tickling my nose.

My dizziness faded.

"Thank you," I said, begrudgingly.

He gave a stiff nod, a muscle ticking in his jaw. "It's not a cure. But it'll keep your symptoms at bay until after training. Then you'll go see Sam."

I nodded, knowing there was no other response he'd accept, especially with shadows slithering around him, wrapping tighter with each sharp line of his body. His eyes remained black, hiding the tempest of emotions swirling beneath the surface. I had a feeling Rune would be accompanying me after training.

General Ronen closed his eyes, took a steadying breath, and walked to another group, observing them with Alexei.

What the hell was that about?

I shook my head and took the blade Ichi handed me, throwing it at the target. It hit. Not a bull's-eye, but close. I repeated the motion, landing several solid throws, and felt a deep sense of gratitude for the general's help.

Without the dizziness, I'd successfully completed a station.

At archery, I performed terribly until Ichi gave me a bow with a lighter draw weight. It made sense. My arm felt like it would fall off every time I pulled the string, and I still needed to build muscle. When we rotated to swordsmanship, I straight up said, "I can't use my right arm anymore."

She smiled and shrugged. "So use your left."

Girl crush gone. She was a demon.

Unable to help myself, I glanced over at Oliver, pride warming my chest. He fared about as well as I did. Ni had him knocked to the ground, but as he glared up at her, his eyes lit with emerald flames. His hand twitched, as if about to touch her with a power he despised.

He was trying. Whether for me or his sister, I didn't know, but it was a small step in the right direction.

Ni responded with a flaming finger, wagging it as if to say *Oh no, you don't.* Oliver let the green flames dim.

"We don't believe in using powers against fellow angels—unless absolutely necessary. We see no honor in it," Ichi said.

Honor? I didn't know anyone here even used that term.

"So you've never used it on your squadmates in the showers?"

Ichi watched Cyrus and Theon. "No. And because we refused to participate, Moira had us replace the two we were meant to punish. She ordered Cyrus to choke me with his vines. But before he could kill me, Ni retaliated. She blocked Theon's water strike and scorched Cyrus with her flames—burned him without hesitation. They underestimated us because of how we chose to live in death. But they learned their mistake that day."

She turned to me with a solemn, determined expression. "My sister and I will pay our penance to be redeemed by participating in this military and her squad. But we will not add time to our sentence. You can always be recycled for your sins."

"So you just stood up to Moira and that's that?"

"Bullies can only bully you if they believe you're too weak to retaliate." She panned her gaze from my boots to my shirt. "I don't believe you're too weak, Lucy. So, may I ask what you're hiding?"

I stiffened. But her honesty and warmth pulled at something deep within me, urging me to trust her. "Nothing I'm at liberty to share without getting myself in deeper trouble."

"Does it have anything to do with why you won't use your powers? From the ring in your eyes, you're at least part angel. So you must have them."

"Yes."

Respect glimmered in her grin, like she enjoyed that answer.

"Well, if you can't prove your strength with power, let's build your warrior skills. And when challenge week comes, you can challenge Moira."

I'm sorry—*what* did she just say?

Stunned, I had no protest or retort as she handed me a sword.

Ichi was insane.

CHAPTER 23

Lucille

After training, Rune and I walked to the healers' wing. As expected, the general followed along through their connection.

"I said I would go. You should trust my word."

Rune barked suddenly, making me jump.

I'd heard her growl, pant, and whine before, but never bark. I had a sneaking suspicion that was the general's special way of responding through his Soulhound.

"You don't have to apologize, General. Just don't make the same mistake twice," I said sweetly.

Rune growled in response, but it wasn't aggressive—more like a sulking child who hadn't gotten her morning pets. I wondered if she could control it or not. Because if the general controlled it, I was sure it would've been a vicious growl.

I twirled the end of my low ponytail, a grin tugging at my lips. "Seriously, General. I forgive you."

The thought of his expression—glaring into space, steam practically coming out of his ears—nearly sent me into a fit of laughter.

Rune growled again, this time deeper.

"Hey, now. Don't go seething in those little boots of yours," I teased. "You wouldn't want Moira thinking she's bad in bed. We wouldn't want a dead general on our hands."

I had no idea if he was with her or not, but it was my best guess.

Suddenly, Rune—or, most likely, the general—sprang in front of me. I tripped over her, crashing into the carpeted floor with a burst of laughter. She sat back on her haunches, tilting her head side to side as if listening intently to my amusement.

"I'm teasing," I said, laughing. "I bet she's great in bed, and I guarantee you are too." I froze. "I mean you're— You have—"

My cheeks flushed, and I shut my mouth, scrambling to my feet and making sure to avoid eye contact with Rune.

Why did I say that?

The rest of the way to the healers' wing was filled with an uncomfortable silence, which didn't even make sense. It wasn't like he walked beside me. But the thought of him hearing those words— of him knowing what I'd said—while also remembering how he felt about me, how he was my superior, and how I was trying to make him respect me, made my stomach twist.

I scurried through the doors, relieved that Rune couldn't follow me inside. I approached a healer and asked for Sam. She led me to a bed, her footsteps quick and efficient, and told me to wait.

I lay down, trying to focus on the sounds of the healers bustling about the large hall—murmurs, the faint jingle of necklaces, the rustle of bandages and herbs—but none of them were Sam.

I stared up at the ceiling, feeling the faint weight of my thoughts pressing in. My mind racing from one worry to the next—the general and what he thought of me now. My mother and when I would be able to dream-walk to her again. Cato and knowing about dream-walking. Lucifer and the greenhouse. The possibility that we might be stuck here for more than a year.

The urgency inside me surged, making my fingers twitch with restless energy.

How could Aspen endure Lilith for another year? How was he now?

I must've drifted off while waiting, because when I blinked my eyes open, I stood in our field. The thick air carried the sweet scent of grass and wildflowers, their whispers brushing against my skin in the blue moonlight.

"It's been a day," Aspen said. "And still, my heart aches from the deep longing to see your face again." He smiled, rising from the ground below the oak tree.

I raised an eyebrow, a playful smirk tugging at my lips. "That's all you've been doing, isn't it? Sleeping, hoping I'd appear in your dreams?"

He shrugged, but something flashed in his gaze, the twilight hiding it from me. I was tempted to shift the dream to daylight, to see him better. Instead, I shifted the color of the moon to silver and placed stars in the sky. And he dressed me back into the green dress.

"Isn't that what every female wants to hear? That the male she adores spends every moment in slumber, hoping she'll visit him there?"

I made my way to him, switching the dress for a pair of leggings and a loose long-sleeve. Aspen sighed, as if disappointed, then reached out, pulling me into his embrace. With his free hand, he twirled a lock of my hair between his fingers, his touch sending a shiver down my spine.

"Maybe," I whispered. "But I'd rather have you here with me in the waking world than in the hazy blur of dreams."

His lips brushed against mine, slow and tender. "This," he murmured, his breath warming my skin, "feels pretty real to me."

I pulled back just enough to meet his eyes, forcing out a half-hearted smile. "You know what I mean."

He sighed. "I do. Have you found any way of escape?"

I stepped out of his arms and turned toward the trees. "We thought we had," I said, my voice tinged with frustration. "Hell has Portal Lake, but it only responds to the king's blood—just like the gates. And neither one has answered him in years."

So, we found nothing.

Aspen's arms encircled me from behind, pulling me close again. His finger brushed the sensitive skin beneath my breast through the thin fabric of my shirt. He lowered his lips to my neck, his breath a warm kiss against my eager skin.

"Have you found anything else?"

I stiffened.

Yes. His dead lover. I still hadn't told him.

"What?" His tone sharpened, and he turned me, searching my face. He looked desperate. And he should be, right? He wanted me out of Hell and probably thought I'd found something small to help with that. "What else did you find?"

I hesitated. What good would it do if I told him? He wouldn't be able to see her. Telling him would only rip open old wounds, bring him more pain.

"Sweetheart," he prompted, lifting my chin. "Maybe I can help if you tell me."

I swallowed hard, the words heavy on my tongue. "Have you found Michael yet?" He told me he'd help me with that too, and I've yet to hear of his progress.

"No."

"You're still looking, right?"

He stared straight at me and smiled, his eyes tightening. "Of course."

I bit my lip. I didn't believe him. His smile was forced, his tone higher than normal. He was hiding something. But was it about Michael... or something worse?

"I'm just having a hard time finding him, sweetheart. That's all," he reassured. He grabbed my hands when I remained quiet. "Really, sweetheart. I'm stuck at the moment and didn't know how to tell you."

"Okay." It wasn't like we'd be able to kill him until we rescued Aspen and... Melanie. I bowed my head. There were too many moving pieces to figure out.

"There's someone else I need you to search for."

He ran a finger across my bottom lip, pulling it from between my teeth and tilting my chin up. "Who?"

"Melanie. Oliver's sister." I steadied myself, gathering the strength to speak the words. "Lilith took her when she took you. Oliver believes she's still alive—somewhere in the Tenebrous Kingdom." If we were going to save her, we needed someone on the inside. "Put finding her above finding Michael," I said, my voice a weak whisper.

After all this, I'd promised myself I'd do everything to help my mom—everything. But Michael was most likely out of our reach, while Melanie was hidden in Aspen's kingdom. And I wouldn't let my best friend wait another year for his sister, even if he currently hated me.

A haunted look passed over Aspen's face, so raw and sudden it felt like he was drowning in something unseen.

I reached out, my fingers brushing his arm. "Hey—"

The air around us vibrated with outside noise, breaking apart the dream. Someone was waking me up.

No! I didn't want to wake up. I needed to figure out what was going on with Aspen.

He crushed his lips to mine, devouring my mouth in a desperate kiss. "I'll do what I can to find them," he murmured, his voice muffled against my mouth before the dream-walk unraveled and our midnight field faded.

"Lucille." Sam sighed as I opened my eyes. "What have you done to yourself now?"

I rubbed my face, aggravated. It wasn't Sam's fault. The whole reason I came here was for him to check on me. I just wish he'd waited a little longer before waking me up. More importantly, I wished Aspen would—I didn't know—be more open and honest about what was going on with him. Wasn't that what a relationship was supposed to be like? Or love, for that matter? Unless this wasn't love. Unless—

"Lucille." Sam shook my shoulder. "Are you okay?"

I dropped my hands and sat up, pushing away my thoughts. "Yeah, I'm fine. I just have a concussion from running."

Sam shook his head, ripping the yellow amulet from around his neck. "Let me guess. Instead of going to one of the many healers here, the general demanded you seek me out—again."

I raised a brow but nodded.

He pinched the bridge of his nose, holding his amulet in front of my face. "I'm an elite healer, Lucille. Concussion, muscle aches, and frozen toes are for the grunts without yellow or white amulets."

"I was just doing what I was told."

Sam's lips tightened as he wrapped a fist around the crystal. With his other hand, he pressed gently on my forehead.

Scalding heat shot through my skull, and I yelped, squirming beneath the intensity before it cooled into a soothing, steady warmth. Energy surged through my veins, chasing away the fog from my brain and the ache in my muscles.

I perked up, feeling refreshed and brand new. "Thanks," I said, swinging my legs off the bed.

But Sam didn't move. I glanced up, finding him frowning.

"What's wrong?"

His eyes narrowed as he studied me. "Your energy levels were as low as a human's."

"I gather that's bad?"

He quirked a brow, placing the amulet back over his head. "Humans don't have enough energy to sustain angelic powers."

I didn't understand, and my face must've shown my confusion.

"Yes, Lucille, that's bad. Your energy dropped dangerously low. If you'd tried using your powers before I healed you, you could've died."

"Oh."

"Oh?" He scoffed. "Your body needs breaks and rest. If you're training physically, then don't train magically, and vice versa. It puts too much strain on your energy. Also, if you feel even the slightest bit lightheaded, you stop what you're doing and rest. Don't push yourself to run ten miles if you can't."

"You do know I'm training with the Tormentors, right?"

Sam grabbed my shoulder. "Yes. And still, I'm hoping you heed my expert advice. Understand?"

I understood that what he was saying was impossible, but sure. "Yep."

He pinched his nose, then shooed me with his hand. "Go. I have other patients to heal."

I walked out of the healers' wing with a skip in my step, feeling more energized than I had in days. It was wonderful. So wonderful, I figured it'd be a great time to run. I had a goal to reach.

The sun hovered behind the winter-burdened evergreens, painting the landscape in pastel pinks and blues. Cold gusts stung my face, forcing me to shield my eyes as I ran. I wasn't having half the fun Rune was having as she chomped on the drifting snow beside me. Her shadow fur swirled around her body, dancing with merriment. She really was made for Hell. And although I was the daughter of it, I felt no connection to the icy land or its inhabitants.

Sam's healing did a number on me. At the halfway mark, still feeling energized, I ran a few blocks into Hoar Hollow with Rune following. The icy buildings glistened in the torchlight lining the cobbled road. Very few souls, either dead or blood-banded, strolled the streets or flew in the air. Only one sleigh with a Hellcat rested at the curb. The couple of souls we passed seemed pretty tame and unthreatening, if I ignored the scars marring their faces.

We turned at the end of the block and sprinted back, passing the same set of strangers. The winding road stretched ahead, flanked by darkening woods and looming trees. As our footsteps crunched in the snow, a quicker set ran behind us.

I shot a glance over my shoulder, noticing someone in a Hell Squadron uniform, their face too difficult to make out.

I picked up speed, determined to prove I could finish this ten-mile run without getting lapped. My breath came in shallow gasps as my legs ate up the distance. Four more miles to go, and the energy Sam gave me was giving way to my inadequate strength.

Another glance. And a curse slipped past my lips.

It was Ni, and she was gaining on me.

Putting on an extra burst of speed, I managed to keep distance between us, but at the cost of my burning lungs. I wanted so badly to finish a warm-up run at the same speed as my squadmates. I was so close.

Come on!

The sound of her footsteps grew louder, the air shifting with her speed. She was closing in. I looked over my shoulder one more time—and she was gone.

What the hell? Did she lusceler?

Before I could process what had happened, a wall of fire erupted between me and Rune, and I was slammed into the icy ground, the world spinning. Pain radiated through my back as I hit the snow, and the last thing I saw was Ni's fist, flying toward my face.

Then, darkness.

Searing pain sparked in my hand, and I jerked awake, crying out. Ni straddled my chest, pressing me into the rough ground while my head and the palm she carved into dangled over a cliff.

"What are you doing?" I yelled, straining to throw her off and pull my hand back.

She leaned onto my wrist, halting my movement. The cliff edge dug into my skin, straining my joints as Ni sliced another line into my palm.

"Ni, stop!" I smashed my fist into the side of her head, gasping when her knife dug deeper. I did it again, cringing. I didn't want to hurt her. I liked Ichi—and by default, her twin—but I didn't know what she was trying to do to me.

She ignored my punches and words, continuing her painful carving. I squirmed, arched my hips, tried to wrap my legs around her head, but nothing worked. My Glory prickled beneath the surface, gaining strength with each failed attempt.

I tried to close my hand, cringing from the sting and pool of blood dripping off my skin.

Ni twisted her head, baring razor-sharp teeth and revealing black veins crawling up her neck.

My stomach dropped.

The Doors of Moirai hadn't show me her past. They'd shown me her *future*.

But how had she transitioned so fast? Yesterday, she had no markings or razor teeth. And what was she turning into?

"Get off!" I screamed, kneeing her in the back. Thousands of needles pricked my skin, my Glory climbing in its painful ascent.

Ni slammed the butt of her knife into my temple, twisting my head to the side with the force of the blow and stopping my fight. A black lake with flecks of white blinked in and out of my vision. It looked like the night sky on Earth—but in a bottomless pit, as if the bowels of Hell had swallowed the stars.

Another stab brought me out of my throbbing daze, sending a line of excruciating pain up my arm. I shrieked as my Glory shoved through my body.

Ni noticed the change in my eyes before I erupted and burned away my clothing—and reacted like the warrior she was.

My white flames collided with her red ones, sending her flying. She landed on her back with a loud thump, but quickly got to her feet. I mirrored her, standing on shaky legs.

"I don't want to hurt you, Ni."

Nor could I unless she came closer. I didn't have control of my Glory. I had no idea how to make a fireball like Aspen. I was naked, standing on the edge of a cliff with blood dripping down my arm, pleading to Ni with my palms raised in surrender.

She tilted her head and smiled, sending goosebumps down my spine. Half her body was illuminated by a glowing blue forest on her left, while shadows from the evergreen forest on her right left her in darkness. Her empty eyes flared with red flame, taunting me.

What was wrong with her?

She fisted her hands in front of her and created two long, red fire whips.

"Ni," I begged, taking a hesitant step forward. "You don't want to do this."

She struck, the line of fire racing toward my stomach. I dove to the ground, stone scraping against my arms and chest, and my Glory scorched the area. Her fire cracked just inches from my head. Before I could gather my breath, she lifted her hand and flung her whip down. I rolled, feeling the spray of rock. She did the same to my other side, forcing me to roll back, then roll again, closer to the edge.

I stood before she forced me off the cliff and jumped over her whip just in time—only to be slammed in the side. I teetered on the edge, my heel pushing off loose bits of rock. My stomach plummeted as I stared at the drop. It was steep enough to steal my life, and there was a line of jagged rocks below.

Swallowing, I regained my balance and lurched forward, taking another fiery hit. My Glory protected me from the flames, but it still felt like a fierce punch.

"Ni, please!"

Maybe I could just wait this out. Maybe she'd tire of me.

My naïve thoughts were quickly extinguished by repeated attacks and dodges. But her whips didn't just slam into me; they tore into the ground around me, chipping away at the stone as if she wanted me to fall into the lake.

But if she wanted to kill me, why not do it when I was unconscious?

I flung up an arm and protected my neck from her attack. Our fires battled each other, but my Glory had the upper hand, shielding me and forcing her red flames back. Encouraged, I took a step forward, fighting her whips. Every inch I gained, she increased the ferocity of her attacks. Holding the foot I'd gained away from the cliff, I absorbed her strikes, thinking *I could do this. I could hold out until the General got here.* He'd know something was wrong once he connected with Rune, *as long as she was okay.* But even then, he would know. I just needed to hold out for a little longer. *I could do this.*

Then I felt the pooling sand in my legs.

My Glory was draining me.

The edge of the cliff shrank.

I didn't have time.

CHAPTER 24

Ronen

I walked to my shower, shucking off my Dark Seraphim uniform, which I'd received from Heaven. Stepping into the shower, I sighed—grateful, for once, for the frigid water.

The door to my bathing chamber squeaked open. "Did you want some company?"

I stiffened at her sultry voice, glaring at the black marble dripping with water, refusing to turn around. "No, Moira. I'm almost done, and I need to see the king."

She padded closer and pressed her warm, naked body against my back. "Too late."

My shadows revolted, pulling at their tight leash, demanding I throw her off.

I turned off the shower, stepped out of her arms, and snatched a towel, wrapping it around my hips.

"Ronen." She grabbed at the soft fabric.

"What part of *no* did you not understand?" I threw an extra towel at her. "Get out."

She pouted, letting it hang loosely in her hand, her wet body on display like she thought it would tempt me. Unfortunately for her, she lost that power the moment the hellion entered my life, and our intimacy had suffered for it. I'd been dragging my feet in ending this, not wanting to face the fallout.

I figured if I didn't seek her out, she'd get the hint. We were never dating, only fucking. I should've known she'd want more. They always wanted more, and I could never give it to them then, let alone now.

"Moira, this isn't happening anymore," I said, pointing a finger between us.

She dropped her towel and walked into my space, her breasts brushing against my chest. "You say that now, but I guarantee I'll be seeing you soon."

"No."

Moira circled her nipples as she backpedaled to the bathroom door, opening it. "Yes," she said, smirking as she left.

I huffed, shaking my head. When did Moira start having such issues with listening? She'd always been bold and stubborn, but lately, it seemed excessive. So much so, I questioned her position as a leader.

But Moira's behavior could wait. I had more pressing matters to attend to.

I changed into a sweater and slacks, then left my rooms to meet Lucifer in his chambers. We had the Damned to discuss.

At his door, I waited until the knob thawed, allowing me entrance.

His seating area had different chairs, and a smaller desk had replaced the larger one I was familiar with. "You redecorated."

Lucifer stood in front of the black-and-red marble fireplace, holding a crystal tumbler half-filled with amber liquor by his side, staring into the massive flames. "Happens when your powers continue to lash out and destroy your furniture." He sighed. "They may have severed our cordistella bond, but it's almost like the effects haven't let me." He said it so quietly, I wasn't sure the words were meant for me.

I wanted to ask about the effects. I only knew the basics of a cordistella bond. But if he knew his daughter was the other half of my soul, our relationship—and my safety here—could be jeopardized. I wouldn't risk that.

Hell hid me from Etan and the council, along with a very powerful rune I had Lucifer hide among my tattoos. He carved it into my skin every year to obscure any specific details of me from the minds of any soul or blood-banded that left Hell. Unless the council traveled to the very dimension they despised, they'd never know where I was. They'd never control me again.

"No change?" I asked, walking over to his well-stocked bar and pouring myself a drink.

"No," he stated, still staring into the fire. "Saraqael is still attempting to survive off my daughter's energy."

My shadows lashed out inside me. *Saraqael wasn't the threat—Michael was,* I reminded them. But that didn't stop the urge to chain the hellion to her bed every time she pushed herself to unhealthy levels.

I stepped up beside him, noticing the wrinkles in his suit and his mussed hair. "Do you think she'd let go if she knew what she was doing to Lucille?"

Lucifer slowly turned his head, eyeing me like I'd just threatened him. "I won't let her."

I didn't know what that meant, but I could see the fierce protection in his gaze. "And what about Lucille? You want her to train, but her energy levels are always fluctuating."

"Cato and I have it handled. We're implementing a solution tomorrow morning. But I didn't ask you down here to talk about my bonded or daughter." Lucifer ran a hand through his hair, turned, and sank into a red leather chair next to me. "The Damned."

I took a sip of my bourbon, forcing my questions about his *solution* down with the burn of alcohol.

"The Damned remind me of Lilith's demons, except hers have never been able to spread an infection."

"I agree." He paused, twisting the band around his ring finger that bound Lilith to him. "Let's say it is her. She's been stealing angels and stripping their powers, replacing the ones the council took. She's the only one we know of who has been able to create demons." He sat forward, deep in thought. "But she isn't an angel. She can't carve runes, and these Damned had runes on them from their creator."

"How do you know they're from their creator?"

"Because the second mark on Silas's back was a symbol, not a rune. A calling card, of sorts. A Seraphim by the name of Bran from the original council used to carve his mark into demons' backs before he killed them. This was the same. The scrolling symbols were initials—L.M."

"Maybe she teamed up with an angel," I suggested, wondering who would want to be part of her ploys—and why.

"Maybe."

"But if that's the case, why would Lilith need a calling card if she's behind this? Wouldn't she assume we already suspect her?" I settled into a chair opposite him, heat from the fire brushing the side of my face.

He shook his head. "Unless she's gloating. Souls are required to go through me before they're allowed in the Redemption Circle, just as they are with the other circle lords. Her creations are bypassing us and infiltrating our circle when we can't even determine a way out."

I ran my hand along the lip of my tumbler. "We've patrolled every part of our circle and haven't found a portal, a runed doorway, or a hole in the ground—nothing."

It was the same old song and dance. Any Damned we found would rather bite off their tongue or sing their song than speak. Torture didn't work, seeing as most had come from the worst agony of their lives. Even my Soul Swords didn't work. They had no fear.

"Then start searching homes. I'll put out a mandatory order. And bring in the next infected."

I nodded. We fell into silence, both lost in our thoughts. Eventually, mine drifted back to *her* and Rune walking to the healers. I couldn't help but replay the scene, remembering the melody that had come from her lips as she taunted me, knocking the breath from my lungs. Seven Hells, *that sound.* And that *joy* that had eased the constant stress lurking in the lines of her forehead. They were fucking seared into my brain, forever branding me. And I hated it—how it made me feel, the flutter that had responded in my chest. Even more, I hated how I was thinking about it again. But my shadows didn't. They devoured it like a starved Soulhound with fresh flesh.

An uncomfortable sensation thankfully pulled me from the useless memory. I rubbed at my sternum, wondering if my shadows were throwing a fit at my thoughts. The sensation tugged harder, making me grimace. Suspicious, I lowered my mental barrier to Rune, and her emotions tore into me. Without a thought, I connected with her senses, and the glass in my hand shattered.

Lucille was at the edge of a cliff, fighting—bloody and naked—against Ni. She was a pillar of white flame, consumed by her Glory as she fought off vicious red fire whips. They lashed out, attempting to wrap around her neck but were extinguished on contact.

Get to her! I bellowed at Rune.

She picked up speed. The glowing trees of the Eternal Forest and the dark evergreens of Verdant Forest lined up on either side of her— a runway of shadow and light to the fiery battle at the cliff's edge.

"Bloodhound?" Lucifer placed a hand on my shoulder.

I ripped myself away from Rune's senses, and Lucifer came into view in front of me.

"Your daughter is being attacked at Portal Lake," I snapped, then stormed out. He called after me, but I ignored him. He threw up a wall of ice in my path that I shattered with my shadows.

I had one destination, and nothing was going to stop me.

He wanted me to keep her alive.

This was me keeping her alive.

I luscelered to the nearest roof, manifested my wings, and flew like the Horde of Hell was at my back. Lowering my barriers to the hellion, I let her emotions flow through me, but they were muted. Even her pain, I could barely feel.

I didn't understand, and my throat tightened.

Did she know about the bond?

Was she blocking me?

I didn't like not knowing. I didn't like the nerves that vibrated beneath my skin, insisting I fly faster. I didn't like that the bond was somehow muted, and I wasn't controlling it. Even after not wanting it, even after the ways the bond had already pushed me to certain actions, the mere thought of its absence shot a fierce dread into my stomach, forcing my shadows to the surface of my hands. They tightened around my palms, begging me to hurry, my worry eating me alive.

Another sensation ripped at my chest, and I dropped in flight, battling the sudden, unexplainable pain. For a second, I thought I was finally feeling the hellion, but her emotions seemed even more muted.

I put on a burst of speed and reconnected to Rune. She'd reached the line of trees before the large open area leading to the cliff. Growling, she lowered her head and lunged for Ni's body. A wall of fire burst from the ground, and she slammed her nose into the blistering heat, yelping.

Opening my essence to her, I let her pull from my shadows. She used them to suffocate Ni's flame enough to breach her wall, only to have a fiery whip come lashing toward her face. Before it landed, a wall of Glory erupted as a shield, stopping Ni's attack.

And then I felt a sharper pain in my chest, like someone had stabbed me. The hellion's emotions were nothing but a whisper in my mind.

Look at Lucille! I demanded.

Rune turned her head to the cliff's edge. Lucille swayed on her feet, dropping to her knees, her eyes fluttering like they couldn't stay open. She glanced behind her and back to Ni, then down to the ground, frowning at something.

Put Ni down, I ordered Rune, snapping out of our connection just as I cleared the tree line, and Ni slammed a line of fire next to Lucille.

The cliff edge crumbled beneath her, and she plummeted.

My shadows dove for her, racing with a desperation that matched my own. Her unconscious body careened toward the starry black lake, and time seemed to stretch as I watched her fall. My shadows caught her moments before she hit the water, curling around her fragile frame like a protective cloak.

I swept her into my arms, holding her tight to my thundering heart, each beat too fast, too hard.

Her fading warmth intensified the painful tug—and it hit me. This wasn't the first time I'd felt a pull from the bond. It was just the first time it had brought me pain. I usually kept our bond blocked.

Like when she collapsed after her run and Rune brought her to the infirmary. At the time, I didn't think anything of the pull. But if I had let my barriers down, I guarantee I would've felt a similar agonizing warning.

It was Divine Wasting. She had overused her powers, pushing her body and soul to their limits.

My shadows darted into her nose, frantic to find any way to help as we raced toward Sam. I couldn't heal, but I could stimulate or suppress parts of her brain. That didn't mean I could wake her from unconsciousness or ease the agony tearing through my chest.

"You do not get to leave me before I've had a chance to know you." I brushed her wavy hair back with a shaky hand, needing to see her face. "Do you hear me, Hellion? Please, open your eyes."

I touched different neurons, sending energy to them, hoping it'd do something. Her toes twitched. Her fist squeezed in her lap. But nothing helped. Nothing stopped the weakening of our bond as she faded.

I had witnessed plenty of death, most of it caused by my own unwilling hands, bound to the will of a power-hungry angel. One drop of blood from my victims allowed me to rip into their minds. Two drops paralyzed them. Three could shut down parts of their brains. The more blood I had, the more I could strip them of everything they were. I watched them die. I watched my best friend die. Each death left a mark—a wound carved deep into my soul and onto my back.

But never, until this moment, had I felt the agony of half my soul dying.

It didn't compare.

Nothing ever would.

Just hours ago, she'd been laughing, filling my chest with that fucking flutter, making me question the bitterness I'd carried toward her. Now, she was taking with her a part of me I hadn't even known I needed.

"Be a pain in my ass, Hellion. Give me a reason to be irritated," I whispered, clutching her close as I tried to steady my breath. "Just open your eyes. We're not finished."

Suddenly, her fist burst with a bright yellow light, cutting through the shadows that covered her like clothing.

And then I felt them.

The throb of pain in her hand. The scrapes on her body. The ache in her face and feet. I felt her exhaustion. Her soul, a little more energized. But more than anything, the sharp, suffocating rip in my chest faded.

I closed my eyes, drawing in a deep, shuddering breath, then dropped my forehead to hers, feeling her warmth slowly return.

"Seven Hells." I inhaled the sweet scent of winter berries, the familiar fragrance grounding me as it steadied the chaos in my heart and calmed the shadows within me.

I didn't lose control. I didn't dive into emotional fits of rage. I didn't worry beyond clear thought. My power and position didn't allow for that. I had painstakingly built a wall between my emotions and thoughts so I would never be ruled by my them again.

But that wall was crumbling—and it was all because of her.

Once we arrived at the healers' wing, I shouted for Sam, only wanting the best to care for her.

He snapped his head up from a half-hidden bed, handing off items to another healer before rushing down the line of cots and privacy curtains.

"Let me see, General," Sam demanded, searching through my shadows.

I pulled them back—but kept them covering her private areas—listing off the events, her injuries, and ending with the yellow light in her fist.

Sam unclenched her hand and pulled out a small translucent crystal, visibly relaxing. "I gave her my energy to use if she ever needed a boost."

"Thank you," I said, the words tasting unfamiliar on my tongue. "It saved her life."

He nodded, then extended his arms to take her from me. I hesitated, overcome by a surge of irrational fear.

His gaze softened. "Let me do my job, Ronen. Or the little energy keeping her alive will have been for nothing."

Reluctantly, I released her, every muscle in my body protesting as I followed Sam into a private room at the back of the large hall. He laid her on a bed with care, his pendant glowing faintly as he pressed his hand over her heart. A stream of yellow light shot into her body, causing her to arch and her mouth to open in a silent scream.

I turned away and tuned into Rune instead, tightening my hold on my shadows before they did something stupid.

Rune walked beside Lucifer, her attention fixed on Ni, who was restrained in ice, her hisses muffled as Alexei and MJ dragged her toward a cell in the dungeons.

"Get General Ronen down here, and find out the state of Lucille," Lucifer snapped to Alexei and MJ, standing in front of the thick black bars. "This demon will answer for her crimes after we bleed the truth from her."

Demon?

I frowned, nudging Rune closer to the scene, and finally saw the black veins crawling up Ni's neck.

She had turned.

CHAPTER 25

Lucille

I blinked open my eyes to a ceiling of angels with brilliant white wings standing on fluffy clouds, surrounding a star of glowing light. I tensed. This wasn't my room. But the longer I stared at their serene faces, as if the light alleviated all their stresses and pains, the more I relaxed.

Crystals dangled in the window, scattering rainbows across the stone floor and bed. I smiled, feeling at peace in this healing room. Then I glanced to my other side and stiffened.

The general slouched in a chair, sleeping right next to me.

I squeezed my eyes shut, then opened them again—he was still there. His head rested in his hand, the tattoo of the Greek word *truth* peeking out from under the sleeve of his black sweater. The soft, sculpted planes of his face held me captive. This wasn't the version of the general I knew.

He twitched in his sleep, and I smiled. How many people had seen General Ronen so unguarded, with soft rays of light hitting his cheeks? He wasn't in uniform, nor did he have his swords. Not even Rune was here. It was just him, vulnerable and at ease. Something fluttered in my chest as I took in this rare, gentle sight. He looked almost young. Approachable. Unthreatening.

I held back a snort. *As if.* Maybe in his sleep, if I ignored the dark tattoos spiraling down his neck, expanding across his muscular torso, and forgot all our previous interactions—the cold, unimpressed looks, the doubts he voiced about me—then *maybe* I could almost believe there was a tender male beneath that lethal, unfeeling shell.

I panned down to his wrinkled slacks and large leather shoes. *Hmm...* I honestly thought they'd be bigger. I snorted, covering my mouth to muffle the sound, and traveled back up his sculpted body, pausing on the dark spots staining his sweater, then met piercing gold eyes.

My smile dried up.

General Ronen straightened, the softness melting from his features. *There* was the general I knew.

We stared at each other in silence. My heart picked up speed under his unrelenting gaze. He didn't blink. He didn't move. But his nostrils flared, and the muscle in his jaw ticked. My palms turned clammy, and I didn't want to be the one to break the silence. Like I didn't want to be the one who always broke eye contact. But I couldn't handle the anxiety thrumming through my body. He was too intense.

"Is that blood?" I asked, pointing at his sweater.

"Yes," he growled, standing to his full height.

I shifted in bed, sitting up straighter. "Mine." I assumed.

His eyes flashed black, and he nodded, narrowing his gaze to my hand with Ni's cuts. He glared at the healed scars like they were a personal affront.

"Do you know what this is?" I asked, analyzing the sharp angles and details etched into my palm.

He brought his heated glare back to my face, the muscle in his jaw pounding. Every line in his body pulled taut, like he was seconds away from exploding. My fingers twitched on the bedspread, wanting to shield myself from the wrath I knew was coming.

"Has something happened to your tongue, General?"

His hands splayed at his sides like he was physically restraining himself from choking me. His glare turned downright murderous.

I swallowed my nerves and looked away. "Have I done something to upset you?"

His hand shot out and gripped my chin, forcing me to meet his pitch-black eyes. I wrapped my sweaty palm around his wrist, tugging against his grip.

"Did I hurt Rune or Ni?"

I didn't think I had. I'd tried to protect both. But why else would he look like he wanted to kill me?

He shook his head.

"They're both alive, then?"

His chest heaved, his shadows snaking around his hand and brushing every inch of my face. The touch was silky. Affectionate. The opposite of his tight hold and unforgiving attention.

"What's wrong?" I asked, a little more bite in my words now.

"What's wrong?" he whispered, his voice a vicious, soft snap. "What about the fact I told you not to push your limits? What about the fact that you shielded Rune and left no energy for yourself? What about the *fucking* fact I had to catch your unconscious body while it plummeted off the cliff!" His voice rose with each word. "You almost *died*!" He released me and turned, pacing in front of the bed.

"Rune needed—"

"Rune would've been wounded, but she would've survived. *You* almost didn't!" He turned back to me, the wooden footboard creaking beneath his punishing grip. "Seven Hells, Lucille."

I startled at my name. He never used it.

He straightened, crossing his arms. "I don't know whether you lack skill, intelligence, or any sense of self-preservation."

My face flushed at his accusation. "I was protecting myself and Rune."

"Except you weren't. If Rune hadn't signaled me, you would've either died from Divine Wasting or drowned in Portal Lake."

I turned away, my cheeks burning with shame, hiding behind the veil of my hair. He was right. I'd pushed myself too hard. With Rune, yes—I couldn't bear seeing her hurt—but the rest had been instinct and fear. I hadn't wanted to burn Ni with my Glory, so I'd shielded instead. But that was where my strategy ended, and the weight of my power caught up to me.

"I didn't know what else to do," I whispered, eyes fixed on the open book on the end table beside the chair.

"So we'll train until you do."

I frowned. "We'll?"

"Yes. You got your wish. I'll meet you at your rooms tomorrow evening." With that, he turned and left.

I sat frozen, dumbfounded by his change in tune. And that was when Lucifer walked in.

"Lucille, you're awake."

I nodded, still trying to process the words—or more accurately, the tirade—I'd just endured.

"I assume the general briefed you on your additional power training sessions?" Lucifer asked, clasping his hands behind his back as he looked down at me with narrowed eyes.

"Yes."

"Good. From what the general and healer reported, you need them." The disapproval in his tone was unmistakable.

I clenched my jaw and dropped my gaze to his shiny red shoes. I didn't need another lecture.

"How are you feeling?" His voice softened slightly, but there was still a sharp edge to it.

"Fine." Nothing hurt, and I was sure Sam had replenished my energy once again.

"I'm sure those two days of rest did you well."

Two days?

"Did anyone visit me?"

Lucifer gave me a curious look. "The general and I came by a few times."

I sighed, feeling a slight tug in my chest. But I nodded, accepting his answer even though it stung.

Lucifer sank into the chair beside me, reached across the space, and took my hand. He flipped my palm over, aligning it with his own to reveal a mark etched into his skin—one that almost mirrored mine.

I glanced up at him in surprise. "What are they?"

"After all your reading and our conversations, what can you tell me?"

He was testing me now?

I refrained from rolling my eyes and thought back.

The only time Lucifer had mentioned cutting his hand was when describing the process of opening the gates or using Portal Lake. I'd assumed he meant a quick slice. But now, seeing his palm, I realized it was far more intricate. The lines carved into his skin were a mixture of old and new scars, some faded, others still raw. A pattern emerged—strikingly similar to mine—woven into the red of his recent wounds.

Portal Lake bridged the circles. To travel to a specific one, he'd need a way to connect with it.

"They're sigils," I said. "They guide your travel to the circle of your choosing."

"Yes. My most recent sigil represents Earth. Yours represents the Immolation Circle."

I snapped my head up. "Why would Ni try to send me there?"

Lucifer's jaw tightened as he dropped my hand. "That's what the general is working on now."

"But why would she even think it would work?" I pressed, my mind spinning.

Unless Ni knew how Portal Lake worked—and she knew I was Lucifer's daughter. But for that, someone would've had to tell her.

Lucifer's stern expression told me he already suspected who that might be.

"I haven't told anyone!" I protested.

"Someone did," he replied, sitting back and crossing his arms. "Perhaps your Nephilim friend?"

I shook my head. "No." Oliver would *never* do something so reckless. He knew the stakes. Still... he had a tendency to run his mouth when he wanted, and he *did* enjoy gossip. He could've let something slip while training with Ni. "I don't think so," I muttered, less certain now.

Lucifer stood, the rings of his irises glowing. "Well, you better find out who else he spoke to, or a maimed palm will be the least of our problems."

He left without another word, and I collapsed back onto the bed in frustration.

A few moments later, Sam walked in. He started scolding me again, but his was different. Less angry. More concerned. He handed me another small crystal.

"Why only one?" I asked, eyeing my saving grace.

"Because," Sam said with a shrug, "it's a fragment of a dead Virtue's pendant. They're rare and difficult to come by."

Angels didn't die of old age. That meant this crystal had come from someone who'd been killed. Possibly someone close to Sam.

I swallowed, feeling the weight of the unspoken loss. "Thank you," I murmured.

He gave me a small smile, followed by another scolding, then released me on the condition that I'd take better care of myself.

I sighed and picked up the book on the end table, reading the cover. I recognized the title.

I smiled.

So he did visit me.

CHAPTER 26

Lucille

I searched high and low for Oliver. I checked my rooms, his, the arena, the library, random hallways, rooms I didn't even know existed, the kitchens—then I did it all over again. Hours passed as I combed through the entire castle, and it wasn't until my second round of searching that I found him.

There he was, sitting on the counter of the pastry kitchen, legs dangling and casually munching on a lemon bar, powdered sugar all over his navy sweater.

No one else stood in the pastry kitchen, but chopping and sizzling echoed from the other side of the wall, the main kitchen preparing whatever dinner we were about to have tonight.

I narrowed my eyes at his knowing grin. He didn't even look up in surprise, like he'd been expecting me. "You knew I was looking for you."

"Yep," he replied, unbothered.

"You've been toying with me."

His grin widened. "Seems I can shadow against you if I concentrate."

I grabbed a spatula and chucked it at his head. "I've been searching for *hours*!"

Oliver dodged. The spatula crashed into a line of hanging pans with a loud clatter. He shrugged. "Wanted to see how badly you wanted to find me."

Dorus, the head cook, whipped her head around the corner of the pastry hall. "You mess up my kitchens, and I'll make you scrub every dish by hand until your fingers bleed."

"Sorry, Dorus," we both chimed in unison, sheepish expressions on our faces.

I shook my head at Oliver once she left. "You're impossible."

Oliver took the last bite of his lemon bar, popping his fingers into his mouth to lick off the sugar. "Pot," he said, gesturing to himself. "Meet kettle." He waved his hands dramatically toward me.

I rolled my eyes and crossed my arms. He was right. Lately, I'd been just as impossible to deal with. That was actually what I came here to talk to him about—not just that, but to apologize again.

"I'm truly sorry for what I said about your sister, Oliver."

His legs stopped swinging, and he gazed down at the stone. "Don't. You're right. I have been struggling to find Melanie. You'd think in ninety-five years I'd have more than just a king's deal to help with that, *whenever he can*," he said, rubbing the rune still inked into his wrist.

How did he admit that so easily? The thought of saying *he was right* put a bad taste in my mouth.

Oliver dropped off the counter, facing me with a sudden seriousness that made me swallow hard. The playful, easygoing version of him flipped, catching me off guard. "But I don't want your apology for *what* you said. I want it for *why* you said it. You wanted to hurt me because you didn't like the truth I made you face." He raised an eyebrow. "Right?"

I scowled.

"And now," he continued, "after almost dying from Divine Wasting and getting yelled at by the general, your father, and Sam—yeah, I was there the entire time, yeah, I shadowed and eavesdropped on those conversations," he said, noticing my confusion but barreling on, "you're thinking maybe your best friend *knew* what he was talking about. And now you're coming to me with your tail tucked between your legs, fighting the words, '*You're right, Oliver,*'" he finished in an exaggerated, high-pitched voice.

I gritted my teeth. "Okay, fine. But if I say it, I want an apology for leaving me high and dry on the hill."

Guilt tugged at his lips. "I'm sorry I didn't help you up the hill or take you to the healers, but I wanted you to see the error of your ways." Oliver shook his head, walking toward me and pulling me into a tight hug. "I just want the best for you," he said softly. "As a best friend should."

I gave a small, relieved laugh, nodding against his sweater. But the more I thought about that run and my training, the more somber my thoughts became. "I don't know how to stop, Oli. It's like this obsessive need. Like if I don't do *everything* in my power to be stronger than everyone else, Aspen will die. With Ni, it was more about not knowing how to use my Glory effectively, and my mother draining me. But the rest... it's this constant urgency I can't shake. I thought it would ease knowing the general would train me, but it hasn't."

He pulled back. "I've felt that way before too, Luce. You need to find a way to manage it. I'll help, and I'm sure the general will too. Just don't bite our heads off when we do."

"So you forgive me?"

Oliver snorted. "Yeah, and you didn't even have to say '*I'm right*'. You should feel so special."

I smacked his arm, rolling my eyes.

He glanced down at my attire, his grin returning. "You *do* know you're still wearing pajamas, right?"

"I wanted to find you more than I wanted to change. *You* should feel so special," I teased back.

Oliver smirked, throwing his arm around my shoulders as he guided me deeper into the pastry kitchen. "Well, now that we're best friends again, I think it's only fair I show you all of Dorus's chocolate truffles that she makes just for *you*."

I gave him a suspicious side-eye. "*Me?*"

"Yep. Dorus can sense a person's favorite foods, least favorites, and even allergies. As long as you're within range—meaning anyone in this castle—she's got you figured out."

I eyed the remnants of powdered sugar on his sweater. "Lemon bars?"

Oliver's eyes twinkled. "Now you know my weakness."

"I'll make sure to use it for evil. Don't worry."

He gave me a playful hip bump, making me laugh. I popped a truffle into my mouth, feeling the familiar warmth settle in as everything finally felt back to normal between us.

On our way out, we swiped a tray full of chocolates and lemon bars, snickering like master thieves, fully aware they were meant for us—well, at least *some* of them.

Once back in my rooms, I changed into sweats and curled up with Oliver in my sitting area. We recapped the past few days, catching each other up. It wasn't until I finished my side of the story of what happened with Ni that I remembered my father's accusation.

Dread pooled in my gut, and I worried my lip. "Oli," I said, taking his hand. "I promise I won't be mad, but... did you let something slip to Ni about who I am?"

Horror swept across his face, draining the color from it. "Not exactly."

"What did you say?" I exclaimed.

"I hardly told Ni anything! I just mentioned having a friend who's high up in the world, and I *might* have glanced your way, but it's not like I blurted out, 'Hey, Lucille is Lucifer's daughter.'"

I heaved a sigh and flopped back. "You might as well have," I said. "Think about it. We got into the Tormentors because of the king. They know that. They also know that *never* happens, and the general sure doesn't show us any favoritism. And here we are, living in the castle. It doesn't take a genius to put your words and the signs together and come to the right conclusion."

Versus the wrong one, where they thought I was having sex with my father. I shuddered.

"I'm so sorry, Lucy," he said, sounding as if I'd gutted him. "I didn't think—I—"

"It's okay. It's not like she was trying to kill me. She just wanted to send me to the Immolation Circle and have me burned alive for eternity," I said with a laugh.

"That's not funny."

I shrugged. "Maybe not. But she failed. And Lucifer wanted to know if we needed to worry about anyone else."

"Ni and I weren't near anyone when we had the conversation, and she can't exactly talk, so I think it's safe to say no."

Relief washed over me as I settled deeper into the cushions, turning my palm this way and that. "It wasn't a bad guess on her part, though. Honestly, I wished it would've worked... well, until I ended up portaling to a circle of Hell."

Oliver, still looking a little shaken, nodded. "Yeah, that would've made things a lot easier."

We sat in a comfortable silence, the warmth from the fire a soothing presence.

"Why'd you use your Glory on Ni and not your Infernus?"

"Because I woke up to a knife slicing me open. Fear was my first instinct."

Oliver nodded, his expression softening with understanding. "Michael."

"Yeah. And I've never actually trained with my Glory."

He patted my leg. "Well, that's about to change tomorrow. Better get some rest for our long day ahead."

I raised an eyebrow. "I didn't know you were invited."

"You bet your ass I am. The general just doesn't know it yet."

I snorted. "I'll bring the popcorn."

Oliver scoffed and shoved a pillow in my face before dashing off to our room. I laughed and scrambled after him, hurling decorative pillows in his direction.

CHAPTER 27

Lucille

I sat on the heated bench in the greenhouse, nibbling on a roll as I waited for Lucifer. He was late, which left me to wonder about Ni.

"Daughter," Lucifer greeted moments later, taking his place next to me and pulling me from my thoughts. His eyes were bloodshot, his hair stuck up in disarray, and he had bags beneath his eyes like he hadn't slept in weeks. The only part of him put together was his immaculate white suit.

What happened between yesterday and this morning to make him look like that?

I slowly chewed and swallowed the rest of my roll. "Father," I said, testing the word. It didn't exactly make me cringe, but neither did it feel natural coming out of my mouth.

"How has your morning been?" he asked, although by his emotionless tone, I wasn't sure if he was curious or just going through the motions.

"Fine. Oliver and I are close to completing the ten-mile run."

He grunted, as if unimpressed.

I gritted my teeth, not sure if I was more frustrated with him or myself. "And yours?"

"Fine."

He sure *looked* fine. But I didn't comment.

"Today—"

"Did the general find a bite mark on Ni's right shoulder?" I interrupted.

Lucifer peered at me, questions in his narrowed eyes. "Yes."

"So the black veins are some sort of demon infection."

He turned in his seat, fully facing me. "How do you know the infection was from a demon?"

"I don't. But the Doors of Moirai showed me an image of a male with white hair and horns sinking his teeth into what I assume was Ni's neck. He looked pretty demon-like."

His forehead creased faintly. "The Doors of Moirai showed you that?"

I nodded.

"They showed you, but not me?" His lips pressed into a thin line.

"Is that bad?"

"It's—" He paused. "Unnatural. We're connected. They should only respond to me. Their mosaic images are their secondary power. They show me important scenes that will have an impact on the future."

"Maybe because I'm your daughter?"

He didn't look convinced, but I had no other explanation.

"So the doors were warning me about Ni."

"Not just Ni. The white-haired male who infected her will play a part in the future, if he hasn't already. You didn't see his face?"

"His hair covered most of it."

Lucifer tapped his fingers against his lips, staring unseeing at the frozen flowers.

"But if he is a demon, how is he here?"

Lucifer considered me. He knew something—or at least had a theory. But would he tell me? Another moment passed.

"We think one of Lilith's new creations has somehow infiltrated the Seven Circles and is spreading this demon infection."

Lilith?

I sat back, staring out the frosted glass windows.

"But why? If Lilith is behind this, why would she want me in the Immolation Circle if she thinks I'm the key to her cage?" Something wasn't adding up. If I were burning up in Hell, that wouldn't help her. If she wanted me dead, I'm sure she would've put that command in Aspen's Hell Rune.

"That's why she wanted you?"

"You didn't know that?" I thought he had eyes and ears everywhere.

His expression tightened. I'd kept my snark in check, so I knew it wasn't my tone that irritated him—more likely, it resulted from the fact that I had questioned him.

Lucifer held up his hand, showing me a black ring on his finger. "This is what locks her in the Tenebrous Kingdom—a binding ring. As long as I remain in my lands, she is a prisoner to hers."

If that bound Lilith to her lands, then why did she see me as the key to her cage?

"It looks like a wedding ring."

"Yes. It's a similar ceremony to what humans do when they wed. But with some tweaking and powerful runes, it can bind two people and control their movements. After our battle with Lilith and her demons, this is what the council decided to do."

"You couldn't kill her?"

Lucifer had been a Seraphim, after all, and they made up the council—the most powerful angels.

The temperature dropped, my breath coming out in white puffs.

"Do *not* question me or the past when you have not lived through it," he said, a dangerous edge to his tone.

"Fine," I muttered, dropping it. "But if that ring is what keeps her caged, then why isn't she after that?"

"It's possible she is. Only, it can't be forced from my finger." He pulled on the dull black metal, and it didn't budge.

"How does it come off, then?"

"My blood and death," he replied, a haughty challenge ringing in his voice.

"Does she know that?"

"Regardless of whether she knows or not, it'll never happen."

"But say she did—and she created the demon infection—why wouldn't she use me as leverage against you to get the ring? How does killing me do anything?"

His silence served as my answer. After another minute, I realized he wasn't about to admit he didn't know. I sighed. Maybe Aspen would.

"Have you ever considered she's the one behind Hell's lockdown?" I asked. "Maybe she's using Hell as leverage and is waiting for you to realize that to strike up a deal."

Lucifer raised a brow. "I see you're improving on your studies."

I lowered my chin, hiding my smile.

"But you're missing the finer details to make that theory work."

Of course I was. "What details?"

"Why would Lilith seal Hell for the first four years without any correspondence or gloating? It's only leverage if we *know*. And if she sought to hold power over us, she would never open Hell."

He had a point.

"I do not want to discuss this any longer. It's time for your lesson."

A cool presence entered my mind.

"I'm disappointed to find your shields are not already up, daughter. Have I not instructed you to hold them daily?"

I gritted my teeth and swarmed my mind with flames, his presence receding for a moment. Then a blast of ice shredded my efforts.

He grunted. "That's tolerable. Now, I'm going to create a hallucination, and I want you to twist the events without me knowing."

"How do I do that without you knowing, if it's your hallucination?"

"Listen to the whispers of your Infernus. They will tell you."

"The whispers of my Infernus are random sounds." They told me nothing.

"What did I say about doubting yourself?" His cold presence expanded, twisting the colorful, icy greenhouse into... nothing.

It stayed the same.

"Are we starting?" But he was looking over my shoulder, ignoring me.

The door to the greenhouse squeaked, pulling my attention to the general in his full armor, dual swords strapped to his back.

"Lucifer, we need you in the dungeons. We found another infected." He walked down the path to stand in front of us.

Lucifer nodded, rising to his feet. "We'll have to pick this up later, Lucille. In the meantime, I'll have the general step in, and you can attempt to hold your shield against him."

General Ronen straightened. "And the infected?"

"I will question them first. You can join me in a half hour," Lucifer said, raising his chin and walking out without another word.

"I guess our training starts now," I mumbled, having nothing else to say.

He sighed, removing his swords and leaning them against the bench as he sat. "I guess so."

I pulled at the flames of my Infernus, surrounding my mind, feeling a sudden cold before warmth replaced it. I glanced at the general. "Was that you?"

He reclined back, throwing his arms along the back of the bench, his hand brushing my ponytail. "Was what me?"

I frowned. "Did you enter my mind?"

"No, Lucille," he said, tugging playfully on my hair. "When I enter you, you'll know." His tone sounded serious, but his hand traveled to my neck and grazed down across my shoulder.

My stomach did weird things, fluttering and twisting in equal degrees. Swallowing, I leaned away. "What are you doing?"

He moved in, curling his hand into my hair, and tilted my head back. His lips were inches away from mine, his warm breath fanning across my face. "What do you want me to do, Princess?"

The fluttering in my stomach died. Something wasn't right. The word *princess* coming out of his mouth sounded wrong.

I stared into his golden irises, finding them dull and ordinary— no pull, no warmth. I inhaled, smelling nothing. The spicy balsam was absent. Even the distinctive winter smell of the greenhouse wasn't present.

This was Lucifer's hallucination—an odd choice to use the general in this way.

But now what? I figured out he was playing with my mind. How did I twist this?

I shut my eyes, acting as if the general's proximity moved me, and dove into my Infernus. Their icy hot tendrils coiled around me in welcome, whispering contradictory sounds. Out of all the noise, I picked up on the three I was familiar with. The rest, I didn't recognize.

How did I pull on the sound of the Hallucination Circle if I didn't know which one it was?

I was wasting time.

The general shifted closer, his nose grazing the line of my neck, startling me.

Focus, Lucy. The whispers.

Lucifer said to trust myself. To trust my Infernus.

Okay. I settled into the sounds, letting them swirl around my mind in a cacophony, mentally seeking the hallucination whisper.

The sound that came to me bounced and dived, grew in volume, then softened, almost like it couldn't make up its mind. Trusting my Infernus, I focused on the changing melody, wrapping it around myself. But what did I do next?

He wanted me to twist it so he wouldn't know. But this was his hallucination. I didn't understand how he wouldn't notice if I tampered with it, if I even *could*.

Unless I didn't. Or acted like I didn't.

Not knowing what I was doing, I sent an image to the melody of me in the general's arms, like I was. Then came the hard part— removing myself from the bench without my father seeing.

But maybe I was overthinking. This was a mental construct. None of it was physically real.

I pulled my consciousness from the illusion of myself and sank it into the shadows of the greenhouse. Physically, I sat there in the form of my doppelgänger, but mentally, I hid in the darkness of the illusion, watching Lucifer's scene unfold.

If I had a face in this incorporeal form, I would've frowned as the general pressed his lips to my doppelgänger.

Why was my father giving me this hallucination?

I shouldn't like the look of us together. I shouldn't want his lips on mine. And I didn't—I wanted Aspen's. But why didn't I stop the kiss? And why couldn't I rip my eyes away from the general cradling my head and devouring my mouth like he was?

Focus!

This wouldn't be a success until I entirely removed myself. I could do that with a shield, but my father would know. That must've been what the shock of cold was—Lucifer.

Could I follow his presence in my mind to his mind?

I felt around for his cold touch. It took me a few seconds, but eventually, once I pushed away the imagined warmth, he was there. I reached out a hand and grabbed hold of the cold. Then everything dissolved, and I was sitting next to my father.

"Close. But next time, touch my presence with your song, not your hand."

I nodded, feeling warmth from his *almost* praise. That was probably as close to a compliment as he'd get.

"Let's continue."

The next few hallucinations, fortunately, didn't include the fake general kissing me again. Unfortunately, I didn't manage to twist a single one without him knowing. It was a wonder that I almost succeeded the first time.

"You have to subtly remove yourself from the hallucination by continuing the actions I would expect from you using your illusioned self," he said, bringing me back to the here and now after another failed attempt. "The moment you do something out of character for the scene, I know. You must know your opponent's thoughts and expectations to trap them in their mind. That being said, crafting an illusion is more difficult than directing your power to an emotion and allowing your opponent to craft the illusion based on their subconscious."

I leaned my elbows on my knees and rested my pounding forehead in my hands. "And why didn't we start with the easy version first? You think I know your thoughts and expectations?"

"You did in the first hallucination," he said in a pointed tone.

I twisted my head to the side. "You think something's going on between me and the general?" But my question was redundant. Of course he did. That was why I was able to almost succeed on my first try. He expected us to kiss.

He raised a critical brow. "Is there?"

"Not at all. Why would you think that?"

Did he think I was lying? The general barely tolerated me, and I only had eyes for Aspen.

"Our lesson is concluded for the day," he said, standing. "How's your energy?"

"Good." My head might be pounding, but I didn't feel drained after using my Infernus. Odd, but nice.

He nodded, like he knew that'd be my answer, then walked toward the doors. "I'll see you tomorrow morning for our next lesson. Remember to continue shielding every day."

I groaned the moment he closed the doors behind him, dropping my head back into my hands.

The day was only beginning.

CHAPTER 28

Ronen

My Dreads and I trudged through the slush of Hoar Hollow and split up into pairs, knocking on residents' doors. We entered the homes of blood-banded and souls, searching through every room for a portal, a runed doorway, any kind of evidence to show us where the demons were coming from. The majority obliged without issue, but some put up a fight despite Lucifer's orders.

After the first line of homes, we regrouped, and all my Dreads reported the same thing—nothing.

I sighed. "Break up and continue searching. We'll meet back here in two hours."

My Dreads dispersed, leaving me with my second and third.

"Well, this would be a bust if that gorgeous female hadn't asked for a date," Alexei commented with a smirk.

"You know, Lex, with how much you get around, I'm surprised any ladies want to *date* you," MJ countered.

"Let's go. Today isn't over yet," I said, leading them out of the Upper City and toward the edge of the Lower City.

"Ronen." Alexei nodded ahead.

"I see it."

We stopped in front of an unremarkable corner house—same shingles, shutters, muted colors, snow-covered roof. Even the light post matched the ones lining the street behind us. But unlike the others, this one was lit.

It didn't seem significant—not at first. Hell's skies were always weary and gray, the sun hiding like it knew the sinful here didn't deserve its warmth. But in the Lower City, where souls outnumbered the blood-banded, lamplight was a luxury. They had to pay to keep them burning, and even then, it typically only lasted through the night.

I walked up the stone steps and knocked on the door.

No answer.

I knocked again, refraining from pounding in case I alerted them.

Nothing.

I tried the doorknob. Locked.

"MJ," I said, nodding her over.

She slid next to me, grabbing the knob. Red and orange flames swarmed her hand, heating the metal. Slowly, after a few minutes, the knob melted, oozing down the wood and letting us in. I eased the door open, staring into a long, dim hallway. I silently signaled them to assume formation, search, and follow. Alexei positioned himself at my back, and MJ almost entered first, but I gripped her shoulder, forcing her behind me.

We crept past an empty living room and down a hallway of closed doors. A sickly, rotten scent crawled into my nose and mouth. Death resided here. I turned around, motioning for them to stay alert. They nodded.

I sent out my shadows. They slithered through the door cracks and searched ahead for heat signatures. There were none on the first floor. I was about to send them upstairs when the smell became cloying.

Stopping, I surveyed the door to my left. The only thing out of place was the blood leaking beneath it. I motioned for MJ to open it, knowing nothing living was on the other side. She twisted the handle, and the door creaked as she pushed it. Decay shoved into my lungs, begging me to cover my nose, and we laid eyes on four dead blood-banded.

Each body showed different states of the demon infection. A couple had razor teeth, and one had horns. But what they all had in common were the black veins and chunks of skin sliding off their bodies in a slurry of red and black blood.

"Did the infection kill them?" Alexei whispered.

"Yes. Just like it did Bonny," I answered.

"So blood-banded don't survive the infection."

MJ wasn't asking a question. I nodded anyway, eyes still on the corpses. But why? What did souls have that blood-banded didn't?

Footsteps creaked overhead. We readied our weapons and followed my shadows upstairs. As we reached the landing, they registered a heat signature right as the humming began. That eerie song drifted through the corridor, leading us to the end of the hall.

We fanned out and burst through the door, surrounding an infected female. She sat patiently on a bed, meeting our eyes with an expectant, lipless smile. Hairless, with black veins threading through burns that likely extended beneath her thick dress, she was clearly from the Immolation Circle—like the rest we'd found.

Her humming paused, and she tilted her head, never dropping her smile. "Did you find my mess?"

"Yes," I replied, leveling a Soul Sword at her neck.

"Pity my followers didn't survive." She frowned, then perked up again. "But we have others."

"Where? And who's *we*? Lilith?" I demanded.

She tilted her head the other way, revealing an oozing soul wound that sliced up her neck and head. "Maybe. Maybe not, Ronen."

My shadows attacked the black gunk, and I braced to ingest the disgusting substance.

"You'll find nothing in my mind. Haven't you been listening to us, General? We were prepared for you."

"Who?"

She hummed her song, swaying on the bed in answer.

"What do you want?" Alexei snapped.

She paused. "We seek the depths of torture and the heights of light, and all the lies between." Her perky grin changed, and a taunting evil curled her lip. "But we'll start with Lucille first."

My grip tightened on my Soul Swords.

"Why do you want Lucille?" I demanded.

The female stuck out her tongue and chomped through it. The small, black muscle dropped to the floor, and she smiled with ichor coating her razor teeth.

She was done answering questions—and I was done holding back the cold rage tightening my body. I swung without hesitation, crossing my Soul Swords. The moment her head separated from her spinal column, her soul dissolved to ash and sifted into my blades to live in torment forever.

"Lucille? The recruit who was placed with the Tormentors? Why would they want her?" MJ asked. "Because she's servicing the king?"

"Watch your words," I warned.

"Strategically, it's a good plan."

I didn't know whether Alexei meant gaining the king's favor through sex or using Lucille to get to the king, but I had a feeling it was the latter.

"You're saying the rumors aren't true? You would know," MJ said, fishing for information.

I wiped my blades on the white coverlet, clenching my jaw. Of course everyone thought the hellion fucked the king to obtain her place. They even whispered rumors about us—only they made sure to do it behind my back. If I caught the words coming from their mouths, I'd consider taking their lives, or just demoting them to the Bowels. But I never corrected Alexei or MJ's assumptions, knowing that if I did, there would be more questions.

I left the room without a word, descended the stairs, and entered the room of death and gore. I wish I could have MJ burn them to recycle, but we didn't know enough about the demon infection. We couldn't risk that they'd recycle as a demon soul, or something worse.

After sliding my swords against their necks, I had MJ scorch the floor, burning away the blood.

We met up with the rest of my Dreads. Xavier and Alessandro reported interrogating an infected before killing it, but they gathered no intel.

I nodded. "Continue searching and report back to MJ."

They dipped their heads and left.

"And what will you and Alexei be doing?" MJ inquired, crossing her arms.

Alexei raised a brow, as curious as MJ.

Lucille would need extra protection. And if Ni's attack hadn't proved that, this Damned sure did.

I summoned my wings and nodded at Alexei. "We're training the hellion."

CHAPTER 29

Lucille

Oliver and I ran another nine miles straight with no breaks, but it still wasn't good enough. We would still end up in the showers with water pelting our bodies tomorrow. We were their daily drug to curb their addiction to inflict pain. At least we no longer ran with wet hair. Moira had Ni dry us off before each run, but today she had to have Ichi pull the water out, since Ni wasn't there.

We paired off, and Ichi led me to the archcry station.

She handed me a bow with a shaky hand, keeping her eyes on the ground, saying nothing. Then she did the same with the arrow, stepping away and turning toward the target. I stared at her, taking in her oily hair and the bags beneath her flushed cheeks.

I opened my mouth, then shut it.

Sighing, I notched the arrow, pulled the drawstring back to the corner of my lip, and released. It flew over the target and clipped the stone wall.

"Shit," I muttered, taking another arrow from Ichi without looking, accidentally touching her hand.

She jerked back and bowed low, the end of her long hair resting in the dirt. "I'm so sorry."

My brows knitted together when she didn't come up from her bow. "Ichi?" I touched her shoulder, and she flinched.

This wasn't the place to bow and shake. I surveyed the arena—most of the warriors were busy training, but some were exchanging words and glances.

"It was dishonorable," she whispered.

This wasn't about accidentally touching my hand. But she couldn't do this here.

I latched onto her shoulders and lifted her. She kept her chin down.

"I don't blame you or your sister for what happened," I murmured.

Still, she kept her gaze lowered. "I didn't report the bite. I reported that Ni was attacked and asked for a day off to care for her. I told the general she was fine but needed rest, and he never questioned me." She paused, taking a shuddering breath. "But I didn't report the bite and lied. That is dishonorable."

"You were protecting your sister. Is that not honorable?"

Ichi shook her head. "Not if it's at the cost of your tamashii."

"Tamashii?"

"Soul," she said, finally meeting my gaze with her one good eye. "Tamashii is sacred in our culture. To let it be corrupted is more than shameful. It dishonors your whole bloodline." Her lip wobbled, and her eye turned glossy.

I stepped toward her to pull her in for a hug, and a clattering sword reminded me where I was.

"Your sister didn't corrupt me. And I would never associate either of you with the word dishonorable." I stepped back and brought up my bow. "It was the infection. It wasn't her fault."

I released the arrow. It hit the outside ring of the target.

Ichi handed me another one, going through the motions. "It doesn't matter what you think. The stain is on our souls. We can only hope laying our swords down at your feet will be enough to ease the stain so we can cycle to the great resting place when it's our time."

I jerked, my arrow flying wide and grazing the target next to mine. "What? No. That's not necessary."

She stayed silent and held out an arrow. After a moment, I notched it, drew back, and let go. But right as the drawstring twanged, Ichi luscelered and whipped her hand up directly in the path of the arrow, impaling herself.

"What the Heavenly Hell?" I shouted, dropping my bow and rushing over to her.

Her face creased with lines as she pulled it out, the feather fletching scraping through the hole in her hand. "A soul wound will remind me every day about our debt."

"Why?" I gaped at the exposed muscle and lack of blood.

"My sister marked you. It's only fair that you mark me."

"I didn't want to mark you!"

Ichi dragged the arrow through the dirt, rubbing off the remains of her hand before giving it back. "Our debt has now been sealed. Let's continue with your practice."

"What? No—"

"I have made much of a scene," she interrupted, gazing around at the warriors who were staring at us with confusion—but not concern. The only person in the entire arena who witnessed what happened and looked remotely concerned was Oliver. "And I have said all that needs to be said. The debt has been made and sealed. It's done. Now, ready your bow and keep both eyes open as you aim."

It took me a second to bring my mouth up off the floor, unlike Ichi, who held out an arrow with her wounded hand, waiting patiently for me.

Maybe Ichi was crazy. Who impaled themselves on an arrow to seal a debt?

I brought up my bow, having no words.

She watched and critiqued every arrow I shot. All her attention was on coaching me, with minimal eye contact. When we changed stations, it continued, only joining in when she needed to instruct or when it was a two-person lesson, like hand-to-hand.

At the end of training, she escorted me and Oliver to the doors leading into the castle.

"Things will be different tomorrow. See you then," she said cryptically, bowing low before leaving.

Oliver and I walked into the hall, the heavy doors closing behind us.

His eyebrows shot into his bangs. "Fuck-a-duck, what was that today?"

"Penance, I guess," I replied, rubbing my forehead. "Today wasn't what I expected."

Oliver snorted and flung an arm over my shoulder as we walked down the window-lined hall. "Wait, you didn't expect Ichi to impale herself on your arrow? Really? I expected a five-act drama with a sword to the gut and some rain for atmospheric effect."

I shoved him away. "I hope training with the general won't be as... well, whatever that was."

"Insane, bizarre, psychotic, some twisted twin shit. I'd probably start with those descriptors."

"Yeah."

"Don't worry, I bet we'll have a splendid time," he said as we approached our door, the sarcasm thick in his voice.

I groaned and walked into our rooms, then abruptly stopped.

General Ronen and Rune were in our sitting area.

"You really don't know proper etiquette when it comes to people's rooms, do you?" I said, noticing two Hell Squadron uniforms lying on the settee.

Oliver perked up. "Is one of those for me?"

I glanced at the general, confused. "But we haven't earned them."

"I'm the General of Hell. I get to determine who receives one and who doesn't. Plus, these will regulate your temperature so you don't have to worry about the cold, and the material serves as a conduit for power, allowing it to flow freely without the risk of deterioration."

"You had me at cold," Oliver declared, striding over to grab his uniform.

I hesitated.

"Do you not want it?" the general asked.

"I wanted to earn it." We were finishing week four of the Infernal Sixty, and I had only slightly improved. My angelic blood helped to accelerate the process of gaining muscle and endurance, but not to the caliber of our squad. This almost seemed like a slap in the face with how easily he just gave them to us. I'd been training hard to build myself up and knew I still had a way to go.

He walked over and leveled me with his gaze. "We're going to be training outdoors, and I don't want to have to worry about regulating your temperature or constantly seeing you naked."

Something glimmered in that golden gaze at the end of his words, but I didn't look too far into it. He made good points.

"Okay."

"Both of you get changed. Rune and I will meet you outside."

"Oliver's coming with?"

"He wants to rank too, doesn't he?"

There was something knowing in his tone that I didn't understand, like his words had a double meaning of some kind.

"I thought you said we wouldn't rank."

He lowered his head inches from my face. "I did. And I still believe it. But for me, this is less about you ranking and more about you learning how to delegate your energy, so you don't do something foolish like *die*." Shadows danced in his irises. "This way you'll have a friend through your failures, and you'll learn control."

I gave him a tight smile, holding back the urge to snap back. He wasn't exactly wrong, and he had a lot of proof to back up his doubts. But it was still a bitter pill to swallow. Somehow, some way, I would show him not to doubt me.

He straightened, and I swore a smug smile twitched on his face. It threatened to unglue my tongue from the top of my mouth. When he finally left us to change, I closed my eyes and heaved a breath.

"Oh, this is going to be fun." Oliver rubbed his hands together in glee.

"It's going to be something, alright."

We changed into the body-hugging uniform and met the general and Rune outside our doors. His face darkened as he gave me a once-over. Not Oliver—just me. His unwavering attention forced me to glance down at the stiff leather.

"Is it okay?"

"It'll do," he said, barking at Rune and turning.

He led us through a back stairwell and to a door hidden in a wall. The general snapped and pointed. Rune descended obediently, her claws clicking against the stone steps.

"Where is she going?" I asked.

"A different way."

"A different way to where?"

He pressed a hand against a specific stone, opening the door.

"You'll find out."

A blast of cold air hit my body. Immediately, my uniform heated, taking away the chill; even the gloves and boots that came with it warmed. The only part of me left unprotected to Hell's icy chill was my face.

"Yeah, buddy, I could get used to this," Oliver said, striding out the door with a giant grin.

We walked out onto a roof where Alexei stood with dappled white wings.

I followed the spotted ends, nearly brushing the snow, to the tips that projected a couple feet above his head. I never realized how large angel wings were, but it made sense if they had to carry all that mus—

Strong arms scooped me up, and we launched skyward.

I flung my arms around his neck, pressing my body against him.

"What are you doing?"

"We were on a roof with no way down. What do you think I'm doing, Hellion?"

"We can't get to wherever we're going a different way?" I protested, my palms slick in my gloves.

"This is your first lesson on delegation. We could lusceler, but that'd burn too much energy. We could walk, but that'd take too long. So we'll fly."

We hovered high above the roof. His magnificent black wings flapped as my stomach flipped. Loose strands of my hair whipped in the wind created by his wings, and my feet dangled over open air. The tops of the snowy evergreens were hundreds of feet away. Souls and blood-banded stood as dark specks against the white snow.

I pressed close to the general's body as I continued to stare at the ground, wondering why I was doing this to myself.

He chuckled, and I whipped around, thinking he was mocking me.

"Yo—"

The retort died in my mouth. He wasn't laughing at me. He wasn't even looking at me. He was staring down at where I presumed Alexei and Oliver were. But I didn't follow his line of sight. My curiosity vanished the moment I saw the creases near his eyes and the joy lining his mouth. In the healers' wing, watching him sleep had done strange things to my heart, but here, seeing his laughter transform the planes of his face, *stopped* my heart. I had never seen him smile. And damn me to Hell, but I loved the sight—and I shouldn't.

I turned away, feeling a heaviness overtake the fluttering, and finally looked at what caught the general's attention.

Alexei held Oliver as they launched into the sky next to us, keeping as much space between them as he could, like he was a bag of stinky garbage. Oliver, on the other hand, beamed up at Alexei, completely ignoring the open air beneath him.

"Nephilim, wipe that smile off your face," Alexei said, scowling.

Oliver didn't.

"Ronen, tell him to stop looking at me like that."

The general's chest vibrated, but he pursed his lips, keeping the smile off his face but not out of his eyes. "Why would I, when it clearly annoys you so much?"

Alexei turned to eye the general, his expression screaming *you'll pay for this later.* "Where are we going?"

"Follow me and find out."

The general beat his wings and pushed us through the air. At first, it was alright, until he dove. I screamed. My Glory surged, stabbing at my skin, and I tightened my arms around his neck, practically strangling him. He laughed, that stunning, playful smile of his returning and distracting me for a second. Suddenly, we banked hard upward, missing the tree tops by feet, and leveled out.

"That wasn't funny!" I gasped.

He shrugged. "I thought it was. I quite liked your scream."

Just like that, my Glory quieted, and my Infernus whispered in my ear. I coated my finger in purple flames and poked his cheek, hoping to frost a little bit of it. But my purple flames did nothing to him.

He seemed just as surprised as I was.

"Are you in my mind? Are you controlling my power?" He better not be, but nothing else could explain why my powers weren't working. Lucifer said I'd have enough energy for the day.

"Second lesson—only use your powers when necessary, especially in the state you're in."

I opened my mouth.

"Retaliating for scaring you is not *necessary*, Hellion. Save your energy."

"Fine. But stay out of my mind, please." See, I even said *please*. I could be nice even when he was being an irritating menace.

A few minutes later, the general landed, spraying up snow. It tinked against large, clear icicles jutting two feet from the ground. They spread across a large clearing in various widths, their sharp points reflecting the low sunlight—a crystal sea of deadly weapons.

The general let me down, and Alexei landed with Oliver. Rune ran out of the dark forest behind them a second later, her fur whipping around as her tongue lolled out happily.

I smiled, and she dashed over to me and the general, her shadow tail curling as she weaved around us before sitting down right in the center.

I scratched behind her ear, then looked up just as Alexei unceremoniously dumped Oliver on the ground and strode over to us. I stifled a laugh at the open-mouthed outrage on Oliver's face.

"A simple *no* would've sufficed," he called out.

Alexei ignored him and beelined for the general, his wings disappearing like they were never there. "The Shard Field, Ronen?" He looked to either side of him, then back at the forest of black, spindly trees. "I don't see the king anywhere, so should I expect to become pulverized male-meat soon?"

The general crossed his arms. "We don't need the king."

"Right, because you can scare off Veil Forest's wind and prevent a Shard Storm from taking us out. Sorry, I must've missed your coronation," Alexei remarked, exaggerating a bow.

"We don't need the king because we have Lucille."

My brows shot up. "Me?"

"Her? The innocent Nephilim who can't handle her alcohol, let alone a ten-mile run?" He flashed me an apologetic smile. "No offense, beautiful."

I glared back at him. "Offense taken."

Oliver snorted, brushing off his bottom and joining our circle.

"Don't get me wrong. You're improving. But that doesn't change the fact that only the King of Hell can prevent Shard Storms. He holds the power over the Glaciation Circle."

"So does his daughter." He gestured toward me. "Lucille."

I shot the general a look that said, *What the hell?*

"Bullshit." Alexei glanced between me, the general, and Oliver, acting like he was waiting for the punchline.

The general side-eyed me and nodded toward Alexei. "Show him."

"Lucifer—"

"Wants you to have extra protection. Alexei's my second and trustworthy."

"Yeah, Luce, show him what you got. Encase him in ice," Oliver urged, rubbing his ass.

I shook my head but sank into my Infernus, plucking the cord of ice. The whisper came, then the itches, and a second later, purple flame swallowed my hand. Slowly, an icicle the size of a carrot formed in the center of the flames. It took little effort.

"Happy?" I asked them, showing off the icicle.

"No," Oliver grumbled.

Alexei's eyes sparkled, his grin widening while he gazed at my hand. "I'm more than intrigued, beautiful."

Oliver crossed his arms and shook his head to the sky.

"Stop being salty, Nephilim. I'm sure there are plenty of other males who'd want you to join in on their *playtime*. I'm sorry I don't like dick." Alexei plucked the icicle from my hand and tossed it at Oliver. "But if you're so lonely..."

Oliver glared at Alexei as it hit his chest and plopped onto the snowy ground.

"It's the size, isn't it? Maybe our beautiful princess can make you a bigger one."

The general and I shared a confused glance, clearly missing some conversation they'd had earlier.

"Or maybe you could get over the performance issues you talked about and try it out. You know what they say—it's not the size of the dagger, it's the way you wield it," Oliver said with furrowed brows and a slight frown, nodding toward Alexei's groin.

The general snorted.

Alexei's face flushed. "Trust me, Nephilim. There is no issue with its size or my performance." He returned his attention to me, a flirty smile dancing on his lips. "Lucille, beautiful, would you give me the honor of proving the Nephilim wrong tonight?"

I quirked a brow. "Oh, so now you know I'm the Princess of Hell, you want me in your bed?"

Alexei tilted his head. "No. I wanted you in my bed the moment I saw you. I'm just going to try harder now, is all."

Rune growled and forced herself between us, pushing Alexei back. He lost his flirty smile and analyzed the general with a shrewdness I didn't understand.

The general stared back, leveling a severe gaze at his second.

"So this is why you involved yourself with Theon and their fight?" Alexei asked, but he made it sound like he'd already made the assumption.

I peered up at the general. His eyes flashed black before settling, his expression hard and unreadable.

"The king wants her trained, not dead."

"Of course not," Alexei agreed, but suspicion lurked beneath the depths of his sharp smile. "Well, if we don't have to worry about a Shard Storm, then let's get to training. I call dibs on being Lucy's partner."

"Sorry, but Lucy has already been dibbed, heartthrob hustler," Oliver said, slinging his arm over my shoulder.

Alexei groaned. "Please never call me that again."

"It's nicer than what I call you," the general offered.

"Yes, but you're not after this." Alexei gestured to himself. "I'd rather the Nephilim insult me."

Oliver shrugged. "If that's your kink, I can do that too."

Alexei threw his hands up. I caught Oliver attempting to hold back his smile and was glad he found a way to brush off Alexei's taunting refusals.

"We're training as a group," the general said, bringing us back to why we were here. "But first, we all need to understand what each of us is capable of. Alexei, you start."

Alexei grinned, his blue irises flashing with blue and silver flame as he held up his hand, tiny bolts of light zinging between his fingers. Then he tilted his head to the sky, and a cool breeze ruffled his golden hair before dancing in my waves. Oliver and the general didn't receive the gentle wind. Instead, rain drizzled onto their heads. Both of them glowered.

"You're a Sky Power." I laughed.

He nodded with a grin, ceasing the rain and wind. "One of three."

"There's only three Sky Powers?" Oliver asked.

"Yep. Would've been two, but the Ethereal Military banished me before I could kill my superior."

"So you didn't end up here because of a debt with Lucifer?" I questioned.

Alexei shrugged. "I ended up here for multiple reasons. But that's a story for another time."

"Nephilim?" the general inquired, putting us back on track.

"You know, you can just call me Oliver. I'm assuming these training sessions aren't going to be a one-time deal, and I really don't want you to call me *Nephilim* every other second."

"Fine, Oliver. What can you do?" Both he and Alexei leaned in closer.

Oliver ran a hand through his hair. "I sense and control fear. It's always there, and I can sense the signature from a distance."

That was how he knew Marcus was in those woods when he first found me, and how he knew those Powers were gaining on us. It was like a tracking beacon.

"That's the easy part of my power," Oliver continued. "That, and shadowing. It's like an invisibility cloak. The worst part of my power, and the one that takes the most energy, is my ability to make you relive your worst fears by the touch of my hand. If I'm not touching you, I can still make you witness lesser fears. But I have to witness them with you."

Alexei whistled, and Ronen raised his brows, both impressed and both taking a step back.

Two high-ranking military warriors were afraid of Oliver's touch. I smiled and hip-bumped him, proud of my friend.

"That's a high-level power for a Nephilim," the general said.

Oliver nodded. "Yeah, my father is an Archangel."

"Really? Which one?" Alexei asked.

"Gabriel."

The general's face paled, and Alexei shot him a concerned glance.

"Do you two know him?" I asked, feeling a strange urge to comfort the general.

"We did. Once. But that was a long time ago. I hardly remember him anymore," Alexei said nonchalantly, then changed the subject.

"What about you? Miss Princess of Hell."

I glanced at the three of them.

Alexei eagerly waited for my response. Oliver pursed his lips in a frown, looking half-distracted as he stared at the side of the general's face. And the general... His gaze was distant, and his hands were fisted so tightly they were shaking.

He'd known Oliver's father.

But Oliver didn't press the general for answers. I remember him saying something about his deadbeat dad, with whom he had no relationship, so maybe he didn't care to know. If he didn't press, then neither would I.

However, I couldn't stand to see the general so caught up in his mind.

"General," I said.

He didn't respond.

I grabbed his gloved fist. "Ronen."

He jerked to face me, his throat bobbing. I wanted to ask him if he was okay, but I wasn't sure how he'd respond to that. Instead, I squeezed his fist a second time, staring at him as I said, "I have the powers of the Seven Circles of Hell, and the Glory of an Archangel."

It had the desired effect of distracting him—distracting them all.

"No, you don't," Alexei said, shaking his head at the same time Oliver chimed in, "You never told me that!"

I released the general's fist, but after I did, something shifted in his gaze, and he nodded at me. I gave him a small smile and turned to the others.

"When Lucifer was created as the King of Hell, lords were created with him." Although I wasn't sure how. The books never stated the ceremony Lucifer went through, or where the lords came from, or what they were. "He had to give away his power to the lords so they could reign efficiently in their circles. But he was able to keep the power of the two he had the largest affinity for, having enough for both him and the other two lords. I haven't given away any of my powers and have already developed affinities for four out of the seven circles. It's safe to say, eventually, I'll develop them all."

"Holy fucking shit." Alexei gaped.

"I second that." Oliver nodded.

"She's almost as scary as you, Ronen."

"Is that so?"

CHAPTER 30

Lucille

Shadows shot out, covering the Shard Field, the creepy forest, and all the light. My stomach fluttered—not because I couldn't see in front of my face, but because of the immediate peace I found within the wispy darkness.

"They created me with the Weaver's Book to be a tool for torture."

I stilled. *They?* Who the hell were they?

"Their goal was simple—render the sinful useless. So they made me with the ability to knock someone unconscious with a shadowball. Clean. No blood. Just silence them."

His unnerving tone felt like a warning, meant to intimidate us. His chilling words should've made my skin crawl. I should've wanted to run as far and fast as I could out of his shadows. Yet, his voice wavered the slightest bit, as if haunted by the *they* who created him or by his powers. I felt no fear—only a tightening in my chest.

"But knocking the sinful unconscious wasn't enough," he whispered. "They demanded blood. Pain. Power. So they made me with shadows that could touch, maim, and bleed the body."

Someone grabbed hold of my chin, tilting it up. I stared into undulating darkness, searching for a spark of gold. I tried to grab his hand, feeling an urge to soothe his ghosts and ease the drop of bitterness in his voice. But he wasn't there, only his shadows were.

"They designed them to absorb blood, infiltrate minds, and drown them in the darkness I ruled." His voice slid through the air like a silk-wrapped blade—nowhere and everywhere at once. "So my victims felt the tampering of their minds as I shut off functions, burst blood vessels, and stopped their hearts."

"Only if their shield isn't strong enough," Alexei said gently, as if he, too, picked up on the general's nearly imperceptible shame.

"And they rarely are," he uttered quietly.

"Ro—" Alexei started.

"You've seen the extent of our powers. Now, we'll recreate the attack," the general interrupted, his voice all business. "Alexei will be Ni, and he will be attempting to get the hellion over the border of the Veil Forest. Hellion, your goal is to either escape Alexei or knock him out. Oliver can help you, but Rune will sit this one out."

I bit my lip, holding back the questions burning on my tongue. I wanted to know more about his past, but he likely didn't want to confide in me—nor would he welcome the consoling touch itching in my fingers. So I let it go.

"Am I only allowed to use my Glory?"

"Yes. That's what this training is about."

"And your shadows?" I asked.

"Me and my shadows stay as they are, easier to protect you from Alexei's lightning strikes," he explained. "And easier to remove feeling from Oliver's limbs when you misallocate your energy."

"Excuse me?" I narrowed my eyes. "Why punish Oliver instead of me?"

"Because I'm well aware you'd risk your life without thinking," he snapped. "This is an exercise in restraint, precision, and control. Understood?"

A shadow-hand tilted my chin up, lacking warmth and the rough texture of the general's glove. I glared up into the wisps. "Understood."

Warm breath tickled my cheek near my ear, spicy balsam hitting my nose.

"Good," he whispered, his lips brushing my skin and the heat of his body warming my back. "Because you're not fucking replaceable." He stayed there a moment longer than necessary, his angry words hanging in the air.

My stomach fluttered at his nearness, only to be replaced by crushing guilt. I shouldn't be affected by his scent or love the vehemence of his words. I shouldn't want to press my back flush against his or feel the need to console him with my touch. I was just a job to him. His words didn't mean he cared about me. He was right— I wasn't replaceable. As the first and only Princess of Hell, he needed to keep me alive for my father. And just because he stood close didn't mean he was drawn to me—craving my scent like I craved his. He most likely wanted to intimidate me. My frivolous attraction to him was shameful. Aspen was my priority.

I stepped away from the general, straightening my spine.

"Alexei!" he shouted. "Let's begin."

A flash of lightning split the sky. I latched onto Oliver's arm, yanking him toward the Shard Field. The plan? I didn't have one. I needed one.

"Do you have a plan?" I asked, bumping into the wall of icicles.

"I could try to touch him."

"If you can catch me," Alexei taunted from nearby.

Shit.

I dragged Oliver farther down the icy wall, cringing with each crunching footstep. A flash of lightning briefly lit our surroundings. Trees bordered the edge up ahead—cover. If we could make it there, we'd have more obstacles to hide behind.

"Beautiful, you do realize I'm taunting you, right?" Alexei called from our left, lighting up the sky. "I can hear your footsteps. I can see you."

A bolt slammed into the path ahead, snow exploding into the air, proving his point. I gasped, freezing in place. Glory prickled beneath my skin—a good sign. I needed to use it. But if it surfaced, how could I stop Alexei without burning him alive? My heart pounded as I fought for a solution. But I didn't have one.

"Lusceler to the trees, Oli."

"You're going to do half my work for me? I could just kiss you." Alexei chuckled.

Another bolt crashed to my right, shattering ice. Shards sprayed our uniforms. Before I could react, another struck inches from my boots, hurling me into Oliver.

Through the ringing in my ears, I swore I heard a low grow—from wherever Rune was—but then jagged plasma ruptured the Shard Field again. Strike after strike hit, and Oliver flipped me over, shielding my body with his own. I stared at his bloodied face in horror, seeing all the nicks and cuts. I touched my own and found nothing.

The general was protecting me. But not Oliver. He was Rune in this scenario.

Would the general go so far as to let Oliver get struck by lightning? Or just ice?

It was one thing to agree to the general numbing a limb, but I didn't think... I guess that was it. I didn't think. The general needed blood to infiltrate Oliver's mind, so of course, he'd have to bleed somewhere.

"Roll over, Oliver," I said, flinching with each lightning strike. I tried to push him off, but he resisted. "Oliver!"

"I'm trying to protect you! Alexei is just ahead."

"I don't need protection!" I shouted, gesturing to his face. "You do!"

"Fine, I suppose I can't disagree there. But this exercise is about you getting taken. We only win if you don't."

"No. It's about using my Glory. But it's never surfaced on command, and I have no idea how to wield it without killing Alexei."

The general had miscalculated. He didn't realize that my skill level with Glory equated to a child's. Did shielding Rune against Ni give him the impression I had more control? Or was this how he normally trained his Dreads?

"Well, that's problematic. What if I scared you and—"

Time slowed.

A bolt cracked through the sky, zigzagging toward Oliver's back. My eyes widened. Needles pierced my skin. I didn't think.

I threw out my hands and screamed as my Glory shredded me apart. Blinding white flames arched around us, colliding with Alexei's lightning in a resounding boom that blasted apart every shard of ice within a ten-foot radius.

Oliver cringed from the heat, sinking closer to my body. I pushed my flames higher, expanding the sphere. Ice sizzled. My vision blurred. My arms trembled.

Sand weighed down my limbs, threatening to drag me under. I released my power, slumping into the muddy ground.

Oliver groaned and rolled off me. "That was almost as bad as the tree incident—except this time I felt like a slow-roasting squirrel."

"Sorry," I muttered, letting my head fall back. "But you're okay, right?"

"Just peachy."

The undulating darkness cleared, revealing the silver moonlight of Hell, the face of the general with Rune at his side, and Alexei's bloody face.

My stomach dropped. "I'm sorry."

He only grinned. "You knocked me on my ass, so I'd like to say you won, but..."

"You failed," the general stated coldly.

I stared him dead in the eye. "I will never let harm come to those I love. I will always put them before myself. I thought you gathered that after I protected Rune."

Alexei's grin fell. "Lucy, I would've never hurt Oliver. I was about to pull the bolt back."

I shot him a hard look, then turned back to the general. "How was I supposed to know how far you'd go? I understand you don't think I'm replaceable—but what about him? This is Hell. Suffer or die, right? And if you can't stand me—if it took you until today to stop calling him *Nephilim*, like he wasn't a person, like you didn't respect him—then why would I believe the General of Hell and his second gave a rat's ass about his life?"

My head pounded, my eyes ached to close, and I knew what I did wasn't safe. But Oliver was all I had.

Alexei looked down, unable to hold my accusing gaze. The general, on the other hand, continued to stare at me, but his anger shifted. He no longer looked at me with disapproval. Instead, it was like he was regarding me in a new light.

"I should've known that was how you'd train me—scaring me into action. Or maybe this session served only to see what I could do." My head flopped back, resigned. "But I don't know how to calm or wield my Glory when I'm scared," I admitted. And knowing it might help, I decided to give them another piece of myself.

"There are five tally marks on my back. They started when I was five. One slice for every time I accidentally used my Glory, knowing Michael was coming. His special gifts to me—for sensing something evil and disgusting in my power. He didn't know he was talking about my Infernus. The only one who knew was my mom.

"When I was ten, he bound my powers. Thirteen, when I broke out of my binding. And still, my mother lived in fear someone would find her miracle child if I used them."

A tear trailed down my cheek, but my arms were too tired to move. I couldn't even wipe it away.

Oliver took my hand and held it, which only made the ache harder to blink away. It wasn't reliving the past that caused my tears, it was just being so tired of all the shit I constantly had to go through. And knowing it wasn't over.

The general crouched next to me, pulled off his glove, and gently wiped my cheek. That didn't help either. If anything, it made it worse. Alexei kneeled in the mud and grabbed a handkerchief from a pocket, handing it to the general.

"Females cry a lot around me." He winked. "And it's clean, I swear."

I laughed, shooting him a grateful smile. Then Rune decided to help and licked a long line up my face. I grimaced, laughing harder.

I looked back up at the golden irises that kept flashing black, as if the general was unsettled by this entire conversation.

"General—"

"Ronen," he interrupted, brushing away my tears and Rune's slobber with the soft cloth.

"Ronen," I said. "I'm behind. I'd only just begun learning to control my Infernus in Elora, while my Glory remained blocked," I explained. "I need more than training that throws me into the deep end." I closed my eyes, hating to admit this aloud—to the two most skilled warriors in Hell, and to two people who had doubted me. "I need you to teach me the basics as much as the harder lessons."

Warm fingers brushed my cheek, and I opened my eyes to Ronen nodding, a solemn expression on his face.

"Okay," he whispered.

"That easy?"

Alexei squeezed my other hand. "We'll teach you the basics of your angelic power, beautiful. Your Infernus..." He trailed off.

"My father is helping me with that."

"Then it's settled," Ronen murmured, scooping me up into his arms. "And it's time we get you and Oliver to Sam."

I rested my head against his shoulder, catching one last glance of Alexei picking up Oliver.

"Thank you."

"No, Lucille. Thank you."

"For what?"

His beautiful black wings unfurled, and he launched us into the night sky.

"For existing."

CHAPTER 31

Lucille

Later that night, I couldn't fall asleep. I should've been trying to connect with my mom or Aspen, but Ronen's gentle touches and soft gaze kept taking over. The more I thought about it, the more I beat myself up for reimagining it. Over and over the thoughts circled until I slipped out of bed and padded to the library in my slippers and pajamas. If I couldn't sleep, I might as well do something to help Aspen.

I clenched my fists, standing in front of the library doors. I wanted to smack that sickening smile off Michael's face and rip him to pieces. My Infernus whispered in my ears, its familiar tune calling to my vengeful heart, begging me to pull at the black flames and seek him out. But I didn't dare touch the haunting melody.

What was the point of showing me an image of Michael holding a dagger and me exposing my back to him? Did the doors want to anger me?

Heavenly Hell, I didn't understand them. Or Cato, who refused to say a peep about my dream-walking powers. Lucifer couldn't even pull anything out of him—or so he claimed. Sometimes, I wasn't sure if I could trust his word.

I opened the doors and froze.

Ronen lounged in a chair near my mini library, a book in his hands. He wore dark sweatpants and a baggy sweater, and his usually styled fade was messy, brushing his forehead. I hadn't thought he could look any sexier. I bowed my head, feeling like I was betraying Aspen for even thinking that. I'd come here to get away from thoughts of Ronen, not run into him.

I took a step back.

"Rune's never been great at protection detail when she's sleeping."

Of course he noticed me. Sighing, I walked over to my table.

He glanced up, his gaze slowly roving over me. His lips twitched. "Is that your normal attire when you come to read?"

I internally cringed, remembering I'd come down in no bra, a silk camisole, and shorts, with fuzzy slippers warming my feet. "It is in the middle of the night, when I assume no one else will be here." I plopped into my chair out of habit. Unfortunately, one that was closer to Ronen than I liked.

He made a noncommittal noise and returned to his book.

That was it? That was the extent of our conversation?

"Do you need something, Hellion?"

I looked away, my cheeks flushing. "No."

I pulled a random book from my stack and opened it. A moment later, the library doors swung open. Dorus entered, carrying a tray with a steaming teapot and a slice of chocolate cake.

"You didn't tell me you had company tonight, Ronen," she chided, setting the tray on a small table beside his chair.

"It seems she found my hiding spot." The smile in his voice did regretful things to my heart.

"Maybe some company when you can't sleep would be a nice change for you?" A motherly smile tightened her crow's feet as she patted his shoulder. "I'll grab another cup and slice."

I waved a hand. "That's not necessary."

"The tea will help your racing mind, honey." She cut off my next protest and quickly strode to the doors. "I'll even add some chocolate truffles to your plate," she called back.

I sighed, knowing she had me there.

Ronen chuckled and sipped his tea. "Dorus isn't one to take no for an answer."

"Is this a nightly occurrence for you?" I gestured to the tea and library.

He lowered his steaming white cup, shadows sheathing his palms as he rested it in his lap. "Yes, when someone isn't passed out on her books."

I opened and closed my mouth, having no reply. Heavenly Hell, I hoped he hadn't seen me drool.

His lip twitched. "Helps settle my mind."

"Does it work?"

Seconds ticked by as I waited for his reply. Butterflies fluttered in my stomach under his silent attention. I shifted in my seat.

"Sometimes the Greek legends of Earth help." He nodded to the book on the arm of his chair. "But I'm beginning to see there are other things that prove more effective."

"Like your chocolate cake?" I teased.

"Among other things."

Heat touched my cheeks, and I glanced at his book, desperate for a new focus. "I always liked the legend of Jason and the Argonauts." I wasn't well-versed in Greek myths, but that was one of the stories my mom read to me as a child that I connected with.

"Really?" His brow quirked.

I realized then that I'd been going about earning Ronen's respect all wrong. Looking back on last night, opening up to him had changed the way he viewed me. He gave ground because I'd given him a piece of myself. I smiled. No, not just a piece—a truth. And while I wasn't ready to hand over all my truths, I could offer a few and hope that, in time, it'd be enough to win him over.

"Yeah," I whispered, my clammy hands fidgeting in my lap. "When my mom read me the story of Jason going off on dangerous adventures, building friendships, and seeking an item that could give them immense power and protection—what abused, isolated eight-year-old wouldn't connect to that?"

Ronen leaned forward and stilled my hands. He kept his head bowed, and I couldn't help myself. I inhaled a lungful of his intoxicating scent. My eyes fluttered and flew open when he grazed a finger along the scar peeking from my shorts. I shivered. It almost felt like it vibrated against my skin. He did the same to my other thigh.

"Our wounds shape who we are. They're our dark stories that either haunt or empower us." He looked up, gently taking my chin in his hand, drilling his gaze into my soul. His lips were close—too close.

Why was he looking at me like that? Where was the disdain? The disrespect? This reminded me of my father's illusion. Had he picked up on something I hadn't from Ronen?

Except the tip of Ronen's finger grazing up and down my thigh couldn't be imagined. Nor the heat pooling in my core. I didn't understand what was happening and hated myself for wanting to. I should pull away, scoot back, but I couldn't.

He placed his other hand over my heart, and I stopped breathing. His hand covered most of my chest. My nipples protruded, pressing against his touch. We stayed that way for a tense moment.

"Don't let him haunt you, Lucille," he whispered.

"I'm not."

"Then why do you let your fear control your Glory?"

I swallowed, having no answer. I couldn't think with him this close, touching me like this, drawing me in with his openness.

I lifted a shaky hand, intending to push him away. Instead, my thumb stroked the stubble of his cheek.

"Lucille?" His tone was a soft plea, barely audible, as if he feared disrupting whatever this was.

"I found some—Oh, dear me."

Ronen and I jerked apart.

Dorus stood near the doors, looking everywhere but at us, holding a plate filled with chocolate and another teacup. "Should I come back later?"

Ronen cleared his throat. "No, Dorus. Now is fine."

She nodded and walked over. She scooted my open book to the side, set down my cup and plate, then took Ronen's teapot and poured me a cup. "Cato would have my head if any one of his precious books got a crumb on it. Good thing he goes to bed early. But please do be careful, honey." Dorus patted me on the shoulder, gave me a wink, then left us to sit in awkward silence.

I ate a chocolate, sipping my tea in intervals while I stared unseeing at my book. I didn't know what the hell I was thinking. Why did I touch him? Why did I let him touch me? *Why did I like it?*

I gulped down the rest of the tangy tea, picked up my plate of chocolate, and stood. I needed to get away from him—and sleep. In that order.

He grabbed my wrist before I stepped past my chair, the heat of his touch branding me.

Hell, I didn't want to like it.

"Think about what I said. It'll be important for tomorrow."

"Okay." I kept my gaze fixed on the exit.

He held on for a breath longer before letting go.

CHAPTER 32

Lucille

I widened my stance and palmed a dagger. My mom mirrored me, our footsteps crunching in the snow as we circled each other. The full moon, tinted purple from my dream-walking power, shone a spotlight on our front yard.

She brushed my hand, sending a concentrated dose of love to influence me, but it stopped short, hitting the flaming barrier surrounding my mind.

When I didn't immediately tackle her in a hug, she raised a brow. "Your shield is impressive."

I shrugged. "Lucifer taught me well. It also helps I saw Sam not long ago." His extra energy served as a jump start to my power, making everything easier.

My mom lowered her hands. "Sam? Hell's head healer?"

"Yeah." I went for the cheap shot and slashed down with my knife toward her shoulder.

She dodged, narrowing her eyes. But I wasn't sure if it was from my attack or my response.

"Why did you need to see Sam?"

"To replen—" I stopped myself. My mom wouldn't like knowing she was siphoning most of my energy.

Except, I'd lasted all day before the drain hit me at the end of training with the guys. Whatever my father was doing definitely helped.

She swiped my legs from under me, and I slammed into the snow-packed ground. She used the opportunity to straddle me, holding her knife to my throat. "To what?"

I let her stay there, smirking. "Sucks not being in the know, doesn't it, Mom?"

"Lucille Chiara, tell me what I want to know."

"Not until you answer some of my questions," I said, flipping her over with a maneuver she showed me and leveling a knife to her neck. "Are you a dream-walker?"

Her brows lowered. "No."

"Then where did my powers come from?"

"Sweetie, powers can manifest based on the Weaver's design."

"Even for me?"

She nodded. "I'd assume so."

But she didn't *know*. "What about your research? What did you find?"

Her hesitation made me suspicious. Mom only hesitated when she was trying to avoid the truth or soften the blow.

"Only a few lines about a rare type of angel."

"What did they say?"

"Lucy—"

"What did they say, Mom?"

She stood and sheathed her dagger. "Dream-walkers were a rare type of dark angel that could invade dreams and memories and alter the known and unknown. But there was nothing more detailed than that."

I sat up. "I thought there were only seven types of angels. Are you saying I'm a dark angel?" Whatever the hell that meant.

"No. You are a born angel with similar powers to a dark angel, it seems." But something in her tone made me pause.

"What aren't you saying?" The soft rustle of tree branches filled the quiet as I waited for her answer. She chewed on her lip, and I scoffed. "Stop thinking about a way to sugarcoat it and just tell me."

"Their book said they were taken care of for their sinful natures."

"Taken care of? Like killed? Tortured? Put on an island, runed and bound, never to be thought of again? Whose book did you read this from?"

My mom tilted her head to the night sky, searching between the stars with a fierce stare. "Michael gave it to me when I asked him to find books on the history of angels."

"Like he's a reliable source," I muttered, sounding like my father when I confronted him and Cato. "Why did you choose Michael? I understand the prophecy scared you, and that's why you hid me from Lucifer. But why him? And why let us suffer through his abuse for so long?"

My mom turned toward our house. "I was told it was the only way."

"The only way for what?" I stood, rubbing my face.

"I made decisions that I believed were for the greater good, and realized I was wrong too late," she whispered, her voice strained. "All I want is to protect you, Lucille, and prevent what's to come. I'm trying to make this right." She gestured between us, still unable to meet my eyes.

"How are we supposed to prevent anything if you won't tell me what you're hiding?"

She gave me a smile that didn't reach her eyes. "Some of my secrets are too shameful to share."

"Sometimes we have to do what we don't want to," I shot back, ready to scream.

"I have given you as much as I can. Tell me why you've been to Sam?"

I closed my eyes, squeezing my hands into tight fists. Every cell in my body thrummed with frustration. I wanted to throttle my mother. To rage at her until she revealed all her dirty secrets. She answered some of my questions, but not *nearly* enough.

"I don't know how to control my powers and used too much too fast, so Sam had to give me an energy boost," I gritted out.

Maybe I was petty or a hypocrite, or perhaps I knew nothing good would come from telling her the whole truth. But at least it wasn't an outright lie.

"Does that happen often?"

"No," I lied anyway. But my response was too fast, and she caught it, her eyes narrowing.

"Lucy—"

The dream dissolved, and I woke to a slobbering wet tongue attacking my face, saving me from an interrogation.

"Okay, okay, I'm up!" I exclaimed, pushing away Rune's big head.

Oliver lay stretched out on top of the bed, clothed in winter running gear with a smug smirk gracing his face.

I shot him a glare. "Were you the mastermind behind this?"

"The wake-up call, no. Poking Rune and encouraging her to lick you with her nasty smelling drool, possibly." He shrugged, smiling. "Alexei and Ronen are waiting outside our door to run with us."

"Why are Ronen and Al—" I cut off. "Extra protection," I answered for myself, staring at our canopy as thoughts of last night swirled uncomfortably in my mind. My palms began to sweat just thinking about it, my heart rate picking up speed. How could I face him today after...

Hell, after nothing! It's not like we did anything wrong. We exchanged a few words, and he gently touched my scars. That was it. I groaned. *Why couldn't that be it?*

Rune whimpered, snapping me out of my thoughts. She sat on the bed, peering down at me with her cute tail coiling.

"We're all waiting," Oliver sang.

I responded as any best friend would—with the middle finger.

He snorted, then proceeded to rip off my covers and shove me off the bed.

I landed in a heap on the hardwood. "Ass."

"The prettiest ass you've ever seen." He leaned over and gave me a noogie.

"That's debatable." I swatted him away.

"Too right. We have the heartthrob hustler and the scrum-diddlyumptious general on the other side of the door."

Rolling my eyes, I stood, then walked to my closet and changed, wishing my stomach wasn't in knots.

Despite my nerves, our run with the general and Alexei wasn't half bad. Ronen led us at a steady pace, teaching us breathing techniques and how to hold our bodies when we got tired, while Alexei chimed in behind us. With their help and encouragement, we ran the entire ten miles. Although we had a slower time, I didn't feel the slightest bit drained—but my lungs still burned.

Afterward, I met up with my father in the greenhouse. He sat next to me, hunching over in his nicely pressed suit.

I touched his shoulder. "Are you okay?"

Dark bags sagged beneath his bloodshot eyes. "I'm fine. Shield."

"I am," I said hesitantly.

Lucifer nodded. "Good. Escape my hallucination and twist it into one of your own."

He started the same way he always did, using my reality against me to make it seem like it wasn't a hallucination. But this time, I felt his cold presence behind the scenes. Whether intentional or not, I didn't know.

I waited on the bench for the illusion to play out, staring at the clear ice glistening in the golden sunlight. Rays refracted rainbows against the stone path. A smile tugged at my lips, enjoying the warmth at my back and the prism of color. But then the scene blurred and everything changed.

If I hadn't already felt my father's tampering, I would've known it was a hallucination by that alone—and the fact that I no longer sat in the greenhouse. Instead, I stood in my seven-year-old bedroom, and Michael had his black dagger raised right above the younger version of myself's exposed back.

My father decided to let my subconscious take over instead of controlling the illusion.

"Do you know why you're being punished?" Michael asked, lowering his mouth to my ear. "Helpless wimp."

Young Lucy trembled, clutching at a stuffed animal rabbit. "Because I accidentally used my powers again?" she whispered.

I closed my eyes, wrapped the melody of my hallucination power around my mind, thought about fear, and pushed it toward the cold presence lurking in the background. My purple, frilly bedroom faded, replaced by the greenhouse and my father holding his head in his hands.

"Lucifer?" I touched his shoulder. Had it really been that easy to remove myself and push my power on him?

He didn't move or even acknowledge me.

I let go of the song whispering in my ear and touched him again. "Father."

He twisted and blinked. The movement was slow, his eyes glossy as if he wasn't mentally present. Standing, he wobbled and steadied himself on the bench arm.

"You did a good job, my sweet Lucille. But I need some rest. We'll practice in the Shard Field tomorrow."

Did he just compliment me?

"Do you need help? Should I take you to Sam?"

He shook his head. "No. Get to training. I don't need any help."

I frowned after him, watching his retreat.

"Oh, Moira did *not* look happy after the general told her we were skipping training to go with him and Alexei," Oliver said as we walked down the hall. "I bet tomorrow our punishment is gonna suck. Well—" He paused. "More than it usually does."

"Mhmm." I nodded absentmindedly.

Was my father sick or just extremely stressed? Was that why he switched the hallucination to the easier version?

Oliver said something as he pushed on the stone to open the hidden door that led to the castle roof.

"Mhmm, yeah," I replied, not paying attention.

Something was up. Any other day, I would've never been able to escape *that* fast. Sure, he was my teacher, but he was the master of hallucination.

Oliver said something else.

And I nodded, hoping it was the correct response.

Could the King of Hell get sick?

We passed through the door, our Hell Squadron uniforms heating instantly, and walked toward Ronen and Alexei, who stood waiting with their massive wings on display.

Should someone check on Lucifer just in case?

"Can you go make out with Alexei for me and tell me how it is? I feel like that's a necessary duty as a best friend."

"Mhmm," I replied on autopilot. "Wait, what?" I twisted toward him, but he had already dropped behind me. Then he shoved me.

Startled, my feet tangled together, and I fell into Alexei's body. He caught me and scooped me up into his arms, smiling down in triumph.

"What the hell, Oliver?"

He smirked, standing near Ronen. "That's what you get for ignoring me. Now kiss him and tell me how it is."

Alexei brought his face closer to mine. "I'd be more than happy to help out with that."

I leaned away from Alexei's advance. He adjusted his hand, almost brushing the underside of my breast, and curled me inward.

Oliver shook his head, pressing his lips together. "Pucker up, Luce!"

Ronen looked on with an unreadable expression, drilling his gaze into Alexei's hand placement.

"I'm sorry I ignored you. I just had something on my mind," I admitted.

Heavenly Hell, I hope Ronen didn't think it was him.

Alexei's warm breath hit my cheeks, and I shoved my hand into the gap before his lips could connect.

Oliver laughed, enjoying my torment. "I could tell."

Alexei kissed my palm, his blue eyes shining with mirth. "Don't worry, Princess, you'll be begging me for my lips soon enough."

"Watch your words," Ronen warned, a cold edge in his tone.

Alexei's amusement evaporated, and he lowered his head in a nod.

Ronen waited a tense second before picking up the still-smirking Oliver and flying off the roof.

"Is he always that intense when he scolds you?" I teased, tucking my face into Alexei's neck as he jumped off, preparing for the blasting wind. But there was none. I frowned before remembering Alexei's powers—he'd created a wind shield.

Alexei's forehead wrinkled like he was trying to puzzle something out. He stayed that way for most of the flight.

"You're going to get frown lines if you continue to do that." I poked his creases.

He tilted his head toward me, his expression smoothing out. "Beautiful, I'm two hundred thirty-one years old, and this face is as angelic and handsome as the day it popped into existence. There will be no ugliness in my future."

"No." I laughed. "Just a bigger ego."

Alexei twirled us in the air and winked, then landed in the Shard Field in a spray of snow. "Ladies love my ego. When you want to take a spin with the heartthrob hustler, just let me know."

I brought a hand to my mouth, attempting to keep my mocking laugh in, but it spilled out.

He rolled his eyes and set me down. "Yeah, okay. I blame your friend for that one. But I had to test it out."

"When you're done flirting, we can begin," Ronen barked, right as Rune came barreling out of the Veil Forest and into Alexei, knocking him on his ass.

"You know, Ro, I see a boxing match in our future—along with an interesting conversation." Alexei lay on the snowy ground, spread-eagled.

Ronen strode over, stepping above his head. "It will be a pleasure to rough you up a bit, Lex," he challenged, holding out a hand.

Alexei took it, and Ronen brought him up, both of them pulling each other in for an aggressive embrace and back slap.

"Don't forget about the conversation."

Ronen smacked him harder. "No words need to be said." Then he released him and turned to me. "Did you think any more about your Glory?"

I opened my mouth, and my thoughts fluttered away to the library—his fingers tracing my thighs, his hand over my chest, brushing my nipples.

"Lucille?" he prompted.

Heat spread up my neck. Heavenly Hell, this was so much easier when we ran. At least then I had Oliver and Alexei between us.

"Kind of," I mumbled. "But I don't understand how Michael is a part of it. I wasn't thinking about him when I erupted yesterday. I was just... scared."

"They aren't just related—they're intertwined. You fear your Glory because of him. You were taught not to accept them. But our powers are created to protect us, so every time you're scared, they signal to you, and your fear doubles, making them erupt without your control. You've been conditioned into a dangerous cycle."

I crossed my arms. "I accept them. I just can't control them."

Ronen took a step toward me, raising a dark brow. "Then why'd you scream?"

What did that have to do with anything?

"I was scared."

"That was not a scream of fear. That was a scream of pain," Alexei said, lightly touching my arm.

Rune pressed close to my side, licking my hand as if trying to comfort me.

I shrugged them off, stepping back and bouncing my gaze between the three males. "So? You're saying your powers never hurt?"

Alexei shook his head. Ronen's lips pressed into a soft, sympathetic frown.

"Oliver, you puke after you use your power," I said, bringing him into this.

He ran a hand through his hair. "Yeah, but that's a hazard of living through someone's worst fear, not me rejecting my powers. I don't scream like I'm being ripped apart."

"It always hurts that much, doesn't it?" Ronen's words were less of a question and more of a statement.

I nodded, tightening my arms around my body.

A hint of sadness clouded Alexei's crystal-blue eyes, his brow momentarily furrowing. I couldn't tell if it was pity, sympathy, or both. Oliver stared at me with a similar gaze, shifting like he wanted to hug me.

"Stop looking at me like that. I've been through things. I bet we all have."

Alexei flicked his attention to Ronen, then back to me. "Yes, but you're the second person I've ever met who had such extreme consequences to rejecting your powers." He took my hands in his and squeezed them, a gentle awe overcoming his words. "We are taught upon creation to cherish them, honor them. They are our sacred right to use to protect people."

He beseeched me with his searching, kind eyes. There were no winks, no playfulness twinkling in his face. This was a male who was proud of what he was, *who* he was. This was a male who had accepted himself and wanted to help others do the same. Alexei wasn't just a flirty playboy. The passion and confidence pushing back his shoulders and moving through his face showed me another reason why Ronen made him his second.

"Your Glory is a beautiful gift. Don't let that sick bastard influence you to punish yourself with it."

My gaze fell to our boots. "Did that speech work on the first person you met with this problem?"

"No, it didn't," Ronen stated.

I jerked my head up, meeting his gaze.

"Haunted or empowered?"

He gave me a small, knowing smile. "It's a battle every day. But I've been winning more."

Alexei released me and patted Ronen on the back. "He's come a long way under my tutelage. Was a stubborn little bastard at some points, but we got through it once he finally started to listen to me. Now we're the best of buds," he joked, but I could tell Alexei was proud of Ronen.

"Okay, *Master* Alexei," I teased. "So if you helped the big, bad general, how are you going to help me?"

Alexei beamed, and Ronen shook his head, that slight smile still there, tugging at my chest.

"Well, beautiful"—he knocked my chin up—"what's the best way to overcome fear?"

I refrained from rolling my eyes, but couldn't keep the deadpan out of my expression. "To face it."

He turned my face toward Oliver. "Exactly."

CHAPTER 33

Lucille

"Wait a minute now. I did *not* volunteer for this!" Oliver exclaimed.

Alexei shrugged. "Ronen and I both agreed this would be the safest and fastest way to solve Lucille's issue. Plus, she trusts you the most. You have a chance to ease her suffering. Don't you want to help with that?"

"Through *more* suffering?" Oliver ran his hands through his moppy hair.

"She either suffers now with all of us in a controlled area or she suffers later and hurts herself or others," Ronen asserted. "We never said this would be easy."

"Lucy," Oliver pleaded.

I worried my lip. I didn't want to force Oliver into something he didn't want to do, nor did I want to relive my fears. But what other choice did we have? He'd been so close to using it on Ni, and I knew this scenario was different. But we could get through this together.

I walked up to him and grabbed his shaking hands. I was sure his were as clammy as mine beneath the leather. "I'll be brave for you, if you can be brave for me."

He shut his eyes and took a deep breath. "You're sure about this?"

"Just think of it as a sneak peek into my mental diary," I teased, forcing a smile. But I could see my fear reflected in his eyes. I wasn't sure about this. He knew it. My hands shook as badly as his. This would be extremely hard on both of us.

He touched my cheek and nodded solemnly. "I'll be brave for you, if you can be brave for me."

A lump formed in my throat. He truly was my best friend. Blinking away the tears in my eyes, I twisted toward Ronen and Alexei. "So, how do we do this?"

Ronen stepped up beside me, his shadows circling his palms. Alexei moved to position himself next to Oliver, and Rune placed herself on the other side.

"Focus on your Glory. Thoughts, feelings, memories. I don't care, just concentrate on that. Then, Oliver, you'll touch her with your power. Hit her with a hard punch of it. Better get the worst one done first," Alexei instructed.

Oliver dropped his head back to the gray, dull sky, clutching his head. "Sounds like a blast."

"Ronen will be on standby with his powers in case your flames get out of control while you're reliving your fears," Alexei said to me.

"And I'll be extra protection for Oliver—plus your amazing cheer-leader."

"You'll make sure we're safe?" I asked, needing Ronen's confirmation.

"Always, Hellion. Face your scars and focus on your Glory."

"This is going to be taxing on both of you. We're going to be at this all day." Alexei gestured to a wicker basket left near the edge of the black trees and snowy clearing. "Rune brought us some of Dorus's food when you want to take a break."

"Not sure I'll have the stomach for it," Oliver mumbled.

"Then we'll force-feed you." Alexei smirked.

Oliver didn't even have a quip for that.

"Together?" I asked him.

His green eyes burst with flame. "Together."

I nodded, and Oliver reached out with a shaky hand, touching my shoulder.

The lights on my ceiling blinked and sparkled from my rotating nightlight beside the bed, like the stars my mommy and I sometimes stared up at. They switched from pink to purple to blue, then stopped. A moment later, the lights turned off, and the room went dark. I clutched Thumper and pulled the covers up to my chin. Something pushed at my tummy. It was warm, and it felt funny. Similar to the feeling that my mommy's tea gave me. But she didn't give me any tea tonight.

A door slammed, and I jumped. The warm feeling shot from my fingers, and a white light hit my bunny's head. I yelped, throwing him off my bed.

"What was that?" I peeked over the edge at Thumper. He seemed okay.

"Michael," my mom whispered on the other side of my door. "What are you doing here so early?"

"I decided I wanted to spend the whole day with my daughter. Is that so bad?"

I tucked myself back into bed and closed my eyes, pretending to sleep.

"She won't wake up for another couple of hours."

I heard my doorknob twist. "That's fine. I'll just sit next to her and watch her sleep."

No, no. I didn't want Daddy to watch me sleep.

"Fine. I'll be in the kitchen."

Daddy opened and closed my door. Then it sounded like he was scratching on the wood. I peeked open an eye. He was writing on my door with a giant white feather, and the letters glowed. Afterward, he turned around, and I quickly shut my eyes.

His boots were loud on the wood and quiet on the carpet by my bed.

"I know you're awake, Lucille. I felt something come from your room."

I squeezed my eyes shut and stayed still.

"You did this to your rabbit, didn't you?" he asked.

I shook my head.

"You know not to lie to me. Now open your eyes." He used his scary tone. So I did, scooting back.

He held Thumper in his hand, rubbing his thumb against the blackened fur on top of his head.

"Tell me the truth. Did you do this?"

"I—I think so. But I don't know, Daddy."

He tossed Thumber against the wall and grabbed my arm, ripping me from the covers.

"That hurts," I cried, trying to pull free.

"What comes next will hurt even more. Lift your arms."

I did what he said, my lip wobbling. "I didn't mean to hurt Thumper."

Daddy pulled off my shirt and took out a big black knife with a large, shiny red stone in the center.

"I promise," I said, sniffling, wiping tears from my face.

Sometimes, if he didn't see them on my cheeks, he wouldn't hit me.

But it didn't work.

Daddy hit me, and I held my face, crying more.

"Daddy, please."

But he didn't hug me like Mommy did when I cried. No matter what I said, Daddy was always mad at me. I tried to be good when he came home. I tried to make him love me with flowers and smiles. Mommy loved those. But he never did.

"You were never supposed to be born. So I will unmake you."

He stuck the knife in my heart, and I screamed.

I screamed so loudly, I didn't know why Mommy wasn't coming to the door. "Stop!" I cried, feeling a warm and cold pull.

Daddy shook his head, his eyes wide like he was confused. He pushed on the knife, and I fell asleep for a second, then woke up to a funny sensation. A flash of bright light blasted him and the knife back.

I rubbed at my heart, crying, but there was no blood, and it no longer hurt. I was okay.

"Why'd you do that, Daddy?"

He stared at me from the floor, holding the knife, which now had a black stone instead of red. Sitting up, he put the scary knife away and reached for me. I moved back, hitting the wall.

He took out the big white feather and climbed into my bed, pressing the tip to my chest. "Daddy made a mistake. But we won't tell Mommy about this, okay? Or Daddy might make more mistakes."

I nodded.

"For now, we'll hide it with my magical feather. Understand?"

I nodded again.

Before I could feel the pain of his rune, a comforting darkness overtook my mind, soothing me into a gentle sleep.

I woke up staring into concerned golden eyes, resting in Ronen's lap on the warm ground.

"Are you okay?" He smoothed back the hair sticking to my forehead.

I sat up with his help, my bottom and hands hot. I looked down to find a large circle of scorched dirt and, farther out, mud and melting snow.

"What happened? Did I hurt anyone?"

I searched for Oliver. He stood in a corner near the Shard Field, heaving his guts up beside Alexei. He patted Oliver's back as he surveyed us, his dappled wings jutting into the gray sky. His feathers looked a little ruffled, but neither he nor Oliver appeared injured. I slumped back into Ronen.

"Lucille," Ronen pressed. "Are *you* okay?"

Was I?

I touched my chest. Michael had tried to kill me at four, and my mother never knew about it. My four-year-old self had shoved the memory into the deepest, darkest corners of her mind—never to remember it again, never to bring it up.

My Glory must've protected me, but it was also the cause.

I bit my lip and touched the warm dirt.

"What happened?"

"Your Glory. I had barely enough time to put up a barrier between us and them."

My heart lurched. I twisted around, scanning his body for burn marks.

He gently touched my face, pulling me from my hunt. "I'm fine. But are you? You were screaming." Shadows flickered in his irises, swallowing the momentary worry creasing his face.

I shifted my focus before I drowned in his gaze. But that almost made it worse. His skin pressed more firmly against my cheek, warming me, vibrating like his body constantly hummed with power. I wanted to hate it. I didn't want to be affected by him. But Heavenly fucking Hell, I'd be a liar if I said I wasn't. The only hate I had was toward myself.

I pulled away. "Why do you care? You're only supposed to be keeping me safe, not looking out for my emotional well-being."

It was unfair to say after these last few days. But it had the desired effect.

His mask dropped back into place, and I almost sighed in relief.

So what if it was a step backward? I couldn't handle my attraction to him, especially not when he acted like he cared.

Rune butted my hand, and I used her to help me stand, putting distance between me and Ronen.

Oliver and Alexei made their way back to my burn circle. Alexei went straight to Ronen, taking him aside for a hushed conversation. Oliver, pale-faced and glassy-eyed, came straight to me and pulled me into the biggest hug.

And that was what did it.

My lip trembled, and I pressed my face into his chest, hiding the tears. "I'm sorry you had to see that." And I was so glad Alexei and Ronen couldn't.

"Not another word out of that mouth of yours, Lucy. Not a fucking word," Oliver said, his voice breaking. "I will make him live through his worst fears every day, puking my guts up for what he did—and has done—to you."

I sniffled against his stiff leather, squeezing him tighter. "How about we just find and kill him?"

He gave a rough laugh, laying his chin on my head. "That works too."

I stepped out of his hold, and we both wiped each other's cheeks, smiling as we did. "Are you ready to see more?"

Because I wasn't done.

I wouldn't let that sick piece of shit control my Glory. I was taking back that part of me. I would train until it not only didn't hurt, but I could use it ten times better than Michael. And when his time came, I'd show him what my *disgusting, sinful* powers could do to him.

We practiced late into the day, taking breaks when we needed, or when my Glory got out of control. Ronen was able to prevent it from causing any damage to anyone, but the same couldn't be said for our surroundings.

Oliver hugged me after each session. Alexei, ever the cheerleader, reminded me that my powers were a beautiful gift and urged me to find the good in them.

Ronen... his jaw throbbed, and his body seemed to tense tighter with each passing hour, Rune pressing against his side as if she sensed he needed her.

By the time night fell, I thought he'd explode. But instead, he sighed like an unbearable weight had lifted off him.

"You did it. You didn't scream."

"I actually think she smiled," Alexei said, coming up behind me and hugging me. Oliver joined in, and of course, Rune as well, jumping up on our group hug. Ronen just crossed his arms, but there was a lightness to his expression.

I laughed. "Does this mean it won't hurt anymore?"

Alexei and Oliver pulled back.

"Try it and find out," Ronen said.

"How?"

"You just spent the whole day with it. Close your eyes and feel it," Alexei said, gesturing passionately.

I shut my eyes and thought about the first time. My Glory was a warm and energizing presence that zinged beneath my skin like a playful puppy. I accepted it. I loved it. And in turn, I could almost feel the love it had for me.

"Open your eyes, Luce."

Small, white flames flickered playfully across my hand, and I didn't feel a single piercing needle.

"We did it," I said in awe, smiling at each of them.

"No, Hellion. *You* did."

CHAPTER 34

Lucille

Firewings swarmed the ancient, vined arches, their otherworldly orange glow muddied by the purple ring around my vision. I turned, cringing from the sharp, dry grass digging into my feet. With a single thought, I imagined boots and crunched my way through the moonlit clearing.

I frowned, finding Aspen's spot beneath the oak empty.

"Aspen?" I called out.

No answer.

I searched the area, and something dark flickered in my peripheral vision, right behind the trunk's shadow. But when I looked directly at the tree, nothing was there. I twisted my head again with the same result.

Creeping toward it, the hair on my arms stood on end.

"Aspen, where are you?" My nerves danced as my voice carried over the quiet. "We need to talk."

I needed to ask him about Lilith and what he presumed her plans were with me. There was a missing puzzle piece in Lucifer's theories. I just couldn't get past why she'd want me in the Immolation Circle after everything Aspen went through to get me to her.

What if Lucifer was wrong? What if Lilith wasn't behind the demon infection or trying to kill me?

But if not her—then who?

The oak taunted me with its ominous darkness, only showing me what it hid in its shadows when I turned my head. I shouldn't even be able to see it at all, not with the oak's large branches halting the light of the moon. But my dream-walking haze distinguished the difference between the shadows and the pulsating mass.

Something invisible brushed against me at the same time I smelled it. The cloying sweet scent overwhelmed the air, shoving down my airways and making it difficult to breathe. I wheezed and stopped in my tracks, then took a few steps back until fresh air filled my lungs, landing at the halfway point between the arches and the oak.

What was that?

Frozen with apprehension, I waited to gather the courage to investigate further.

Something latched onto my hips, and I screamed, the ring around my vision eclipsing my eyes and drowning my surroundings in purple.

"Gotcha," Aspen whispered in my ear, arms encircling my waist.

I would've whipped around to hit him, or chastise him for making my heart murder my sternum, but the purple-hued blob was no longer a blob. It looked almost like a figure.

"Is someone else here?"

He tightened his hold, placing a kiss on my neck. "Not that I know of."

"You don't see that figure behind the tree?"

He attempted to twist me, but I wouldn't let him. I wasn't about to turn my back on the figure-like dark void that suffocated me the closer I got.

Aspen sighed. "No, sweetheart. I don't see it. Is that even possible? This is my dream."

"Yes, it's possible."

Ronen had somehow managed to come into a dream with us, most likely because he had power over the mind. But this wasn't Ronen. The pulsating shadows weren't wispy and curling. They didn't give me a sense of peace and solace. No, these were heavy and unsettling, devoid of life—a soul-sucking blackness with a barrier of smothering air.

"You said we need to talk? Did you finally find a way out?" he asked hopefully, stepping in front of me and blocking my view.

I frowned at his dismissal. That wasn't like him.

"Why—" I stopped short and raised my hand, brushing it along his full beard, then trailing up to the wavy brown locks almost covering his dull eyes. "You look... different." It hadn't been that long since I last saw him... had it?

He rubbed the side of his face, smiling with no lips. "Haven't had time to shave. Did you find a way out?"

That question again? The figure didn't concern him at all?

"No, we're still looking," I replied, peering around him and toward the trunk.

It wasn't there. Nor did it lurk in the field or behind the ancient arches. But I still picked up on a whiff of that terrible smell.

Aspen framed my face, stopping any head movement. "No progress?"

I opened my mouth, hesitating. My gut wasn't playfully nudging me anymore—it was screaming.

He dropped his hands and grazed a thumb over my palm, his eyes tightening. "Still floundering, sweetheart?"

That damned word pressed against the cracks in my belief—one breath from breaking. I shut my mouth, analyzing him as he rubbed my scarred palm. Just the one, sending a tingling shockwave of dread to my heart.

"You always think I'm floundering." I pulled my hand to my chest.

"I have a lot of reasons to believe you are."

"Because I was betrayed and locked in your cuffs in Elora?"

It wasn't the question I wanted to ask. It wasn't the question burning like acid at the back of my throat.

He shrugged, giving me a once-over. "Among other reasons. But yes. That wasn't that long ago."

I rubbed my thumb over the palm he had been touching, not sure if I was trying to take away his tingling touch or press it into my skin. My thoughts descended to a dangerous place, twisting my stomach into knots. A stinging pricked my eyes, making me blink rapidly.

I had to stay strong.

"There will be a day when you will no longer be able to think of me as a damsel in distress." I reached up, cupping his face, a lump rising in my throat from the tingles of our bond. "I've been practicing my powers every morning. And today in the Shard Field, I'll learn even more." I ran a thumb across the dark bag beneath his eye. "If you saw what I could do now, I bet you wouldn't call it floundering."

He held my drilling gaze before lowering his mouth to mine. "I hope you're right," he mumbled against my lips, then he gripped the nape of my neck and crushed me in a tingling kiss, pressing his body into me.

I refrained from pulling back, from falling into the words that screamed in the back of my mind. *Helpless. Helpless.* Instead, I took my hurt and desperation out on our kiss, biting and slamming my mouth against his. He met every angry nip with his own, trying to take control. But I wouldn't let him. I grabbed his long, greasy hair and yanked him back.

"Have you found Melanie?" I demanded, already knowing the answer.

He shook his head, breathing hard and gripping my waist in a way that'd leave bruises.

I nodded. I didn't want to be here any longer. I couldn't. And like my dream-walk heard me, I woke up.

I ran a hand through Rune's fur, soothing myself as the tears I'd held back slid down my cheeks. This couldn't be love. It wouldn't hurt this much—would it? Would it make you go out of your mind, questioning every single moment together?

Because that was what I did. I forwent sleep to tear apart my dream-walks and every moment we'd had together.

The guys and I ran our circuit in the early morning. Snow fell from the dark sky, and our boots filled the quiet with our crushing steps.

Oliver made jokes, Alexei gave it back, and Ronen tolerated it. But I couldn't concentrate on their words when Aspen consumed my thoughts.

At the end of our run, Oliver flung out a leg, and I went flying into a pile of snow right before the arena doors. I landed on my forearms, preventing a total face-plant and tensing at the immediate cold melting down my back.

"Oliver!" I heaved.

He hunched over his knees, gathering his breath. Alexei and Ronen stood near him, both breathing deeply but more composed.

"Out with it, Luce," Oliver said, waving his hand expectantly.

"Out with what?"

"Oh, I don't know," he deadpanned, straightening. "Whatever has your panties in such a twist that you've ignored my joking, Alexei's flirting, and Ronen's scowling questions?"

I brushed off my uniform and stood in my snow crater. "Nothing."

At least, nothing I wanted to explain to any of them. I could already hear what Oliver would say. I could already see the judgment in all their eyes. I was barely holding on to the tiny ball of hope I had. No, I wouldn't say a thing until I was sure.

"Seriously, it's nothing. Just reliving all my Michael memories did a number on me."

It was a lie. As hard as it was to face every time I was abused by him, afterward, I felt purged of my past and even more determined to train and kill him.

I touched Oliver's arm. "Really."

Oliver pulled me in for a hug and nodded. I glanced at the other two. Alexei stared at me with sympathetic eyes, while Ronen's face remained unreadable.

I gave Oliver a small smile. "Go on with Alexei. I need to talk with Ronen."

Oliver quirked a brow, and I shoved him when he didn't move.

Alexei unsheathed a dagger and started to flip it. "Now we're more than intrigued. You've been silent and dazed this entire run, and then you want to talk to Ronen?"

I groaned, dropping my head back to the pre-dawn sky. "You two are insufferable. I'm not going to say a word to him while you're here."

I should've thought that over better. Of course King Nosy and Ronen's loyal second would want to know, but I didn't have the time to wait to ask Ronen, not when we were almost back inside the castle and I was about to train with my father.

"Leave us," Ronen commanded.

Alexei sheathed his dagger and snatched Oliver's arm. He had to be dragged through the doors, his head flopping back over his shoulder with a pout. I would've laughed, but all my energy was holding up my glass ball of hope on a shrinking needle.

I turned to Ronen. "In twenty minutes, I'd like you to meet me in the Shard Field. Lucifer and I are practicing there after this, and I'd like you to come watch, to critique me."

Lie after lie, I couldn't stop. But I also couldn't tell the truth. At least this way, if nothing happened, he couldn't question why I wanted him there. Then my hunch would be wrong, the stinging that continued to threaten my eyes would subside, and the fissures slowly spreading through my heart would stop.

But if something did happen, I'd want Ronen by our side. My father struggled in our last session for whatever reason, and I didn't want to take chances if he was in a similar state this session.

Ronen quietly watched me in that unnerving way of his, like he was analyzing my every word. I fidgeted as the silence dragged on. Did he understand the power he held over me with that gaze? Could he hear my heartbeat?

"I figured a second pair of eyes would benefit me," I added, needing to fill the silence.

After the longest moment of my life, he finally nodded.

My father stood in a fearsome armored uniform a few yards away. Spikes protruded along his arms, gaining length at his slouched shoulders. They were red-tipped, as if decorated in the blood of his enemies. A black skull sat at the center of his breastplate, red paint dripped from the eyes and mouth, seeping into the interlocking armored plates beneath like a gruesome ribcage. The color bled into the armor at his legs in long drip lines, as if the skull had ruptured his heart and pooled down his body.

Red for blood and black for death—Hell's colors.

I stood straighter, glad he didn't have a helmet or mask that went along with his gear. Without one, he wasn't as intimidating; in fact, his hunched form made me wary. He looked worse than yesterday.

"Are you sure you don't want to move our session to a later day, or we could have Ronen take over?"

"General Ronen," he snapped, his eyes flashing.

Wind whipped around us, creaking the Veil Forest's branches, pulling my hair loose from its bind, and swirling fresh snow at our feet.

"General Ronen," I replied slowly, my brows furrowing.

"Shield," he demanded, raising his arms.

A whirlwind of ice and snow gathered in front of him. Shards glinted in the hazy light, threatening me with pain. He directed the storm at me, and I felt a cold finger scrape across my mind.

I had seconds to both solidify the fiery barrier surrounding my thoughts and defend myself against an ice storm, so I sank into my powers, asking my Infernus for help. It responded without hesitation, adding layers of fire to my mind. Then, I coaxed my Glory to protect me.

I thought it'd be easier after yesterday, but I'd only intentionally wielded my Glory on my hands. Now, I'd need to use more of it.

I gripped the humming strands of my Glory, feeling no pain, only sweat sliding down my forehead from the effort to drag them to the surface. A piece of ice sliced against my cheek just as my Glory flamed across my skin, stopping me from becoming hamburger with a sizzling hiss.

The cold pressure against my mental shield abruptly stopped as the tornado of ice and snow picked me up and threw me back. I tensed, my heart beating out of control as I laid all my energy into my Glory, eliminating my mental shield as I waited for the impact with the Shard Field. Two long seconds ticked by, then I felt a moment of pressure before I slammed into a hissing puddle of water.

Breath punched from my lungs. The steam scalded the back of my neck as my Glory flickered. I jerked up, tugging harder on the humming strands, but not before the whirling ice picked up speed and nicked my face.

When my white flame fully covered me again, the storm eased.

I squinted through the twirling snow and ice. My father knelt on the ground, with one shaky arm thrown up. Concerned, I shot up and jogged through the gentle snowy wind.

"Lucifer?"

"I'm fine."

He squeezed his eyes shut and held his stance for a moment more, then dropped to his hands and knees. The wind disappeared, and the snow and ice plopped to the ground.

I released my Glory, and he exhaled slowly. Frowning, I realized—besides the sweat trailing down my neck, the ache in my head, and my uneven breaths—I felt like I could go again, just like I had yesterday.

Could I be—

No.

Testing a theory, I called to my Infernus. Purple flames erupted on my hands, but my father didn't react like I thought he would. He remained on all fours, taking deep breaths.

"Are you sure? What's—"

Shadows flickered behind the crooked trunks at my father's back, cutting off my words. I froze, my gaze zeroing in on the moving figures gaining length and width, coming closer.

Was it Rune and Ronen?

I hoped it was. I hoped my hunch was wrong.

But the shadows split. Instead of two, there were four. Then six.

"No," I whispered.

The needle balancing the last of my hope tipped, shattering it—and my heart.

CHAPTER 35

Ronen

The heavy wooden door loomed ahead, reinforced with Ember Metal and runes. The sight of it never ceased to unnerve me. I unlocked the door with my key and blood. The back of my neck prickled. My muscles coiled, knowing precisely what would happen when I hit the bottom of the stone steps. I fisted my hands. After the numerous times I'd been down here, you'd think I would finally be rid of this fucking anxiety—but not once over the years did it let up. I never went down here if I could help it. But being the general didn't always allow for that.

In the dungeon, the long hallway of dark cells flashed before my eyes, taking me back to my past. No longer were the bars bare Ember Metal; now they were painted white, along with the stones beneath my feet, the wall sconces, and the walls themselves—everything glistened with sickening white. All that was missing was Gabriel and his encouraging smile.

"You plan to stand there all day? I mean, I don't mind. You're a nice piece of meat to look at, but could you walk closer to the flame so I can see you better?" Anya's voice snapped me out of the past.

Usually, I couldn't take myself out of the memory for minutes. It typically played out to the very end, forcing me to relive his death all over again—a death that could've been prevented if not for that fucking controlling bond.

I rubbed my wrists, my shoulders easing, grateful for Anya's rasp—our resident, no-good, annoying soul who'd gotten herself thrown in here until her next Judgment Day.

"Are you still planning to rot in here instead of redeeming yourself?"

She leaned her head back against the damp wall and stretched out her legs. "Safer in here than out there."

"And what would you know about out there?"

Anya was only a human who used to practice divination on Earth. I never believed humans had much skill, or any power at all, really. That was reserved for angels and demons. But then Anya would say something that made me wonder if she did have some foresight.

She shrugged. "Only that it's best not to get attached to anyone or anything. Things are changing, baby—as you well know."

I almost indulged her by asking another question, but I caught the mischievous glint in her expression. She was egging me on. She wanted me to get sucked into her words. Even if she did believe it was safer down here, she received little engagement. She didn't need to eat or drink. She wasn't sneaky enough to require a personal guard, and the closest prisoner was six cells away without the ability to talk. Her socialization came from me.

I didn't understand how she wasn't insane after all these months. If I hadn't had Gabriel, I would've lost my mind. I would've completely given up.

He was the only reason I was able to escape.

Sighing, I took out a pencil and my piece of runed parchment, tore off the rune to deactivate its connection to the ranking board, and shoved them through the bars. It wasn't much, but it could help her void of boredom and loneliness, at least a little.

Anya glanced at my offering, then up. "Why?"

"Because I know." I dropped it in her cell. She could use it or leave it. Then I strode back to Ni.

She smiled the moment I stepped into view, or whoever had control over her did. She crinkled her runed parchment and set it aside.

I sent a shadow into her cell, forced it into a solid, sharp point, and sliced just above her neck. Black gunk oozed out. Internally cringing, I let my shadows absorb the abhorrent substance and brought it to my lips. I entered her mind, standing in the center of the shattered pieces.

Her thoughts and memories resembled Silas's—even her manic smile. What didn't was the way she responded.

"Who are you?" I demanded for... honestly, I'd lost count of how many times I'd asked that question.

On the outside, Ni only smiled, but inside, the pieces of her mind collected to form a clear thought: *What makes you think I'm one person?*

I tried to latch onto the thought and follow it to memories, but it slipped through my fingers as if it hadn't come from Ni at all. Not for the first time, I wondered if she was still even in there.

We didn't understand the demon disease. It killed blood-banded. It gave control over the soul. It changed their blood, their appearance, fractured their minds. But that was as much as we had figured out.

"Are you Lilith?"

Laughter vibrated through Ni's brain, shaking the pieces before coalescing into a thought: *Oh, darling, I'm not going to tell you. It's so much more fun to keep you guessing.*

My hands curled around the bars of her cell, squeezing until the Ember Metal dug into my skin.

"How did you get into this circle?"

Technically, we didn't. Just our infection did. But I know what you meant, and it's pretty clever on our part. I'm not surprised you or your king have failed to figure it out.

I glared at the whirling colors of Ni's mind.

Don't beat yourself up, darling. You'll figure it out—once it's too late.

Her thoughts lacked sound, but I could feel the confidence in her words grating against my mind.

"Why do you want to kill Lucille?"

Kill her. Burn her. Steal her. Bleed her dry. So many options, but only one will suffice for our bigger picture.

I gripped the metal bars with bone-crushing force, refraining from unlocking the cell and cleaving her head from her shoulders. Each time I interrogated her, she gave us breadcrumbs—just enough new information to make us keep her alive, but not enough to act on. And each time, she said shit like that to rile me up.

I leashed my shadows before they could rip apart her brain, but just as I left her mind, she gave me one final thought: *Her time's about up, General.*

Her words slithered into my chest, coiling tightly and squeezing. I glared into her smiling face, then stormed out of the dungeon.

"Don't get attached," Anya called after me.

She didn't have to tell me twice. There were only two people in this dimension I cared about. Who I trusted with my life. Two people I knew wouldn't betray me, use me, or die because they had no choice but to step in front of a sword to protect me.

Two people... and another slithering beneath my skin.

But it's not like it meant anything. It was only self-preservation. I didn't want Lucifer condemning me for slacking on his daughter's protection, and I sure as hell didn't want to feel the physical pain of her death. It was nothing more or less.

And yet, if she was just a charge to watch and train, why couldn't I control my emotions around her? Why was she always on my fucking mind? Why did my chest ache with worry?

Seven Hells, I didn't want another useless bond. But no matter how hard I tried to push her away—to remind myself she was nothing but a job—she snuck through my barriers like a stealthy shadow. She looked at me with those agonized, breathtaking eyes, shared her story, her scars, and turned me into a male who wanted to comfort her and torture every sick bastard who'd been a part of her trauma.

I strode through the dungeon door, finding Rune waiting where I'd left her.

"Meet me at the Shard Field."

Immediately, Rune raced down the hall. I luscelered to the roof by my rooms, manifested my wings, and shot into the sky.

I wanted to say Anya's words, and those controlling Ni, didn't affect me. I wanted to say the worry clenching my chest was an over-reaction. But after this morning's run—seeing Lucille so distracted, feeling her growing distress, and then hearing that from Ni's mind—it felt orchestrated, not coincidental.

Dropping my shields, I let some of Lucille's emotions through. The coiling in my chest turned into crushing. But the excruciating pressure couldn't be physical pain. If it were, she'd be dead.

She was with Lucifer. They were most likely undergoing an extremely difficult training regimen that put strain on her chest. She was safe with him.

I sped up, despising the fact that Lucifer never wanted Rune around. In his position, I understood not wanting to be spied on by your equal, but fuck if it didn't drive me insane right now.

Gritting my teeth, I slammed my barriers back up, flying as fast as I could. Even if I didn't want to be bonded with her, I still needed to keep her safe—for Lucifer, and for my sanity.

Staying low, nearly brushing the treetops, I reached the edge of the Shard Field. I dove into the forest and weaved between the trees.

I spotted her through the trunks. The tightening in my chest eased as she stood on steady legs. Then I laid eyes on Lucifer, hunched on all fours.

Seven Hells, what happened?

I landed behind the tree line, dematerializing my wings, unsure if I needed to intervene.

Lucille's hand flickered purple as Lucifer collapsed. She gave him a quick, panicked glance, then raised her arm, showing off a glinting icicle in her palm. Before I could comprehend what she was about to do, she twisted back and threw it with precision. The icicle sliced through the air and into the Veil Forest. Seconds later, a male fell out of the foggy woods, landing on his knees. A deranged laugh croaked from his lips.

A deadly calm sluiced through my veins as I eyed the horns protruding from his scarred face. I unsheathed my Soul Swords, my lips curling at their satisfying shing.

"Good luck, Princess." The impaled male laughed. He dug his hands into the ground as his eyes flashed green. Vines erupted through the snow, wrapping around Lucille's ankles. Then five more stepped out of the forest.

Shadows pooled out of my body, carrying my chuckle and filling the clearing with darkness.

"She doesn't need luck, demon. She's got me."

CHAPTER 36

Lucille

His voice vibrated through the darkness, and the tension in my shoulders melted.

He was here.

The vines holding my ankles were ripped from the ground, releasing me. I reached out to feel for Ronen, but he wasn't there. It was his shadows, then. The grunts and hisses to my left more than confirmed that.

Safe within his wispy power, I sank to my knees and felt for my father's neck. It only took me a couple of tries before I found the cool, unprotected skin. I bowed my head when I felt his pulse—faint, but there.

Fire flashed at the edge of my vision, and I whipped my head up. A mangled face with curling horns appeared. He smiled at me, tilting his head while he held an orange fireball. The toothless, black grin made my skin crawl—evil, lifeless, stretching across his glistening, grotesque scars. My Glory moved beneath the surface of my arms, and my Infernus whispered in my ear.

The male stepped toward me and began humming "London Bridge." The nursery rhyme crawled down my ears and over-pumped my lungs.

Keeping my eyes on the demonic male, I formed two foot-long icicles in my palms and planted myself in front of my father's body.

"Get back," I warned.

He tilted his head the other way and took another step. A low growl rumbled behind him. He raised his ball of flame higher, illuminating the scene, and his humming grew louder.

Then the tune sprang up on either side of me, growing closer with each passing second. He was calling his group—to me.

One of his followers appeared on my right. But she wasn't humming, nor did she wear that creepy smile. Instead, skin molted off her face in a gory mess of red and black. The horns on her head were crumbling, and I swore I saw pain in her eyes.

She snapped her arm out, trying to wrap it around my throat. I easily sidestepped.

"Don't kill!" the eerie male rasped.

His follower didn't listen. She unsheathed a dagger and sliced it toward my chest. I dodged, swept her legs, and followed her to the ground, shoving one icicle into her neck and the other into her chest. They were quick, efficient strikes. My mother would be proud.

Mixed blood spurted out, splattering my gloves. Her skin slid away from the puncture at her neck and plopped to the snow, completely detached from the muscles beneath, just like the skin on her face.

"Burn me," she gurgled, a haunting clarity in her eyes.

I frowned.

"Burn—" She choked on her blood, and her body relaxed.

A sharp squelch, like a sword piercing flesh, cut off one of the hummers. Then another. And another. Their tune quieted with each of Ronen's kills.

I stood as the demonic male crept closer, ignoring the predator at his back like he was mindless. The infection veining his neck had stripped him of clarity, unlike the dead female at my feet.

With effort, I wreathed my hands in Glory just as Rune materialized from Ronen's shadows, her teeth dripping with drool. Still, the robotic male ignored her, focusing only on me.

"Goodbye," I said sweetly.

Rune's jaw unhinged, opening wider than I'd ever seen. She snapped her mouth around the male's torso, crushing bone and severing his spine. His chilling tune ended as, in his dimming flame, half his body folded backward, tearing away from his pelvis.

I would never unsee that. Nor unhear the sound of Rune munching on his leftover remains.

More sickening slaps of a blade slicing through flesh echoed through the clearing, until there was nothing left but blissful silence.

I sidestepped the female and sank next to my father. Ronen's shadows brushed along my face and tickled up my nose—probably checking if I was physically okay—then cleared.

I blinked against the sudden light and found Ronen lowering his blades. I expected to see bodies at his feet, but there was only snow. Even the male I impaled with an icicle was gone. A blot of black substance dotted the ground where he'd been, the same black ooze dripping from Rune's maw and saturating the snow beneath the female. Except hers was more red than black.

Ronen resheathed one of his swords, then strode toward me. His posture was rigid, his gaze fixed on the dead female. He lifted his blade.

"Wait. I was going to burn her."

I wasn't sure why. I shouldn't care about the female who tried to kill me. But the clarity in her gaze made her seem less demonic, and I couldn't help myself.

He narrowed his eyes. "We can't take that risk. We don't know enough about the disease. The blood-banded could cycle with a demonic soul." Then he cleaved her head from her body. A second later, she dissolved into ash, and his sword absorbed her. "This way she'll never cycle."

I sat straighter. No wonder Theon peed himself.

Ronen sheathed his blade and sank in front of me, grabbing my chin. He twisted my face back and forth, his nostrils flaring.

"Are you okay?"

"Don't you already know the answer?" I gestured toward my nose, where his shadows had just been.

His golden irises flashed black.

"I'm fine."

"Are you lying to me, Hellion?"

"No." At least not in any way that mattered to him.

On the outside, I had a few insignificant slices on my face. But inside, everything was pain—like someone had reached into my body and squeezed all my organs to the brink of rupturing.

I just hoped I could hold back the scream clawing my throat for the rest of the day. If I allowed my thoughts to take form for even one second, I wouldn't be able to hold it together. And I still had to train with the Tormentors.

I ripped my chin from Ronen's grip. "Something's wrong with Lucifer, and I'm not sure if it's my fault or something else."

"Why would you think it's your fault?" he asked, gently rolling Lucifer onto his back. He checked his pulse, nodding when he felt it.

"Because I have more energy than I used to, and he seems to have less."

Ronen unbuckled the armor on Lucifer's arms.

"What are you doing?"

He ignored my question, yanking off Lucifer's arm braces. "Has he runed you?"

"No. Why?"

Ronen pushed up Lucifer's sleeves, revealing five active runes carved into his arms. One I recognized: the Ligamen Rune between him and Oliver—his end of the deal not yet complete. The other four were the same symbol, just in various shades of gray, their power fading.

"What are they?"

"Transference Runes," Ronen said grimly. "They work like a Wrath Rune, transferring energy to another person. They're used in battle. When some of our warriors are weak, the stronger and refreshed ones give them a portion of their energy."

I didn't have any new runes. So he wasn't giving energy to me. But who—

"My mom," I answered aloud. "He's giving his energy to my mom."

"Which means she's taking less from you."

And every time Lucifer used his powers, he drained himself.

I almost sighed with relief. For a moment, I thought I'd caused his sickness. But in a way, I did every time we trained. Which meant we'd have to stop. At least until we killed Michael.

Ronen grabbed Lucifer's arm, twisting it before taking off his glove and grazing a finger over the raised marks.

"What?"

"I need to get him to Sam."

There was more he wasn't telling me. I could tell by his furrowed brows and calculating expression.

"What aren't you saying?"

He shook his head. "Nothing I'm sure of yet. Do you have another of Sam's crystals?"

I pulled out the little yellow energy boost I took everywhere and handed it to him.

He placed the crystal in the center of Lucifer's hand, cupped his palm, and helped him squeeze. A burst of light flared between their knuckles, and color rushed back into Lucifer's face. The bags under his eyes lightened, and he already looked healthier. But he didn't wake.

"You better get going."

But Ronen didn't move from his crouch beside me.

"What are you waiting for? His death?" I joked, though it lacked any humor. Beneath my chaotic emotions, a sliver of worry crept in.

Ronen gave me a long, irritated look. "I can only carry one person while flying."

"So?"

He had to leave. I needed a moment to gather the pieces slipping through my fingers, to build up a more substantial wall for the rest of the day. I couldn't do that while he was still here.

His expression darkened.

"I'll be fine. We killed them all."

He didn't look convinced. I saw the indecision warring in his face, pulsing in his jaw.

"He's the King of Hell. His life is more important than mine. Plus, I have Miss Soul-Consumer over here." I hooked a thumb at Rune.

Her shadow tail curled with speed, knowing I was talking about her. She stared into the foggy forest ahead, watching for threats and refusing to acknowledge us any more than that.

"If I were anyone else, you'd already be gone."

"But you're not anyone else," he growled.

I blinked, too emotionally spent to interpret it.

"He tasked me to keep you safe."

"Exactly. You answer to him. So you need to save him."

What was he waiting for? Sam's crystal only lasted so long.

Ronen stood, rolling his tongue across his teeth as he glared down at us.

"I answer to no one, Hellion."

"Last I checked, there was only one King of Hell—one ruler. Unless I missed something, you're a general. A large step below a king."

Maybe his big ego was talking. But I didn't care. I just wanted him gone.

He refrained from commenting, breathing deeply like he was gathering patience.

"What if there are more infected souls?" he asked.

"Then Rune will eat them, and I'll sit back and plug my ears while she does," I replied. "You should already be in the air. *Leave.*"

His shadows tore out of him, sliding chaotically around his body and infusing his irises. He unstrapped one of his swords from his back and threw it at me. I caught it before it could smack my nose and held it like it might unsheathe itself and slice my head off.

"Stay on Rune," he said, his voice sharp. "And only use my sword if you absolutely need to."

I frowned, glancing at the beastie as she lowered to all fours. "Stay on Rune?"

Ronen swooped down and picked me up before my mind caught up, then quickly placed me on Rune's back.

"Really?"

"Run fast and stop for nothing," Ronen urged, patting Rune's side, ignoring me altogether.

She took off before I could snap something back. I yelped, tensing my legs around her body and shoving my arm through the sword strap before ducking down. I latched onto her fluff, wishing there was more substance to hold. But at least most of my attention was on staying on and not the thoughts threatening to pull me under.

The trees in the Veil Forest creaked and rattled from a punishing wind, swirling the fog Rune ran through. My brows lowered as I glanced at my still hair. Shouldn't the wind be hitting us? It was hitting everywhere else. Everywhere but our warm little bubble, as if we had some sort of shield while we ran.

The black, leafless trees merged into a shapeless haze, leaving me unable to discern any details. If the infected lurked behind the trunks or hid in the fog covering the ground, I would never know. Rune never paused in her stride, never stopped. She sprinted out of the forest, past Hoar Hollow, and continued until she passed the castle gates.

Her lungs pumped rapidly beneath my legs as she carried me up the hill, finally slowing down. I eased my hold on her, letting her breathe more deeply, and rubbed behind her ears.

"You did well, Rune. You can put me down now. We're safe."

Her fur coiled around my fingers like a wispy hug, and then she plopped herself down on the snowy road. I slid off her back right as Alexei dropped from the sky in front of me.

"Well, I'm glad you're in one piece. Ronen made it seem like you were fighting for your life in Veil Forest." Alexei huffed.

I took off Ronen's sword, grabbed the unusually warm hilt, and held it out to Alexei. I was glad I didn't have to use it. "He overreacted. We didn't run into any trouble."

Alexei's face blanched. His gaze darted between me and the sword.

I offered it, hoping he'd take it, and he jerked back.

"It's Ronen's."

He laughed, but it sounded a little high and strung out. "I know whose sword that is."

"Okay, well, can you give it back to him?"

I was sure he was still with the king or doing whatever damage control he had to do, and I needed to get to the arena. I didn't want to be carting this heavy, giant, soul-absorbing sword around while I trained.

Alexei shook his head, taking another step back and pointing to Rune. "Give it to her. She can give it back to him."

I didn't have the energy or time to dissect Alexei's weird behavior. Walking to Rune, I held out the sword. She opened her mouth wide. Taking a guess, I placed the sword sideways, resting it against her five-inch canines. She bowed her head as if in thanks and closed her mouth over the sheathed blade.

Alexei quietly led me to the arena, leaving Rune to cool down. Something about Ronen's sword had his flirtatious tongue in a twist. Maybe Ronen never lent out his special sword.

His dappled wings snapped out of existence once we reached the doors. He opened them to reveal Moira standing too close to Oliver. She turned, her irises flashing with blue fire, and her mouth popped open as she saw me step through the threshold. Her shock quickly transformed into a tight, vile smile, like it did when she was about to punish us—but worse.

I left Alexei with the redheaded Dread, who eyed me up and down, judgment clear in her gaze.

"What the hell have you and Ronen been up to?"

"You want answers, MJ, ask him."

I caught the sharp tone of her reply as I walked toward my squad leader, hoping I didn't have another Moira on my hands. One was enough.

"Let's get this over with."

"Theon and Cyrus," Moira sang, brushing her hands across my shoulder pads like she was tidying my uniform, "follow us. The rest

of you go to our station and pair up while I deal with our imposters."
She squeezed my shoulders, unable to take her eyes off my body.

Heavenly Shit. I forgot to change.

Moira slid her arm around my shoulder like we were friends and led us through a sea of red and black. But she kept our pace slow, giving every warrior, new and old, time to see what I was wearing. I couldn't keep count of how many lips curled in disgust or how many ran their fingers over their weapons and smiled like they couldn't wait to rip into me and show me how much I hadn't earned the colors of Hell.

Once we reached the showers, Moira shoved me into the back wall with startling force. My shoulder took the brunt of the pain. Oliver luscelered to my side, rage in his flaming emeralds.

"Are you okay?" he whispered.

I gritted my teeth. "Yeah." I was fine. Only pissed.

"Did you fuck him for that uniform? Or did you service his Dreads like you serviced the king and earned it that way, Hell-whore?"

She picked the wrong time to taunt me.

"You would know." I lifted my chin. Something moved in the shadowed hall behind the trio, hiding in the doorway of the changing rooms. I scrutinized it for a split second before giving my full attention to the queen bitch. "Wouldn't you, Moira?"

Oliver squeezed my arm in warning, but I ignored him.

"You must've given him great head for a second-rate whore like you to earn the Tormentors position. It's no wonder he turned to me."

I still didn't know what giving head meant, but I could only guess it was sexual.

Her face pinched into an ugly mask. "Cyrus! Bind them."

Vines shot from the tiled floor and walls, wrapping around our wrists and ankles. A few weeks ago, I would've started hyperventilating. Now, I raised a brow, enjoying the way they cut into my skin.

I tilted my head and smiled, loving how it made Moira's face flush a cherry red. "Hit a nerve? Ronen not letting you in his bed anymore?" I pouted in mock sympathy.

"Lucy, stop," Oliver discreetly whispered through his teeth.

A dagger from Moira's belt came beelining for my head. I dodged it, laughing as it bounced off the tiled wall and dropped near my feet.

"But I was just getting started. The bitch needs to know who she's speaking to," I taunted.

If only I could tell her. Better yet, *show her.*

The dagger on the floor rose, hovering near my stomach. Moira shook as severely as her dagger did, showing her rage. But she couldn't stab me—not unless she wanted to risk the wrath of Ronen or his Dreads. We weren't to harm our squadmates. Lightly torture, fine. But if I came out of this bathroom with a stab wound after she gave such a show to half the warriors in the arena, it'd be her ass, not mine. If she wanted to punish us, she'd have to do it the same way as always.

I saw her internal battle. She wouldn't risk it. Not if her relationship with Ronen was already rocky. And by the way she reacted, it was. I smirked and opened my mouth to rub salt in her wounds.

Oliver shot me a severe glance. "Don't."

"It's okay, Oliver. She should know I've replaced her. He's no longer hers." Oddly enough, I liked that thought. "Poor thing."

"Theon!" she shrieked. "Shut her up! And suffocate them."

I winced. Heavenly Hell, she almost blew out my eardrums.

Oliver groaned, dropping his head. Most likely thinking I was insane. But he should've learned by now that I'd never let anything happen to him. He also should've been more observant.

Theon grinned, raising his hands to form head-sized water spheres, oblivious to the water coalescing behind him. He taunted us, wanting to stoke our fear.

But it was difficult to be scared when three water dragons reared up behind their backs. They were expertly crafted, from the frills along their faces to their glistening teeth and scaled bodies. They almost looked real, if not for their transparent, wavering forms.

I rested my head against the tile, unconcerned and smug.

Theon's nostrils flared, and he chucked his spheres at us. Before they could so much as move a foot, the dragons attacked. One cleaved through the air, swallowing Theon's water, and the other two swallowed Theon and Cyrus.

Before Moira could overcome her shock, the third dragon reared up tall, opened its maw, and devoured her. The three of them dropped to their knees, suffocating.

Cyrus's vines released us, and we stepped away from the wall.

"Doesn't feel too good, does it, Theon?" I mocked.

Theon bared his teeth, his face as red and angry as Moira's. Both of them glared at me while Cyrus desperately clawed at his face, more concerned with fighting the water than plotting revenge like the other two.

There would be hell to pay later. No doubt about that. But I didn't care. We were done being their punching bags. If they wanted a fight, we'd give them a fight.

Eventually, the three of them passed out on the shower floor. The dragons splashed to the ground, running toward the drain. Ichi stepped around their limp bodies and approached us.

"You're a badass, Ichi." Oliver grinned.

I dipped my chin to her. "Thanks."

She bowed her head in response. "I'm only following my word. They'll wake up in a few minutes. Let's not be here when they do."

CHAPTER 37

Ronen

I luscelered through the healers' wing and into the private room in the back, placing Lucifer on the bed. Then shouted for Sam.

He stormed in, ready to chastise me for yelling—until he saw Lucifer.

"He's suffering from Divine Wasting from four Transference Runes carved into his arm."

Sam snapped his head toward me and ripped off his amulet. "That's suicidal!"

It was. If Lucifer weren't the King of Hell, he'd be dead already.

Sam shook his head and placed a hand over Lucifer's chest. Yellow light shot into his body, pressing him into the mattress. Seconds passed. Then minutes.

What was taking so long?

Was he dying?

I couldn't become king. We didn't have my feather for the ceremony. Even if we did, I didn't know how to perform the transference of power. And then there was the matter of my past. If he died, I'd be exposed, and things would turn dark fast. That wasn't even factoring in all of Hell's other unresolved problems.

"Seven Hells, I shouldn't have taken so long to bring him in," I muttered.

A second later, color returned to Lucifer's face. Sam's yellow light faded, and his hand dropped limply. He turned to me, sweat soaking his brown hair. As he gripped his dark amulet, yellow flames flickered in his irises.

"You did what?"

That was a first. I'd never seen him angry before.

"We ran into an incident at the Shard Field. I had to make sure Lucille was okay."

"Assuming by the fact she's not here, no harm came to her, correct?"

"Yes."

"Then the king should've been your priority, General!" he shouted. "Instead, I've hit my limit and can't heal anyone else today!"

"I—" Had nothing to say to that.

Sam scoffed and left, slamming the door behind him.

Fucking Lucille.

The more time I spent with her, the harder it became to distinguish between Lucifer's order, my obsessive shadows, and my intrusive desires. The worst part? I didn't know if the urges I felt were mine or the bond's. Did it really have that much control?

I could ask MJ. But that'd only lead to more questions, and she knew how to get the truth out of me. Alexei was already breathing down my neck as it was.

"I didn't take you for a daydreamer, General," Lucifer rasped.

My focus snapped back, and I sat straighter in my chair. "Nor did I take you for someone who'd risk all of Hell just to give Saraqael and your daughter more energy."

Sam came back in at that moment, shutting the door firmly behind him. He wore his full disapproving healer expression—from the lines on his forehead to the tension pressing his tongue into his cheek. He clearly wanted to lecture Lucifer but kept it buried beneath professionalism.

Lucifer dropped his head back and sighed at the painted angels on the ceiling. "Saraqael is degrading fast. I don't know what changed or why. Originally, I only carved one Transference Rune, and it helped—but then it started to fade. One moment she was stable, the next, her complexion faded to a sickly gray. She lost weight exponentially fast, and her heart nearly stopped."

Sam approached the bed. "Based on what little you've told me, and all the healings I've been doing, I'll surmise Saraqael realized she's risking Lucille's life by draining her energy to survive. As a result, she's either trying to take as little as possible... or she's giving up entirely, so your daughter can live." He looked pointedly between Lucifer and me.

I stiffened. Sam wasn't supposed to know that. Lucifer leveled him with a considering gaze. Seconds passed as they stared at each other, an unspoken conversation unfolding in the silence. Then, finally, they both nodded.

The steel in Lucifer's expression crumbled, leaving only exhaustion in its wake. "How do we keep them both alive?"

"Explain their situation. Which type of Wrath Rune is it? Two-way or three-way?" Sam asked.

Lucifer tugged at the neckline of his healer's gown. "Three-way."

"The carver wanted to kill Lucille and give Saraqael her energy." Sam didn't assume or guess. His words were confident. He was not only the best healer in Hell, but one of the most intelligent angels.

"Yes," Lucifer confirmed.

"I can only think of one potential way. Notice I say *potential*, because Lucille is an anomaly in this situation. That being said, if we treat this like a normal three-way bind, then your best option is to limit Lucille's power use to a designated time frame—*that's* when you can use a Transference Rune, Lucifer. But one. Not four," he warned. "Every time Lucille uses her powers, she's taking energy away from Saraqael. Not stealing it, but using it before Saraqael can. That could explain some of her decline and why she's draining your energy as fast as she is. It's also why I think you should cut her physical training in half. That will give your Transference Runes more potency."

Lucifer grimaced, and the temperature dropped. "I can't cut her training. Give me a better solution, Sam."

"Why not?" I asked, crossing my arms. "Are we not the ones who dictate who trains and who doesn't?" I wanted her strong, and cutting back to keep her and her mother safe didn't sound like a bad idea.

The icy glow of Hell overtook Lucifer's gaze, and frost crept along the walls. "Another solution, Sam."

I stepping forward, planting myself beside the bed. "Why *can't* you cut her training?"

My shadows writhed inside me, demanding release to wrap around his throat. Lucifer wore that same calculating expression he had when we first saved her, and they could sense something dangerous in his words.

"I've made a deal. And part of her demands was to train Lucille—hard and fast."

"A deal with who?"

"That's none of your concern, General."

My fingers twitched, itching to either crack my knuckles or grab my sword and threaten him until he explained himself.

"If you won't tell me who. Then tell me the *other* part of this deal."

"*You* are not the king. And until you are, you will not question me. Lucille has a predestined fate. As do you. I'd remember that, General. Unless you want your creators to know where you've been hiding."

I tightened the leash on my shadows and clenched my jaw before I said something that would ruin everything.

"Since you can't talk to Saraqael and convince her she's not hurting Lucille, then the only other solution I can recommend is complete cessation of your power use," Sam said. "I can continue to give Lucille energy crystals, and you can continue to carve *one* Transference Rune twice a week. But that's not a permanent solution."

Sam's words pulled Lucifer's scrutinizing gaze away from me.

"That's not a solution at all," I countered. Lucifer needed his powers to judge souls.

"Thank you, Sam," Lucifer said with a nod. "General, if you say a word of this to my daughter, there will be consequences. You're dismissed."

I shook my head and forced my feet to carry me from the room, my shadows pounding at my skin, desperate to be released. I could only imagine the terrors they wanted to create. I'd been in Lucifer's mind once, back when I was proving he couldn't use me like the rest had. He learned quickly to fear my power, just as I learned to fear his. But he still had the upper hand.

A part of me wanted to fuck the consequences and rip apart his memories until he showed me what he was hiding about Lucille.

He made a deal that decided her fate.

But what kind of fate would that be?

CHAPTER 38

Lucille

"This session will be a lesson on problem-solving, control, and teamwork. My shadows are covering all of the Shard Field and this clearing. You three are tasked with escaping them. But you have to use the least amount of power you can, you have to escape together, and you can't bleed. If you break any of my rules, I'll render a part of your body immobile. You have an hour. Begin," Ronen said, his voice echoing through the darkness. "Also, there's a solid wall of shadows you'll hit before entering Veil Forest. Good luck."

My shoulders sagged. After watching my back during training—and Oliver's—after going through the motions with Ichi and straining to keep my thoughts on lockdown, holding onto the numbness, I just wanted the day to be over. I didn't want to do this. I didn't want to think or move. Or maybe I did. Whatever would help the pain.

Why were we even back near the Shard Field? Wasn't Ronen concerned about demons?

Obviously not. Nor did he care that no one seemed to want to be here. Ronen turned into a snappy ass right after I asked how Lucifer was doing. Alexei couldn't stop shooting glares at Ronen or scrutinizing glances at me. And Oliver continued to yawn like he had overexerted himself and needed a nap.

But instead, we were here, holding hands, unable to see, and hoping we could get through this drill fast.

"Does anyone have any bright ideas?" Oliver mumbled, sounding as happy as I felt.

"Fifty-seven minutes," Ronen announced behind me.

I twisted my head, but only wispy air caressed my face. Through the endless dark, I swore I met a pair of golden eyes. But they didn't reel me in like they usually did. I felt nothing and was grateful for it.

"I could throw lightning at them until they crumble," Alexei suggested.

I turned toward his voice. "That's using the least amount of power?"

He shrugged, moving my hand. "If I say it is—" He hissed. "Fuck you, Ronen!"

"What'd he do?" Oliver asked through a yawn.

"Little bastard cut and paralyzed my hand."

Tiny bolts of static lightning zapped through my fingers as Alexei held them, before a larger bolt streaked through Ronen's power, briefly illuminating our surroundings. Alexei searched left and right. "Stay in your little hidden corner and out of our plans, you secretive ass!"

His other hand went limp in mine, and he cursed again.

"Guess lightning is against the rules," Oliver concluded.

"Most of our powers that could get us through the Shard Field seem to be against the rules. Which doesn't make sense." Wasn't the point of this training to learn how to use my powers?

"So if we can't use our powers, then how do we get across a giant field of pointy, killing ice or a solid wall of shadows? While in said shadows?" Oliver asked.

"We don't," Alexei answered.

"We don't?" Oliver said in disbelief.

I understood his frustration, but something in Alexei's tone made me pause before reacting. I replayed Ronen's directions in my head, analyzing each word. He had said to escape his shadows. He never said anything about escaping this area. That was just the first thought that came to all our minds—the easiest one. But we didn't have to attempt to break free to escape. We had to somehow stop him from using them.

"We have to fight him."

Alexei barked out a short laugh. "Beautiful, I can barely beat him in a fistfight, and currently, those fists are out of commission." He lifted his arm and my hand that held his useless fingers. "So, how do you suggest we accomplish that, especially knowing he can hear every word we say?"

I thought for a moment, going over my own experiences and the books I had read. "Alexei, wield another bolt of lightning."

He did, revealing a quirked brow before sending us back into darkness.

"Was that pretty easy?"

I felt rather than saw him nod. "For the most part. It's harder when I direct it."

"Oli, stay right there." I released his hand.

"Staying."

I stepped into Alexei's space, placing my hands on his chest. "Do it again."

"Anything for you, beautiful."

Static zinged across his uniform, gathering to be shot into the sky, and tingling my fingers. As he focused, I pressed against him and slid my arms around his neck. I buzzed with the energy vibrating through his body, my hair standing on end.

His throat bobbed against my palms. "What are you doing?"

I tiptoed up to his ear. "Where's your lightning, Alexei?" My breath fanned across his neck, and I smiled when I felt his chest pounding.

"I'm having trouble concentrating."

"Oh? Really?" I enjoyed teasing him more than I should've, but not only did it prove my point, it gave me a good distraction.

Something grabbed my shoulders and ripped me away from him. I stumbled back and whipped around, reaching toward the culprit, finding no one.

"Oliver?"

"Still here, standing about, waiting for our great plan."

If it wasn't Oliver... "Ronen?"

"Your time is running out." He enunciated each word with a cold, harsh snap. His voice sent a shiver up my spine.

"I think I'm finally picking up what you're putting down, beautiful." Alexei reached out, hitting me with his limp hand, and walked into me. He dragged his arm up my body. "I think I have a plan. Where's your ear?" His search conveniently stopped on my chest

"Clearly not there," I deadpanned.

"I mean, I can't feel anything, so you never know," he muttered with a flirtatious hint, then yelped. "Hey! You were all over me, no need to hit me."

"Wasn't me." I sighed, grabbing his hand and holding it against my ear.

"Wasn't me either. Still just standing here, waiting for the dream team to stop fucking around and come up with something before I die of boredom or take a nap," Oliver chimed in.

Alexei whispered his plan, and I almost hit him myself. "Not going to happen. Nor would it work."

"Can't you tap into that circle? Shouldn't take too much power, right?"

"No. I only attempted it once, and it was an accident." My stomach rolled at the memory. "No. Think of something else."

Alexei hummed while awkwardly holding my head. "Then do it to me."

I smacked him.

"Hey!" he exclaimed.

"Of course you'd suggest that."

"Anyone mind cluing me in to what we're discussing?" Oliver asked, his voice sounding like he was sitting on the ground.

"Get your ass up and get over here if you want to know. We're not going to shout it across the bastard's shadows and alert him to our awesome plan."

"Or lack thereof," I mumbled. "I said I didn't know how to use those powers."

"You don't need to. Do it for real," Alexei said. I could hear the smile in his voice. "Trust me on this, I have a hunch it'll work."

"What will?" Oliver said, a lot closer now, his hand smacking me in the face. "Sorry. Can't see anything."

Alexei scoffed, and I reached out for Oliver, pulling him right next to our faces.

"Say your hunch is right, Alexei. Wouldn't he see it coming since he's already infiltrated your mind?"

"Depends if he's still in there—and that depends on how much blood he took and how much time has passed. But I've reinforced my mental shields and don't feel him. Trust me, I think the plan will work."

"And he can't hear our conversation through his shadows?"

"Not unless he's standing close, or he'd have to be in our mind to know more. He can only sense our heat signatures and movement."

"I want to know the plan," Oliver whispered right next to my cheek.

Alexei proceeded to tell him.

"Of course."

I had a feeling Oliver was rolling his eyes as much as I was. But he knew Ronen best, so if Alexei had a hunch, then it could work. Add in the fact that Ronen ripped us apart—for reasons I couldn't think about—and it was our best bet. The only problem was I didn't think it'd be a big enough scene to disrupt his shadows, nor was I going to willingly make out with Alexei while he *teased my breasts*—his words, not mine.

"I have a better idea, but it'll be much harder." I shifted both their heads so my mouth was at their ears and explained.

"No, I like my plan more."

"Me too. Haven't I puked enough in these stupid lessons?" Oliver groaned loudly.

I smiled, knowing wherever Ronen hid, he had to have heard that.

My ears popped as something changed in my environment, and wings rustled to my left. Curious, I slid my hand over Alexei's shoulder and ran my fingers through his heavenly soft feathers.

Alexei moaned. "Are you sure you don't want to go with my plan? Because you pretty much ran a finger along my cock. And I'm trying really hard not to get turned on right now. But a guy can only do so much."

I jerked my hand back and wrapped it around his neck. "Sorry."

He laughed and scooped me up after figuring out his arm placement. "There's a reason our wings don't stay out. So please, keep your hands and feet inside the vehicle at all times, or we're going with my plan."

A fierce, cold breeze snapped at my face as Alexei shot us into the air. He only went so far, staying within the shadows, but I knew the drop would kill me either way.

"You think this is really going to work?" The palms of my hands were slick with sweat, and my pulse quickened.

"Yes. And so do you, or you wouldn't have suggested it. He'd never let anything happen to you," Alexei admitted softly.

He made it sound like I meant something to him. Maybe I did. Maybe I didn't. If I did, I should've been ecstatic. That meant he might actually help me. Too bad it no longer mattered.

"Ready?"

"For this day to be over? Yes. For free-falling over the ground— or worse, the Shard Field—no."

Alexei huffed. "Enjoy the fall."

I swallowed. My nails dug into my hands, refusing to let go.

"Catch her if you can!" Alexei shouted as he released me. Even if I wanted to hold on to him longer, my sweaty hands slid, and I fell.

A shriek clawed up my throat. This was how I died. My stomach jumped into my mouth, and I flailed. It didn't matter if this was our plan. Images of my body impaled on icicles invaded my mind. Surely Ronen had retreated to some far-off corner. He wouldn't rescue me in time. Hadn't I already been falling forever?

Strong arms closed around me, and I was gasping for all the air I could get.

"What are you playing at, Hellion?" Ronen snarled, suspicious.

We flew for a moment, and I pretended I was gathering my breath to speak. Although it wasn't completely faked.

I didn't have time to make up an excuse; I didn't even have one on hand. Instead, I used all my focus and my father's training to imagine the hallucination Alexei suggested and burrowed deep into my power.

We landed.

"I'm proving I'm as scary as you." Then I shouted, "Now, Oliver!"

We touched Ronen at the same time, and I dove into his mind.

Ronen's barriers were a fortress of solidified darkness. They had no cracks, holes, or weaknesses at all. I knew force wouldn't get me through—not unless I was mentally and physically stronger than him. Which meant I had to try the way my father taught me.

I visualized warmth and safety, making my mental presence appear as nonthreatening as it could. If I wasn't a threat, there was a chance I could slip through. I softly touched his walls with my mental hand. At first, nothing happened. Then a shadow broke off from the wall and sank into me.

That never happened with my father. Did I screw up?

Nervous, I pressed harder and fell through to the heart of his mind.

It shouldn't have been that easy. But I didn't have time to question it. I needed to perform the next step of our plan.

Ronen

"I'm proving I'm as scary as you," she said, touching my face.

I couldn't see her, but I could feel every inch of her. My shadows wrapped around her body. Her warmth penetrated my uniform, just as her winterberry scent struck my nose. Overloaded by her addictive smell and intoxicating heat, it was difficult to concentrate on anything else.

"Now, Oliver!" she shouted.

I knew this was coming—I'd heard Oliver give away part of their plan—and yet he still managed to touch my back.

I collapsed, dropping the Hellion, and fell into my fear.

"Hey! You were all over me, no need to hit me," Alexei complained— the flirting bastard.

Maybe it wasn't such a good idea to tell them to restrict their power if all they were going to do was flirt and waste time. But if Lucifer wouldn't, then I would wherever I could. She'd never forgive herself if she killed her father or mother. Their lives were more important than Lucille practicing her powers every day. She could learn this way, slowly and with limitations. If she knew the truth, she'd agree, if not outright quit. At least this way, she'd receive some training.

"Wasn't me." She sighed. Her heat signature pressed closer to his.

"Beautiful, has anyone ever told you that you smell divine?"

Seven Hells, I wished Alexei would shut up—or at least lower his voice so I didn't have to hear him from here. I'd put enough space between us to give them an advantage. But they sure weren't taking it.

My shadows rippled, signaling a slight movement. But I couldn't pinpoint which one of them moved or the direction of their movements; their heat signatures were too close together.

"Lucille."

I frowned at Alexei's tone.

"What would you do if I kissed you right now?" He wasn't flirting. He wasn't joking. He was serious.

I waited for her to laugh or deny him.

She whispered something back that I couldn't make out. She had to have said no to him.

My shadows rippled again. I gritted my teeth, so close to dropping my power. But what if this was part of their plan?

Alexei knew me too well. He had to be taunting me to try to prove his suspicions right.

Seconds passed with more small ripples and whispered words. Hopefully, they were finally planning. I focused on Oliver. He sat on the ground. Small pulses surrounded his hands. Was he fidgeting?

Playing with snow? I refrained from scoffing. This was supposed to be a team effort.

A bigger ripple pulled me away from Oliver and back to Alexei and Lucille. I frowned at the oddly shaped heat signature on the ground, trying to process what I saw. In hindsight, I already knew, I just didn't want to believe it. Once the red glow dimmed from the items, I forced myself to look at their combined signatures. Then she moaned.

My ears rang as I dropped my shadows, and it felt like someone shoved a hot fire poker in my gut.

Alexei, half-dressed, leaned over Lucille, nipping at her breast. He held her up as he thrusted his fingers into her core. Her hair pooled down her naked back as she gasped to the sky.

For a second, I just stood there. Alexei flirted with everyone. He also stuck his cock into any gorgeous body that'd let him. But I didn't think Alexei would ever touch her, not after all his prying questions and suspicions. Even if I shut them down, I never thought he'd go this far. I never thought she'd let him.

Unholy heat seared through my stomach and boiled my blood. My shadows consumed my eyes and whipped out in a chaotic storm. Lifting my chin, I luscelered to Alexei and ripped him back by his neck.

His hands gripped the arm I had secured around his throat. "I'm sorry, Ro," he croaked. He didn't even fight me as I squeezed tighter.

I didn't want his apology. It was worthless now. He did the deed. After berating me with questions and assuming what she was to me, he still fucking did this.

The hellion hit me from behind, begging me to let go, but I couldn't. The pain stabbing through my chest wouldn't let me.

This wasn't supposed to happen. Not with the male I'd shared all my hardships with. Not with someone I called my brother.

Seven fucking Hells, her scent was all over him. Another shot of rage seared through me.

I squeezed tighter.

"Ronen! Stop! Don't hurt him!" the hellion screamed behind me.

Bile gathered at the back of my throat.

Then the scene dissolved and shifted.

We were at the Shard Field, but Alexei stood fully clothed next to Oliver, and Lucille was next to me, pulling her hand from my face.

I should've been relieved. Oliver never touched me. It wasn't a fear—it was a manipulation.

Dread dug its claws into my chest. A voice—*his* voice—slithered through my thoughts, echoing in my ears. My lungs seized. My hands trembled. One moment they were clean—the next, coated in blood.

Seven Hells. Not again.

This wasn't real.

A distant voice pierced through his oily, controlling words—familiar and warm. I snapped my head up.

Alexei's face flickered—golden and concerned, then pure white and apathetic.

No. He wasn't here. He didn't know I was in Hell.

Unless I wasn't here.

Snow crunched beneath my shifting boots. In a blink, it was gone—replaced by blinding white marble.

"Ronen, are you okay?" It was her voice, distorted and echoing, but it was *his* face. "I didn't mean—"

I jerked away from her—*his* touch.

Lucille

Shadows wrapped around his heaving chest, brushing his face as if trying to soothe him.

"Ronen, are you okay?" I touched his shoulder gently. "I didn't mean—"

He jerked away like my hand burned him. His expression broke something inside me. He'd never looked at me like that before—like I was something vile.

Alexei had known his plan would work. But I would never willingly let Alexei kiss or touch me, so I had to weave a convincing illusion. The only way I figured Ronen wouldn't suspect me was if Oliver acted like he was forcing Ronen into his fears.

I should've been proud. I'd successfully infiltrated the mind of the second-most powerful angel in Hell. Instead, I felt sick.

He couldn't think it had been real... right? I'd never do that to him.

But if it wasn't that, then why was he trembling? Why did he clench his fists until his knuckles cracked?

His fear gutted me. His distance made my feet twitch, wanting to comfort him.

"Ronen, look at me." Alexei reached out to grab his shoulders.

He luscelered back, shadows bristling, and unsheathed a Soul Sword.

"Hey," Alexei said, palms up. "It's just me. Alexei."

Ronen's gaze darted between the three of us, eyes gleaming with panic and rage. His hands shook, white-knuckling the hilt. His shadows lashed out, forcing us back.

"Come any closer and I will kill you."

I stiffened.

Kill us?

What had I done? Did something go wrong when I was in his mind?

"Ronen, you're okay," Alexei said, voice soft, coaxing. "You're safe. You're with people who care about you."

"I am not your slave anymore!"

His wings burst free in a violent flare of power, and I stumbled back, shaken by the ferocity in his voice.

"Don't—" Alexei lurched forward.

But Ronen was already gone, shooting into the gray sky.

I stood there, breathless, heart hammering, watching the dark blur of him disappear.

Devastated.

CHAPTER 39

Lucille

I woke up in the last place I ever wanted to be. My chest ached as little firewings zapped around me, their vibrant color warning me back. If they landed on my bare skin, they'd bite and swarm, devouring me in heat and torment. Still, that wouldn't compare to how I felt on the inside.

"Take me out," I whispered to my power. "Let me leave, please," I begged.

Why was I even here?

I dropped my head.

I knew why. Aspen had told me.

He told me how to tap into them because he knew how. Then he covered up his confident words with lies and kisses.

My gut warned me, and I ignored it for *him*, blinded by my feelings instead of logic.

"Sweetheart?"

I flinched, the shards of my heart grinding together.

"Lucille?" Aspen touched my shoulder, attempting to turn me around.

"Don't touch me." I wrenched out of his hold, biting my wobbling lip hard before facing him. The taste of copper trickled into my mouth, but I barely noticed.

Aspen searched my face, then thoroughly scoured our surroundings before the concern tugging on his lips flatlined. "So you finally figured it out."

Finally, as if I should've known from the beginning—and I should've. I should've known all of this was too good to be true, that his behavior was different. But I wanted to believe I was with the real Aspen—the one without secrets, hidden agendas, and uncontrolled by Lilith.

"I'm not sure. Are you actually even Aspen?"

"Good question." He imagined two chairs and plopped himself in one, sitting back. "I'm the Aspen you were with in Elora."

At least he wasn't Lilith. Something clicked into place at that thought, and I laughed, the sound a broken, half-version of itself. He may not be Lilith, but I *guarantee* the figure I saw in our last dream-walk was—and I bet that wasn't the only time she showed up. Which meant she either had some rune or power to infiltrate dreams, or she was a dream-walker, and *that* was where I got my power from. Not from my mother, father, or their Weaver—from the evil bitch who made my birth possible.

"Let me guess, Aspen. You're Hell Runed."

He switched his leather uniform for a short-sleeved tunic and pants, looking at his wrists. "No, I'm not."

He kept his arms turned up and rested them on his legs, revealing two red-black Hell Runes, showing me his lie, and confirming Lilith controlled what he could and couldn't say. Did that mean she controlled what he *did* too?

A lump traveled up my throat. He did things to me I'd never done with anyone else. I was vulnerable and nervous, but I'd felt like it was okay. He had me. He'd guided me through my nerves with that desire in his eyes and those gorgeous dimples. I had trusted him, given a piece of myself to him that no one else had. I thought it meant something to him.

Clearly. Fucking. Not.

"Did she watch us?" My voice cracked.

He flinched like it hurt him. His usually vibrant blues seemed to hold shame. But as great as it was to see, it didn't make me feel better.

"Did you put on a good show for her? Did I?"

He dropped my heated stare to his hands, stomping on whatever remained of my heart.

"She commanded you to be nice to me too, didn't she? So I'd spill all my secrets?" I yelled, searching his face for the answers, knowing it was the only thing that made sense.

I was so fucking naïve. And stupid.

"Glad you're not floundering anymore, sweetheart," he whispered, sounding sad and exhausted.

I tilted my head to the overcast sky, blinking back the stinging in my eyes, covering my mouth, and locking my knees from buckling.

Every part of me wanted to drop to the grass and scream, to grieve the fake male I fell for. He was an illusion. One big, fat lie.

I held tightly to our tender moments in Elora, to who he *could* be, and his poisonous words snuck into my weak heart.

I should've listened to my gut.

Knowing I couldn't hold it all in much longer, I forced my tears back and looked at him again. I waited until he met my gaze and told him the one secret I'd been hiding, wanting to hurt him as badly as he'd hurt me.

"Your first love, Nalini—she's living in Hell now, and she'd be so disgusted with you."

Aspen's face blanched right before he cried out, and the runes on his wrists pulsed with light—the same old song and dance.

"Enjoy rotting with Lilith," I snapped, then forced myself out of the dream-walk.

I quietly slipped out of bed, put on a robe, and left Oliver to his sleep. Tears trickled down my face as I walked through the halls, half-aware. When I reached the hidden doorway and stepped out onto the castle roof, I ignored the snow burning the bottoms of my feet. I fell to my knees, and they cracked against the dark stone. Then I tilted my head back to the black sky and screamed.

It was low and wet, vibrating out from my crushed heart and tapering off into whimpers.

Through my softer sounds, a bellow rang out far in the distance. A foreign pang tightened my chest—almost like I could feel their hurt, like their pain was my pain.

For some reason, the thought that I wasn't completely alone in my grief, that someone out there was hurting as much as I, made me feel a little less lonely on this cold, dreary night.

The next few days, my nerves were a chaotic mess. I needed to apologize to Ronen and make sure he was okay, despite Alexei's reassurance. But neither he nor Rune showed up—for anything.

Instead, it was just Alexei and Oliver at every run and training. Nothing felt the same anymore.

Lucifer never used his powers on me, saying my mother needed his extra energy, which I confirmed with my own eyes when I saw her skinnier and paler than usual. I tried to dream-walk to her afterward, but it never worked. I asked Cato again, but he refused to speak of it and luscelered away to wherever he hid.

Then there was Oliver. My heart was in pieces from Aspen, and I was scared to tell him. He'd been right. Aspen had been lying to me the whole time. But how did I admit that to my best friend? After spending night and day trying to strengthen myself and find a way to Aspen—choosing him over my mom—only to ignore my gut and discover I was just a pawn *again*. How did I get those shameful words out? Worse, how did I tell him a part of me couldn't stop thinking about Aspen?

I couldn't. So I withdrew as much as possible and put on a show that I was okay. If only I were.

At the end of the week, after training, I strode up to the dais where Alexei stood. I'd finally had enough. I didn't think their absence would hurt this much, at least not Ronen's. But each day that passed, I found myself scanning the arena for his golden gaze, analyzing every shadow like a hopeless fool.

"Where are they? Is he okay?"

Alexei finished writing the rankings on his parchment, then gave me a small smile. "He just needs time, beautiful."

"It's been a week. Can you at least tell me where he is? So I can apologize—or help, or something?"

Alexei grabbed my shoulder. "An apology won't fix anything because this isn't about you. Ronen needs time to think and heal. Give him that."

I didn't completely believe him. I knew I'd struck some chord within Ronen, one Alexei refused to enlighten me on, but that didn't mean it still wasn't my fault. I had infiltrated Ronen's mind. I'd made him live out that scene. The pain that twisted his features and bled through his voice gutted me, and I needed to see for myself that he was okay. I cared about him—more than I ever thought I would.

Over the next few days, I badgered Alexei with the same questions, only to receive the same result.

To distract myself, Oliver and I read every night, searching for a way out of Hell. Sometimes I found myself picking up a book on the Tenebrous Kingdom, feeling a strange urgency in my blood. I'd think about Aspen, ease the gnawing need for him in my stomach, then slam the book shut.

At one point, I searched the library for books on relationships or guardian bonds, trying to comprehend my twisted feelings. It was like something inside me still wanted him, still desired to save him. But why?

How could I possibly still care about him?

This shame and want couldn't be love, could it?

None of the books told me one way or another. I'd never been in love, but I knew I'd been falling for him.

But maybe that wasn't what this was.

Perhaps it was the overwhelming guilt that came with remembering Miriam's words, asking me to save her son.

Or maybe it was the bond we shared, the one I couldn't just cut away, no matter how much I wanted to.

After two weeks, Ronen and Rune were still gone, and I coped like I had every previous night. I went to the library hoping to see him. Not sure why. It was a pointless hope. Ronen wouldn't be sitting in his chair reading. He never was. Yet I still came at this time, just to see— and to have some of Dorus's tea and chocolates.

Before I opened the doors, I paused in front of them. Their colorful pieces shifted from the symbol they had been displaying daily—a symbol I still couldn't decipher—to a new image: Michael's dagger in Ronen's hands.

My stomach churned as I remembered every instance that blade had drawn my blood. At four years old, it had nearly killed me. At five, six, seven, eight, and nine, it marked my birthday "gifts." At nineteen, Michael tortured me with it. But I didn't think the doors were showing me the dagger to just reminisce. There had to be a purpose, some kind of significance.

Thinking, something I had forgotten came rushing back. Her words—the female from my nightmares, the one who invaded my mind in Elora—trickled into my memory:

"If you ever want to save Aspen, steal the bastard's knife."

Part of me wanted to save him as badly as I wanted to breathe. But another part ached with self-hatred at the thought.

"What is wrong with me?" I whispered, opening the library doors.

I stopped short at the entrance.

Oliver lounged at our table, plopping chocolates into his mouth with his fuzzy slippers propped up.

"Didn't I leave you in bed?" I padded down the marble floor and took a seat opposite him.

He smiled, his teeth covered in *my* chocolate truffles. "Haven't heard of the old pillow trick?"

"I wasn't that sheltered. But why are you up this late?"

He took his feet off the table and leaned forward, grabbing my hands before they could reach for a book. "We need to talk."

I quirked a brow. "Breaking up with me, Oli?"

"You know, that would've actually been kind of funny if not for your monotone voice and dead eyes. Now what the hell is going on with you?"

I pulled my hands back. "Noth—"

"I'm going to lose it. I will shriek like a girl and wake up Cato, and we'll get the scolding of our lives. I'm your best friend. Just talk to me," Oliver pleaded.

I stared at my fidgeting fingers, unable to meet his eyes. "Have you ever been in love?"

Oliver's chair shifted, and I peeked up at him. His silence told me he hadn't expected that to come out of my mouth.

He shook his head. "No. Searching for Melanie took up all of my time. I had flings and flirted. But falling in love has never been on my mind."

"What do you think it feels like?"

Oliver let out a puff of air. "Everything. I think some days you'll wake, roll over, and look at them in bed, and a feeling of unadulterated joy will fill you up. A small smile might stretch across both your faces, because in that moment, you both feel like the luckiest person alive. Other days... it'll ache. It'll squeeze your chest in an unbearable grip. They'll frustrate you. They may even hurt you in ways you never expected. But love isn't just beautiful, it's brutal. Soft and sharp. But worth it when you find the right one."

I narrowed my eyes. "Are you sure you haven't been in love?"

"I'm sure I have eyes and ears and have lived a long enough life to have witnessed it." He clasped his hands and placed his arms on the table, leaning forward. "Is that what this is about? Aspen?"

"Maybe."

"We'll find a way out and get to them. Don't worry."

That was the problem, wasn't it? I was worried. I shouldn't want to rescue him.

"This'll cheer you up. Alexei told me to tell you to meet him on the roof tomorrow morning. Something about seeing the sulking general. So you can apologize and then get back to wooing him over to our side."

The urgency whispering in my ear practically hummed with contentment at the idea. The thoughts lessened the strangling of my organs.

Was this what love was? I almost hoped it wasn't.

"You're not coming?"

"Wasn't invited. But I believe in you."

I didn't.

How in the world would I woo Ronen to our side after I apologized?

CHAPTER 40

Lucille

I dream-walked, and it wasn't the type I liked. I invaded someone's body.

At first, I didn't know whose. But after thinking about the questions I had before bed—and feeling the extra appendage in our pants—I had a hunch.

We stared down at a sobbing female kneeling on blinding white floors. Threadbare cloth swallowed her malnourished form, vibrating with her cries. Her eyes pleaded with us as blood trickled from the cut along her neck.

I confirmed my hunch when black shadows reached out and absorbed her blood.

Ronen and I delved into her mind, watching her memory unfold like a high-speed movie, revealing every beautiful and tragic moment. We saw her as a cheerful child, watched her grow up and raise a family, saw their prosperity. Then their home was destroyed, their belongings taken, and their family left destitute, trying to make ends meet. The last image we witnessed was of her stealing from a local market.

We popped out of her head, black shadows seeping from her nose and dissipating.

"She stole a couple loaves of bread and some meat," we said, turning our head and glancing at a male beside us. He sat in a golden chair with luminous white wings jutting from his white robes, his long hair just as devoid of color. Disdain twisted his lips as he sneered at the female at the bottom of the dais.

He stood and glided to the edge of the stairs, stopping right in front of her. Unfolding his hands from his robed sleeves, he reached out and hovered a finger a few inches beneath her chin.

"Such a sinful creature," he said.

The female lowered her head and almost brushed the male's hand. He jerked back like she was diseased.

"Kill her."

Ronen flinched like an invisible blow had struck us. The next thing I knew, we were mentally battling a cold, all-consuming force that eclipsed every emotion he had. He fisted his hands, trying to hold onto his boiling rage, to fight against the force.

"She only stole food for her family, Etan. She isn't evil. She's starving!"

He tried to resist, pushing back against the force that urged his shadows to obey, but then Etan luscelered and grabbed his wrist. Pain seared into our skin.

I knew that pain. I knew that movement. Etan was carving a rune into Ronen's inkless wrist.

"I didn't ask for your opinion."

The invisible force he struggled against cooled his rage and silenced his desperation. His fists relaxed, and an empty, cold feeling took over. There was no more emotion, no thought, no trace of the beautiful light that had filled his mind.

A light I hadn't even noticed until Etan carved it away.

Who Ronen was—who he truly embodied—shrunk to a pliant shell.

Etan pointed at the female. "Send her to Hell."

A fierce command shot into our mind, and black shadows launched out.

I wanted to scream *Don't do it*, but I was just a spectator.

I tried to close my eyes, to shield myself from the horror to come, but I had no control.

So I watched.

Ronen's shadows slipped into her nose, eyes, and ears. She screamed, then seized. Blood dripped from every orifice, sliding down her face in a gory mess.

Heavenly Hell, that poor female. She had a family. She had been innocent.

And Ronen—my chest tightened for what Etan forced him to do.

"Wrath to the sinners," Etan said, shooting a searing blue flame at the female's corpse, reducing her to nothing. "Come. There are more to execute."

We followed the angel, and my heart raged in time with Ronen's as he killed ten more lives that day. Every time, we tried to resist Etan's commands. But the Hell Rune wouldn't let us.

So, we watched their bodies burst. Rot. Burn. Over and over.

Of the ten, only one person deserved it.

The rest were innocent, just trying to survive.

I woke up gasping, chills scattering across my skin. That was what I had felt on his wrist in the Hoar House—a Hell Rune scar.

It had destroyed all sense of self. His mind felt like I was drowning in a black hole of nothingness, ready to be filled with Etan's machinations.

The fear and panic, even the way Ronen looked at me, made sense now. I had worked my way into his head and manipulated him just like Etan did. I'd caused him more pain than I could even imagine.

After hours of lying in bed and thinking of Ronen and Aspen, I dressed in my uniform and hurried to the moonlit roof. Alexei wasn't there.

Did he mean morning, like at sunrise?

That wasn't the usual protocol.

He stepped through the door a few minutes later, and I relaxed. "You're late."

Alexei rubbed his chin. "I still don't know if this is a smart idea. You dug up some of his past demons, and he's struggling to come to terms with that."

Hell's chilly air nipped at my cheeks as I looked in the direction of Portal Lake. "You mean Etan?"

"How do you know that name?"

I turned back to his blatant surprise. "I understand why he reacted the way he did now. That's all you need to know. But what I don't understand is—if you knew about Etan, knew about Ronen's past—why didn't you say something? Why would you let me go through with that?"

Alexei pulled at his gloves like they needed adjusting and sighed. "I had to test out a theory."

"About what?"

"About—" He paused. "It's not important right now."

I placed my insulated hands over my ears, protecting them from the wind. "Was it at least worth it?"

Alexei grimaced. "I guess we'll see."

He scooped me up and shot us into the air. We flew over a forest of dark evergreens weighed down by snow. The sharp scent of pine stabbed my nostrils, triggering a relentless sniffling. It was annoying, but not as bad as I imagined it'd be without Alexei's wind shield.

After a few minutes, we rose higher, flying over a shadowed hill, and my jaw dropped at the top.

The harsh, icy grip of Hell's snow-covered landscape melted into a surreal, glowing forest. The trees stretched taller and broader, their thick trunks more imposing than the brittle ones we'd just flown over. Their bark pulsed with radiant blue light. The soft glow wove through the branches, reaching for miles and casting an otherworldly hue over the land.

As we crossed the invisible threshold marking the end of one forest and the beginning of another, a blast of warm, floral-scented air hit me like a gentle slap. My uniform instantly cooled, adjusting to the change in temperature.

"Welcome to the Eternal Forest, beautiful. The only warm place in the Redemption Circle," Alexei commented, a smile in his voice.

"It looks like Damatha Forest."

"They're connected. That's why."

"How—"

"When angels are buried in Damatha Forest, a piece of their essence infuses the earth and transfers to the Eternal Forest, and vice versa. They are spiritually connected. A way to always honor our dead."

"I didn't know Hell honored anything but suffering."

Alexei laughed. "Hell would never exist without death. Of course Hell honors it."

Right.

We continued over the warm, glowing graveyard, the blue canopy fighting the moon's light for dominance. A little further out, the Eternal Forest met a border of lightless evergreens. Alexei steered us toward that dividing line and dropped us between the towering trunks, weaving through the two radically different environments.

One moment, I felt warm, cast in a blue hue, a slight hum vibrating across my skin. The next, my nose and ears stung from the cold. But I smiled through the strange ride, enjoying the contrast until we landed in the Eternal Forest.

Alexei set me down on a carpet of lavender blooms, which stretched far and wide and mixed with orange moss. I couldn't get enough of the sight or smell. Their light, sweet scent soothed part of the ache in my chest—and my nerves.

"He should be out there."

I lifted my head to Alexei. He pointed at the dark spot through the gaps in the trees.

"You're not coming with?"

"Nope. I already apologized and got thrown off the cliff."

I worried my lip between my teeth. "Is he going to throw me off the cliff?"

"I highly doubt it. But if he does, just scream 'beautiful,' and I'll catch you." He winked.

That didn't reassure me in the slightest. What was I even going to say to Ronen? How did I approach this?

I took one step forward, then another. The guilty sensation eased the farther I walked, but my heart rate increased.

Eventually, the forest opened to a flat expanse of snow-speckled rock, leading to the cliff I'd fallen from and to the silhouette of Rune and Ronen.

I stopped.

His magnificent black wings unfurled from his muscular back, stretching wide, a breathtaking span of power and grace. The deep, onyx feathers shimmered with a blue sheen, kissed by the forest light. They were sleek, radiating strength, much like every line in his body.

When he leaned into the wind and fell off the cliff, I held my breath, watching as he sliced through the air, his wings snapping open to carry him into the sky.

He flew high, then low, spun, and dived. At one point, his wings disappeared completely, and he plummeted. My eyes widened, and I dug my nails into my hands as he sped toward the ground.

When he passed the cliff's edge, I sprinted out into the open.

But of course, I had nothing to worry about. He snapped open his wings and banked up, the moonlight catching slivers of his tattooed back.

It took a second for my raging heart to settle. Then he did it again, and again, like it was some kind of game.

It was fun *for him.* He seemed to enjoy every second in the air. And it wasn't just the playful way he flew that made me know he loved it, but Rune's swishing, happy shadow-tail and her perky, tilting head as she watched him.

This was his.

The illuminated space. The open air. The beauty I imagined he witnessed when he flew over the lake and trees. This was all his.

A place where he came to unwind and be free from the obligations of being a general, and whatever else the king made him do. A place his friends left him alone to think and be himself.

It was just him, Rune, and his gorgeous wings.

And I was intruding.

He noticed me when he lowered back toward the cliff's edge. Rune did a second later, whipping around and barreling across the few yards separating us. She knocked me off my feet, straddling my entire body while she smothered me with her stinky slobber.

I laughed, trying to dodge her large tongue.

"Okay, yes. I missed you too, beastie."

She continued to lick even as I pushed her head away. Ronen snapped his fingers, and she finally stepped off me, but my face was a casualty of her saliva.

I stood, wiping my cheeks, and my breath caught at the artwork detailing his muscular torso.

Life and death wove around a large tree right over his heart. Half the branches were empty and skeletal, while the other half grew leaves and flowers. The tree stretched toward a night sky, but where the lifeless branches touched, there were no stars, as if death had sucked out all their light.

But what really tugged at my heart was the angel with broken wings, kneeling at the base of the trunk, his head bowed and his clasped hands raised to the heavens.

Ronen said nothing as I openly stared at his body. His silence crept down my spine and forced my gaze up to his face. I refrained from fidgeting under his emotionless attention and approached. His cold mask tracked every hesitant step. I had to keep reminding myself that his expression was no different from before, but for some reason, it seemed different.

It *felt* different.

Despite my nerves begging me to shy away, I kept my eyes locked on his and stepped into his space. There was no gold to get lost in, only black—like he was putting up a barrier between us. I tried to work up the courage to say something. But my tongue wouldn't move. My mouth wouldn't open. I needed to apologize. I owed him that much. So why wouldn't the words come?

His feathered wings ruffled in our stilted silence. My fingers twitched, curious to feel how soft they might be. But knowing their sensitivity, I grazed a finger along the dejected angel's tattooed wings right above his pants instead. A gentle vibration hummed against my fingertip. He tensed, and my Infernus sang to me, but I didn't understand the noise.

"I never wanted to hurt you," I whispered, pulling back.

He grabbed my hand before I dropped it and placed it on his chest. He held it over his racing heart like it served as his anchor, like he *needed* my touch. My own heart fluttered, proving I could no longer deny the warm feelings slipping through my barriers.

"If I had known..." I trailed off. It wasn't the right time to tell him that I dream-walked to his memory. "I'm sorry, Ronen."

He searched my face, the corners of his eyes softening, and I was trapped. His mask melted away, leaving only the quiet strength of a male who no longer hid behind the warrior. His thumb moved back and forth against my hand. The rise and fall of his breaths, the warmth of his skin, grounded me, quieting thoughts of Aspen and the punishing need to rescue him.

I wanted to stay in this quiet, gentle moment. I wanted to bask in his golden gaze and forget everything else.

But then he had to speak.

"Is that the only reason you're here, Lucille?"

My name sounded like a prayer on his tongue—beautiful and reverent. And I had a feeling the moment I opened my mouth, I'd lose that tender baritone.

"I..."

His mask dropped back into place, and he let go of my hand, stepping back.

One word, and I was no longer talking to Ronen—but to *General* Ronen.

"I didn't think so." He crossed his arms, exposing what looked like a tattoo of Rune along his forearm. "Let's finally hear it. I've been curious when you'd ask."

"Ask?" My insides fluttered with unease.

He tilted his head. "Well, I'm assuming the main reason you wanted to apologize was so we'd be on better ground for when you demanded my help for Lilith's little pet."

"How do you know about…"

Ronen nodded down at Rune. "If you're not counting the time your powers lured me into a dream-walk of you and him, then it's probably best you know Rune doesn't need her eyes open for me to be able to listen in on conversations."

I stepped back. "You knew this entire time?"

He followed me, chin tilted up. "Since the day I accused you of being a traitor."

I stepped back again, shaking my head. Had *anyone* in my life not kept secrets from me?

At each step I took, he mirrored me, as if we were two ends of a string.

"For a moment, I thought you were going to admit to it at the tavern. I tried to drive it out of you, but then you asked me to train you instead."

I scoffed. "So that's what the whole truth thing was about. Does your tattoo even mean truth, or was that just part of the manipula—"

My back hit a glowing tree trunk, and my breath hitched when Ronen stepped into me, leaving only a couple inches of space between us. His heat swallowed me whole. His intoxicating aroma of spicy balsam and clove sank into my senses, biting my tongue and infusing my lungs, causing my eyes to flutter in ecstasy.

Why did he smell like home?

His knuckle grazed my chin, slowly tilting my head back.

"I never lied to you. It means truth. I respect honesty."

"Obviously not that much, otherwise you would've told me you already knew what I was going to ask you."

"I was waiting for you to come to me." He smiled, but it lacked warmth and had a taunting edge to it. "Ask me."

I frowned. "About Aspen?"

He nodded. "Yes. Say the words you've prepared."

Was this a trick?

"Will you help me rescue Aspen from Lilith?"

Shadows seeped from Ronen's body, wrapping us in a dark cocoon. The wispy tendrils brushed against my hair and face. He lifted his hand and wrapped it around my neck as he brought his lips centimeters from mine.

My Infernus perked up, excited. Heat pooled in my core, and all I could do was stare at his lips. All I could think about was what they'd feel like against mine. My pulse raged with the urge to know. He was a breath away, daring me to find out how he'd devour me. He just needed to bridge the gap.

His hand squeezed a little tighter, and his thumb brushed my pulse point as if he could feel the desire racing through my veins.

"I would rather run my Soul Swords across my neck than help a male who kidnaps and murders females," he finally whispered.

He stepped back, dropping a bucket of cold reality over my yearning daze.

An invasive urgency shot into my body, taking away my breath and reminding me of Aspen. "He needs our help, Ronen."

"Sounds like an interesting dilemma."

He started to turn, and I lurched forward, grabbing his wrist. "Wait!"

The moment I touched him, Aspen—the urgency—it all quieted to a much-needed relief. It was only Ronen and the humming power beneath his skin that tickled my fingers.

He shook off my touch, and I felt it again. The unexplainable desperation screamed in my head—relentless and demanding. *Save Aspen. Save him.*

"Ronen, he has a Hell Rune like you did. You're the only one who can remove it."

He straightened, clenching his jaw. "Did Alexei tell you about that?"

"No—I—"

How did I tell him I invaded his mind again, but this time unintentionally?

"Of course he did." He shook his head. "Him and his damned hunch," he said to himself. "We would know if Lilith had my feather."

"I know! Believe me. *Trust* me."

"You expect me to trust you when you're sleeping with the enemy? I wouldn't be a good general if I didn't take into consideration that he might have his claws in you—and you might not even know it."

My mouth opened with a retort, but nothing came out. Aspen *did* have his claws in me. He used me, and still I *needed* to help him. It wasn't a want. It was a burning, screaming, destructive demand.

"That's what I thought."

Ronen turned his back on me, his wings snapping out. Rune trotted over, butting into his side.

"Ronen, Lilith's using him like Etan used you! You're the only one who would understand. *Please*," I begged.

He stiffened, every inch ramrod straight, and Rune whimpered.

"This conversation is *done*. Have Alexei take you back, and don't seek me out again."

His wings gave a sharp flap, and he shot into the rising dawn, his shadows swarming around him.

CHAPTER 41

Lucille

I wove through the dimming trunks, the soothing scent of the lavender flowers lost on me. Up ahead, Alexei leaned against a tree, flipping a dagger, not a care in the world while mine was thoroughly fucked.

When he spotted me, he flipped the dagger back into its sheath and tilted his head. "How'd it go?"

"Terrible."

Alexei grimaced. "Care to elaborate?"

I shook my head. "Not really."

He pulled me in for a hug, and I let him, my arms hanging limp at my sides.

"Don't worry, I'll bring in the big guns next."

"The big guns?"

"MJ. The redhead you see around us. She's Ronen's third and knows all the tricks for getting under his barriers. She also knows more about his past."

I sighed, leaning more of my weight into Alexei, exhausted. That might help Ronen, which I wanted, but it wouldn't help me or Oliver.

"Let's just go, Alexei."

He leaned back, looking down at me with concern in his warm eyes. "He'll come around, beautiful. He just—" He paused. "He's just haunted right now. The last time this happened, Lucifer managed to infiltrate his mind, and that was another ordeal MJ and I will never forget. For some reason, I thought it'd be different with you."

"Why?"

Alexei picked me up and manifested his dappled wings.

"The fact that you have to ask means Ronen needs MJ to knock some sense into him more than I realized."

"That doesn't answer my question."

"It's not my answer to give."

Oliver and Alexei noticed my volatile mood during our morning run, but surprisingly, they refrained from commenting on it.

I didn't think my mood could possibly get any worse—until Ronen showed up. After all his time away, he finally decided to grace his military with his presence. Oh, and Moira was right next to him, practically petting his chest.

My Infernus came alive at the sight, its whispers more like hisses in my ear. I ignored them. Before he could spot me walking through the arena's doors, I turned and veered toward our squad.

"Hey, Ronen's back," Oliver commented with enthusiasm.

I hadn't told him about my early morning failure. "I can see that."

He raised a brow.

"Let's just get this day over with."

Since Ichi attacked Moira and Theon, they'd stopped taking Oliver and me back to the showers. It didn't seem like Moira was the type to let something go, so I had a feeling her payback would come when we least expected it. But not today, not while she was trying to fuse herself to Ronen. He shook her off more than once, but the desperate harlot didn't seem to understand when she wasn't wanted.

Oliver and I partnered up, facing off with Ichi in a hand-to-hand match. We threw combination after combination at her, and with Oliver's help, we both lasted longer than before. The match was a vicious whirlwind of equally matched power, which said a lot about Ichi's skill.

She smiled. "You both have improved," she said, right before sweeping Oliver's legs and sending him to the sand.

I smirked at my best friend, but it was cut short. Ichi was on me a second later, never letting us catch our breath. I threw up my hands to block her punches. Oliver jumped up and kicked at her kneecap. She stumbled, and I thought we finally had her, but then she did something completely new.

As Ichi caught herself, her arm blurred, slamming into my ribs and Oliver's chest. I flew back and hit the ground with an oomph. But the impact didn't compare to the throbbing in my ribs.

"You okay?" Ichi asked, hovering above me.

"No," Oliver moaned from my other side.

I assessed the damage and concluded she didn't break my ribs, but she most definitely bruised them. Before I could answer, shadows brushed my face.

I flicked my attention to Ronen and Moira. He glared at the hand on my ribs, then shot a dark, threatening look at Ichi. It made me want to protect her. But she stepped in front of me, her body angled not toward Ronen, but toward Moira.

Moira's expression was more murderous than Ronen's, and all that jealous heat was aimed squarely at me. I couldn't help the smug smile tugging at my lips. Her male was paying more attention to me than to her. That had to sting.

"Moira looks like she's going to blow," Oliver said, crawling across the arena floor and sprawling out beside me.

"She won't." Not in front of Ronen. She'd wait until no one was watching.

I held Moira's gaze in challenge.

Try it. I dare you.

Her face flushed like she could hear my taunting thoughts, or maybe it was just my smile. She stepped forward, and my Infernus sang.

"Better watch out. Challenge week is just two days away," Oliver warned.

His words struck a nerve. I was so sick and tired of watching out. Every time we entered this arena, we had to be on edge. Every time we trained, we had to anticipate every movement. We couldn't run alone. We couldn't walk into the barracks or a dim hallway without fear. We were cursed at, spat on, tripped—and the only reason other squads hadn't killed us was Ronen's interference with Theon.

It had to end.

I was done waiting for someone to plunge a dagger into my back.

I sat up, the pain in my ribs already gone thanks to Ronen. "Ichi, show us how to do your neat little trick. I'm going to need it when I challenge Moira."

Oliver laughed and patted my back.

"I'm not joking."

He stopped laughing. Ichi grinned.

She moved us outside, away from the rest of the warriors, and started from the beginning. It turned out it took a *lot* of concentration to channel luscelering energy into specific body parts. And eight times out of ten, Oliver and I completely sucked at it. By the time we finished, my mood was in the dumpster.

When we got back to our rooms, we found Rune waiting at the door. She perked up as we approached, bounding across the last few feet.

I stepped back, refusing to touch her. "Go back to the general."

She whimpered, nudging my hand. I pulled away.

"Alright, Luce," Oliver said, kneeling to pet her, "I know something happened—and I have a feeling it has something to do with the big, tall, and pissy shadow male showing up at training—but that doesn't mean you get to take it out on Rune."

"She's been spying on us for her master," I snapped, ignoring the way Rune's ears and tail drooped.

Oliver stood and shot me a warning look. "And? That's not news. What's with your piss-poor attitude?"

"He said he wouldn't help us, Oli."

His expression softened, and he pulled me into his arms. "Come on. Let's go in and you can explain." He glanced at Rune with a grimace. "Rune, you're going to have to go back to Ronen tonight. It's Lucy's turn for time alone, okay?"

Rune whined, but bowed her head and ambled back the way she came.

Oliver guided me through our door and onto the settee, covering me with a blanket before sitting beside me. "Talk."

I told him what happened, but left out the specifics about Aspen. I did admit how Ronen made me feel.

"Finding Ronen attractive isn't a crime. I think it'd be a bigger crime if you *didn't*. Or you'd just be straight-up blind."

"It's more than that. I wanted to kiss him."

Oliver laughed. "So? I probably would too."

I fiddled with my fingers, staring into the fire. There was so much more I needed to tell him. But I was scared.

"Do you love Aspen?"

Heavenly Hell, how was I supposed to answer that?

I bowed my head. "Oli, I don't know what love is. I don't understand these feelings—for Aspen or Ronen."

Oliver pulled me to him. I leaned against his side, resting my head on his shoulder.

"Luce, don't put pressure on yourself to figure it all out. We're rescuing Aspen and my sister regardless. Yeah, it might be harder without Ronen's help, but we'll make it work. Don't let the idea of how Aspen or Ronen will judge you mess with your head.

"Maybe you're in love with Aspen. Maybe you're not. Maybe you've got feelings for the dark, tattooed god, or maybe you don't.

Stop shaming yourself for feeling anything at all. That's not what emotions are for. They're here to inform you, and to help you *live*."

He pressed his cheek to my head, and for a moment, I believed him.

"And... did you ever think maybe you're holding back on falling in love with Aspen because you're still trying to figure out who *you* are—and who *he* is? He's been runed and controlled his entire life, and you've been caged away without the freedom to fully explore your own likes and dislikes. Not to mention, it's been danger and secrets between you two from the beginning. Not exactly the best foundation for a relationship," he said, nudging my side. "Am I right or am I right?"

I gave him a small smile.

He sighed. "Life and love are never easy. But I *do* know they're easier when you know who you are and what you want. Right now, neither of you is in a place to figure that out. Not until the drama of our lives settles a little.

"As for Ronen... attraction messes with the mind. But so does having someone who protects you and helps you grow. I've seen the pride on his face when he watches you train, and he only has that expression for *you*."

"That's not helping," I admitted as my stomach fluttered. But he wasn't wrong, I'd seen it too—and loved it.

"I'm just saying... he doesn't always have that unimpressed, pissy look on his face. And even when he does, he still looks out for you. Hell, he protected us from your father from the very beginning, and he hasn't stopped.

"He cares about you, Luce. And he's showing it in better ways than Aspen ever has. I think you *see* it, and I think you *know* it—but you're scared of what it might mean. So your subconscious goes haywire whenever he's around, and then your guilt attacks you. You don't let yourself *feel* it. And that's why you wanted to kiss him."

I lifted my head and pulled back to look at him. I should say it now. He needed to know about Aspen.

"How did a goof like you become so wise?"

But I couldn't do it.

"Do I need to remind you how old I am?"

"No, but you *can* start using all that wisdom on our rescue plan, now that we don't have Ronen's help."

"We first need to find a way *out*."

I leaned back against his shoulder, feeling like the worst friend and the worst daughter. The only person I seemed to be looking out for was Aspen.

"That we do."

CHAPTER 42

Lucille

Alexei pulled Oliver and me from the last training day with the Tormentors. We luscelered to the Shard Field, but this time we had company.

MJ leaned against a line of sharp icicles, arms crossed and a dry expression on her face. Her fiery red hair lay in two perfect braids over her Hell Squadron uniform. She stood when we approached and scrutinized me from head to toe. She didn't look at Alexei or Oliver— only me, like she was attempting to delve into my soul.

A couple feet away, she removed an arrow from her quiver while keeping that unrelenting stare on my face. I had the strange urge to flee but refrained, stepping forward with the guys. Without warning, she whipped up her arrow and pressed it to the pulse point at my neck.

"MJ," Alexei warned.

"So you're her," she said, ignoring him.

I held up my hands.

What did that mean? *I'm her?*

"Sure," I breathed. I'd be anything she wanted me to be, as long as she didn't impale me.

"What she means," Alexei said, giving MJ a pointed look, "is that you're the one who challenged your squad leader, Moira, to a no-rules fight."

I raised my chin. "Yep."

Alexei gestured to MJ. "And that's why she's here. You need every advantage. And so does Oliver, because he's been challenged too."

"What?" Oliver and I said in unison.

"I'm surprised *you* didn't have anyone challenge you," MJ commented, digging in the arrow to the point of pain. "It was bad enough placing you two in an elite squadron. But then little miss here had to flaunt her unearned uniform to Hell's military. Although I'm guessing everyone assumes Moira is going to kill you, so there'll be nothing left to challenge."

I gritted my teeth, her hard smile strumming the cord of my Infernus. "Ronen gave it to me."

"On a first-name basis with your general? And he *gave* you a highly coveted uniform? What did you give in return to receive all this special treatment from him?"

"I didn't fuck him, if that's what you're insinuating." Itches spread up my arms, and pressure strained my eyes. I didn't care if MJ was Ronen's third or part of his Dreads. My emotional stability was hanging on by threads, my Infernus wanted an outlet, and I had half a notion to give in. Exposure be damned.

MJ's smile widened. "I want to see if you can prove yourself worthy of the challenges to come." She dropped the arrow from my neck and unhooked a bow from her back. "Then," she said, turning her attention to Alexei, "I'll do what you asked of me."

She luscelered to the edge of the Veil Forest, notched an arrow, and aimed it at me.

"Is our lesson starting now?"

"MJ!" Alexei snapped. "What are you doing? This is *my* lesson."

MJ released her arrow, disregarding him, and I dove to the ground.

"Our challenges are ruthless. They're unfair. Moira will fight dirty and use any means necessary to kill you. No one'll help you. No one will rescue you. Of course, you can forfeit and be placed in the Bowels. You can give up entirely and ask the king for a different area to work off your debt. Or you can see what you're made of. Understand?"

She notched two more arrows and waited for me to decide.

The fiery warrior wasn't playing around, but she didn't know who I was or what was going on. My father wouldn't allow me to give up. He wanted me trained, as did I. And despite the shit I kept going through, and Ronen unwilling to help us, I still wanted to rank. I wanted to prove to myself I could beat the blonde who had somehow caught Ronen's eye.

I wasn't weak anymore. And it was time I showed them all.

"Release it."

A sliver of respect glinted in her eye, and she nodded, letting go of her drawstring. I had expected the arrows to fly toward me, but they veered toward Oliver. I reacted without thought, tackling him to the ground, and was up a second later, dodging more.

MJ didn't let up—and neither did I.

"Alexei, stop babying them and throw those daggers you love."

A moment later, an arrow came at me from the front and a dagger from the left. I dropped, but unlike the last few times, MJ didn't let me stand. She shot arrow after arrow, and I rolled. Snow and ice sprayed my face, the tips of her arrows skimming past my head and driving into the ground.

I couldn't roll forever. Alexei's dagger sliced my cheek, and I stopped just in time to miss an arrow that would've sunk into my side. MJ was ruthless.

"Don't stop! Stand or roll the opposite way, Luce!" Oliver shouted.

MJ tutted. "Nephilim, that's helping. Her opponents may very well come after you in retaliation."

I hissed as Alexei's dagger cut my other cheek with precision. The fact that he could wound me without injuring me severely was a testament to his skill—and our budding friendship. Ignoring the sting, I moved to help Oliver, but I didn't need to. He luscelered out of the way, smiling, and brushed imaginary snow off his shoulder.

"Don't ever be persuaded by the taunting words of your opponent, beautiful. If you have help, trust them to take care of themselves, or suffer the consequences."

Before I could ask about the consequences, an arrow sank through my hand, and I screamed.

"MJ!" Alexei shouted, flinging a dagger at her. She moved aside, giving Oliver time to lusceler in front of me—a barrier between me and the fierce redhead.

"She'll heal, Alexei. You know Moira. If she can kill her, she will. You want her to survive? Stop coddling her. You know who I'm doing this for. If they choose it, she'll need to know how to fight while in constant pain."

Who was MJ doing this for?

Oliver glanced down at me, analyzing the arrow in my hand and the blood slowly dripping onto the snow. "You okay? We can stop and go to Sam," he said.

I reached out my good hand so he could help pull me up. "No, we can't. Can you hold your own, though?" I asked, knowing the answer, but it was hard not to worry about him.

He grinned and let his fear power flame in his emerald eyes. "I've been holding my own longer than you've been alive. Do what you've got to do. I'll be fine."

"Okay." I clenched my jaw and held back a scream as I pulled the fletching through the hole. I knew it'd make me bleed more, but if I had to roll or drop, I couldn't have anything slowing me down. Which meant I had to end this soon. Angels heal fast, but not *that* fast.

I slid out from behind Oliver and found even more respect in MJ's amber eyes. "Let's go again, Redhead," I taunted.

She notched two arrows. Alexei palmed two daggers, surveying Oliver and me. We dodged the projectiles and attempted to go on the offensive. But it seemed every time we tried, the next knife or arrow would stop us. Alexei aimed for the head; MJ for our limbs. I tried to avoid the arrows more than the knives, mostly because Alexei kept going easy on me, which meant my face continued to sting with cuts.

But MJ didn't care how I fared with Alexei. If I avoided all her arrows, she came faster. It took all my focus not to get impaled, but I did. Then I gave her a cocky little smile.

That was a mistake.

Her arm blurred as she luscelered to notch more arrows and release them. They flew toward me and Alexei. It happened so fast—too fast.

Alexei crouched to retrieve his daggers, his back turned to MJ. I knew she wouldn't kill him, but she *was* testing me. I didn't have the time to reach him. I had a choice to make.

Right or wrong, I called to my Glory and gave it one command—*protect.*

Perfectly crafted spheres of flame covered both of us.

The arrows hit and burned instantly.

Oliver turned to me with a giant grin. "Hell yeah!"

I smiled back. I'd been working hard on those.

Alexei shot up, taking in his flaming protection and the ash on the ground, then glared at MJ. "Were you trying to kill me?"

She formed a red fireball. "I had a backup plan."

Alexei scoffed. "You are *insane*, MJ."

"And it seems you two have been holding out on me," she said, looking over my shoulder.

I released my Glory, and a shadow tickled up my nose. My pain vanished, and pressure descended on the hole in my hand.

Ronen was here.

"Leave, before I do something I'll regret," Ronen bit out, his words sharp and cold.

Goosebumps scattered down the back of my neck, and I stepped forward, away from the wrathful energy he exuded.

MJ smiled. "You have a lot of explaining to do."

"Leave. Now!"

A beautiful pair of auburn wings burst from her back, and she shot into the air.

Ronen came around me and surveyed the cuts on my face. His shadows brushed my wild hair back, and his expression narrowed.

I didn't think Ronen's energy could get more menacing—but it did. The pitch black of his irises writhed with barely restrained rage.

"Did the Archangel do that to you?"

"Do what to me?"

He grazed my tipless ear with a shadowed finger.

Oh.

Self-conscious, I pulled my hair in front of my ear. His shadows didn't seem to like that and pushed it back again.

"Who the fuck did that?"

"A fallen angel named Brockalian," I whispered.

Ronen's nostrils flared, but he released me and stepped back.

"Oliver, take Lucy to Sam," he said, dismissing us and turning to his second. "Alexei, I thought I banned the use of powers in her lessons. Has she been using them all this time?"

Alexei's silence answered for him. We'd started these trainings to practice my Glory. Alexei and I saw no reason to stop, so we ignored Ronen's unusual order. Of course, I probably should've questioned using my power with MJ here. But as Ronen's third, I assumed she was as trustworthy as Alexei.

Ronen's large black wings expanded as he drilled his gaze into Alexei. "Inform MJ to meet me tomorrow."

He shot into the sky with those parting words, taking his pain-reducing shadows with him and leaving me unsteady.

"What the hell was that?" Oliver asked, staring after Ronen.

Alexei rubbed the back of his neck, looking tired. "That was Ronen under the influence."

My eyes widened. "Under the influence of *what*?"

"Powerful, hellish alcohol?" Oliver offered.

"No." Alexei sighed. "Something more powerful than that. Get Lucy to Sam—she's bleeding all over the snow. We'll practice more tomorrow, but I'll lead instead of MJ. Especially if Ronen ends up killing her."

I assumed that was a joke, but I couldn't be sure.

"Sounds good to me," Oliver chirped, lifting me into his arms and luscelering to Sam.

That night, Oliver and I went to the library, determined to find our way out. He grabbed the large door handle, then paused when he noticed I was staring at the mosaic.

It was still the image of the black dagger.

Oliver scanned the doors up and down. "Why do I get the feeling you're not seeing what I'm seeing? Unless you've grown overly fond of staring at black and red swirls."

"The doors show me things," I admitted.

He released the handle and stood next to me, scrunching his eyes like that would reveal the mysterious image. "Is it demons again?"

They show me important scenes that will impact the future.

If you ever want to save Aspen, steal the bastard's knife.

This dagger. There is only one of its kind. Its name is Tsal-mawet.

Their words circled in my mind, each sentence clicking into place and forming the borders of the puzzle. Could it be that easy? Was this our answer?

"Oliver, remember that voice I told you about in Elora?"

"Yes. Why?"

"She told me the way to save Aspen's life was to steal Michael's dagger."

"I'm not following."

I pointed to the doors. "The mosaic is of that same dagger. And these doors show images that will impact the future. What if she knew we'd be stuck in Hell? What if she knew the only way to escape and rescue Aspen was with that dagger?"

Oliver ran a hand through his hair. "Then why not just tell you that?"

"She was never forthcoming with information. She only gave me little bits, like telling me to find you and Magda."

"Yeah, and we both betrayed you and handed you over to the enemy. I wouldn't say this mysterious female in your head is trustworthy."

I turned to him and touched his arm. "But, Oli, if I never did what she told me, how do we know we'd ever end up in this position like we are? I have a best friend now."

His disbelieving expression softened, and he pulled me into his side, giving me a noogie. "Yeah, you do." Then he kissed my forehead. "But she might've had nothing to do with that. Her intentions could be more sinister than we realize. All I'm saying," he added before I could protest, "is to be wary of her suggestions."

"Well, she's been quite silent lately." *Except for that time I had the same three nightmares a few weeks ago.* But that was nothing like Elora. Why was she so absent now? Was it the same reason why I couldn't feel Aspen anymore? I had a feeling that had more to do with his Hell Runes than anything else.

"That could very well be a good thing."

"Maybe. Regardless, I think the dagger is our key. There are too many coincidences."

He sighed. "Okay. Then where's our door?"

"Let's go look for it."

Later, Oliver and I were hunched over a book about Tsal-mawet. Unfortunately, there wasn't much about it—only a single paragraph:

The Weaver's blade: An artifact of legend, the Weaver's Blade is a sentient black dagger, distinguished by the bloodstone set within its center. This weapon is said to hold the ability to unmake and remake through the act of sacrifice. It is written that the Weaver alone possesses the skills to wield this blade, for it is a living entity with a will of its own. Only the Weaver can command its tendencies to create or destroy when the stone turns black.

Oliver dropped his head on the table. "That gave us nothing."

I sat back. Why couldn't we get one straight answer? I stared at my hands and the scar that filled my palm. If Aspen had never touched it, if he hadn't brushed his thumb across the raised wound and insulted me with his words, it would've taken me longer to believe my suspicions. *But did he do it on purpose?* Aspen was smart. What if he was working around the rune and Lilith? He'd done it before. What if he egged me on so I would figure it out? He wanted me to know Lilith controlled him. Something about that needled at my mind. Something I was missing.

"What was it?"

Oliver turned his head, his cheek smooshed against the wood. "What's what?"

I glared at my scarred palm, thinking back to everything Aspen said.

Don't worry about me. Worry about getting out.

Just find a way out.

If you find a way out, come to me.

Have you found any way of escape?

"Lilith controlled him," I said to myself. *That* was it. She controlled his words. I had thought he wanted me to escape *for him.* But he wanted me to escape for *Lilith*, which meant I was right. Lilith didn't want me to die. She wanted to steal me. That was why Ni didn't kill me.

"What was that?"

I panned between my hand and the paragraph. A dagger that could unmake and remake. *Like remaking a portal where one used to be?*

"Maybe it would've worked. Maybe Ni just used the wrong knife." The puzzle was slowly coming together, but I still couldn't place the part about the Immolation Circle.

Why send me there?

I needed answers, and there was only one person I could ask.

"Lucy!" Oliver grabbed my shoulders, shaking me. "What the fuck did you just say?"

"About Ni?" I asked.

His eyes flickered with fire. "No. Who does Lilith control?"

I felt the blood drain from my face.

He tightened his fingers on my shoulders. "Say it."

"Aspen."

CHAPTER 43

Ronen

Flying away from the hellion yesterday—and leaving her with Alexei, who maimed her face, although minimally—took more strength than I realized, especially with the rage boiling inside me from what Brockalian did to her ear.

I had to force myself to fly to Portal Lake to calm down. Anytime her pain punctured my barriers, it sent my shadows into a frenzy. I hadn't registered the slices on her cheeks, but the arrow through her hand, I noticed that immediately. I might not want to be near the hellion right now, but I also wouldn't stand for her to be in physical danger. Although I didn't expect *my third* to be the cause of that danger. MJ was lucky she left when she did.

It was getting harder to control myself the more I was in proximity to the hellion. My shadows wanted to connect with her... and it *terrified me*.

That afternoon, I flew out to Portal Lake, knowing that if I didn't, it'd cause me a bigger headache than I'd like. Sitting on the edge of the cliff, lost in my thoughts, something slammed into my back. I fell off the ledge, my wings burst free, and I banked upward.

My shadows lashed out and wrapped around MJ's neck. They didn't choke her, but they made it pretty damned uncomfortable. And like the insane female she was, she smiled. She always fucking smiled.

"That's for not telling me Lucille was the daughter of Hell," she rasped.

"Alexei—"

"Said nothing." She tucked her chin and grasped at my shadows. "Lucille admitted to it this morning."

"I planned to tell you today," I said, resigned. After Lucille's brilliant display of control over her Glory, I knew MJ would demand an explanation.

I let her suffer for one more second before releasing her.

She coughed, rubbing her throat. "Yeah? Did you also plan to tell me that Lucille is your damned cordistella?"

I almost forgot to flap my wings. Hearing it said out loud sounded entirely different than hearing it in my head.

"Alexei," I accused again. We would have words. First, he disobeyed my orders with Lucille's training. Then, he revealed a truth that was never his to voice. The first, I understood, even if it filled me with dread. Lucille didn't know what damage she was inflicting on her parents. I wanted to tell her. I thought about it daily, but doing so would jeopardize my life. And still, I considered giving it up for her every damn day. But to tell MJ before I had the chance?

"Ronen!" MJ snapped me out of my thoughts. "I love to blame Alexei as much as you do, but do you really think Alexei told me? I've had a cordistella. He hasn't. I know what the signs are, dumbass." She shook her head and stared long and hard. All the fiery fight eased out of her eyes, and her face relaxed into something tender. "I promise not to kick you off the cliff again if you come here and talk." MJ plopped herself down.

I hesitated. I didn't need to talk about anything.

"How much do you actually know about the cordistella bond, Ronen? Do you understand what happened yesterday?"

My silence was answer enough.

"I'll do the talking until you're ready, okay?" She gave me a small smile and nodded to the spot next to her.

This side of MJ always got to me. Her rare moments of tenderness were reminiscent of a time when she had a soft heart. The moment her cordistella died, so did the majority of that softness.

"I know the basics," I admitted, snapping my wings in and settling next to her.

"Then I'll enlighten you on the finer details."

The way she unintentionally paused between her sentence, her voice softening at the end, made me reach out and squeeze her hand. I could only imagine this conversation hurt.

"The first thing you need to understand about the bond is that they weren't originally intended for love. They were created for battle, but we turned them into something more. If you start at the beginning, we were created to destroy evil, were we not?"

I nodded. Sometimes I forgot MJ was older than me. She didn't always appear or act like it, but when she shared the knowledge of the past, I remembered.

"For us to be proficient in our mandate, they wanted us in pairs, and they figured the best way to create expert killers with less potential for death was to create angels that came from the same soul. As a result, the bond has certain attributes." She gestured to her hand. "For example, I imagine it hurt when I shot Lucille through with an arrow."

Seven Hells, she didn't even sound guilty.

My shadows shot out toward her neck, but I stopped them before they could circle. "Careful."

She chuckled. "That right there is your praesidium. I used to tell Knox his surly bastard was coming out to play."

"And I'm sure as you insulted him, he swooned at your feet."

"You bet your ass he did."

"So what's the purpose of the praesidium?"

"It's a part of the bond. Any threat to the other half of your soul, and your soul will demand a reaction. Even if you hated Lucille, you'd have no choice. A part of you will always defend your other half. It can be seen as romantic or pragmatic."

"So she'll be affected by this too."

MJ nodded. "It's a safety mechanism, just like the ability to feel each other's emotions. The more you know and can sense about each other, the better odds you'll survive." Her voice became soft at the end. "Sometimes, stronger bonds can develop a mind-to-mind connection, but it takes practice, trust, and power. Knox and I never achieved it, but we were content with what we had."

A mind-to-mind connection... I wasn't sure if I'd enjoy that or hate it immensely. I had shields up at all times. The fact that she even infiltrated them unnerved me.

"Is it normal to be unable to hurt your cordistella?" I asked.

"Yes. You have to think of the bond as how can we keep each other safe at all costs? Physically hurting each other will never work. Emotionally, on the other hand, is a different story. You won't die from hurtful words."

Which was probably why her powers were able to work on my mind.

"Do you know about the scars?" she asked, grabbing my hand and flipped it over, removing my glove.

"It's the result of full acceptance, isn't it?"

Her finger brushed a barely visible red mark in the middle of my palm. "Yes. Which I see you haven't completely done."

I pulled my hand back. "No." And I wasn't sure I was going to.

MJ pressed her lips together, looking like she wanted to comment but refrained. "The moment you both share scars is the moment you share your souls. It's the ultimate sacrifice and ultimate reward. You become whole again. You'll always take half of their pain and share your energy when theirs is low."

"What if only one of us accepts the bond? Can you still share pain and energy?"

"Yes. But it'd be one-sided, and what you experience now will multiply until your other half accepts. It could cause issues, and you can't take it back. Which is why you decide *together* to accept or decline the bond."

I ignored her pointed remark. "What happens if their energy is depleted?"

MJ sat there quietly for a moment. I almost regretted asking.

"Depends on the severity of depletion. But if you can't make it to a healer, you have a choice to make. You or them," she whispered. "Knox chose me." She pressed a kiss to her hand and turned, blowing it toward the Eternal Forest.

"You'll see him again, MJ."

One way or another.

She took a heavy breath and nodded. "Even if you're connected soul-to-soul, you won't die when they do. You'll just never feel that wholeness again. You'll never be with someone who knows you from the inside out again. You'll never touch their energy and feel their joy or their tingles on your skin." She paused, closing her eyes and lowering her voice. "Your heart and home are destroyed forever, and you will crave death."

I pulled her into my side, having no words. Lucille and I weren't connected yet, and still, I lost control when I thought she was about to die.

"I want us to have a choice," I admitted.

"Who says you don't have a choice?"

"You just said the praesidium forces you to protect. When she's hurt, it's like I lose all intelligence. I feel out of my mind. I try to block the bond from myself and her—"

MJ grabbed my hand, stopping me. "First, the praesidium only wants your other half safe and free of pain. I'm assuming you'd want that for Lucille regardless of the bond?"

I nodded.

"Second, the cordistella bond doesn't force emotions. What you feel is all your own. You may be acting out of character because, well, honestly, Ronen, have you ever had romantic feelings for someone? Alexei and I have only ever seen you with females you can have physically, but who have rotten personalities."

Ever since I came to Hell, I'd avoided relationships. I didn't know the first thing about them. Connection and getting close to people always unnerved me. It took me years to accept MJ and Alexei as more than warriors I commanded, and a lot of trust.

The unfamiliar emotions of anxiety, worry, and... hope had slithered beneath my skin. I didn't know what to do with the feelings. But the hope—the little bits of light I'd received from watching Lucille grow—was addictive and terrifying.

"Third." MJ smacked me on the back of the head, and I grunted.

"You can't block the damned bond! She deserves to know, and you can't continue to use your powers to hide from uncomfortable things. You shouldn't even be allowed to block it. The fact that you can is unnatural."

She grabbed both my shoulders and tugged, forcing me to meet the weight of her gaze.

"You speak of choice." She picked up my tattooed wrist. "You value truth. And yet you don't honor *either*? You're better than this, Ro. Tell Lucille."

I remained silent, burdened by my hypocrisy, but even more by my fear.

"What are you so scared of? Falling for her?" She grazed a finger over the red circular mark on my palm. "I think you're already on your way. Or is it Gabriel?"

I straightened and pulled back.

"It won't be the same as what happened with him."

"You don't know that."

She sighed. "Ro—"

"It doesn't matter. She loves another."

The heat of MJ's quiet stare burned into the side of my face. I knew she wanted me to talk about him. She always did.

"I wonder if she still would if she knew the truth," she commented instead.

"I thought you said the bond doesn't force feelings."

"It doesn't. The cordistella bond is still a choice. But the call to home is difficult to resist in proximity."

Didn't I know.

She stood and manifested her auburn wings, stretching them wide. "Ronen, don't let your past control your future. Feel, be scared, love, connect, *heal*. No one can control you anymore—no one but yourself."

MJ was right, as usual, and yet I still suffered from battling my scars. Allowing another being inside my head, even if it was just emotions, made my skin crawl. But I wanted to heal, and maybe the first step was lowering the block on the bond.

"Tomorrow—" MJ paused, pulling me away from my teetering decision. "Don't interfere. It'll be hard, but Lucille needs this—or the rest of the warriors will come after her. She can handle Moira."

Shadows circled my palms, squeezing and releasing repetitively. Tomorrow's challenge would be the longest day of my life. "I know. I'll stay on the sidelines. Just make sure she doesn't use her powers."

MJ nodded, standing at the edge of the cliff. "Oh, and if I ever see you with someone like Moira again, I will personally flay your balls." Then she shot into the sky, a streak of red slicing through the dimming daylight.

Staring into the starry lake, I brushed a finger through the layer of shadows I kept between me and the bond.

Allowing the hellion in would be like spitting in Etan's face. It would be a step toward healing. If Gabriel were here, he would've given me shit for not already doing it. And then I'd give him shit back, since part of this was his fault.

"Selfless bastard." I scoffed. If that was what I should call it. I glanced at the large trees glowing softly, brightening with each passing second. "You better be in Heaven."

Then I closed my eyes and lowered the wall.

The hellion's emotions flowed, filling my head and softening the tension in my muscles.

One step.

The next would be to tell her—then release the block on my emotions.

CHAPTER 44

Lucille

Today was the day that I either kicked ass or got my ass kicked. Knowing Moira, more than likely *dead*. I'd need to use all the skills I'd acquired and then some, since I couldn't use my powers—or at least not the ones anyone could see.

If I managed to defeat Moira with my hands essentially tied behind my back, then I could finally stop doubting my worth in this military. It would mean not only that I was a warrior, but that I had the ability to save the people I loved.

I stepped out of my room, clothed in the colors of Hell, and gave Oliver a small smile.

He gave me one back.

I'd explained what had happened with Aspen after he found out, which—unsurprisingly—didn't shock him. But once I told him I still wanted to rescue Aspen, I received the scolding of my life. We argued late into the night and eventually came to a truce after I started to beg and cry. I think my desperation scared him. It scared me too.

Oliver knocked my shoulder with his fist. "Today's the day."

"Let's hope we survive."

He pulled me into his arms and gave me a noogie. "Luce, we're going to wipe the floor with them. I'm not worried."

That made one of us.

We walked to the arena and met MJ and Alexei at the doors.

"The Nephilim's up first," MJ informed us, stepping boot-to-boot with Oliver. "I don't care how many times you puke. If you can put them down, do it."

Oliver straightened and saluted MJ. "Brought my barf bag, Sergeant."

MJ's eye twitched. I was pretty sure she wanted to stab him with one of her arrows.

Alexei smacked his back. "Dig deep and tune out the images, got it?"

"Got it." Oliver twisted his head. "Kiss for good luck?"

Alexei shoved him toward the door.

I hugged Oliver and whispered in his ear, "I'll be brave for you, if you'll be brave for me."

He pulled back and kissed my forehead, murmuring the same words against my skin. Then he pushed his shoulders back and entered the arena. We followed close behind.

BO hit me like a slap in the face as I passed the stands, and sweat instantly beaded on my forehead. The arena was packed. Angels, humans, and half-breeds sat shoulder-to-shoulder, filling every inch of the cement seating. Warriors stood on the ground level, circling the outer edge, waiting for the next match.

"Be brave, Oli," I said as we split off from him. We pushed through to the front row, and a coppery tang slowly overpowered the BO. Sliding up next to Ichi, who conveniently stood beside Rune and Ronen, I found out why.

Blood decorated the open circle as if someone had taken a few buckets of paint and splashed them onto the ground. Some poor Bowel recruit currently poured fresh sand over the gory scene before Oliver and the Trencher approached the center.

As the final grains fell, Oliver strode toward his opponent at the heart of the arena with his chin raised and a mischievous smile twisting his lips. His smile never faltered, even as the large, bald warrior sauntered down the opposite path, receiving pats on the back, encouragement, and weapons.

I was proud of him.

"Marcel, a blood-banded human from the Trenchers Squadron, has challenged Oliver, a blood-banded Nephilim from the Tormentors Squadron, for his spot," a male announced from the dais. "Let the challenge begin."

That was a surprise. The majority of elite squadrons were made up of angels and angel half-breeds for a reason.

Marcel twirled his sword in a flashy maneuver. "Let's go, Nephilim. I'll send you where you belong."

Oliver laughed in disbelief. "Did someone put you up to this?"

Marcel blinked. He seemed confused by the question, or maybe by Oliver's nonchalance.

"If so, you gotta get better friends, man."

Marcel jabbed his sword toward Oliver's stomach, and Oliver jumped back.

The crowd booed. But I wasn't sure if they were booing Marcel or the fact that he didn't stab Oliver.

"No? Don't have any friends? Then are you just a complete moron?"

Marcel attacked again, and Oliver dodged, shaking his head. His eyes flashed green, and Marcel dropped his sword, flinging his hands up to his face. He dug in the heels of his palms as if that'd stop Oliver's power.

"What are you doing to me?"

"Not much." Oliver shrugged.

"Make it stop." Marcel fell to his knees. "Make it stop!" he screamed, clawing at his face.

Remembering the first time Oliver used his powers on me, I could only imagine what Marcel was seeing. Whatever fears Oliver dredged up had reduced him to a sniveling, bald baby. And he didn't even touch him. This was a mild fear.

Oliver picked up Marcel's sword and placed it against the Trencher's neck. "I could make it a lot worse, if you'd like. *Or* you could use the last brain cell you have and run along before the images turn darker, or you die."

Marcel flipped over and scrambled on his hands and knees back the way he came. Either Oliver had gone deeper than I thought, or Marcel was just that pathetic.

"The challenge goes to Oliver," the announcer shouted.

Oliver winked at me, and I rolled my eyes. That match was nothing.

But it made an impact. The crowd didn't cheer, but they didn't boo either. Neither did the warriors. Everyone stood in stunned silence, unable to comprehend what Oliver had just done.

"Up next, Theon, a blood-banded angel from the Devils Squadron, has challenged his own squadmate, Oliver."

Oh, shit.

The warriors thundered their approval, hollering, pounding their chests, and shooting bursts of flame and water into the air. The crowd, caught up in the excitement, followed suit.

"You two sure know how to make friends," Alexei commented.

"Hard to make friends with angels that suffocate you daily," I replied.

Alexei flipped his dagger, considering Ichi. "Is that so?"

Ichi turned and gave him a slight bow. "I wasn't a part of it, but I stopped it."

"You should've said something, beautiful."

I crossed my arms. "Why? So the big bad Dreads could come to our rescue and make us look weaker?"

He had no response to that—because he knew I was right.

Theon luscelered into the ring, pumping his fist in the air, and the cheers grew deafening. He paraded around as the crowd threw flowers and coins at his feet, even a few lace panties. I wanted to find those females and tell them they were better off saving their panties for someone who wasn't a rotten piece of shit.

Oliver leaned on Marcel's sword, looking as unimpressed as I felt. Not that my opinion of Theon could fall much further—it was already seven circles under.

Theon reached down and picked up a red lace thong, sniffing it as he grinned.

Heavenly Hell, he made me sick.

Still crouched beside his new pile of panties, Theon raised his hand—and water slammed into Oliver's chest, knocking him flat. He never saw it coming. *I* never saw it coming. Theon had played into our expectations.

He luscelered, blurring across the short distance. He double-fisted his axe, raised it high, and swung for Oliver's head with everything he had. No pause. No hesitation. Theon wanted to take Oliver's life—fast and viciously.

"Roll!" I screamed, my skin itching.

Oliver didn't.

Instead, he whipped up the sword, and steel clanged against steel, ringing through the crowd's noise. Theon bore down on him. Metal screeched as Oliver held the axe at bay. Blood bloomed through the glove of his left hand as his arms strained against Theon's burly strength.

Why didn't he just roll? Oliver's muscles were half Theon's size. And he was fighting from his back.

Theon's axe pushed lower, inching toward his neck.

"Use your power!" I shouted. He should've done that from the start.

What was Oliver playing at?

He didn't listen. Theon grinned, and water swallowed Oliver's face—a green light refracted through the liquid.

So, he was using his powers. But they weren't enough. Either they didn't affect Theon, or he had a strong mind shield, and Oliver couldn't penetrate.

The axe lowered further.

I lurched forward, only to be stopped by Ichi. "We don't intervene."

"I'm not going to let Theon kill Oliver," I snapped, trying to shake off her tightening grip.

But she held onto me, even when Oliver lost the struggle.

It all happened so fast. Oliver's right arm dropped as he shifted his head. Theon's axe veered off-center, sinking into his shoulder. Water muffled his cry, just as the cheering crowd drowned out Theon's laughter when he yanked the weapon free. It was over. The next swing would drive through Oliver's head, and I'd lose him.

I wrenched out of Ichi's hold, about to pull at my Infernus, when Theon stumbled back and dropped his axe. He clutched at a dagger protruding from his stomach.

"How's that feel?" Oliver rasped, standing, no longer suffocating on water. But his brows were drawn, and he covered his wound while his right arm dangled uselessly at his side. "It took me a few seconds to figure out where I wanted to stab you. The stomach seemed the best place for putting on my show."

His show? Did Oliver plan this, or was he making it up as he went?

Theon's nostrils flared as he shot out a blast of water, but it faltered, losing momentum. Oliver jerked out of the way and winced. *That* small movement hurt, and he thought he could put on a show?

"See, I could've slammed it through your ribs, hoping to nick your heart. But then you'd miss out on my favorite part." Oliver laughed. "Heart, part. I like that."

Theon didn't. He ripped the dagger from his stomach and charged Oliver. A second later, Oliver used a maneuver we learned from Alexei to dodge the knife, then slid up behind Theon and fisted his orange hair. Water instantly encased Oliver's head. But with each passing second, it thinned, revealing his nose, his smug smile, and blazing green eyes.

"Enjoy," Oliver taunted.

Theon collapsed. I sagged in relief. *Finally.* He jerked in the wet sand, soft whimpers escaping his mouth. Looking absolutely green, Oliver sank to his knees next to Theon's head. For a moment, I thought he was about to puke on him. But instead, he unsheathed a dagger at his hip and held it to carrot-top's throat, signaling he could take Theon's life if he wanted.

He *should* kill him. He should rid the world of Theon's stain. But I knew in my gut he wouldn't. And after seconds of tense silence, everyone else knew it too. Which meant Theon would wake up and come back for revenge. Maybe not today or tomorrow, but someday.

"The victory is Oliver's!" the announcer yelled, riling up the spectators.

The stunned crowd roared to their feet, shouting and applauding. The warriors, on the other hand, had a mixture of emotions. Some seemed apprehensive, others skeptical, and very few regarded him with begrudging respect.

But I was proud.

Oliver stood on shaking legs and walked over to our group on the sidelines. The dagger dangled from the fingertips of his good arm while blood dripped down the other. He still looked ready to spill his breakfast.

I refrained from hugging him and smiled instead. "You were brave, Oli."

He smiled back with tight lips.

Alexei pounded his back, and Oliver winced. "Nice job taking that calculated wound! Showed your mettle and strategic intelligence."

Oliver only nodded.

I quirked a brow. "Did you puke in your mouth?"

He nodded again.

Ronen stepped up beside him. "I'll take you to Sam and find a bucket along the way."

We still had a weird tension between us and barely spoke. But I gave him a grateful smile nonetheless.

Oliver hesitated.

"Go. There's one match before mine. You won't miss much, and thinking about you holding your puke in your mouth is making me nauseous."

He gave a pointed look to Alexei.

"MJ, Ichi, and I got our beautiful girl, don't you worry. Go do what you gotta do."

That pleased Oliver enough to follow Ronen out of the arena. Someone eventually dragged Theon out of the ring, and the next match started. During it, Alexei, MJ, and Ichi drilled me with reminders.

"You either kill her or severely wound her so she won't get back up. Got it?" MJ didn't blink, didn't even flinch. Her voice was cold with expectation.

I gave her a sharp nod.

Alexei slung his arm over my shoulder as we watched a female from the Devils Squadron beat in Cade's face—one of my squadmates. "Remember, Moira's—"

"A telekinetic. She'll try to use her powers against me. Keep my head on a swivel."

Cade stabbed the female repeatedly in the thigh, back, and sides, and used his flaming hands to burn her. But nothing stopped her metal-coated fists. I'd never seen anyone, let alone a soul, so unfazed by pain. And since souls didn't bleed, she wouldn't die from blood loss, nor did she care about her charred skin. He needed to sever her neck or tendons. He figured that out a second too late.

"She favors long-range combat. Anything that prevents her from getting her hands dirty," MJ explained for the third, maybe fifth, time. "But if you can avoid my arrows, you can avoid her attacks."

"But be mindful of the weapons that return," Ichi added in her soft, rhythmic accent.

The Devil shoved Cade to the ground, and he slashed weakly at her heel. His feeble attempts hardly grazed her boot, and she retaliated by smashing in his face. Brain matter and blood splattered on the sand. I had to avert my gaze, unable to stand the sight. I couldn't believe the female named Rissa had just murdered Cade with her bare hands and a pair of brass knuckles, winning her spot in my squad.

"Stay mindful, head on a swivel, avoid her weapons. Sounds easy enough," I said over the announcer's voice and the bloodthirsty cheering.

But I knew it wouldn't be. Moira was a vindictive, power-seeking harlot—but she also had the skill to keep her spot as leader of the Tormentors. It should've made me reconsider, made me back out. But I needed this. If not to show everyone my worth, then to prove to myself I could be more than the naïve, whimpering female from Elora—from Earth.

"Lucille, a blood-banded Nephilim, has challenged the Tormentors' leader, *her* leader, Moira, a blood-banded angel."

I took a deep breath. My Glory and Infernus hovered just below the surface, awaiting a call that wouldn't come.

"Go get her, beautiful."

I stepped into the ring, and Moira walked calmly out of the background of warriors. As expected, she held her head high, hips swaying, the most smug smile I'd ever seen gracing her face. Her weapon of choice: daggers.

Close. Bloody. Personal.

Or they would be, if she weren't a Dominion.

"Did you finally figure out he no longer wants you?" I mocked, pouting.

Moira threw a dagger at my head. The thick blade wobbled through the air, and I easily sidestepped, smiling as it missed me.

She smiled right back, unsurprised. Why—

I moved right as Alexei shouted, "Duck!" Flattening myself to the ground as three daggers flew over my body. She must've pulled two from the weapons wall.

The crowd booed, disappointed they didn't see blood. Part of me wanted to fling a middle finger at them, but I didn't have time. Moira's hovering daggers were zooming back for me. They dove again and again.

I searched through the thin cloud of grit hanging in the air and found something to help. I rolled to the edge of the circle until I hit the boots of warriors, then jerked up and ripped away a warrior's shield just in time for Moira's blades to thunk into the wood.

By her flaring nostrils, she definitely didn't like my quick thinking. Behind her, though, stood my smirking, healed best friend—and Ronen, with pride in his eyes and a smile on his face.

That smile had my heart racing more than the fight did. After the other night, I didn't expect that reaction from him. But his belief in me made my soul sing and gave me the courage to offer him a nod of gratitude in return.

Moira twisted to see who I was looking at, and I used the moment to strap the shield onto my back and lusceler closer. I didn't have the luxury of endless weapons like Moira. If I threw my knives and missed, I'd be at a disadvantage, which was why Alexei gave me throwing knives a Dominion couldn't steal.

Moira turned back just in time to take two blades to her shoulders, right in the joints. I hoped Ichi was proud.

Moira screeched like an incensed demon, and things took a turn for the worse.

I threw two more knives toward her legs, hoping to immobilize her, but they both missed. Her fingers twitched. The weapons wall rattled at my back, and the daggers at her hip lifted from their sheaths.

Oh shit.

I couldn't dodge all those. Not unless I used my Glory. For a moment, I considered it. But I had another option before I chose that path.

Something hard struck my wooden shield, jolting me forward. Then a knife plunged through my arm. I cried out, luscelering in a zigzag pattern. It made it harder for her to land attacks, but some weapons still nicked me. A few slammed into the shield at my back while I dodged the ones coming for my front. But I played a dangerous game that wouldn't last.

My Infernus surged beneath my skin. I strategically called to the bouncing melody as I ran for my life. It answered. The next thing I knew, I was smashing apart her perfectly crafted brick wall and spearing into Moira's mind.

I didn't have time to craft a hallucination, so I sent her subconscious a shot of fear and pulled out. Right before I opened my eyes, searing heat stabbed into my stomach.

I looked down to find Moira shaking on the ground and a dagger protruding from my body.

Gasps and cheers rang around the arena as I dropped to my knees. Oliver and Ichi shouted something, pulling my attention. I frowned. I couldn't make out their words in all the noise. And why did it look like Rune was sleeping at their feet?

But what really confused me was MJ and Alexei.

They were shouting too—but not at me.

At Ronen.

He jerked in Alexei's hold, his eyes pitch-black as MJ attempted to turn his head away from us. I didn't know what she said, but I knew it had something to do with Moira. Because the way he stared at her—

the way his shadows squeezed every inch of his rigid body, darkening with each second—made me think he wanted to kill her. His lover. Or former lover.

Moira groaned on the sand, and I mentally smacked myself.

This wasn't over.

I glanced down at the knife in my stomach. It should hurt, right? But even the knife in my arm didn't throb nearly as badly. I think I was in shock.

I moved an inch, then something wrapped around my boots, pinning me to the ground.

What the fuck?

I felt along my boots, unable to twist and see. A vine? Where the hell—

The vine wove around my hands, securing them to my ankles. I couldn't move. I couldn't grab for weapons. I was completely immobilized.

Cyrus. It had to be him. Who else would help Moira cheat?

The crowd ate up the new development. I wasn't sure they even knew what was happening— or if they could see the vines hogtying me as I leaned awkwardly back over my legs. Oliver and the rest of them knew something was wrong, but they couldn't see either. Especially when Moira stood and blocked their view.

She smiled down at me and gripped my hair, forcing my neck back. I didn't think her grin could get any wider—until she ripped the knife from my gut, drank in my cries, and pressed the blade against my throat.

"Even when you try, you're worthless."

I don't think *hate* fully encapsulated the emotion I felt toward her. But not because of her words. I couldn't care less about what she thought of me. The only person I imagined she had anything good to say about was herself. No, I hated her for her horrible personality and the position she was in. She shouldn't be a leader of a Hell Squadron.

"That's funny."

Moira's eyes narrowed.

"You think I give a damn about your opinion?" I pressed into her knife.

Let her think she had me. Let them all believe I was helpless and at her mercy. When it came down to it, I wasn't about to let this bitch kill me when I could burn away Cyrus's vines and run her through with an icicle.

A part of me wanted to win with skill alone. A larger part didn't want Michael or the council to find me. Nor did I want to put anyone in danger. But I refused to die.

Only, when I called to my Glory and my eager Infernus, it wasn't the crackling ice of the Glaciation Circle that answered—or any melody I was familiar with. It was a new one.

The rushing of air whispered in my ears. It whooshed in, then quieted as it whooshed out, like breathing. But what stunned me more was the purple cloud in front of Moira's mouth, darkening and lightening with each exhale and inhale of her breath. A tiny line of purple trickled toward my face, and I pressed back, only to be stopped by Moira's grip.

She laughed, thinking I was just trying to struggle against her. She must not be able to see what I did. When the trickle of purple air touched my lips, I had the sudden urge to breathe deeply. I gave in to it, and Moira gasped. She released my hair, dropped the knife, and clutched her throat, choking.

I tapped into the power of the Suffocation Circle. And I didn't have to reveal my powers.

Although I was still tied up. But maybe...

Before I could second-guess myself, I forced my body to still and focused on Ichi's teachings. It took longer than I liked and a couple tries, but eventually I pulled at the live wire in my core, imagined gathering a bright ball of energy, and directed it at my hands and feet. Then I luscelered my limbs out of Cyrus's restraints.

I whipped out two knives and stabbed Moira in the back of the knees. She couldn't even scream as she fell to the ground. And just because every step I took jostled the agonizing wound in my gut, I repaid the favor.

"Hurts, doesn't it?" I rasped.

Before she could pull another dirty trick, I pressed my knife to her neck and waited for the announcer. Moira wasn't getting up. She wasn't tapping into her powers—not while I was pulling the air from her lungs.

I won.

Alexei, MJ, Ichi, and Oliver all smiled at me, each wearing a different shade of pride. But Ronen—his shadows softened just enough to reveal stunned wonder in his eyes. No one had ever looked at me like that, like they were genuinely moved by what I could do.

He may have doubted me before. Hell, I had doubted myself.

But now, after defeating an elite squad leader without using all my power, I did it. I was a warrior. More importantly, I had a real shot at rescuing Aspen, stealing Ronen's feather, and beating Lilith at her own game.

And even though I would rank after this, I knew Ronen wasn't about to change his mind and help us.

But maybe he'd give me Tsal-mawet instead.

"Lucille has w—"

An arrow shot through the announcer's neck.

Then there was movement in the shrieking, confused crowd.

A male with a gruesome soul wound on his freckled forehead parted the warriors with his bow and a notched arrow. He stepped into the challenge circle with Cyrus and Theon behind him.

"Ready for round two, Hell-whore?" Cyrus taunted.

Vines erupted from the ground and wrapped around me, holding me in place once again. The freckled male aimed and released his arrow. My powers raged beneath my skin, almost bridging the surface—when a wall of shadows blocked the arrow, ripped apart the vines, and shot into my nose, silencing my pain.

Ronen stepped into the circle. "This is your warning, Lou."

Lou hesitated, lowering his bow an inch.

"The Hell-whore doesn't deserve to be our leader!" Cyrus shouted, and Theon nodded.

Oh, Heavenly Shit.

That never registered. I wasn't doing this to be their leader. Oh *fuck.*

"Lucille won. This challenge is over."

"No."

I turned just in time to see Moira drop her hand. I must've lost my grip on my Infernus. The knife hit a solid wall of shadows, and then darkness bled through the arena, rendering everyone quiet.

"Ronen." I raised my hand, searching for his body.

Shadows tenderly brushed my face in answer. Usually, they soothed me, but I could practically feel their rage this time. It was vicious and thick, chilling me to the bone.

Metal slid against sand before I heard a wet slice, then a thump. I swallowed, wishing I could see. A moment later, I heard another. Then another. And another. The last one sounded closer and ended in a gurgled choke.

Slowly, Ronen's shadows pooled back into his hands, revealing five decapitated bodies and a torrent of blood seeping across the ground. They were all dead. Moira, Theon, Lou, Cyrus—every single one of them lay in a pool of their blood.

"Holy fuck," Oliver whispered next to me.

"He did warn them," I said weakly as Oliver helped me to my feet.

Moira had a gaping space between her throat and neck. A couple tendons still connected the very back of her head to her body, unlike the rest, whose heads were several feet away. Ronen didn't make it a clean cut. She had to be the one who choked on her blood.

Ronen gazed around with pitch-black eyes. He twisted Theon's axe in his hand like he was ready to take on more. He waited, leveling every member of his military with an expression that said: *try and see what happens.* Not a single person moved or even twitched—except for MJ, who smiled as if she wasn't surprised in the least by Ronen's behavior.

"I do not allow insubordination." Ronen chucked the axe to the ground. "Understood?"

No one said a word.

"Understood!" he bellowed.

The warriors of Hell frantically nodded, shouting, "Yes, Sir!"

He turned toward the crowd in the stands. "I hope you all enjoyed the last of the challenges. Please go and enjoy the ball that will start in an hour and reward your warriors with your generosity and support."

Ball? Heavenly Hell. I'd spent the last several days so focused on trying not to die here today that I'd forgotten about that. Whose bright idea was it to have a formal ball after challenges, anyway?

The stunned crowd stood and filed out, but Ronen had already turned his back on them and everyone else. Now, his dark attention was on me.

He strode over to me. He reached out and gently brushed away some of my hair. "Moira punctured your spleen. You'll be okay, but you need to get to the healers' wing."

I nodded, placing my gloved hand over his. "Thank you."

The black in his eyes lightened the slightest bit. "For what, Hellion? You won. I was just doing my job."

"Hell yeah, you did," Oliver chimed in. He adjusted me in his arms, taking more of my weight.

Ronen's lips twitched like they were on the brink of a smile. "Both of you ranked, you know."

I lifted my head to the board and saw our names in first and second place.

"Didn't I tell you, *General*?" I reminded him.

Ronen did smile then, and it was filled with unadulterated pride.

I studied every inch of his smile, searing the image into my mind. It transformed the hardened, threatening lines of his face, softening his fierce aura. It brought warmth and life to his eyes like I'd never seen before. I wanted to reach out and graze a finger against his tilted lips. Butterflies swirled in my stomach when the rest of his shadows gave way to the gold I loved so much.

"I know what I want as my favor."

His smile dropped, and I couldn't help but be disappointed. He probably thought I was going to ask for his help again.

"I want the dagger you found on me when you first rescued me."

He frowned. "Why?"

"Well, for one, you stole it from me. And two, I just do. Is it on you?"

He seemed to want to ask more, but refrained. "No. I'll see what I can do."

Good enough—for now.

"Before you go, tonight, I'd like to talk to you after the ball, if that's alright?"

"About?" My heart rate picked up at the seriousness of his expression. What could he possibly want to talk about? The night we argued? Aspen? Or something to do with today?

"Later. Go to Sam," he said, giving me one last stare before leaving.

"If we're going through with this, then it sounds like tonight would be the best time," Oliver murmured.

"I agree." I followed Ronen with my eyes, memorizing his walk, his stance, the way his shadows wove around his uniform. I held the image in my mind, next to his smile that I craved to see again.

Except... there was a chance I wouldn't.

CHAPTER 45

Lucille

"Why are you here, Lucille?"

I faced Aspen. My thoughts warred against each other. I wanted to leave and forget him, but I also wanted to reach out and soothe the exhaustion weighing down his shoulders.

His unruly hair lay tangled and limp on his head. His beard appeared bushy and unkept. But the most concerning was his lifeless, dull eyes, as if Lilith was sucking away his soul.

The invasive energy that haunted me surged into my toes, urging me to move. I knew what it desired. What it always desired—Aspen.

"Why the Immolation Circle?" I asked, forcing my boots to stay planted.

"Don't," he hissed through his teeth and clutched his wrists.

"Why does Lilith want me there?"

Aspen gripped his head, squeezing his eyes shut. "I'm begging you."

"Stop fighting her influence and tell me."

He crumbled to his knees. The Hell Runes peeking from his uniform strobed between black and red light. He was in pain. I remembered what it felt like to press my hand to those runes—and this time, he had two. Digging my nails into my palms, I refused to bridge the distance and help him. I didn't want him to fight. I needed him to give me the answer.

Lilith wanted me badly. There was no doubt in my mind that she would've commanded Aspen to do everything in his power to either gather information that could help them steal me, or influence me to find them.

"Is there a way to the Tenebrous Kingdom through the Immolation Circle?"

"No," he gasped. But his face twitched like the time I asked about Michael.

He was lying.

"Where's the entrance?"

He groaned, trying his hardest to fight her.

"Tell me!" I shouted. We didn't have time for this.

"P—" He stopped, shaking his head and clamping his mouth shut. But the harder he resisted, the darker his runes grew. "Portal!" he blurted.

"Where's the portal?"

He pressed his hands against his mouth, trying to muffle his words. Sweat slicked his forehead as he curled into himself. "Caves."

"Where are the caves?"

He said something, but it was too muffled. I bridged our space and shoved his shoulders back.

"Where?"

"Past fire field," he whispered. "Use the Ember Metal."

I said nothing, ripping myself from the dream-walk. I opened my eyes to Oliver snacking on some food a maid brought to our rooms.

It was time for our next step.

"Let's steal the dagger, Oli."

His head flopped against the settee. "Oh, goodie, our suicide mission can commence."

I sat up and grabbed his hand. "You don't have to come. Let me risk it alone."

Oliver turned his head to face me, pressing his lips together, and nodded. Then he ripped out a decorative pillow from behind his back and whipped it at my head. "That's for the stupid shit that came out of your mouth." He hit me again. "And that's for the previous time you suggested that."

"There's a good chance we won't find your sister, and we'll end up dead, Oli. I'd rather risk my neck for Aspen alone. I don't—"

Oliver hammered me with the pillow, forcing me back into the couch.

"Okay. Okay!" I raised my hands to block his attack. "I'll shut up."

"Music to my ears. Now let's strap on some weapons and let the chaos commence."

Unfortunately, the only weapons we had were the two daggers Oliver always kept with him. Fortunately, I guaranteed Ronen had an arsenal to steal from.

All ready to break into his room, we opened our door and immediately had a problem.

"Rune? Why aren't you with Ronen?"

She sat in front of us, her tongue lolling out and shadow fur moving quickly as if excited.

"What do we do?" Oliver whispered into my ear.

She headbutted my chest, seeking pets. I scratched her beneath her muzzle, thinking. Maybe it'd be as easy as just telling her to leave. It had worked before.

"Rune, we have things to do. You need to head back to Ronen."

She tilted her head, looking as if she knew we were up to no good. At least her eyes were lightless, but we had to ditch her before that changed.

"Go to Ronen, Rune."

Rune didn't budge.

"It's not working."

"Clearly."

There was only one solution I could think of, and it was barely a solution at all.

"Let's rest a second, Oli." I grabbed his arm and forced him back through our door, opening it wider and ushering Rune in.

She sprang through the threshold, her excitement palpable as she eagerly joined us. A tight knot twisted in my chest at the thought of what I was about to do next.

Placing my back in front of the doorknob, I turned the lock, and her ears twitched. Before she could react, I shoved Oliver out of my room, followed after him, then slammed the door shut. Hopefully, that'd hold her long enough to retrieve the dagger and leave. She whimpered, her paws scratching frantically at the door. I felt terrible. I hated when she cried.

Then the pawing stopped, and in the next second, she rammed against the wood.

"Rune's going to contact Ronen! Probably right before she blows through your door!"

"I didn't know what else to do!"

Oliver snatched my wrist and pulled me away right as Rune's next slam created hairline cracks in the wood. "We'd better hurry."

Ronen's room was a short run down the hall. Oliver rushed to open Ronen's door and hissed, jerking his hand back. "What the fuck kind of doorknob is that?" he asked, sucking the fresh blood on his palm.

"One protected by his shadows." I reached out, felt a prick on my skin, then the lock clicked.

Oliver's eyebrows rose.

"No clue," I answered, walking into Ronen's immaculate sitting area.

Oliver whistled, turning in place. "Huh. This suits him."

"It does." I pointed to Ronen's wall of weapons. "It's right there."

Thank heavens it was. I'd played a tricky game asking for it. But we needed to know if he had it on him, and hope he wouldn't take it to the ball.

Oliver luscelered over and grabbed the dagger. "What the—" He yanked harder, then used two hands. "Lucy, we may have a problem."

My stomach dropped. *No.*

I marched over and grabbed the top of the sheath while Oliver grabbed the hilt. "One, two…"

"Three," we said in unison, pulling as hard as we could. The knife gave easily, and we both toppled to the floor, Oliver knocking into one of Ronen's chairs.

I glared at him.

"I swear it was stuck!"

It hummed through the leather, vibrating my skin. "Weird," I mumbled, feeling the urge to unsheathe the blade, take off my glove, and press it against my hand. I'd forgotten how magnetic it felt to me.

Oliver stood, then helped me up. "Come on, let's go. If we're lucky, no one heard that."

"Wait, we need more weapons." I snatched a few daggers off the wall, placing them in all my empty loops. Oliver tried to do the same, but he couldn't remove them.

I handed Oliver a blade, confused. "I don't understand."

"Neither do I, but we don't have time. Let's go."

We hurried toward Ronen's door, and right as we stepped out, Alexei turned the corner. He was dressed in a black suit with a floral tie that matched the blue of his eyes. He even had a matching pocket square. His hair was combed back into flowing locks, and his golden skin glowed. He cleaned up nicely.

"Aren't you two supposed to be changed and at the ball by now? Why are you in Ronen's room?"

"Ronen had to talk to us, and we were in there longer than we realized," Oliver lied smoothly.

"He's in there now? I wanted to ask him something."

Oliver opened his mouth, but I beat him to the punch. "Yep, he is!"

"Great. Well, hurry up and get changed. I'll see you two down there."

We moved out of the way, and Alexei went in, calling out Ronen's name and shutting the door. I grabbed the handle and coated it in a solid block of ice.

"Like that's going to hold the lightning wielder for long." Oliver latched onto my hand, jerking me into a run.

"Did you have any better ideas?"

Oliver grumbled under his breath, which meant no.

We passed a few maids and castle staff carting around food and drink trays. They lurched to the side as we barreled through, and Oliver cursed the entire way. We were leaving a trail of witnesses, but we couldn't very well run down the main stairwells. They'd gossip about it, but what could they actually say? It's not like they'd report to the king that his daughter was missing. I was inconsequential to them.

Once we burst through the back doors of the castle, our uniforms heated. We sprinted to the barn, scurrying inside and slamming the big wooden doors shut.

I leaned my head against the wood and sighed. We were almost there.

Oliver elbowed me in the side. "Uhm, Lucy... turn around."

Two sleighs led by Hellcats appeared just beyond the barn's opening. Each held a couple dressed in dark fur-lined cloaks and overcoats.

"Neither one of us took into consideration that this might be the drop-off spot for couples coming from the city to celebrate the ball."

"Nope," Oliver said. "But we weren't sure how to call Alexei's Hellcats, so this might work out in our favor. Follow my lead."

From experience, Oliver's lead usually involved lying and theatrics. But as much as I didn't want to go along with whatever plan he was concocting, I had no choice.

"Welcome to the Twilight of the Warriors Festival," he said, walking up to the first couple and helping them out of their sleigh. "We will take care of your sleigh and cats for you."

"It's about time the king employed a stable boy to help with the festival. Last year, we had to do everything ourselves," the male griped, brushing off the imaginary snow on his shoulders.

Yes, a *stable boy*, in a Hell Squadron uniform.

"At least they have good food and servants for the ball. Otherwise, we wouldn't have come."

Right. By their fancy, old-fashioned clothing and the open wounds marring the side of the male's face, I presumed they were entitled souls from the Victorian era—with a few sticks shoved so far up their asses they were blind, dumb, and full of themselves. She sure looked like it with that upturned, snooty nose.

"Yes, he must've seen the error of his ways. Luce, will you get the door for this pleasant couple?" Oliver motioned toward me. I resisted grinning at his veiled sarcasm.

"Why, of course." I opened the barn door, and the couple walked away. It gave me great satisfaction to see the female stumble in the snow.

The next couple had already moved their sleigh to the side and unharnessed their Hellcats, placing them in an empty stall. They walked up to us, wearing modern dress.

"I would've said entitled pricks, but *pleasant couple* is more polite," the male joked, opening the barn door I wasn't holding to usher the female through. "They must've never gotten the memo that the king provides services at the front of his castle, not the back. If you come here, you're choosing to do the work yourselves. That's how it's always been. Enjoy your night," he said, winking, closing the door behind him.

Oliver gave me a questioning look. "Do you think he knew what we were up to?"

"He definitely knows we're up to something."

"Right, well." Oliver ushered me into the pricks' sleigh. "Looks like karma found its next victim. Let's get out of here."

We slid into the sleigh, and Oliver took the reins.

"Here goes something. To Portal Lake!"

Thankfully, the Hellcats responded and took off. Unfortunately, Rune barged through the barn doors with glowing eyes and jumped into our sleigh right as the cats leaped off the cliff and blinked.

CHAPTER 46

Ronen

I stood next to Lucifer, who sat on his throne, gazing at all of Hell's citizens mingling in their finery. The blue bags beneath his eyes and the pallid tone of his face told me he was still transferring his energy to Saraqael. I'd bet if I forced him to show me his arms, he'd have more carvings than he should.

"You're playing a dangerous game."

"When I ask for your opinion, General, you'll know."

My shadows curled around my palm, inching for an outlet. "You can't keep going like this."

Lucifer took a sip of his drink, nodding to a few passing souls. "I will not let anything happen to Saraqael. And I will not stop Lucille's training. Sam is helping me."

"Sam won't be able to keep that up forever, either."

"We don't need forever. We just need until Lucille can save us."

I turned to face him fully. "What?"

Lucifer stood, ignoring me, and stepped down to talk to some dead noble. I had half a mind to rip him away and demand answers. *How would Lucille save us?* Did this have something to do with the deal he made?

Speaking of the hellion—where was she?

Her anxiety brushed up against my mind. She was probably nervous about the number of people who wanted to see the warrior who bested Moira.

My own anxiety was getting the better of me. Tonight, I planned to tell her everything. MJ was right—why not try for something good in my life? Once the truth was out, if she still decided to love the pet, then fine. But at least I would've tried. At least I'd have given her the freedom to choose with all the facts in play.

A sudden shot of guilt speared through her anxiety, along with concern from Rune.

What was up with the two ladies in my life?

After a moment, Rune sent me an urgent emotion, calling for me to link to our connection. Sighing, I followed the thread between our souls and connected with her senses. She stared at a wooden door, whimpering and scratching. Then she barreled into it.

Rune, I chastised.

She ignored me, sending waves of suspicion and worry.

Show me where you are.

She twisted her head back to show me the hellion's room.

Who would've locked her in?

Rune sent more urgency down the bond and slammed into the door again.

Okay, I'm coming. Don't break her door down.

I disconnected, but when I arrived at said door and saw it in splinters, I kicked myself. Rune was no longer there. I was about to reconnect when something exploded down the hall.

Wreathing my hands in shadows, I strode toward the source, only to find Alexei walking through my blasted-apart door.

"What the fuck?"

He winced, then quickly sobered. "Lucille and Oliver locked me inside your room after lying to me about talking to you."

Odd. "They haven't spoken to me since the challenge."

"They were both still wearing their gear," he added.

"I found Rune locked inside Lucille's room." I stepped on my broken door and entered the sitting area, scanning my weapons wall.

Tsal-mawet was gone. She'd stolen the dagger from my runed wall, along with many others.

I didn't take into consideration that she *could* take my weapons. But we were technically two parts of a whole.

"What are you looking for?" Alexei asked, peering around.

"The dagger that created Hell. She stole it."

Alexei's eyes widened. "Barring the fact you didn't tell me you found *that* particular dagger, why would she take it?"

"She asked for it after the challenge."

"What does she want with it?"

There was only one thing the hellion wanted—to save her loved ones. And there was only one way to do that. I didn't know how the knife came into play, but somehow, it did.

"She's going to attempt to leave." My shadows tightened on my hands and pressed against my eyes.

"But she can't... can she?"

I sighed, a terrible feeling brewing deep in my gut.

"We're about to find out." I quickly connected to Rune. "They've stolen a carriage and cats, and they're…" I waited. "At Portal Lake. Get MJ and meet me there."

Alexei nodded before luscelering to find MJ. I wouldn't risk time changing, so I ran to the roof in my expensive suit, manifested my wings, and took off. I reconnected with Rune on the way—and nearly lost all altitude.

"Fuck!" I shouted into the punishing air, feeling the hellion's pain.

She had carved a symbol into the palm of her hand, and the moment her blood touched the lake, it began to swirl.

She opened the portal.

"No!" I bellowed. She couldn't be ripped away from me now. She couldn't enter my life like a blazing star, tearing apart all my barriers, and then disappear.

I put on a burst of speed and disconnected from Rune.

I could finally see the edge of the cliff, making out their tiny forms. They'd just finished backing up and were now starting to run. My heart slammed against my ribs, and worry—unlike anything I'd ever felt—stole all logical thought.

They jumped, and I tucked in my wings, plummeting with only one goal in mind.

Her.

They didn't see me coming, too focused on the swirling mass of light and color. Only a few feet away, I made myself known and threw out my shadows, hoping to create a barrier between them and the portal. They bounced off and stopped, but I hadn't realized how magnetic the pull of the portal would be. The tail end of my shadows was already being sucked in, and I knew I wouldn't be able to yank us back.

I dove and wrapped my body and wings around Lucille just as we were pulled into the vortex.

My name on her lips contorted as the wind stole our air and sense of gravity. We twisted and turned in the unknown force, and all the while, I held her with everything I had, refusing to let go.

No one was allowed to travel with the king to the circles. It was against the laws of Hell. So I had no idea where we'd end up—or what we were about to encounter.

I tightened my already crushing hold.

Seconds later, the lights darkened, and we crashed into warm water. I didn't even have time to put away my wings. Like the clothes on my body, they soaked up the water like a sponge, threatening to drag us both down. I released Lucille and pushed her to the surface, while my shadows helped pull me up as I kicked.

Breaking the surface, I immediately searched for her. She was inches away, staring at me with stunned surprise. Oliver and Rune popped up a moment later, and the lines in her face relaxed when she saw them.

I tilted my head up to the swirling gray sky, then just past the rocky beach to the miles of purple and black flame. Flames that were at least a mile away. But their sweltering heat flushed my face and warmed the lake we treaded in.

I had a feeling I knew where we were.

"Lucille," I said in a grave tone. "Where did you bring us?"

Before she could answer, something splashed behind me. I whipped around, and a piece of the sinking dread lightened.

"Lucy, if Ronen doesn't rip your ass a new one, I sure will!" Alexei shouted, slowly swimming over. His dappled wings dragged behind him, explaining both his slow progress and irate expression.

"Not until you've had your bottle and we've changed your diaper," MJ mocked, swimming with ease beside him. She must've put her wings away right before diving in.

"What am I, just chopped liver?" Oliver added.

Alexei twisted, about to yell at him too.

"Let's swim to the beach, and then you two can explain yourselves."

No one complained about my recommendation. It took a few minutes, but we all swam to the rocky, black beach. I grimaced as gravity tugged at my drenched wings, their tips dragging across the heated stones. I kept the irritation and pain to myself, unlike someone else.

"This is why we don't fucking fly into Portal Lake! This is why we don't fly near water at all! What the hell were you two thinking?" Alexei jabbed a finger at Lucille and Oliver.

Immediately, I felt her defenses go up.

"We were thinking we were doing this alone!" she shouted back. "But you three and Rune had to spoil that."

"Spoil that? *Excuse me, Princess.* One challenge must've gone to your head if you think you can just go portaling into the Seven Circles of Hell by yourself and survive!" Alexei gestured toward me. "Tell them, Ronen."

I wanted to. I wanted to rage at her just as Alexei was. This place—what I was now certain was the Immolation Circle, based on the sweltering heat—was the most dangerous circle of them all. Every instinct I had set my shadows slithering across both our bodies, alert and ready.

But as I stared into her double-ringed eyes, seeing and feeling her resolve, I knew my words would be as useless as Alexei's. She planned to come here and save the pet, and nothing would sway her. She believed a Hell Rune controlled him, and that Lilith had my feather.

Could it be possible?

Lucifer had told me he checked for my feather in their kingdom ages ago, that I never needed to search there. Did Lilith hide it that well? Or did she not have it then? Regardless, if she had it, I needed to steal it back. And I supposed... the pet too.

Additionally, Lucille held the key to Portal Lake. I didn't know how or why, but she was our only way out. We either complied, or she would leave us here. And there was no way in this circle or the next I'd let that happen. Which meant Alexei, MJ, and I better get filled in.

"Tell us your plan—and how we can help."

She scrunched her face, and I regretted the doubt I sensed in her. I'd put that there. I'd forced her away, and now she didn't trust my intentions. But why would she? I knew what she wanted. She planned to rescue the pet, and she knew I hated him. Still, that didn't change the fact that I'd rather be by her side, making sure she was protected, than have her go it alone.

I should've figured that out sooner, along with her plan. But never in my imaginings did I believe someone could escape Hell.

"You said you wouldn't help—"

I stepped into her space, cutting her off. "I will help you rescue Aspen if you tell us your plan and allow us to adjust it so we can make sure everyone escapes unscathed. Okay?"

She searched my face, lips parted slightly. I wanted to kiss her. Or at least allow her to feel the tingles vibrating at my fingertips, the ones I continued to block from her senses. As much as I wanted to tell her, to let her feel what was between us, now wasn't the time. If we were to succeed, she needed to stay focused, not thrown off balance by a secret I'd kept for two months.

"Thank you," she breathed. Her eyes glistened with relief, and I had to step away before I really did kiss her.

Alexei gaped at me. Anyone else, and I'd probably force them to take us back. But she wasn't just anyone, and I wasn't sure I *could* force her to do anything. MJ didn't look surprised. If anything, she surveyed the landscape with eager eyes. Oliver grinned. Rune sat beside him, her shadow fur whipping chaotically. She didn't like it here. This sweltering circle was her birthplace.

Which meant we also had to watch out for Hellfire and Hellhounds.

Lucille turned, pausing as she took in the Hellfire fields. "I believe we need to go through that, get to the base of those cliffs, and find a cave with a portal that'll take us to the Tenebrous Kingdom."

Alexei stretched his sagging wings in an attempt to dry them. "There's no portal to the Tenebrous Kingdom here, beautiful."

"Yes, there is."

I internally cringed as I expanded my own wings, muscles straining under the weight. "The only portal that leads to Elora is Hell's gates."

"Trust me. There's one here."

She *believed* that. I could feel it. "Where did you get your information?"

"Aspen."

Alexei's wings dropped. "That piece of shit prince?" He grabbed her shoulders. "You can't trust a word he says. How has he even contacted you?"

I glanced at MJ, surprised she wasn't chiming in, only to find her scrutinizing me. I could see the gears turning, piecing things together—my silence, what I'd told her earlier about Lucile loving another. She shook her head, lips tight with disapproval. Not for the pet. For me.

"It doesn't matter. But Oliver and I are rescuing him."

"The prince can't be saved. He's a lost cause. If anything, we should drag him here and leave him to burn."

A strange pulse of energy flowed through Lucille, muddying her other emotions. She whipped out a knife and leveled it beneath Alexei's chin. "I'd refrain from saying things like that. If you don't want to come, then stay. We only need Ronen to remove the Hell Runes."

Alexei slowly released her and turned toward me. "What the fuck is going on, Ronen?"

I sighed. "Lucille believes Lilith is controlling him with my feather. If that's the case, we need to get it back. And if we save the pe—prince along the way, so be it."

"Excuse me? I know she's your cor—"

My shadows flew out, tightening around his neck. "Careful."

He gave me a sharp nod, and I released him.

Alexei cleared his throat. "This could be a trap. We could all end up burning here."

"No. Lilith wants me whole. There's no trap here. But there could be one on the other side of the portal," Lucille admitted.

"Then why go through with this?" Alexei pulled a dagger from her belt, nerves clearly fraying.

That same urgency flared in her. I didn't understand it.

"I have no other choice," she said quietly.

"We have to save my sister too," Oliver added. "But we don't know where she is."

Alexei stole another blade, flipping and catching them repeatedly while fanning his wings.

MJ's wings burst free, perfectly dry, and she laughed at Alexei's distress. "Oh, this is going to be fun."

Alexei whipped around. "You *would* think this would be fun! We don't have any battle gear. My wings are almost steaming as they slowly dry. I'm about ready to say screw it and jump back in. We're not even close to the Hellfire fields—and there's most likely a trap waiting for us inside that godforsaken kingdom! And what about the fact that we'll die if we don't have Ember Metal?"

"There will be some in the caves," Lucille said.

"Your trusty prince tell you that?" Alexei snapped.

MJ wrapped an arm around his shoulder. "We'll strategize along the way. It'll make you feel better."

"Hard to strategize when we don't know what we're getting into. No maps. No backup. We'll be sitting ducks walking through that portal. No powers. Might as well just slit my throat now."

MJ rolled her eyes. But Alexei had a point.

"We'll run through every scenario we can with the resources we have before crossing the portal," I said. "We've been through worse."

Alexei scoffed and pointed a dagger at Lucille. "Beautiful, I better not die rescuing that scumbag."

CHAPTER 47

Lucille

Ronen radiated threat as his shadows plucked my knife out of Alexei's hand. "Don't."

Just one word—yet Alexei straightened and dipped his head in compliance. If I didn't know better, I'd think Ronen reigned over this circle. He stood like he commanded the land itself. The perfectly tailored dark suit hugged his body in all the right ways, and the gold accents highlighted the uniqueness of his eyes. His shoulders were pushed back, his shadows curling around his hands. The lethal male was temptation wrapped in a mind-altering bow, begging to be untied and discovered.

Oliver elbowed me hard in the side. "You look like you're about to eat him. Focus!"

I found it ironic—and a little concerning—that the one person who would absolutely join in on the ogling was chastising me. I took his shaky hand in mine, and he squeezed it.

The heat punished my face. My hair stuck to my forehead. Sweat soaked the back of my neck and trickled into my uniform. The Immolation Circle practically suffocated me, and yet Oliver and I had temperature-regulated uniforms helping us. Judging by the glistening sweat dripping from Ronen, Alexei, and MJ's foreheads, the way their wings drooped, and the dark splotches blooming across their formalwear, we needed to move. They were struggling—everyone except Rune and MJ.

Rune seemed agitated but unfazed by the heat, while MJ flashed a smile. Her pantsuit clung to her damp skin, her heels clicked with each shift, and sweat bled through the fabric. Still, a vicious grin played on her lips.

I pointed toward the Hellfire. "Let's go."

"Music to my ears," MJ purred.

Alexei stretched his wings wide, dripping onto MJ's back. "I seriously think you need help."

MJ turned, stepping into Alexei's chest and squeezing his cheeks. "At least I'm not scared."

He jabbed her in the stomach, forcing her back. "Some would say that's a problem."

"Or a strength."

Alexei let out a derisive laugh. "Well, if you're so strong, you can carry Oliver then."

"Carry Oliver, carry the team, save your asses—sounds about right," MJ said with a smug smile. "Oh, don't pout, Lex. Or I'm going to have to go get your binky."

Oliver released my hand, and strong arms scooped me up, startling me.

"What are you doing?" I snapped at Ronen.

"You said to go. I only listened." His wings flapped, spraying droplets of water as we rose into the sky. "Trust me. They'll be bickering for hours if we let them."

Below us, Oliver clung to Alexei as he pushed off the ground after MJ. His neck muscles tensed, and his wet wings slapped with each pump, struggling against the air.

"Is Alexei okay..." The tendons in Ronen's neck were just as taunt, and we flew lower than usual. "It's your wings."

"They'll dry soon."

"How soon?" I hid my face in Ronen's chest, trying to shield myself from the painful heat. We needed to gain altitude before we reached the Hellfire.

As if sensing my distress, Ronen flapped harder. He hissed with each movement until the air thinned and the heat lessened by a couple degrees. But his face, neck, and any exposed skin were flushed pink.

My Infernus whispered a tune I hadn't touched since Elora. The haunting melody sent itches scurrying along my arms, begging me to use its power. I ignored it. How could it possibly help our situation?

Peeling off a glove, I tapped into the Glaciation Circle and coated my hand in ice. I touched his cheek. "Are you okay?"

He pressed into my palm. "Better now."

He captured me—not just with the quiet longing in his gaze, but with the warmth of his words. I felt cherished, like I was the relief he'd been yearning for his entire life and had finally found. But how could just two words do that? How could one look make me feel steadier, stronger, and more than I ever had? My heart thundered, full and fierce, fueled by his attention alone. His scent, warm and spicy, filled my lungs, allowing me to breathe deeply again. And his arms around me? They felt like home.

Truly. Completely.

What was this pull that happened every time we touched or met each other's eyes? Was it just my growing feelings for him?

"Good," I whispered.

My ice continued to melt, dripping down his lips, down his neck, sliding over the swirls of his tattoos. It eased his tight tendons, pulling out a sigh. I bit my lip, following the glistening trail back up to his mouth. What would they feel like, pressing mine to his? Would it be soft and gentle? Or ferocious and claiming? If just touching him made me feel this alive, his lips would be a drug I'd never quit.

"Don't." His breath mingled with mine—his word brushing my skin in a tempting caress. I hadn't even realized I'd leaned in. "Or I won't stop, and your prince will have to pry you from my arms."

I dropped my hand and turned forward. Ronen made me forget about Aspen so easily. We were risking our lives for him. How was it possible he slipped my mind? My feelings for both of them were a tangled mess I had no clue how to unravel.

"Is Rune okay down there?"

She was. But I needed to think about anything else.

"This is where she was created. She's immune to Hellfire."

The beastie zoomed through the purple and black flames at a speed that kept up with us.

"We're almost there."

Moments later, darkness eclipsed my eyelids, and cool moisture kissed my skin.

Ronen placed me gently on my feet. Alexei landed with Oliver, MJ right behind them. Rune sprang through the opening, shaking off her fur as if ridding herself of the flames.

"Man, I could lick that," Oliver said, eyeing a drop of moisture rolling down the cave wall the same way I'd stared at Ronen's lips.

"I'd probably refrain from drinking anything here. This is a circle of suffering, and I guarantee that's not water," Alexei said, scanning the cave. "Have you guys felt the drain?"

"Yes. Since we stepped out of the lake," Ronen answered.

"It's worse here, though."

Ronen nodded. "I imagine we're beneath the prisons of the Immolation Circle. Our powers will keep draining the deeper we go."

In the light from the cave entrance, Alexei's mouth pressed into a hard line, and he gazed back like he wanted no part of this non-plan.

"Looking for your binky?" MJ cooed. "It's probably burning back there with your balls."

Alexei elbowed her. She retaliated by stealing the dagger he'd taken from me. His expression darkened like it physically pained him to part with it. Judging by MJ's smile she knew that.

Oliver drew one of his sheathed daggers and offered it to Alexei. "Will this make you feel better?"

Alexei snatched it. "No."

"Lilith may know I'm coming, but not when. Nor does she know about you guys. We have some advantage if this is a trap." Or so I hoped. There was a reason I told Oliver to stay behind, not that he listened. "Plus, I'll have my Infernus. You'll just have to rely on me. We'll find more weapons soon," I said, like everything would somehow work out.

"How will you have your Infernus?" Alexei asked.

"Not sure. But it's worked against Ember Metal before." I had a hunch my immunity had something to do with Lilith's involvement in my birth. Not that I was about to share that.

Alexei shook his head and shoved MJ away from his ear. I could only imagine what taunting remarks she was whispering.

Ronen gripped Alexei's shoulder. "We've fought under worse odds."

"Yeah, and we learned from our petulant mistakes. This would be repeating them," he grumbled, but threw out a hand. "Lead the way, General. I'm not leaving you or yours—I'm just the voice of reason here."

We walked farther into the dark cavern, and I finally felt the drain they'd spoken of, like part of me was falling asleep, or being locked behind an impenetrable wall I couldn't reach.

"Well, it's all on you now, Princess."

A smack sounded.

"Watch it, Nephilim," Alexei snapped.

MJ laughed.

"Stop being an asshole," Oliver countered. "If you can't deal with the loss of your power, then stay behind. We don't need your fear. We've got enough of our own. So, shut up."

"I think I'm starting to like you, Nephilim. But I'd like you more if you hit him again." MJ bumped Oliver's elbow like they were already fast friends.

I swore I could feel Oliver's grin.

"This shouldn't be here," Ronen said abruptly, and I slammed into his back.

Peeking around him, I saw a black stone archway, framing a gilded mirror. The antique stood out against the dark rock. The mirror glowed and rippled as we approached, distorting our reflections.

"No, it shouldn't," Alexei agreed. "And isn't it just so *handy* that all around the portal are cuffs, bracelets, necklaces, earrings"—he kicked a pile of objects—"and other odds and ends made of Ember Metal that will suppress your power and allow you to enter the Tenebrous Kingdom?"

"Yes, I told you there would be. And unless you've got some demon blood in your lineage, I'd put something on. Unless you'd rather die," I remarked.

"Is he always like this?" Oliver asked.

Ronen sighed. "Alexei gets pre-battle jitters. But he's useful. He brings attention to all the details."

"Hells, I hate when you guys call it that! Makes me sound like a Bowel recruit seeing war for the first time."

"When you act like this, you are."

Grumbling, Alexei sifted through the pile until he found a thick, tarnished chain and placed it around his neck. It clashed with his silk tie. "There. I'm ready to be sacrificed to Lilith now."

"So when does the fearful griping end?" Oliver asked, bending and picking up a bracelet.

"When he kills something," Ronen replied, crouching to retrieve two matching bangles. He handed me one and slipped the other on.

"In all seriousness, this portal shouldn't be here. Neither should this supply of Ember jewelry. The convenience of it all is setting off my alarms—and I don't mean the trap we're expecting on the other side. Something else is going on."

"Like someone—or something—is getting through here," Ronen said, glancing at Alexei and MJ.

Alexei crouched, surveying the ground. "But how are they getting from this circle to ours?"

They?

"That's what we'll have to figure out."

"The Immolation Lord may know something," MJ mused.

"I've thought of that. But we'd need Lucifer to talk to him. We're not even supposed to be here."

Alexei nodded. "So we stay sharp. If we survive, we report our new findings to Lucifer."

Ronen and MJ agreed. But I had a feeling I already knew what they were really talking about.

Oliver and I divided the rest of our daggers among the group. I gave the black dagger back to Ronen, trusting him with it more than myself.

They accepted the weapons without hesitation, securing them in their belts.

"Prepare yourself," Ronen said.

Armed, we all circled the portal.

"Why follow us if you think this is a trap? Why risk yourself for Aspen when you hate him?"

Ronen drilled me with a gaze holding more emotion than I'd ever seen in him. "My soul is already at risk, Lucille. But I'm hoping with all of us, it has a better chance of surviving. And if not"—he stepped closer, grabbing my chin—"then the world will see a version of myself I've hidden away for a very long time."

I could taste the wrath behind his words.

"I don't understand." He didn't answer my question; if anything, he left me more confused.

"You will, eventually."

"On top of all that, this is bigger than a rescue mission, beautiful," Alexei added.

"You're talking about the demon infection, aren't you?"

Ronen nodded and glanced back at the cave entrance—just a pinprick of light in the distance. "This all is very suspicious. We should've seen at least a few souls or Hellhounds on the way here. It's eerie that we didn't. Even if we weren't rescuing the prince or stealing back my feather, we'd need to investigate."

"So if we all die, we can blame you three—since you'd have gone in anyway," Oliver joked.

No one laughed.

"No one will die today," Ronen said, like he could command Death himself. "Lucille, do you know where the prince will be?"

I grimaced. Alexei was going to love this. "No."

"So much for fucking strategy."

CHAPTER 48

Lucille

After a lot of pissy comments, arguing, and planning as best we could with almost nothing, we stepped through the portal. It was different from all the others I'd traveled through. We didn't fall or twist around in a light show. We moved slowly through what felt like sticky, translucent slime that stole our breath, until it felt like we were about to suffocate. Then we popped out, all of us falling to the ground and gasping for air.

"That sucked," Oliver wheezed.

"*That* is what happens when portals are created by someone who doesn't have enough power to sustain them," Ronen said, helping me up.

There was no Lilith. No Aspen. No one else. Instead, we found ourselves in a stone tunnel lined with flaming torches. I turned, looking back at the mirror portal, then ahead. The dim path stretched away, then hooked to the right.

"Well, this is anticlimactic," Oliver muttered.

"Someone lit the torches." Alexei kept his daggers raised and attention locked on the turn, much like Ronen.

"They could be runed to stay lit," MJ countered.

"And what Archangel or Seraphim would have the ability to do that in this kingdom?"

"Alexei's right," Ronen confirmed. "MJ, fall back. Alexei, up front with me. Let's see where this leads."

We all fell into formation and continued. MJ's heels echoed through the damp tunnel, setting my nerves on edge. I squeezed the hilt of my daggers, approaching each new turn, expecting to see a demon, Lilith—even Aspen. But no one was there. She had to be toying with us. That was the only explanation for why we weren't already being attacked. And once we were... then what? I almost hoped we'd be fighting Aspen. At least then we'd have found him. But that would only solve one of our three problems.

Something caressed the back of my neck and tickled the inside of my nose. My anxiety eased.

I glanced at Ronen, assuming it was his shadows, but he shouldn't have any power here. He turned to me.

"We'll find him."

It was strange to hear the earnestness in his voice, stranger still that he refrained from using the degrading name *pet*. His feelings couldn't have changed in a matter of days, yet he was putting aside his hatred for me.

Why?

I focused back on the path and frowned. "Is that—"

"A dead end." Ronen stopped.

How did that even make sense? "The portal can't lead to nowhere."

"It didn't." Oliver pointed at the stone ceiling to a trapdoor.

"Great. A tiny door where only one of us can fit through at a time. Easy pickings," Alexei drawled.

"There better be something on the other side he can kill," I muttered.

MJ patted him on the back. "Does our Bowel babe want to go first?"

Alexei pushed her away. "We should've left you at home."

"Give me your knee," Ronen demanded.

Alexei knelt and cupped his hands.

"Wait. We don't know what's up there. Let me go first, I have my powers."

Ronen brushed a piece of hair from my face. "No way in Hell or Heaven."

A stubborn resolve took hold in my bones, and I stepped closer, about to shove him off Alexei's knee, when Ronen's eyes went pitch-black.

He had his powers. So earlier, I hadn't imagined the brush.

Mirth danced at his lips, along with a smugness that made me want to push him off Alexei for an entirely new reason.

"Be careful."

His smile dropped. "For you, always."

I swallowed. I had no words for what that phrase did to me. The severity of his tone, the fervent way he held my gaze—it struck a chord in my chest. My fingers twitched, aching to trace his cheek, maybe his lips. I wanted to feel his warmth for just a moment. His gorgeous, otherworldly eyes beckoned me. I took a deep breath, filled my lungs with his scent, and stepped back.

He gave me one last long look before stepping on Alexei. My Infernus sent itches along my skin and practically screamed in my ear to act. They hovered at the surface, ready to explode, while Ronen eased open the creaking trapdoor and pulled himself up, his back an easy target. All someone had to do was shove a blade in his spine, and he'd be dead. I didn't take my eyes off him.

He made it through the trapdoor without issue, and we all collectively exhaled. A wayward shadow caressed my face, almost in reassurance, and helped ease the purple flames skimming the surface of my hands.

"Lucille, you're going to want to see this."

Something in his tone made my heart pick up again. He held out his hand, and I stepped onto Alexei.

My head popped through the trapdoor, and I frowned. A large chandelier hung from a gold-inlaid ceiling. Something about it was familiar.

Ronen pulled me up, and more of the luxurious bedroom came into view.

Moonlight deepened the mauve of the gossamer drapery surrounding the floor-to-ceiling arched window. Without looking, I knew that to my left there should be one velvet chaise lounge and a dark wooden coffee table. I swallowed and looked. Dread stole the warmth from my hands. Which meant...

"Is this the prince?"

I knew what I'd see when I turned toward Ronen's voice.

Steeling myself, I twisted.

Aspen lay chained on the velvet bed with his eyes closed.

"Yes."

His greasy, limp waves rested against the pillow, the same length they were in our dream-walks. He even had the full beard and mustache. I approached slowly, taking in his gaunt face and the way his tunic and pants hung loosely on his frame.

"Heavenly Hell," I whispered, brushing his long bangs off his forehead. "What has she done to you?"

Ronen backed away, giving us space and helping the rest of the crew up. I focused on Aspen. Ember Metal wrapped around his wrists and ankles. I twisted his palm over, and the chains clanked. His Hell Rune glowed the terrible dark red of control.

The energy pounding beneath my skin wanted the chains off. It demanded it. But I had to be smart. We didn't have Ronen's feather. If we unchained Aspen and he woke up, things could get ugly fast. I sighed, lifting his wrist to examine the lock, and the chain clattered to the bed.

What the...

"The princeling looks like shit," Oliver commented, stepping closer. "Least he was an easy find."

I ignored him, scanning Aspen's ankles and finding chains loosely wrapped around them, but no locks. That didn't make sense. In my nightmare, the chains were always locked. If Lilith wanted control, she'd keep him secured to the bed. My muscles tensed.

Aspen was the trap.

His eyes flew open. He lunged from the bed, seized my waist and yanked me toward him. Cries of outrage rang out as I struggled to break free. A dome of blue flame erupted, engulfing the bed. I tried to punch him, to reach for a dagger and hold it to his neck, but my hands wouldn't cooperate. They refused to attack him. I *knew* what I had to do, but the very thought of it filled me with crushing dread.

It made no sense.

Instead, I ended up in a headlock, choking on air, facing Oliver while the rest of the group attacked Aspen's barrier.

We all knew this was coming. I practically gave Lilith and Aspen a calling card for my arrival. I just hadn't expected my nightmare to be real.

Had the female in my nightmares set me up? Was she Lilith, taunting me with reality, urging me to act?

I should've known better.

But even if I had... it wouldn't have changed anything. I still would've come. I still would've tried to help him. Now I just needed a plan.

Oliver's inched closer. "Let her go, princeling, or I'll shove this knife into your stomach."

Aspen stole one of my daggers and held it to my cheek. "Stay back, Nephilim, unless you want to add to our pretty princess's scars."

"You fucking spill a drop of her blood, and I'll destroy you." Ronen didn't raise his voice. He didn't erupt in fury. He spoke with certainty, his words a cold, lethal promise. He seemed calm, while his shadows slammed against the barrier. The force shook the room. Plaster rained down from the ceiling. Rune paced back in front of the flames, snarling and snapping her jaws.

"Interesting tricks, shadow-wielder. Your powers must not register as angelic to the Ember Metal. What does that make you? Too dark? A demon? Did Lilith give you her blood too?" Aspen taunted. "Maybe you belong here with us."

Was that why they worked? Because they were too dark? It made a twisted kind of sense. Ember Metal suppressed angelic power, but Ronen's weren't typical. He was a Dark Seraphim. Could the metal not distinguish what he was?

Oliver moved closer while Aspen was distracted.

"Nu uh," Aspen chided, flicking his gaze back to Oliver and digging the knife in. I hissed, and Ronen surrounded the barrier in shadow. Alexei, MJ, Rune, and Ronen all vanished into the dark. They pressed in, and the dome shifted slightly, the grip on my neck loosening enough for me to breathe.

"Aspen," I rasped. "You don't want to do this."

"Sorry, sweetheart. I gave you a chance, and you didn't listen. You should probably give your friends some parting words to remember you by. The queen's waiting for us down the hall."

Fuck that.

I pulled at my Infernus, demanding anything it could give. Most of their whispers were silent, except hallucination and seduction. I called to my hallucination melody, thought about fear, and slammed into Aspen's mind.

I thought it'd be hard. I expected thick, unyielding barriers. But instead, I pierced his mind effortlessly—yet my hallucination didn't take. The emptiness swallowed my attempt. I tried to weave images into his head and recreate the scene so I could manipulate him, but the void consumed that too. His mind was hollow, and it hungered for anything, devouring everything. My powers didn't work.

Desperate, I reached for his wrists, wrapping my hands around them—bolts of searing heat shot through my body. I screamed, nearly letting go, when I felt just a hint of his emotions. It was hardly anything, but it was something. If only I could reach him. If we could get Aspen on our side, just long enough to betray Lilith and take her feather, maybe we'd have a chance. Maybe we could end her.

"Remember my fear, Nephilim," Aspen groaned, his arm tightening around my neck.

Black specks blurred Oliver. The pain of the runes dulled with my weakening hands, Aspen's emotions slowly becoming numbed again.

Oliver looked like he was about to ram his knife into Aspen.

"Don't," I wheezed. I wouldn't let Oliver hurt him. But more than that, we needed to get to Lilith and her feather, and this was the only way. I could be the Trojan horse. "Let me go."

Oliver stared at me like I was out of my mind. But so far, this was the best plan I could come up with.

"Trust me," I breathed, my hands falling from Aspen's runes, my eyes closing.

The last sound I heard was an eruption of rage that felt like it could tear the world apart.

CHAPTER 49

Ronen

"How does he have Seraphim flames?" MJ snapped, fisting her empty hands. She tried to throw her daggers at the pet, but he had erected his dome, encasing Oliver and Lucille, and they dissolved on contact. No ash, no nothing—just melted and gone the second they hit.

I clenched my jaw, swarming his flames with my shadows and squeezing them. He resisted, our powers battling against each other. The pet was strong, but he didn't realize he'd just ignited my praesidium by strangling and knocking out the other half of my soul. The feeling pounding through my blood wasn't the surly bastard MJ had called Knox's. It was a soulless predator. It felt as if the frigid lands of Hell sluiced through my veins, humming a song of unforgiving death—no mercy, no pity. The pet would suffer.

I exerted more pressure, tightening my shadows. His flaming barrier shrank. Someone shouted something at me, but it didn't register. I had one goal. My head whipped to the side, and slowly, pain crept into my cheek.

MJ blocked my view. "The Nephilim is next to the bed. If you compress it any more, the prince's flames will kill him!"

Part of me didn't care. The pet would have to let go of his power if he wanted to take Lucille to Lilith. Maybe Oliver's life would be worth the sacrifice.

MJ backhanded me, then ripped my head back by my hair. "She will *never* forgive you if you don't snap out of this. I promise you we will get her out, but you need to take back control."

Her words sank through the ice, warming me and bringing back a semblance of reason. I pulled back my shadows and placed them around my mind, creating a wall between me and her emotions. They revealed the blue Seraphim flames, and I almost lost my hold on my praesidium when I saw her limp body. I could feel she was alive, but it did little to appease my barely restrained wrath.

The pet stared at me through his flames, something passing through his gaze. It looked knowing, like he'd figured something out. A red light flickered on his wrists.

"What is that?" Alexei asked.

"Hell Runes," I replied. Lucille was right. The pet was being controlled, and that slight flickering I saw was him trying to break free. But he had two. It took me witnessing the death of my best friend to pull free of one. The only person I bet he cared about was Lucille, and I would lay waste to this entire kingdom before I let her die.

The pet stood with Lucille in his arms. He gave Oliver a long look before releasing him to us and shrinking the barrier to cover just them. Then he opened the door, destroying the wood and metal with a single touch.

"I'll see you in the throne room, shadow-wielder. But take your time." He smirked, his wrist flashing. "Your arrival will be a *surprise* to the queen."

Something in the way he said that made me pause. The queen didn't know the rest of us were here. And by the sound of it, the pet wasn't going to tell her. But why? Or better yet—how?

Against the rioting shadows whirling chaotically around my body, I let them leave. Everything in me revolted against my choice. All my muscles were one rigid, shaking line holding my feet in place. I vibrated with the need to follow them. But didn't. I had no idea what was about to happen to her, and I fucking let her go. Why? Because there would be more casualties if we fought. And we came here to save him for her, and to steal back my feather. We needed to figure out a better plan before we stormed after them.

"Why is the prince helping us?" Alexei asked.

"Because he's fighting his Hell Runes." Oliver frowned. "He told me to remember his fear, and Lucy told me to let her go, like she had some plan."

"What kind of plan?" I demanded.

Oliver shook his head. "Hard to tell when her evil lover is choking her."

Alexei dropped his dagger. "Excuse me? Did I hear you right? The prince and Lucille? But—" He questioned me with his eyes, and I answered him with a tight grimace.

Yes, I was aware of their relationship. No, I didn't want to spend a second thinking about it.

"Explain what he meant about his fear."

Oliver glanced at the charred door, looking just as eager to go after Lucille as I felt. "In Elora, I accidentally forced him into his worst fear and made him remember his mother's murder. But it was a fail-safe. It triggered his rune, weakening him and turning him into what he is now. So, I'm not sure why he'd tell me to remember it. Lucille is the only one who could kind of bring him back to himself."

That reminded me of my time with Gabriel. But she couldn't be—no. I pushed that thought away.

"Was he in pain when the rune weakened him?" I asked.

Oliver nodded. "Yes."

Alexei retrieved his dagger from the floor. "What are you thinking, Ronen?"

"The Hell Rune is designed to suppress everything but commands. You don't feel, you barely think, and your memories are hidden out of reach. I broke free of mine when I witnessed a tragedy. My grief and rage swallowed the numbness of the rune and rendered it inactive. But it fought back, and breaking free was excruciating."

"But remembering his mom's murder didn't allow him to break free. It made him worse," Oliver reiterated.

"Did he *remember* it, though?" I asked.

Oliver opened his mouth, then closed it, thinking. "No. He thought it was an illusion."

I nodded. "There's a chance his breakthrough is on the other side of his fear."

"Do you know the details?" MJ asked Oliver.

He bowed his head. "Not sure I'll ever forget the day our mothers were murdered and my sister was taken."

Seven Hells.

I latched onto his shoulder and waited until he met my gaze. A twinge of pain tightened in my chest. His eyes were so much like his father's, it was uncanny. One day, I'd have to tell him about Gabriel.

"Our priority is to get Lucille out alive. If your sister is there, we'll bring her too. But if she isn't, we may not be able to rescue her this time. Can you handle that, and help us break the prince from Lilith's influence?"

Oliver shook his head. "Lucille's always the priority, isn't she?"

I didn't like his tone.

"Yes, but—"

"No buts. My sister has always been put on the back burner, even with the King of Hell. She does not matter to any of you. She will never be a priority."

"I swear—"

"You don't have to promise me anything. Of course I'll help save my best friend. I'll even help save Aspen. But after that, if I have to, I'll search for my sister alone. I owe her that."

Honorable and wise, just like his father.

"Once Lucille is safe back in Hell, I will personally help you find her."

"We'll help too," Alexei said, pointing between him and MJ. She rolled her eyes, but I knew she agreed.

Oliver nodded quietly. "Okay. So I try to remind Aspen about his mother's murder. But how are we going to do this?"

"Blackout. Sense. Gather. Plan. Attack," Alexei advised.

I agreed.

Rune pressed into my side and whimpered. I imagined she could feel something from Lucille, but I couldn't check in. I knew I wouldn't be able to handle her emotions. Not without going off the deep end.

"MJ, guard Oliver. Rune and Alexei are at the front with me."

We got into formation, then followed the discolored footprints in the marble hall. The pet was leading us to them. Either he was fighting the runes and wanted us to rescue Lucille, or this was yet another trap.

The trail turned a corner. I paused our group.

"I don't have my full powers here. My reserves are at half. Blacking out the throne room will take a good portion of that. I'll need to save the rest for Lilith and Lucille. That means you three are on the pet and any other threats." I looked between my second and third, then shifted my attention. "Oliver, focus on breaking him free. Everyone understand?"

They all nodded.

I ran my hand along Rune's jaw, tilting it up. "Eat any threat you see and protect our soul."

Rune bared large canines, sending a feeling of vicious intent through the bond.

A familiar scream pierced through the double doors. My body tensed, every muscle rigid as a drawn blade. A deadly calm washed over me, colder than ice, and in its wake... pure, raw rage. I wanted blood for that scream. And I would claim it—mercilessly, and without hesitation.

CHAPTER 50

Lucille

I opened my eyes to find myself in Aspen's arms. Two large doors loomed behind him, blurred by his blue flames. Dark, haunting marble comprised the walls, veined with red cracks. To the left and right, rows of towering circular pillars framed archways draped in mauve fabric. The curtains whipped in a vicious wind, revealing balconies and the brooding Elorian sky. But the air never reached us, blocked by Aspen's searing barrier.

We were no longer in the bedroom. This room had minimal furniture. Only a couple tables in the spaces between windows, holding candles and statues of females cupping red five-pointed stars.

Where were the others? Did they listen to Oliver and let me go? Or did they fight Aspen—and end up wounded? Or worse... dead.

No. I would know if something happened to them. Aspen wouldn't hurt Oliver. There was still something left in him. And the rest of them were strong enough to protect themselves, even if their powers were suppressed. Right?

My Infernus skittered across my arms as I searched Aspen's impassive face for blood or some sign that he might've hurt them. But would there be any evidence? His flames reduced anything in their path to nothing.

"Are they alive?" I whispered.

Aspen didn't react, keeping his empty gaze straight ahead.

"Darling, bring her here."

I stiffened, resisting the urge to turn toward the sickly sweet voice behind me, then latched onto Aspen's wrists.

"Are they alive?" My words fell into a soft cry as my body arched, taking in the torturous heat. I clenched my jaw, holding back the rest of my screams.

Aspen clutched me closer, shaking as he stayed planted. The barest hint of pain slithered through our bond. I could feel him again.

"Yes."

Blistering heat ripped up my arm, stopping any relief I might've had from his answer. I should've let go. I wanted to let go. But his gaze was no longer impassive. It was tortured and glassy.

"Make me remember," Aspen whispered through clenched teeth, spittle spraying.

Remember what? I wanted to ask him. But I knew if I released my jaw, I'd never stop screaming. The shots of pain were extending up to my shoulder, and I couldn't hold back my whimper. The runes carved fire through my flesh, burning me from the inside out, while the energy that wouldn't allow me to hurt Aspen—that demanded I save him—calmed. It eased beneath the agony like it somehow knew I was helping him, even if I was suffering myself.

"Aspen. Come here," Lilith snapped.

"Make me—" He struggled to get the words out, every inch of him vibrating as he resisted her commands. "Remember."

I dug my nails into his skin, needing him to look at me, to see the question I couldn't voice in my eyes. He had asked Oliver to make him remember his fear. But what fear? The one about his mom? How would that help him?

The last time Oliver had shown him that fear, it triggered Aspen to become a ruthless pawn.

"Obey me!" Lilith's voice rang out, echoing through the high ceiling and slamming against Aspen's flames. The Hell Runes sent a new jolt of agony into my body. I screamed, letting go. His barrier fizzled out, and a coppery rot blew my hair back.

His hold on me lightened, and he moved forward, walking down the open hall toward Lilith. The little emotion I had felt from him was gone. The Hell Runes were now a steady dark red, like the color of blood when someone died.

"Make you remember your mom?" I rasped.

"Why would I need to remember? She's right in front of us, sweetheart." He pointed ahead of him. I turned my head, unable to ignore her any longer.

Lilith stood clothed in a sinuous black dress at the other end of the room. Her long black hair framed her deathly white face and draped over her shoulders. The blood-red rings in her irises stood in eerie contrast to her pale skin, matching the color of her lips and the six-pointed star inked low on her chest. But it wasn't the tattoo that caught my eye. It was the ebony quill, suspended from a chain around her neck and peeking from the V of her cleavage—Ronen's feather.

I had a feeling she'd keep it on her. Someone who enjoyed gaining power as much as she did wouldn't let an item like that out of her sight.

"Darling." She smiled, opening her arms wide in welcome. They angled toward the large white and brown slab before her, as if she were presenting me with a gift.

I had an odd sense of déjà vu staring at the slab meant for me. Michael flashed in and out of my mind. I could almost feel the cold press of metal at my back and the rough chains digging into my limbs. My scars burned with the remnants of the slicing pain.

Aspen led us closer, and my Infernus perked up. The slab, which I'd thought was made of white and brown stone, revealed hints of red. Then, the glistening blood grooves came into view. They outlined the stained slab and led to the half-filled basins beneath.

"Is that—is that blood from the females you've brought to her?"

He shrugged. "Some. I don't normally watch. I just bring them and leave."

He just brings them and leaves? Heavenly Hell, how did I wrap my mind around that? I knew he had a hand in murdering female angels. We all knew. Yet I was the only person who pushed that fact away, blamed it on the runes, and welcomed him with open arms. The rest of them hated him. The rest of them would rather see him dead than alive.

My eyes stung, staring at the large buckets of blood. We were halfway to my slaughter.

"Will you leave me too?"

"Yes."

My chest ached. "Why? Are you scared to watch me die, Aspen?"

His forehead wrinkled before smoothing out.

"Are you scared to watch Lilith murder me like she did to Nalini and your mom?"

Aspen lurched to a stop, yards from Lilith and her sacrificial slab. His grip on me tightened. "Who?"

"Miri—"

I screamed as a cloud of red smoke swarmed me, searing like acid. It scalded my face, ate through my uniform, and left my limbs bare.

"Now, now, let's not go around telling lies. I'm glad the king's sigil worked for you and you made it here, but I'll make this more painful for you if you say another word," Lilith threatened.

My Infernus raged in my ear, and I pulled at it. Purple flames burst free, attacking Lilith's acid cloud and pushing the substance back.

She laughed. "There's that beautiful power I need."

I ignored her, searching Aspen's face and weighing my options. Time wasn't on my side. I could spend my last few seconds of freedom attempting to convince Aspen that Lilith murdered Nalini and his mother, resisting Lilith's attacks as I did, hoping it could help him. Or I could make a plan to steal Lilith's feather, which would save Aspen and never allow him to be runed again. I'd just need to get close to rip it from her chest, and I'd only get one shot.

"What? You're not strong enough?" I taunted, turning to face her.

Aspen stopped next to the slab, holding me over the blood-stained stone. The smell of copper and rot made my fingers itch to reach for a dagger. Instead, I let Hell's melodies flood my senses, each chord a spark, each itch along my skin a promise of violence.

Lilith bared her perfect teeth in a smile. "Very few are stronger than me. Our handsome prince isn't even on that list." She wiggled a patronizing finger near his chin. He didn't react, but I had half a mind to bite it off for him. "I mean, look what I've created." She gestured toward us, gloating. "Just one drink of our magnificent blood and it birthed my first experiments."

Our blood? Didn't she mean *her* blood?

"I thought your first experiment was your demons." I didn't care either way. But she seemed like someone who enjoyed hearing herself speak, and I needed her distracted.

If I let Aspen set me down, I could reach the feather. The slab didn't have any chains to prevent me from moving.

"You and Aspen were experiments of a different kind. A pet project to snub the sanctimonious bastards for twisting the demands I required. But I suppose that's what I get. Dream-walking is finicky."

"So you were the one to give me that power."

Lilith examined her manicured nails. "An unfortunate accident. But no worries, I'll remedy that mistake and take back all I've given you and more." She waved toward the slab. "Darling, I need to start the ritual. Set her down."

I squirmed in Aspen's hold, fighting just enough to convince her I wanted to escape. And I did—just not yet. My Infernus sang in my ears, ready and waiting.

Aspen forced me onto the stone slab, and I pulled at two melodies—glaciation and suffocation. In my head, my plan worked seamlessly. I'd suffocate her and slam an icicle into her stomach, forcing her to bend over where I could snatch the feather and roll off the slab. But there were obstacles I didn't account for.

My icicles formed a second before I could pull on the purple cloud of her breath. She noticed at the same time Aspen did.

"*Attrahere.*" The tattoo on her chest flashed bright red, and my body slammed back into the stone. Not a second later, a wall of blue flame erupted between me and Lilith.

I tried to lurch up, to squirm, but each pull stretched my skin painfully, threatening to tear it from my muscles.

Lilith sighed. "I'm a blood-witch. I specialize in spells that relate to my namesake. Currently, the blood inside your body is magnetized to the dried blood on the slab that we gathered from Michael's torture. My death is the only way you escape."

Fuck.

Aspen plucked the icicle from my hand. It hissed, melting in his flames. Then he extinguished Lilith's protective barrier.

I pulled at my hallucination melody and speared into Lilith's mind, only to hit a solid steel wall.

Lilith raised a brow. "Darling, you won't get into my head, but try as hard as you like. Maybe you'll see your mother then."

"Why would I see my mother?" I released my hallucination powers and tapped into the haunting melody that seduced my rage. I wouldn't be able to hold my Hellfire for long, and I had no idea how I'd hit her with it when I couldn't touch her and could barely move to see her.

Lilith pulled out a dagger with a line of rubies in the hilt. "Because you'll kill her. But she seemed ready to go when I dream-walked to her last, so carry on. Maybe you'll both end up in the same place."

My power stuttered.

"No. I've been feeling fine. My father has been giving her his energy."

"Even better. You'll kill them both." She bent over inches from my face while blood sloshed beneath me, her hands dipping into the buckets. She smiled like a cat watching a mouse caught in its paw.

"You're lying."

Ronen's feather dangled within reach, reminding me what I was here for. I couldn't fall for Lilith's tricks.

Lilith stood, her hands and dagger dripping with dark, gelatinous gunk. "Why would I lie? Because I'm scared of your powers?" She scoffed and reached toward my face. I tried to turn away, but my head had no give against the magnetized slab. "Darling, I benefit whether you use them or not."

A sour, metallic tang infused my nose as she painted my face with her finger, murmuring words I couldn't understand under her breath. She straightened and painted her own. "I almost wish you would. I'd make taking over Hell a whole lot easier."

I thought that when I used up my energy, it left my mom with no choice but to draw from my father instead. He was the King of Hell—he had all the strength to give. More than I did. He told me Sam said this was the best solution. But I never, not once, imagined I was taking energy from both of them. If I had been, someone would've told me. My father would've stopped my training. Sam would've. Even... *Ronen*. Was that why he ordered Alexei to train without powers?

No. He wouldn't. He valued truth. He must've had a different reason.

I shouldn't even be considering Lilith's words. But if that was her goal, then the death of my parents would indeed benefit her.

Except, why warn me? She didn't do that out of the kindness of her heart. She had to be nervous of my powers. Still, if there was a chance that using them was killing my parents... I couldn't. Which left me with only one option.

"Lilith murdered your mom, Aspen! She murdered Miri—"

A cloud of red smoke slammed into my mouth, swarming my lips—blistering and burning. I choked on a scream.

Aspen jolted forward. "Wait." But his face resembled someone attempting to figure out a puzzle.

A sharp pain slid down the length of my arm, and I tried to cry out, but Lilith's power suffocated the sound.

"Aspen, leave. Now."

"But—"

"*Leave*—" Lilith's voice broke off at a loud bang.

The pain in my arm vanished, along with the acid burn corroding my lips and throat. I heaved a breath into the wispy darkness.

But was it from relief or fear?

CHAPTER 51

Lucille

Ronen's shadows eclipsed everything. They solidified into hands, yanking at my wrists and ankles. When they tried to dig beneath my skin, I hissed, and he immediately stopped. It was no use. I'd gotten us into a mess and had no strategy to escape it. Maybe Alexei was right. Moira's match had gone to my head. I'd miscalculated my skill. I was desperate and overeager, and now we'd all pay for it.

"Aspen, I wasn't told we were having company," Lilith commented, her tone conversational. She didn't even acknowledge the power swarming around us. Did she truly not feel the fury clawing through darkness, or was she just that confident?

"I must've forgotten," he replied, sounding off. "I'm sorry."

While they spoke, footsteps padded softly through the sacrificial hall, barely audible over the drip of my blood draining into the metal buckets.

"You can make it up to me, my darling," she purred, like a—

Bile gathered at the back of my throat. Like a *lover*.

"Kill them."

A sharp thud sounded to my left where Aspen stood, and more footsteps, but no response.

"Don't make me ask again. You know how I am when I have to ask twice."

I hoped her words didn't have a double meaning. I hoped this witch spoke like a seductress to everyone. If not—if Aspen—

No. I wouldn't go there.

"Aspen! Obey—" Her words fell off into a hiss. "Enough!"

A storm erupted around Lilith, the billowing edges skimming dangerously close to the slab. It wasn't like any storm I'd ever seen. Rather than black clouds, red smoke roiled, thick and seething. The tang of copper shoved up my nose, burning and suffocating. The air screamed—feminine and eerie—as if it carried the cries of the dead. Lightning crackled within its growing depths, pulsing like a bloody heart, bathing our surroundings in a sinister glow. It radiated menace. Evil.

A knife flew from my left, striking the red smoke and clattering to the ground.

Alexei and Rune flashed in and out of view at the edge of my vision—right where the knife had come from. And Aspen was gone. Just... gone. Did the others take him? He wouldn't have just left. I tried to twist to see better, but the stone yanked at my scalp. Pain shot through my skull as Lilith's spell attempted to rip my skin from bone.

Alexei and Rune snuck closer. The beastie nuzzled my palm, nosing into it like she sensed my desperation. Alexei raised a finger to his lips and grabbed my wrist, but his hand only circled half of it. Still, he tugged, and I cringed. Frustration wrinkled his brow, and he glanced at me with questions in his eyes.

"You need to kill her to free me," I mouthed.

Alexei glared at the red storm, twisting a dagger in his hand and preparing to throw. Static crawled along my skin, the sharp electric smell of ether filling the air. Red lightning shot over me, forcing Alexei to dive to the ground, missing him by centimeters. Ronen's vicious shadows retaliated, engulfing her storm and sending us back into darkness.

He had her. But then it was like watching a balloon slowly inflate. Cracks formed in his smothering sphere, red smoke seeping out. All around us, his black wisps lightened to gray, then flocked to their battling powers, flooding the space with light. They reinforced the cracks and shrank her power. Hope bloomed in my chest.

Alexei stood above me, squeezing his dagger, looking eager to help Ronen. But there was no use. This would soon be over.

Something moved behind Alexei. I strained to turn my head, gritting my teeth as the skin pulled taut. I made it maybe a centimeter before the pain was unbearable, and tears beaded in the corners of my eyes. But I had to see.

The urgency in my mind demanded I try again. At first, the slab gave me no give, but then it released my head, as if Lilith's hold slipped.

MJ had Aspen by the throat, holding him against one of the dark pillars with a hand over his mouth while Oliver whispered in his ear. I jerked, feeling a surge of energy as I watched Aspen writhe in agony.

What the hell were they doing to him?

His legs were bent as if the only thing holding up his contorted body was MJ's hand and the pillar at his back, yet he didn't fight. There were no blue flames. He didn't raise his limp arms or kick out. He subjected himself to the pain.

Alexei touched my hand, bringing my attention back to him. His face softened, on the brink of smiling as he gazed toward Ronen and Lilith. He opened his mouth as if to speak, then his face fell. Something unfamiliar tugged on my chest. The faint pressure almost hurt, but not quite. I glanced down and didn't find anything but the remnants of my uniform.

"Ronen, stop!" Alexei shouted.

I turned back to the warring powers, and my heart froze.

Ronen knelt before the cracked sphere, red smoke bleeding from hundreds of hairline fractures. His body swayed, arms shaking to hold in Lilith's powers. Rune growled, running over to him right as his eyes fluttered.

Something unnameable ripped through me. I thrashed against the stone, wild with the need to reach him. Every muscle in my body snapped taut, straining to tear myself free. A sharper sensation wrenched at my chest, and Ronen's arms fell to his sides.

"Ronen!" I shrieked, raw and feral. My skin stretched, attempting to peel from my muscles as I forced myself to reach him. I just had to. I didn't know why or how. I didn't care about the fucking agony of prying my bloody body from the slab. I needed to get to him more than I needed to breathe.

My Infernus raged in my ear, screaming to be unleashed. I didn't think—just pulled at the first song. Hellfire swallowed my body in black and purple flame. It devoured the slab's hold on me, burning through Lilith's spell, or maybe through my blood.

Bit by bit, the stone released me. Fingers first. Then my back. Ankles. I arched my chest, reaching. I was almost there. I could almost get to him.

"Fuck!" Alexei shouted.

I freed the rest of myself with an agonizing yank, tearing the skin from my biceps and calves. A cry ripped from my throat, for the pain and for *him*. I barely twisted toward Ronen when Alexei crashed on top of me.

Lilith's red cloud burst through Ronen's shadows like a bomb.

"Ronen!" I cried as he folded forward, crumpling like his strings had been cut. My Infernus surged toward him, racing to intercept the acid-laced smoke barreling for his falling body.

Alexei's wings snapped out, encasing me in a soft cocoon. Lilith's power blasted into us. Alexei bellowed. We were torn from the slab, thrown like dolls. I slammed headfirst into the marble floor, hearing a sharp, wet pop.

Then blackness.

Mist curled around the giant, blue-veined trees of Damatha. I tilted my head up into the dark canopy and touched the rough bark. It hummed beneath my hand and glowed brighter, as if saying hello. I followed the curling mist, passing the vibrant mushrooms and moss that blanketed the ground and trees. Eventually, I came upon a path of Celestrus. Their white light and vanilla aroma guided me toward a hidden turquoise pond.

This looked like the scene from my nightmares. But this wasn't a nightmare. It was a dream-walk.

Why was I here?

"Hello, sweetie," a voice rasped somewhere near the pond.

I swallowed, stepping out of the trees. "Hello?"

"It's me, Lucy." My mom sat at the edge of the water, facing me. A high-pitched ringing filled my ears.

In my nightmare, she always had her back turned to me, and she never spoke. I almost wished for that back.

Her cheekbones jutted from her gaunt face, and her eyes were sunken, ringed by deep purple shadows. Her sweaterdress hung off her like a shroud—no longer hugging her chest or biceps.

Exhaustion dulled her jade eyes, and the silky black hair I remembered now lay completely gray and limp down her back.

"Mom?" I breathed.

She stood and hobbled over to me, wrapping me in her arms.

"What's happening? Why am I here? I was just in a battle," I whispered against her shoulder, feeling her ribs dig into my chest. Was this what happened before I died? Some twisted dream-walk illusion to say goodbye? Except I felt normal, and my mom looked like she was the one dying.

My mom took my face in her hands, and I flinched. They were frigid. "You need to listen to me."

Listen to her? To those fragile, fraying words dragged out on an air of breath, like each one might be her last? She wanted me to listen to *that*?

No. This was too convenient.

I stepped back. "This isn't real." This was Lilith. She had to be the ominous female voice inside my head. She had infiltrated my nightmares and my dream-walk again. "You're not my mom."

"Sweetie, we don't have much time. I need you to listen to me."

"Get out of my head, Lilith!"

My mom shuffled forward with watery eyes. "I'm dying, Lucy. My body can't sustain this form for much longer, and neither can yours."

"I don't believe you." But her face looked so honest.

"I used to call Thumper 'Crispy' because of the times you accidentally burned him with your Glory. Would Lilith know that?"

"No." My knees gave out, slamming into the glowing Celestrus. "No! I'd know if you were dying," I said in denial.

They would've told me.

She followed me down, resting her lifeless hand against my cheek. Pain pinched the lines of her face, but that wasn't what gutted me. It was the fucking sad sympathy in her familiar eyes. Like she had already accepted her death, like she was just waiting for me to accept it too.

I bowed my head, unable to stand the sight. "Did I do this to you?"

She combed her fingers through my hair. "No, sweetie. This is Michael's doing, not yours."

"But I'm draining you each time I use my power." It wasn't a question. I already knew the answer and needed to voice the horrendous words out loud.

"As I've been draining you to survive in my coma state."

I whipped my head up. "But that's okay! I'm okay with that! We're going to kill Michael and save you. You just need to hang on for a couple more days."

Her face tightened into her no-nonsense expression. "How many times have you needed Sam to save you from Divine Wasting?"

"That doesn't matter. I've been fine since Lucifer has been giving you more energy."

My mother jerked back as if I'd slapped her. "No, it's not *fine*. I'm slowly killing you, and now your father too."

"I'll just stop using my powers. Then you can take more of our energy, and you'll be okay until we can kill Michael," I said, trying to convince her and myself.

"Lucy," she said softly, pulling me close.

I resisted. I knew that tone.

It was the same tone she used when our dog ran away and never came back. The same one she used after I got sent to the principal's office for punching the kids who mocked my eyes. She hadn't scolded me then. Just held me and gently explained the way of the world.

"Listen to me." She wrapped me in her warmth.

I breathed her in and squeezed my stinging eyes shut, keeping my arms by my side. I couldn't hug her yet. I didn't accept this.

"You are my greatest joy." Her voice cracked.

"Stop!" I jerked back, quickly wiping the tears that had escaped. "This isn't goodbye."

But she continued, ignoring my outburst. "There's a lot you still don't know, and I can't bear to tell you it all now. But once I held you in my arms, I knew I had to do everything I could to keep you hidden, and I might've gone too far. I know that now, and I'm so sorry for taking so much of your life away."

"Just stop," I pleaded through the ache in my throat.

"I'm sorry, Lucille."

My lip wobbled when a few tears trailed down her cheeks. My mom rarely cried in front of me. I could count on one hand how many times it had happened in the last twenty years. She always wanted to protect me from her pain—from everything.

"It's okay." And it was. Earth wasn't all darkness and abuse. There had been joy, laughter, even wonder woven between all the suffering.

"But it's not, sweetie. You deserved to grow, and I didn't allow that because I was scared. I was so scared. I still am."

"I forgive you for the past. But don't you dare give up now." She pulled me back against her chest and rocked me in her arms. "I'll find Michael. Please, just hold on."

"Sweetie, you have been through so much. You traveled through Elora and survived not only its inhabitants but also capture. You lived through Michael's torture. You've persevered in Hell's military. And not once have you given up on me or yourself."

"I don't know how to give up."

She grasped my shoulders and pushed me back. "Exactly. And I never want you to. Do you hear me? I *never* want you to give up on yourself." She tilted her head, her eyes glassy as she touched my face. "You are Lucille Chiara, my beautiful daughter, born from an Archangel and the King of Hell. You, my heart, are a warrior. A *survivor*. And I'm so proud of you."

A sob worked its way up my throat. I clenched my teeth, trying to stay strong for her, but I couldn't stop the stream of fresh tears.

She brushed my cheeks, and I brushed hers.

"Mom, please," I begged her.

"When you wake, I only ask two things of you."

"No. You can ask me when we both wake up."

She smiled through the gut-wrenching heartache I could see in her jade eyes. "Tell the grouchy old male in the library that Saraqael wishes for him to stop being afraid and mentor you. Tell him—" She swallowed. "Tell him you need to find Miriam at the beginning. Where this all started." She glanced to the side, her chin lowered. "When you find everything out, please don't hate me, Lucille."

I tugged her back into a hug, unsure of what she was talking about. "I'd never hate you, Mom. Even after all the shit we've been through. I'd never hate you. I love you."

She nodded against my shoulder before sitting back, her face sobered. "Second, you will use your Hellfire and Glory when you wake. You will use every ounce you have, and you will direct all of it at Lilith. Understand?"

I straightened. "No. I can't. I'll die if I take off my Ember Metal."

"You won't. Your Glory may be more suppressed, but Lilith's blood runs through your veins." She placed her hand over my heart, opening her mouth for the final blow, and I jerked back.

"I won't kill you! You can't ask me to kill you!" I screamed.

My mom sat quietly, patient and solemn. "A daughter does not sacrifice herself for a mother. You do *not* give up. Do you hear me? You will do this for me."

"No. I'm staying here."

Her patient expression hardened—the same expression she got when she was training me.

"Dream-walking might not take as much power, but it still takes some."

She might as well have taken a knife and shoved it in my heart; it probably would've hurt less.

"Why would you say that?"

"Because you need to wake up and fight. Lilith plans to kill you, steal your powers, and take over Hell. The fact that I'm still alive means Lucifer is giving me more energy than he should. He is weakened, and if Lilith gains your powers and reaches Hell, she'll be able to kill him. We can't let that happen."

"But she can't escape her kingdom! Not with Lucifer's ring binding her in place."

My mom shook her head, that sympathy back in her eyes. "Do you know how that ring comes off?"

"Lucifer's blood and death."

She nodded. "You are his one and only blood child. An anomaly that has tipped the balance in the celestial world. Lilith is confident you are the answer to her cage."

I swallowed and looked at the glowing veins in Damatha's trees. "So what," I spat, choking back my tears.

Her cold hand forced me to meet her gaze. "I know my daughter's smarter than that. You know we can't last in this dream. You know I'm dying. Just like you know when you wake up, you'll need to use your powers."

I clutched her hand, squeezing it in a death grip. "I can't leave you. I won't give you up."

"I understand." She placed a soft kiss on my forehead, then stared straight into my soul. "I love you, Lucille. Never surrender, my warrior." Her form dematerialized.

"No." I reached for her fading image, desperate to hold her there. I couldn't lose her—not now, not after everything. My hands passed through empty light, and then she was gone, the glow of the Celestrus vanishing with her. "No!" I screamed, jerking awake.

Reverberations vibrated through my body. I blinked open my eyes. And immediately wanted to close them again. I didn't want this hellscape to be real.

But it was—and they were all about to die.

CHAPTER 52

Lucille

Weeks ago, Oliver had asked me what would happen if I had to choose who to save. I never answered him. But I'd had an answer. A horrific, guilt-destroying answer that ate at me every time I dream-walked to my mom. That was before I knew about Aspen's deceit. And I wished I could say it made a difference. But it didn't. The foreign urgency boiling my blood influenced my thoughts, and the Infernus raging in my ears.

But this choice wasn't just about Aspen or my mom. Oliver, who'd stood loyal and at my side these past months—who'd turned from a betrayer to a brother and best friend—was in danger. So was Alexei, whom I'd grown fond of, and MJ, whose ferocity I admired.

And... *Ronen.*

The male who had me prying the skin from my muscles to reach. The mere thought of the breath leaving his lungs rattled something unfathomable and absolute inside me. A force louder than the urgency screaming at me about Aspen. I would rip the rest of my skin from my body. I would feel the throbbing pain and the blood that oozed down my arms a thousand times over if only it'd save the male who reminded me of home.

And yet, if I chose them, I lost my mom.

Because no one told me I'd been killing her.

Terror burned through me, hotter than the blue fire shielding my body. Terror for my choices. Terror for the scene unfolding before me.

Aspen and Alexei thrashed midair. Red smoke circled their necks, slowly squeezing the life from them.

Below their feet, a flaming blue sphere caged MJ and Oliver. Lilith slammed her power against it, drawing curses from Oliver's lips.

Rune lay unmoving at the base of the stone slab, her fur streaked with blisters and bloody fluids—an agonizing patchwork beneath drifting wisps of shadow. Above her, in another fire sphere, lay Ronen on his back. His eyes were closed, blood soaking his sleeves and drawn across his face, as if Lilith had attempted a ritual on him.

Aspen was resisting Lilith's control. He was helping us.

But how long could that last?

Flickers of blue fire fought against the acid-eating smoke wrapped around their necks, keeping Alexei and Aspen barely conscious, barely fighting. Alexei lifted his burned wings, pain twisting his face as he strained to fly away from Lilith's hold. His choked scream cracked the air—then came a crash like the sky splitting open.

Water slammed into MJ and Oliver's protective sphere. Scalding steam erupted in a violent hiss, drowning their screams. The white haze swallowed Aspen's and Alexei's jerking bodies. But not before their neck muscles pulled taut, their faces blistered, and their teeth bared in raw agony. All the while, Lilith laughed, acting untouchable.

Aspen dropped all our fire-spheres, weakened, leaving us exposed to her will.

I knew what I had to do. All my training, practicing, and learning had led me to this.

"Lilith, darling," I stated, removing my Ember Metal bracelet, "you're in for a fucking treat."

I pushed myself off the marble and flung out my hands, throwing my Glory and Hellfire at her shield. Black and white fire met red—and consumed it.

She released Aspen and Alexei as she failed to reinforce her protection, and they dropped to the ground. Alexei cried out as he landed on his wounded wings, and Aspen heaved as if the air had been knocked out of him.

I wrapped my flames around my body and luscelered through the gaping hole in her barrier. She struck with her lightning, hitting my legs. It tickled. It should've burned. But my flames absorbed her attack the moment it touched me. A stronger bolt hit my pelvis, pushing me back, then my legs again. She wanted to immobilize me.

She wanted my blood, not my death. Not yet.

I stepped through the rest of her barrier, conjured a fireball, then hurled it at Lilith's face, knowing full well it wouldn't connect. I stumbled with the effort. It wasn't faked, but it did play into my plan.

She sidestepped, sneering, "Cute trick."

My protective flames sputtered and died, leaving me exposed. She smiled. My face fell. I backed up like I could escape her, and a thick vine whipped out, snaring my throat. She yanked me forward like a rag doll. I sagged against her, clutching at her dress while drowning in her confident air.

"So much power," she purred, her sharp nail tracing my jawline, "but no finesse. No strength."

Her arrogance was her downfall.

I dropped my fake fear and shrugged. "Who needs finesse—when you can play to your opponent's expectations?"

She leaned back as if trying to reassess the situation, and in doing so, loosened the chain I'd pinched between my burning fingers. The Ember Metal jangled, falling from her neck. I surged upward, smashing my forehead into her nose with a sickening crack. She reeled, and I snatched the feather from her cleavage.

Purple flames burst from my hand, flash-freezing it. "Oliver and MJ!" I screamed, then threw it toward them with everything I had, right as lightning jolted through the vine digging into my throat. My scream tore free, cut short as I fell to my knees, spasming, choking.

Oliver caught it as the doors to the hall slammed open, revealing a demon horde. Half were Cambion Demons, and the other half were souls with black veins crossing through their grotesque scars—the demon infection.

Lilith was their creator. We'd suspected it. But with a group of them here, in her kingdom and under her command, it confirmed it.

"Finally." Lilith gestured to my friends. "Kill them, retrieve my feather, and capture the prince."

The demons charged the four of them, and Lilith yanked on my neck, forcing me to meet her heated gaze.

"You think that was smart? You think your friends can remove that feather from my castle without my demons killing them? You'll listen to your friends die one by one. Give up before you murder your mom."

I gathered my saliva and spat at her.

Her nostrils flared, and she electrocuted me, shocking my gathering power. My body spasmed, but my mind stayed sharp, waiting for the moment to strike.

"You probably shouldn't have said that, darling." That was what I'd wanted to say, but my teeth were clenched so tightly, my words wouldn't come.

An explosion rattled the ground, along with excited shouts somewhere to the left.

"Yes! Throw, then shield!" Oliver shouted.

Another explosion rocked the hall, shaking loose bits of stone from the vaulted ceiling, threatening to pull my attention from the ruby-hilted knife appearing in Lilith's hand as she stood over me. She tightened the hold on my leash.

"Let's begin where we left off," Lilith purred, "and I'll be one step closer to avenging my coven."

She plunged her knife toward my chest. I could've stopped it. But as shockwaves continued to disrupt my powers, I needed the blade to finish this. Taking a lesson from Oliver, I moved at the last second and let it sink into my shoulder—then ripped it from the searing wound and sliced it through her vine, releasing me from her hold.

She conjured more, but it was too late.

"Never surrender," I whispered, and unleashed my Hellfire and Glory.

It was like my mom stood here—coaxing me, steadying me, giving me strength for what came next. I infused my soul with her unwavering love. Her laughter. Her soothing touch. Her annoying jazz music. Her ridiculous chicken obsession that had made her giggle. The steel in her spine. All our trainings. All our nights wishing to the stars. I wove every memory of us into my heart as I pushed my power at Lilith.

My combined flames slammed into her quick smoke barrier. She held me back for a second before I destroyed her shield. She erected it again, reinforcing it while throwing water, lighting, vines—all her stolen powers—at me. But Hellfire and Glory were a bottomless void of destructive power. They burned hot and fast—hot and torturously.

After breaking through again, Lilith smirked. I'd expected fear revealing the whites of her double-ringed irises, not a smug smile. She raised her hand, and a masculine groan sounded behind me.

My heart stilled.

Ronen.

Her powers flew over my shoulder toward him, and something inside me snapped. A feral, merciless harbinger of death ruptured from my chest. It pulled every ounce of Hellfire and Glory from my core and poured out of me. Ravaging black flames, eradicating white flames—they swarmed Ronen and Rune, burning away her attack.

Pins and needles climbed up my legs and torso, and still I called more.

Divine Wasting pushed behind my eyes, threatening to close them, and for one moment, I thought Lilith would win. I thought she'd take them away from me.

Then—a jolt.

Energy swept through my limbs, sweet and euphoric. It filled every inch of me, healing my wounds, giving strength to my muscles and life to my soul. It was like I'd been living with half a working body, and now the other half had come back to life. I shoved that energy into my flames, and it burned through Lilith's power and sank into her skin like an unavoidable infernal parasite.

She shrieked, and I thought she'd burn immediately. But my powers had other plans.

Her flesh ruptured, spilling hissing blood and black ash into the air.

She fell to her knees, screaming and clawing at her neck. Her flesh oozed from multiple gashes as my flames ate her from the inside out. Water shot from her hand, blasting into the fiery cuts. My flames hissed softly, then grew in size, dancing in her water and mocking her attempt to extinguish them.

Her eyes melted, hollowing into charred craters. Feces and some other unnameable scent filled the air, making me gag. Her screams turned into wet gasps, then nothing, as her dress dissolved, revealing organ mush pushing through her burst stomach. My flames consumed the gory mess and every inch of stone where her blood or skin touched, until there was nothing left of her. They devoured every minuscule bit.

I leashed my addictive song and humming Glory. I stared at the corroded stone, the only evidence of Lilith's death. The ground trembled with explosions. Fissures cracked through the hall. Shouts rang out. And yet I couldn't lift my eyes.

Warm, calloused hands cupped my face, and golden eyes filled my gaze. "Lucille, are you okay?"

She was dead.

I opened my mouth to tell him, but nothing came out. My ears rang. My heart faltered. My knees buckled.

She was dead.

"Lucille!" Ronen cried, Aspen echoing him.

Ronen caught my body, his shadows diving into my nose.

"Is she okay?" Aspen asked next to us, his face and clothing smeared with blood and ichor.

She was dead.

"As much as she can be," Ronen replied, scooping me into his arms.

Another explosion rocked the ground, and Ronen stumbled. Aspen's hand gripped his shoulder. A breathless silence stifled the air—possessive, territorial. It wrapped around me in a dominating cocoon.

Aspen stepped back, easing the tension. "The floor is about to cave in. We need to go."

"Grab my Soulhound, Prince," Ronen barked, then limped forward.

She was dead.

That was all I could think. All I could feel. The power energizing my core smothered me in grief. I wanted to claw my way to the center and rip it out. I didn't want it. I didn't want to feel *her energy*.

Ronen pulled me tighter against his chest, as if he could feel my agony.

My mom was—

A scream caught in my throat.

Oliver.

The haze of the Cambion explosion lifted to reveal his body twisted in the rubble, unmoving.

"Oliver," I cried out. I squirmed out of Ronen's arms, stumbling over the shifting ground. MJ made it to him before I did, feeling for his pulse.

"Is he alive?" I choked out, collapsing next to them.

MJ didn't answer me fast enough. I reached out, placing two fingers at his neck, and dropped my head to his chest, the tears I'd been holding back flowing free.

Shoes thudded nearby. "Is he dead?"

"No," MJ answered Alexei. "He's not dead."

Ronen kneeled next to me. "We need to go now. I can carry him. Can you walk?"

I hesitated to move.

Ronen grabbed my chin, his fingers tingling against my skin, forcing me to gaze into his uncompromising eyes.

"I will get him out. But I need you to answer me, Hellion. I know you're in a lot of pain, but I need to know you can get yourself out. Or I'll have MJ carry you."

All I could do was nod and stand on wobbly legs—or no. That was the ground shaking. Ronen picked him up, and we limped, shuffled, and somewhat jogged out of Lilith's crumbling sacrificial room.

CHAPTER 53

Lucille

Two Days Later

My mother's funeral took place tonight, and my father wouldn't even allow us in his room to retrieve her body. Ironic, seeing as he was the one who declared her funeral. Ronen said he'd take care of it, and I decided that while he did, I'd wander the castle. I had nothing better to do.

It was either wander numb, visit Oliver in his coma state and ask Sam for the hundredth time when he'd wake up, or lock myself in my room and let loneliness and pain consume me as I cried morning, afternoon, and night.

Eventually, I found myself using Ronen's key and my blood to unlock the dungeons. My Glory fell asleep the moment I stepped into the long room. Sturdy Ember Metal and three-foot-thick walls crafted each cell.

I walked until I saw him, then slid down the damp wall across from his bars. Part of me wanted Aspen out of his cage, and another part thought he was better off in there. It was safer. The majority of Hell despised him.

We stared at each other, both unsure how to proceed after everything that had happened. His vibrant blues reflected the devastation of his lies and treatment of me, as did the feelings I could sense from him again. And the fact that Ronen said he'd been in Aspen's head—after carving the opposing rune into Aspen's skin with his ebony feather, which MJ had retrieved from Oliver during the mayhem—officially eliminated the Hell Rune's commands. It was a precautionary measure, even though Oliver had already helped Aspen break free of his control. This way, we never had to worry again.

Everything from now on, everything Aspen said or did, was all him.

Aspen dropped his gaze and let his head fall back against his metal prison. "I don't know what to say to you, Lucille. I want to apologize. I want to get down on my knees and beg for your forgiveness. But I don't even think that'd be enough."

"I should've known," I admitted. How many times did I think things were off in our dream-walks? How many times did I push my suspicions away? Or how about the nightmare I had of him being tortured—the one I believed Lilith had controlled?

He shook his head. "If you'd known, how could you have stopped me or Lilith? I mean, yes, you could've prevented me from touching you with my disgusting, manipulative hands and—"

"Stop!" I couldn't take the reminder or the disgust he had for himself. He quieted, but I didn't know what to say. I didn't know how to separate my feelings from my thoughts. His actions and words destroyed me. Yet of course, they were Lilith's actions and words.

But were they?

"How much of it was you in the dream-walks? How much of it was the truth?"

He flinched, and his shame deepened. "A lot of it," he whispered. "But I did it for her, not you. She wanted me to be as close to myself as possible to persuade you to trust me. It was the only way after I told her how you reacted to the Hell Rune in Elora."

"If she wasn't forcing you, would you have gone through with any of it? With…"

"Why does it matter, Lucille?"

"Because of what we…" I trailed off. The feelings I had for Aspen were tainted with betrayal and blame.

He scoffed. "There is no fucking *we* anymore."

Anger heated my blood, and I stood, glaring down at him. "What about our guardian bond?"

"Guardian bond?" He rose to his feet. "I can tell you right now I've never been your guardian. I've only ever hurt you. Might as well forget about it and go on your merry way, Princess."

I slammed my palms against his bars. "How could I ever forget about it? I'm pretty sure our stupid bond put you above my mother!" I screamed. "I chose you!"

The energy beneath my skin had to be from our bond. That was the only explanation I had.

He laughed, self-loathing thick in the sound. "Then why are you still here? Why did you even come down here? You should hate my guts."

I opened my mouth to scream at him again, but the words didn't come. Why was I down here? Because I wanted to make sure he was okay. Because his depressive emotions had seeped through our connection while I wandered the halls, and I couldn't stop myself from wanting to help him.

"What are you holding onto? Those few moments in your Earthly forest when I was kind to you? Curious about you? I was just a passing fancy to settle your need for mystery and adventure, and you were just a distraction from my fucked-up life."

Despite the self-hatred and shame I could feel from him, his words still punched me in my fragile chest. I probably would've cried if my mother's death and Oliver's state hadn't stolen all my tears. I surveyed his tortured expression, his tousled brown hair, and his bony fingers, hoping they'd feed him better here, then turned and left.

Regret instantly shot through the bond.

"Sweetheart, wait!"

I paused. "I never want to hear that name from your mouth ever again." Then continued up the stairs.

"Lucille!" he called out again.

I ignored him and left him to his suffering. I understood his regret and pain, but I no longer wanted to live in it. Oliver was right— I didn't need a knight in shining armor to catch me on the way down, because he wasn't trying to catch me. He was trying to drag me down with him, and I'd had *enough*. I just needed to make sure he was at least breathing. Whether that was because of the bond or my conscience, I didn't know, nor did I want to spend time thinking about it.

Ronen

Finally, after having it out with the king, he released Saraqael's body to be prepared, to be burned and buried in the Eternal Forest. Once it occurred, she'd be able to cycle to Hell or Heaven, and I think that scared him. He would either have to damn his cordistella to be tortured, or he'd never see her again as she ascended to Heaven.

It would be the most difficult judgment of his long life.

I didn't think Lucille even had the chance to consider the ramifications of her mom's death, and what came after. But with the amount of pain consuming her, I refrained from saying anything. She'd need to know eventually, but I needed her to have enough will to get up in the mornings. Rune stuck by her side these past two days, and all Lucille had done was cry and stare off into space.

It destroyed me.

But not as much as when she asked me yesterday to turn it all off, with watery, starry eyes. One look, one question, and she completely gutted me. Of course I wanted to take away her devastation. But turning off her emotions would only prevent her from healing. When I told her no, I had to take out my helplessness on a punching bag with Alexei.

His wounds had shaken me when I watched him stand and stumble in Lilith's castle. But Sam did a good job healing him. He'd had to rebreak parts of Alexei's wings to save them. He'd need a couple more healing sessions and physical therapy before he'd be cleared to fly. For now, he sported a pair of patched-up, semi-featherless wings that still hung weakly at his back, and somehow still managed to use them to lure in the females. Of course, the sob story he gave them helped. Nothing got him down—the insufferable male. But I needed his strength; my own waned.

MJ found me in the hall later. I was happy to see she'd finally had Sam heal her.

"Ronen, with Lilith dead, does that mean the infection died with her?"

"We'd be foolish to think that without more evidence." Every infected soul I'd interrogated said *we*. Unless *we* referred to the infected demons as a whole, Lilith wasn't their only creator. "If she was the source, then what's left of her demonic creations should be mindless without her control, and hopefully incapable of continuing to spread the infection. Regardless, we'll continue to search and kill what's left in our domain."

"And the Tenebrous Kingdom?"

I shook my head. "Once Oliver wakes, we'll regroup, speak to the king, and make a plan before heading back to find his sister. Hopefully by then we'll have more answers."

MJ nodded. I was about to leave for my room, but she stopped me.

"I saw Lucille leaving the castle alone. Just thought you should know."

I sighed. "In what direction?"

"Toward Portal Lake."

I found the nearest roof, manifested my wings, and flew off to find her. It didn't take long. She weaved between the Eternal Forest and the Verdant Forest. I maneuvered into an open spot, scooped her up, and shot us into the skies.

Her yelp of surprise was a breath of fresh air after all the pain I continued to feel from her.

"What are you doing?" she asked, pressing into my body to keep away from the forceful wind.

For once, I didn't use my shadows to create a barrier. She shivered in her leggings and baggy sweatshirt. I gritted my teeth, refraining from protecting her. I wanted her to *feel*, and if that meant forcing her to endure the harsh wind, then fine.

"Flying. What are you doing?"

Before, she would've narrowed her eyes in annoyance. But now, there was no expression.

"Walking."

I gazed down at her, finding her staring out into the cloudy sky. Her eyes were still puffy and red from this morning. I had to look away, feeling my helplessness rise again.

I wanted her out of this state. But it would take far longer than two days. It didn't help that Oliver had sustained a severe brain bleed and remained in a coma until he healed. Sam said he could wake up any day—we just had to wait. I wished that day were today. Maybe that'd give her some joy. Some hope. Fuck, I'd take *anything*.

Flying to Portal Lake, I touched down on the cliff. We sat, our legs dangling over the edge.

"We're preparing your mom for tonight," I said softly.

She flinched, and I cringed. She needed to know.

We were quiet for a while longer, and then she spoke.

"I visited Aspen today," she said, holding out the key to the dungeons.

That got my attention.

"Oh?" I replied, taking it from her.

"It went as well as I expected. He's suffering from self-loathing and did a wonderful job taking it out on me."

I pressed my mouth into a thin line to keep from saying something I shouldn't. His words *hurt* her. I could feel that. Hell, I still remembered skimming the surface of his memories and coming upon some of the things Lilith made him do. I didn't dig too deep, just enough to know she no longer controlled him. After witnessing two instances of him and Lucille together, I avoided the rest. It took an insurmountable amount of self-restraint not to drop him dead right then and there. I only didn't for *her*. But feeling more of her pain, as if she needed any fucking more, I wanted to fly to his cell and give it back to him tenfold.

At my silence, she continued as if I wasn't there.

"I thought we had something."

My shadows swarmed my palms, and my heart ached, but I continued to be a silent body, letting her release her grief.

"But maybe he was right. Maybe I was a distraction from his fucked-up life. Maybe none of it meant anything. Just a passing fancy."

A distraction? A passing fancy?

The moment I laid eyes on her, I knew she would never be something so temporary. Maybe that was why I'd been such an asshole in the beginning—I *knew* she had the potential to change my life.

She would never be just a fleeting indulgence.

I wanted to tell her how utterly she had burrowed into my hardened, fearful heart. How she became the very thing I never knew

I needed. I wanted to take her chin in my hand, force her to meet my solemn gaze, and make her understand.

It took me longer than I liked, but I finally knew—I wasn't trying to find a home on the edge of this cliff or in the silver specks of the lake. No, some part of me must've always known who would come into my life. Someone with eyes like Portal Lake—resilient, radiant, and untamed.

I'd sought the white and purple specks in her gray eyes. She crashed into my life, upending everything I thought I wanted and needed. Found my feather. Showed me that the only time I'd ever felt truly settled was when I was beside her. Whether she chose what I had to offer or not, she would never be temporary. She was the beginning and end for me.

But how did I tell her that?

"He was mysterious, and I did want adventure with the handsome prince who met me in my woods. But..." She bowed her head. "I thought I could be enough to change him," she whispered, like the words weren't meant for me but for the chilling winds of Hell to secret away.

She changed me.

"Do you love him?" I despised the question, but I needed to know. My shadows slithered around my palms like they did when I was agitated. I wasn't above jealousy, as much as I wished I was.

"I don't think so," she admitted on an air of breath.

The tension in my shoulders eased, but something else bothered me, something I didn't understand from earlier at the castle.

"If you don't love him, then why were you willing to sacrifice yourself for him?"

"I couldn't hurt him."

"Couldn't? Or didn't want to? Even if you just stabbed him with your ice, it might've distracted him enough so you could escape. He would've healed." I'd been in his head. I'd felt his power. He was like a Seraphim, but not wholly.

"I *couldn't*, Ronen."

There was that phrasing again.

"You couldn't physically hurt him?"

"No."

My wings tightened, as did every muscle. "Why?"

There were only three instances where I knew one being couldn't hurt another: if they were Hell Runed, which she wasn't. If he were her cordistella. But as far as I knew, cordistellas only came in pairs. The last option made me wish Aspen *was* a second cordistella to her, that the Weaver wanted her to have two, and she could choose between us. Because as much as I wanted to be with her, not one ounce of me would share her if I had her. I was too possessive. But I had a horrible feeling it was the third option.

The one I didn't think was possible.

"He's my..." She laughed and shook her head, as if she didn't believe it. "He's supposed to be my guardian."

No.

My shadows burst out of me, swarming our bodies as if Lucille needed protection. This couldn't be happening. Not again.

"Lucille," I said, dropping deep into the chilling beast who demanded retribution for anyone who threatened *ours*. "This is really important. Can you feel his emotions?"

Seven Hells, I couldn't have found the other half of my soul only for her to be taken from me.

She gazed at all the shadows brushing her body. "What's wrong?"

My heart hammered. "Answer me."

Her brows furrowed. "I do."

I dropped off the cliff and snapped out my wings.

"Ronen!" she screamed. "Wait!"

As fast as I possibly could, I flew back to the castle and sent Rune a command to retrieve Lucille. I should've known. I fucking *felt* it. Her desperation. Her helplessness. And that urgent energy I wasn't familiar with.

The energy almost felt foreign, like it wanted to be a part of her but wasn't. She had the same look in her eyes Gabriel did—like she couldn't fucking help herself. And she couldn't. She would *not* go through what he did. I wouldn't allow it.

I barreled through the roof door, knocking down Alexei.

"Whoa, what's the rush?" he asked, standing and brushing himself off, his breath clouding around him.

"Nothing," I spat, storming past.

He stopped me, gripping my arm. "Right, and I wasn't about to fly off to the bar to find me a nice female to nurse my wounds."

I jerked on his hold, but his grip only tightened.

"You look murderous. I'm not letting go until you explain yourself."

"No."

Alexei tilted his head, raising a brow. "Does this have something to do with our very special prisoner that your cordistella wanted to rescue?"

I jerked harder on my arm, tempted to chuck a shadowball at his chest to see if he'd pass out.

"I'm going to take that as a yes. I'm also going to advise against whatever ideas are hiding behind your shadow eyes."

"Let go, Alexei, before I make you let go."

He stepped closer and shoved me back, standing in front of the door. "I'm thinking no."

I barreled into him, forcing him and his bandaged wings against the chilled stone. He winced, then smiled. "Fine. Go make matters worse."

I only felt a little guilty after he stepped aside.

"Make sure Lucille gets back safely from Portal Lake," I said, striding into the castle. The sky darkened as I passed countless windows and descended the stairs toward the dungeons. With each thundering step, I imagined cutting through his tendons and listening to his screams. I imagined rupturing his blood cells over and over, letting him heal only to do it again until his heart stopped and the threat was gone.

At the dungeon doors, I dug in my pocket for the key, then dug around in the other one.

"Alexei," I hissed. He stole it.

I had a spare in my bedroom on the other side of the castle, if he hadn't gone there and stolen that one too.

I luscelered to my room. My new door remained unharmed, and my shadows were still in place around the knob. I opened it, ran to my desk, and rummaged through the drawers, but the key wasn't there. Then I remembered I'd placed it on the side table next to my bed.

Minutes later, I unlocked the dungeon doors and stalked toward the pet's cell.

He looked up at my approach, but like Lucille, he seemed too numb to care why I was here. I guaranteed he felt my rage. His attention flicked to my swarming shadows, yet he still stayed put on the ground.

After unlocking his cell, I grabbed him by the neck of his shirt and slammed him into the wall.

He barely reacted. "I wondered when you'd stake your claim. I remember what it felt like when my praesidium acted up."

My fist paused midair.

He grinned, but it lacked humor, more a baring of teeth than anything. "Didn't catch those memories, then, I guess. Thought you already knew. I don't normally share that part of me with anyone. Lucille doesn't even know."

At her name, the rage and my protective instinct returned. I drove my fist toward his face, and it crashed into a wind barrier.

"We went through a lot of trouble to rescue the prince's ass. I'm not about to have you throw it back in our faces because something pissed you off," Alexei said, walking down the dungeon hall.

I ignored him, gathering my shadows. Alexei blasted me with a shot of wind, throwing me from the pet's cell. I threw a shadowball at his chest and luscelered simultaneously. He dodged, and I made it into the cell, only to be thrown against the wall.

"I can do this all day. I have backup coming any minute."

I pulled at my shadows and made to attack again, but someone luscelered between me and the pet.

It wasn't MJ like I'd expected, although I could see her fiery hair from the corner of my eye. No, that someone was Lucille. MJ must've flown her here.

"Ronen! What are you doing?" she demanded, eyeing my shadows like the threats they were. That same foreign energy twisted inside her mind.

The fact that I felt it—and now knew what it was—only made my power whip around more chaotically. One shadow lashed out, sliding past her. MJ's flames couldn't burn it. Alexei's wind couldn't blow it away. It circled the pet's neck, cutting off his air.

"Stop!" Lucille cried, stabbing me with an icicle.

It pierced my uniform, but the moment it touched my skin, it melted.

She stared at it, stunned. But her shock only lasted a second, interrupted by Aspen's gasps. Next, she wreathed her hand in Glory and threw a ball at my face. I let it hit me, smiling when the searing heat turned into a brush of warmth, caressing my cheek before it dissipated.

Desperate, she shoved me back. "Ronen, please! Please stop!" she begged me.

It was her begging. She really didn't want any harm to come to Aspen. But it was also the energy prompting her, twisting her insides until she listened to its controlling urges.

I couldn't let the pet live.

Then she did the only thing that could've possibly stopped me.

She grabbed one of my Soul Swords, stepped away from me, and held it to her neck. "Stop, or I'll slit my throat."

"Whoa, beautiful. You've gone too far. Give Ronen his sword back. He won't hurt the prince, right, Ro?"

My heartbeat picked up speed. I knew she wasn't joking. That unstoppable energy would force her to take her life to save him. I'd lived through that horrific scene before.

"Right," I said, instantly releasing Aspen. "Lower the sword, Lucille."

She didn't. "Explain."

Any other moment, I'd admire the steel in her spine and the fury in her face. Right now, her pain didn't control her. But I wouldn't be able to explain anything until she returned my sword, and I killed Aspen.

"Yes, General. Explain," the pet said, realizing something else was going on here.

Out of all of them, MJ was the only one who knew the full extent of my story. Alexei knew most, but not this piece.

"There's only been one other guardian bond in existence," I started. "The first was two hundred and sixty-five years ago when Oliver's father, Gabriel, was bonded to me."

Lucille's arm dropped in shock, and the blade brushed her collarbone. I lost my train of thought while my Soul Sword threatened to steal half of me. Her knuckles were white on the hilt, struggling to hold my heavy blade. I knew she wouldn't let me take it, but I couldn't stand here and say nothing. My shadows slithered across her neck and chest, creating a barrier between the sharp edge and her skin. It wouldn't stop the sword if she used enough pressure, but it consoled me enough to keep going.

"The council needed to make sure their asset was safe at all times." I flicked my gaze to Aspen, and for one split second, I felt empathy for the bastard. "You weren't the first to be controlled by a Hell Rune."

"Etan," Lucille whispered.

Goosebumps spiked down my spine, and I had to tense not to visibly shake. "How do you know that name?"

She took in my reaction and frowned at the wispy darkness seeping across the floor. "I dream-walked to one of your memories."

"Seven Hells." I didn't want to know what she'd seen. "Etan is the head of Heaven's corrupted council. He created me, with the other Seraphim members, to use me as their arm of justice. But I did a lot more than rid the world of demons and sin." Guilt and regret reared their ugly heads, forcing me to crack my knuckles and pause. "I did so well under their control, Etan decided to create another rune. One that would bind someone to me. But not just anyone. Once placed on the skin, the rune would choose the perfect protector. So the next day, a searing burn expanded down my back, and a tattoo of wings emerged. But the only one who could see it was Gabriel.

"The guardian bond didn't seem so bad at first. I didn't want it, but neither of us had a choice, so we made do. Initially, I began to sense where Gabriel was, and eventually, he developed the same sense. We thought that'd be the extent of it. Two homing beacons to each other. But the guardian bond grew." I squeezed my fists.

"Gabriel began to feel my emotions. And then came the uncontrollable urges. Anytime we went on missions together, he'd step in front of any threat. He was my first line of defense, whether he wanted to be or not. Whether it was an intelligent move or not. The guardian bond forced him to always choose me over himself, no matter the cost or injury. And if I went on missions without him and came back wounded, the bond would force him to maim himself for the inability to protect me," I spat, remembering the times my friend had run himself through with an arrow as penance for my wounds.

Finally, Lucille lowered the blade and looked at Aspen. I snatched my sword from her hands before she dared to threaten herself again, and pointed it at the pet, deciding to spell it out and erase the look of confusion on his face.

"You," I seethed, wanting to shove my blade through his chest, "are *not* her fucking guardian. *She* is yours. She will sacrifice her life to keep you breathing. And I will *not* lose my cordistella in service to the likes of you."

CONTENT WARNINGS

-Graphic Violence/Gore
-Verbal Abuse
-Child Abuse
-Physical Abuse
-Swearing
-Explicit Sexual Situations

SIGN UP FOR MY NEWSLETTER TO HEAR ABOUT UPCOMING RELEASES

https://www.msquinnauthor.com/

Or follow me on Instagram and TikTok

If you loved my book, I'd love if you gave it review and spread the word.

ACKNOWLEDGEMENTS

That wasn't too big of a cliffhanger, right? Just a little tease. Don't worry—by the time you finish this book, I'll already be working hard on book three to get it out to you as fast as I can. In the meantime, keep an eye on my newsletter and social media because I have some surprises coming your way.

If you enjoyed *Wings of Darkness* or *Wings of lies*, I'd love it if you wrote a review. It helps me immensely, or even sharing it with a friend makes a huge difference.

Readers, I want to thank you for reading my books. It's amazing to see you dive into my stories and hear what you think. Your enjoyment of my books gives me energy to keep writing. I'm still at the beginning of this journey, but *The Daughter of the Seven Circles* series has been in my head for the longest time. I already know the endings of books three and four, and I even have another series I've started to tinker with. I hope I can make you proud in all the books to come.

To my alpha and beta readers, editors, and cover artist—you all amaze me with how much help and work you put into these books. I truly could not make my stories come alive without your constructive criticism, creativity, and brilliant minds. I can't wait to work with you more along the way.

To my fiancé—thank you for believing in my dream and supporting me throughout this journey. You've been incredibly accommodating with my long writing hours during our busy life, and your reminders to eat and take breaks when I push myself too hard mean so much to me. I love your unwavering faith, especially when imposter syndrome kicks in and I second guess everything I'm doing. You are my best friend, and I couldn't have done this without you.

Lastly, to all the amazing people I've met along this journey who have helped me and who I've built relationships with. I don't think I would've ended up where I am without you. It all started when I joined a writing critique group called New Authors Unite. I have met so many wonderful individuals who have been incredible sounding boards and sources of support. I remember being nervous about joining the group, but I'm immensely grateful that I did. Thank you to each and every one of you for being a part of this journey

ABOUT THE AUTHOR

Makayla Sagami grew up in a little town near Madison, Wisconsin, reading Twilight, City of Bones, Vampire Academy, and many other fantasy romance novels. She graduated college with an art and elementary education degree, which she enjoyed but not as much as storytelling. When not writing, she's most likely reading, spending time with her family and friends, wrangling her cats, or finding a new restaurant to try with her husband.